Other works
by Mary Anne Evans:

Hattie of Crawford Notch

I LV ME: A Spiritual Journey of Healing

Embracing Our Final Days: A Journey of Care to the End
(co-authored with Rebecca McElfresh, Ph.D.
and Lucy Ellen Smith)

Are You Serious?

My Teen Teachers

Something of Value

Millie

of Great Falls

A novel by Mary Anne Evans

ISBN: 979-8-9851642-4-4 (paperback)
ISBN: 979-8-9851642-5-1 (ebook)

I dedicate this book to Grammy Harlow,
my spiritual mentor.

Contents

Prologue

Manuel

The real voyage of discovery consists not in seeking new landscapes,
but in having new eyes.
-Marcel Proust

"I wanna get away from here too," Manny whined, as José gazed dreamily at the ocean, its waves crashing into Ponta Delgada's shoreline. It wasn't that Manny disliked the beauty of Flores. It was certainly an aptly named island, with its wild, blue hydrangeas spread like an ocean upon the land with calla lilies as whitecaps. He accepted the ancient volcanic mountains as a given, along with the many waterfalls that spilled from their heights. He'd heard of the azure and emerald waters captured within each volcano, though he'd never seen them. No, it wasn't that Flores was such a bad place to live; rather that it was terribly small and unexciting compared to lands he and José had heard about. He wanted to see different countries with different sights.

Manny knew José had similar dreams. The difference between them, other than their ages, was that José not only wanted to see other lands but also yearned to be a sailor and hungered to kill the mighty whale. Even now Manny knew José hoped another sperm whale would breach. The majesty and sheer immensity of the animal, as well as the vast expanse of the sea, excited José, while these were the very features that made Manny anxious. He saw the endless sea as obstacle enough toward realizing his dreams, but to have to deal with tons of living blubber too— well, that was just something he'd have to accept if he truly wished to see new lands. What neither boy knew was how long a whaler would stay at sea. It could be just half a year, or three years, or even more. It all depended on how kindly King Neptune was in allowing his whales to be captured.

José was happiest when he could lie back on his elbows in the field, keeping one eye on their flock and the other on the sea. The crowning element of his joy was clear weather like today when he could see Corvo easily, and beyond that the home of all that lived under the Atlantic Ocean. José was curious about the world beyond their island. How many species of fish and mammals swim under those magnificent swells? What mysteries does the ocean hold captive in its cavernous belly? What do other lands beyond this archipelago look like? Are the grand tales the sailors boast really true? Is it true that there are lands rivaling the vastness of the sea? People the color of ebony? Forests so deep and dark they can easily swallow a man? Miles upon hundreds of miles of nothing but sand? Mountains made of ice? It just couldn't even be imagined.

"Pa needs you here," José said, feeling annoyed at his younger brother's persistent chatter and answering his whining yet again. "Who'd look after these sheep? Come on. Let's get something to eat." The boys walked back up the steep hill to their home, checked their shoes for mud and muck, knocked off what they could with a rock, and went inside. The small stone structure, resembling a barn more than a home, was dark inside save for the oil-burning lamps and the two cloudy windows capturing the waning daylight. Since the family spent most of the year outside farming (or playing, in the case of the smaller children) there was little need to change anything. Not that there was money to upgrade their humble home, anyway.

"Sit, sit. Eat," was all Ma said. It was perhaps Ma who suffered most. Her work kept her close to the house, if not inside most of the time. Feeding and clothing a family of twelve was daunting, especially with yet another child coming soon. Ma wasn't one to talk overly much. But then, neither had their own mother been. Housework and childrearing were never fully finished. Talking took precious energy from her limited supply.

José and Manny sat at the rough, handmade table, and Ma filled their simple clay bowls with the hot, brothy, mutton-bone soup she'd made. That and their hard-crusted ration of bread would have to hold them until their next meal, which more than likely would be exactly the same. Around them, their smaller sisters played with one of the cats. The brothers didn't talk, just ate, as Ma had demanded. Both sat thinking of leaving the island on a whaling ship. Only one had the blessing of their father to do so.

The boys often heard their Ma and Pa talking late at night. It was almost always the same strained discussion. Ma would complain about too many mouths to feed. And couldn't the older boys find work in the town? Pa reminded her that the boys were in danger of being taken to the motherland to fight in her wars. Strong, young boys were easiest to snatch in town where the abductor could hide among the buildings. Neither parent spoke well of Portugal. Why would they? Portugal had sent her far-flung Azorean islands the dregs of her society–criminals, rebels, and opportunists who gouged them of all that was good. Portugal had not listened to her islands' needs. Now the islanders suffered the added blows of potato rot and grape fungus. The starch to fill their bellies and wine to wash it down were staples they could hardly afford to lose.

The family had heard tales of riches to be found in America, stories of gold in a place called California, that had reached Ma and Pa's ears. If their boys could only get to this land of riches, they could bring back much-needed money to their half-starved family. The boys knew what was expected of them, but only José was considered old enough to board an American whaling ship as soon as the next one came. Manny would have to tend the sheep and wait his turn at sea.

With the morning's chaos of bodies in the house the following day, Manny and José couldn't wait to find the flock and the relative peace of the open field. Once they'd moved the sheep to better grass, they could sit and talk or dream the rest of the morning. It wasn't the nice day outside that yesterday had been. They pulled their thin coats up around their necks to block the morning's dampness and the insistent wind. At least the air would warm some in the afternoon.

"Awful hard to see anything beyond the island through this fog, let alone our sheep," Manny grumbled. There wasn't much he didn't grumble about these days, so desperately did he want to join José on the next whaler. To keep his brother from complaining, José began telling Manny of the tales of the sea he'd learned from an older friend who'd been to America and returned to Flores. The high adventure of gliding across the endless stretches of water in good weather or crashing through waves higher than the Igreja de Ponta Delgada, the Catholic church where they'd been baptized. Then, just as they'd passed miles of nothing but the froth of ocean waves, a cry would sound…

"She blows! She blows!" Manny blurted, having heard the story many times before. Then José continued, saying that all eyes searched the sea that lay at the end of the sailor's pointing finger as the mighty ship turned to meet her prey.

Manny never tired of hearing José's stories and could think of little else these long days of tending the sheep. His thinking, though mostly repetitive and unproductive, had brought him to one important decision. He shared it with no one.

A few weeks later, as the brothers worked the sheep, José suddenly stopped what he was doing and stood, unmoving, facing south. Manny followed his gaze. Just barely discernible in the great distance was a three-masted ship. José took off running up the hill toward the house with Manny at his heels. They burst through the door, hands on their knees, doubled over, needing breath faster than their lungs allowed. When he could, José stood up and shouted, "There's a whaler coming! I saw the three blinks of light from the bow. It's American!" Then he turned and ran out the still-open door with Manny at his heels. They bolted down the hill to the sheep, where they had the perfect view to watch the mighty ship grow larger. The boys were so intent on the view that they failed to notice their father stride up behind them.

"Are you ready, son?" Pa asked.

"Yes, sir! I am," José answered.

"So am I!" Manny said, standing as tall as he could. He just had to try one more time to convince his father that he was ready to sail with José.

"No, Manny. Do not mention it again."

The beautiful ship would be ready to sail again in three or four days' time, once it was restocked and the weather was agreeable. Some sailors left the ship to seek ale or women before returning. Others left the ship never to go back. New provisions would be stowed away, to hopefully keep the men well-fed until they reached another port. This ship had stopped first on the island of São Miguel and then on to Pico. Its final stop would be Flores before heading back out to the open sea. The people of Ponta Delgada knew which of their men intended to sail on this ship and made a mental note to give the young sailors a quick and sincere blessing when they could.

Whaling was central to life on Flores. Everyone knew someone who was either currently on a whaler, used to be, or wanted to be. Stores stocked food and supplies. Churches were always available to receive those who mourned the loss of a seaman either by death or by decision. Neighbors knew of each other's celebrations or heartaches. Manny knew word would spread quickly when the ship was ready to sail.

A few nights later, when the sky was still inky black just before dawn and only stars patterned the heavens, José left his bed. Manny could just make out the hug Ma gave his brother in the doorway before Pa and José closed the door behind them. Manny heard sniffles, then finally the rhythmic breathing of Ma's sleep. He rose quickly and quietly from his place in the bed he shared with some of his younger siblings. He was already dressed in all but his coat and shoes, which he donned after carefully letting himself out of the house. He raced to the barn and grabbed the small bag he'd hidden in a corner. He'd need to hurry to stay as close to his father and brother as he dared without being seen by anyone who might disclose his presence. He was going to stow away with José whether his father approved or not. He was fifteen years old, and it was high time he lived his own life.

As Manny crept from rock to rock and fence to fence, down the hill and across the fields, into the town and finally the port, he thought about the conversation he'd overheard. Pa told Ma that he'd take José to the ship and that José would be ushered aboard from the dock if the sea was placid enough to tie up at port. Otherwise, if the sea was cantankerous, José and the others who'd gather would be put on a dinghy and rowed to the ship. Ma had said that the whole thing sounded much too dangerous, but Pa assured her that this was really his only option for his of-age son.

In Manny's mind it was the only option for him as well. He felt he would suffocate at home with so many bodies demanding the same stale air. He just knew that life elsewhere would be much more exciting than this monotonous existence. *Any of the other children can tend the sheep,* he thought angrily. *Why should I stay and waste my time here? Why can't Pa understand my need for this adventure?*

Manny fervently prayed that his God above would allow calm seas because he knew he couldn't stow away on a dinghy. His prayers were answered with a calm night. The *Brunswick* held tight to the dock, thick mooring lines wound around the bollards. *The ship wants to be free,* he thought. *Just like me!* He wasn't sure if he was mostly excited, frightened, or nervous. The only part of him that moved were his eyes as he stayed to one side of the growing crowd of young men and their families, losing sight of José and Pa from time to time. He heard the murmured goodbyes and quiet sobs of the women and conceded that Pa might miss him. But Ma wouldn't. She'd never loved him like Pa and his own mother had. His resolve to leave strengthened.

From out of the diminishing crowd, Manny saw his brother hug their father quickly and walk up the wooden gangway. Once on board a man taller and hairier than his father bellowed, "What's yer name?" His command of the Portuguese language was about as developed as José's English. But asking a person's name was one of the first things José learned. Even Manny understood the word "name."

"José Valadão," his brother shouted back. "Follow the others," he said, quickly twisting at the waist to point behind him. Then José disappeared.

Manny knew he had to find his moment soon. He looked around for his father. He didn't want to be seen by anyone who would hold him back, but he absolutely couldn't risk being seen by his father. He gazed inland and saw his father's backside striding away from the dock. Suddenly he heard voices raised and looked back around. He saw a commotion of several, maybe three, boys struggling to step onto the gangway while a woman pulled at one of them. An older man shouted at the woman and pushed her to the side to let the first boy gain a foothold. But the woman only shouted more loudly, crying to regain possession of the boy's arm. Quickly, the man who had asked José's name walked angrily down the gangway to stop the disturbance. While everyone was occupied with this clamor, Manny shot up the narrow ramp, onto the ship's deck, and in the direction he'd seen his brother disappear. He easily slipped past one sailor and then another while they were occupied with their own work. He saw a small doorway and a set of stairs leading below deck. Before he ducked through the door, he looked out across the land past the dock and saw his father's figure heading for their home. With an unexpected lump in his throat and the sudden appearance of tears, Manny disappeared below.

The strong odor below deck made him heave. He was no lover of the smells of gutted fish, blood, or even brine. He hoped he'd get past the instinct to retch. In his mind, the sea was no temptress. What lured him was what lay beyond it. He knew it was different for José. His brother talked of the sea and whaling as if it called to him, as if the Lord, Himself had come calling on José's heart. Even now, as Manny stole a peek, he watched José work with the others as though he weren't a greenhand, as if he'd been whaling all his life. José was so absorbed that Manny knew he was safe where he crouched. José would assume his younger brother was fast asleep at home.

Daylight came. Manny had to be even more careful without the dark of night to shield him. He scrunched himself tighter between the bags of grain. It seemed forever before he finally heard someone above him shout, "Cast off!" Men scurried to untether the ship's moorings, recoil and stow the ropes, and tuck the last of the provisions in the holds. When it appeared all the men were aboard, Manny heard another man yell, "All gone, sir!" Then Manny heard creaks and groans from the ship's hull and felt her movement, a gentle buoyed rise and fall through the water. He knew the magnificent canvas sails were being raised, and with that, the *Brunswick* turned away from port, heading north and out into the open sea. Manny was filled with the excitement of having successfully stowed away. He was headed for America!

He wondered how far from port the ship should be before making his presence fully known. It wouldn't do to be taken back to port. Or worse, thrown into the sea and be told to swim to shore. The embarrassment alone would be devastating. And if he was returned to the island, his father's anger at what he'd done might mean he could never stay in his father's home again. Just to be safe, he hunkered down a while longer.

Part One

Millie

You could spend your whole life looking for love
with your eyes closed.
-Caroline George

One

Missing Jennie

Wednesday, December 25, 1889

Dear diary, I am Mildred Francesca Thomas. I am 9 years old. I live on a farm in Great Falls, Maine. My papa is Manuel Thomas (mama calls him Manny). He came from the Azores where his father rased sheep. So we rase sheep, too. There's Merino sheep that are all white. There wool makes the nicest sweaters. And there's Suffolk sheep with black faces. There meat tastes very good.

My Mama is Julia. She came from Standish. She grew up in a very nice house. She knits our wool. I have two brothers. First is Joe. Mama and Papa call him Josey but I don't. He is 13 years older than me. And Howard (we all call him Howdie) is 10 years older.

Today was Christmas day. The usal good things happened. We had lamb with mint jelly, potatos, carrots and Mama's Christmas pudding. We sang carols. But it wasn't the same without Jennie. She was my sister. She dide in April.

And my feelings are all mixed up about my present from Mama and Papa, this diary, my very first. I'm greatful for it. Mama was happy to give it to me. I told her it made me happy because I did not want to hurt her feelings. But I know twas Jennie's diary first with her pages cut out. And I know tis a waste not to use the good pages. But it feels a little bit rong to rite in Jennie's diary. She always told me not to snoop and read what she rote. Jennie, forgive me for riting in it. I know how preshous it was to you.

I slid the diary under my pillow where no one would see it and undid the ribbons from my braid before my fingers got any colder. I put the ribbons in Jennie's and my ivory hair receiver on our dresser. This Christmas has made me think of Jennie so much. The hair receiver was really hers, but we shared it and the dresser. I had the bottom drawer, and she had the other two. We slept together in this bed like Papa does with Mama. And like Howdie used to with Joe until Joe went off to college. I don't know how Howdie feels about sleeping alone now, but I don't like it. I miss Jennie awfully. She used to bring the bedwarmer upstairs each night. I think she thought I was too little to do it. But now I do it all the time, so I guess I'm not so little as she thought.

I undressed and put my nightgown on as fast as I could in the icy air. Jennie and I liked to pretend that if we weren't fast enough to get under the covers, Jack Frost would slide his fingers underneath the window and lay a blanket of cold on top of our bed. We'd giggle so much our sides hurt and Mama would come upstairs and tell us to go to sleep. Then we'd giggle all the more with our heads under the covers. Now my bed feels too big because there's a Jennie-sized empty space on the left side. At least I get all the warm from the bedwarmer now. I guess that's one good thing.

Thursday, March 6, 1890
    Dear diary, I am ten years old today! I think I'm taller. And smarter now.

"Millie! Are you ready yet? Mama and Papa have started out for the cemetery," Howdie called up the stairs.

"I'm coming, Howdie!" I yelled.

"Oh, blast these buttons! There are ever so many, and they are ever so small," I said under my breath so Howdie wouldn't hear me say "blast." I was doing the best I could. I didn't feel like going to the burying ground anyway. And I'd be late for school because of it.

By the time I walked down the winding staircase and through the house, I had gained control of my agitation. "Thank you for waiting for me. It's these tiny buttons that slowed me down. I'm sorry, Howdie."

I shrugged into my coat and fumbled with more buttons, pulled on my boots, and shoved my hands into the pretty blue mittens Mama made for my birthday. As I did that, Howdie said in his quiet way, "When you're in a hurry, Millie, don't hurry." I gave him a sideways glance of exasperation. I don't think he saw me, but he didn't say anything more after that.

We walked in silence. I did my best to keep stride beside Howdie, but his steps were so long, I had to trot to keep up. The snow was mostly melted on the road, but there were large puddles, some of which were still a little icy, so I had to watch my step. Good thing the burying ground isn't far.

I could see Mama and Papa standing in front of Jennie's grave waiting for us. My stomach felt queasy. Jennie and I used to come here in the spring and eat picnic lunches on the steps in front of a big monument way in the back. We'd make up stories about the lives of people buried there whose names we didn't know. Jennie thought it wasn't right to talk about the people in families we did know. I guess maybe she was right, but didn't we have fun pretending! Mr. Elgar was a rich gentleman who liked smelly cigars, we decided. Miss Arden had a poodle who sat on her lap and ate from the table at dinner. We'd laugh and laugh at such silliness. All that fun and now Jennie is under her own stone. It feels so wrong. That's why I stopped coming here after she died. I just can't think of Jennie down there.

I watched Papa scan our faces after we slipped in beside Mama. He had only half of his children alive now. I wondered if he was thinking that too. Then he bowed his head, expecting us to do the same. He said a prayer for all of us, including Jennie and the babies. But when he asked God to watch over his family, I think he meant just me, Howdie, Joe, and

Mama, so we wouldn't die either. I said some extra words so God wouldn't take Papa from us. He never included himself in prayers. At least not out loud. After he said "Amen," he recited the words that he and Mama had put on Jennie's tombstone, "Blessed are the pure in heart for they shall see God."

I didn't hear what Papa said next because I was wondering what it means to be pure in heart. It sounded like a good thing to be, so I'm sure Jennie was that because she was always so good. Except when she pulled my braids when she got very put out with me. Maybe something like that doesn't count, though. So, if she was pure in heart, she must be seeing God. I wonder if I am pure enough to see God someday. I wish I had been nicer to Jennie and helped Mama more when Jennie was sick.

A tear fell from my eye and when it slid down my cheek it felt hot and tickled my skin. I looked up at Mama. Her face was wet, too. She was looking down at Georgie and Matie's small stones near Jennie's. They were Mama's baby boys who died before I was born. I wonder if it hurts more to lose a seventeen-year-old than a baby? I 'spect so. But I don't know what Mama was like when the boys died. Howdie said she cried a lot, though. When I thought about Mama's loss, I didn't feel quite as sorry for myself and wondered if Mama was alright.

"Manny, I'm ready to go home," I heard Mama say to Papa very quietly. She doesn't call him that very often. Usually she just says, "Papa." Howdie and I let them go ahead. I studied Papa's uneven gait from behind him.

"Howdie?" I asked, "Was Papa hobbled since he was little?"

"You know Papa took a bullet through his leg in the war," he said to me as if I had asked a foolish question.

"Yes, I know that. But was he already hobbled before he left his home in the Azores? I mean, is that why he got shot? Because he couldn't get away as quick as the other soldiers?"

"No. He was fine until the war, I think."

We reached the house, and I grabbed my lunch pail and my slate–a cast-off from an older boy named Willie Hatt–and started walking to school. I knew I would be excused for being late this one day, but I'd rather have stayed home altogether. All I wanted to think about was

Jennie and how much I missed her. I didn't want to do arithmetic and spelling. But Mama and Papa wouldn't allow me to miss school just because I didn't feel like being there, so I walked extra slowly up and down the hills.

I kicked the small granite rocks that were pebbled in the sandy road. When Jennie walked me to school, we'd see who could kick the rocks the farthest or who could hit this tree or that fence post. Jennie taught me how to laugh. It wasn't that I didn't know how, exactly, but she made life more fun. Like the time I couldn't find my primer before school. It just wasn't anywhere that I could see and I was going to be late for school. I got very irritated at the situation and stomped around the house looking for it. Mama told me to stop my stomping. But right then Jennie walked over to me and picked up the book which was sitting plain as day on a little table right next to me. She held it out and laughed and said, "If it twoulda been a bear, twoulda *bit* cha," poking me in the stomach. She wasn't laughing *at* me. She was just laughing because she found it funny. I couldn't help laughing too.

I thought about how it was Jennie, not Mama, who brushed my hair. One hundred strokes before braiding it neatly for the night. I really loved that. We would sit on our bed and giggle and tell secrets or stories or even gossip while she brushed. We weren't supposed to gossip. Mama said it wasn't nice. But we couldn't help it. When Jennie got close to counting one hundred, she'd slow way down so I didn't have to go to bed yet. Now I mostly brush my own hair. Sometimes Mama does it, but she is usually in a hurry, and she doesn't talk to me like Jennie did.

When I walked past Addie Moses' house, I thought about how we'd laugh at their cat pouncing on his shadow, which detached when he was in the air. We supposed the silly animal thought he was going to kill the dark monster that wouldn't leave him alone. A couple years ago, we used to stop and pick up Addie when she was in her last year. She and Jennie walked together and talked. I felt a little forgotten while they talked about things I didn't understand. So I'd walk behind them and pout and scuff my feet real loud so they'd be sure to hear me. They would turn around and look at me and tell me that if I didn't pull my bottom lip back in, they'd hang a bucket on it. They laughed at me then and I cried. I couldn't help it. Then they'd stop to give me a hug, and it was like the sunshine came out again.

Thinking about the sunshine made me gaze up into the sky. Jennie would always say that the weather was going to get better if there was enough blue to make a dutchman's pants once the clouds started breaking apart. I'm still not entirely sure just how much blue one needs to make a pair of pants, but Jennie was always right. A bit of blue and the weather *was* new. But today, not even the sunshine breaking through the clouds could make the grayness in my heart go away.

Too quickly, I reached Moses' Coatshop. I opened the door, ignoring the tinkle of its attached bell, and walked past Mr. Moses to the back room where Miss Brackett was teaching arithmetic. I gave Miss Brackett the note from Mama and then took my seat quietly after hanging my outer clothes on my hook. Then I placed my slate on my desk and reached for a piece of chalk. My hands wouldn't stop shaking, though. Maybe it was because I was cold with the wood-burning stove on the other side of the room or maybe I was still full of thoughts of Jennie. Maybe both. I usually loved school, and I loved to learn. But today my heart just wasn't really here.

That evening, Howdie noticed that I was quieter than usual, I guess. Maybe I was moping around so's Mama would come up and brush and braid my hair. She didn't ask me why I was sad. She only said, "Good night. Don't let the bed bugs bite," like she usually does. It seems like I'm the only one who misses Jennie. After Mama left, I closed my door all the way and put my heavy cat doorstop behind it so everyone would know I was upset and not come in. Only I really did want them to come in if they were willing to listen to me. Mama wasn't gone very long before I heard the doorstop scrape along the floor very slowly. I wondered if she had suddenly realized that I was not happy. I wanted her to realize this. I was ready to have her hold me and I began crying.

"Millie?" Howdie asked softly. I decided to curl up with Tippy and pretend to be asleep. He called out again.

"Yes?" I finally said into the darkening room.

"What's got your heart so twisted, Millie? Wanna talk about it?" I didn't answer.

After a little while, he said, so quietly and slowly that I had to listen hard to hear him, "You know, I was a little younger than you are now when the babies died. I remember being more upset about Maitland's death. I'd thought maybe God had given me another brother to play with since he'd taken Georgie away. But then Matie died too. I was very angry with God about that. Papa sat me down and had a talk with me. If you like, I can share what he said."

At that moment, all I wanted was for Howdie to hug me. I looked into his eyes, and he must have understood what I wanted because he held out his arm. As I scooted closer to him, I realized how much I love him. I love Joe too, but he hasn't been home much, just in the summer. Howdie is gone a lot now too. But he goes to school only ten miles away and comes home when Papa needs his help on the farm. I know how impatient he is to get to college but the thought of both of my brothers being gone except for summer is so painful. Sometimes it feels like my heart will rip in two.

Howdie interrupted my thoughts and said, "Papa told me he thought I was old enough to understand what he was about to say, and I think maybe you are too, Millie. He said, 'When we plant crops, sometimes they live to give us the food we need. But sometimes hail or drought destroys them. We can get angry with God, but it's God who makes our crops grow as well as the hail or the drought. Same with our lambs that don't live. God makes all the lambs, some of which are weaker than others from the start. And so it is with people. It's all in God's hands. All of it. Sometimes the people we love die before we think they should.' So Papa said, 'Learn this now: The Lord giveth and the Lord taketh away and it's just plain wasted energy to fuss with Him.' I didn't want to believe Papa. I thought I could talk God into doing what I wanted him to. But I know now that what Papa told me is true. Jennie is gone, along with the babies. We can't know why and there's just no point in fussing with God. But Millie, crying out my feelings was the quickest way for me to stop being angry with God."

I looked up at Howdie with a question on my face. He understood. "Yes, I cry sometimes too. So, shed your tears, then go to sleep. And tomorrow, live your new day."

I hugged my brother for all I was worth then. I didn't need to say anything and Howdie didn't either. He just held me a little while longer and then kissed my forehead and left my room. I relit the oil lamp, grabbed my diary and pencil from beneath my pillow and wrote:

Wednesday, April 30, 1890

Dear diary, oh God, last year, this very day, my dear sister, Jennie, died of the fever. But you know that. I am so very sad. And I'm also angry with you just like Howdie was but mostly sad. Why did you take my very best friend from me? She was so good. To evryone. Espeshially to me. It isn't fair. Howdie says I mustn't fuss with you so I will say my prayrs tonight but I won't much mean what I say.

Two

A Joyous Spring

The next morning was the first of May and this, along with the brilliant sunshine, lifted my spirits so much that I bounded down the curved front stairs. Oh, how I wanted to slide down that banister, but Mama would not approve. I don't know why I feel so happy today after feeling so gloomy yesterday. But who could feel dreary on May Day? I ran through the living room, the parlor, and the kitchen, and skidded to a stop at the door to check the piazza. Sure enough, there hung two baskets on the doorknob and three more were sitting in the door jamb. I brought them in and laid them on the table. My, but they looked wondrous, what little I could see! What a pity I'd have to wait until after school to thoroughly check their contents. Oh, how the day would drag again, but for such a different reason than yesterday.

All my friends except Luella buzzed with excitement at what each had found in his or her basket that morning. Luella and I stayed away from the rest so as not to hear what their baskets held. We wanted to be utterly surprised. She and I had promised to deliver our baskets together last night, but when she saw me at school yesterday, she thought better of it and suggested we wait a day. We had also decided to wait until after school today to look through our baskets together.

When we were dismissed, Luella and I ran to her house to get her baskets and then to mine. We took them all out to the piazza to look through them. "I think 'twas Harry or maybe Nellie who brought the cone-shaped basket because they both put some nuts in the bottom of theirs last year too," I said, reasonably.

"I got one with two cookies!" Luella chirped, eyeing them ravenously. "I'll bet you did, too! Oh! Look! You did! Do you think your mother would let you eat one of them now? I think it would be alright with my mother. Go ask yours!"

"Yes, you may," Mama said. "But only one. Luella will have to leave soon, anyway. There's chores to do and then supper."

"Yes, Mama." I raced out to the piazza and breathlessly started to tell Luella we could each have a cookie, but by the looks of things, she either overheard or couldn't wait. Half her cookie was gone. So I bit into my own and it was delectable–that's a new word I just learned. "Do you think people will like our baskets too?" I asked Luella.

"Sure they will! Especially with your Mama's penuche fudge in them. But we need to go to the bluet patches in the meadow to lay some of the prettiest ones on each basket. Go ask your mother if we can go right now. Then I'll go home for supper and come back."

With a sigh, Mama gave her blessing, but only if we were quick about it. I knew just where to look, and we ran straight to them. Quick as bunnies we were back, and Luella and I hugged before she ran on home.

"Millie," Mama said after Luella left, "help me finish this last bit of butter now."

"Yes, ma'am. But Mama, Luella will come back after supper, you know."

"Yes. I know that. You will have time to hang your baskets. Now hold the skimmer while I strain this last bit of cream."

I took the skimmer from Mama's hands and held it tightly in both of mine. I watched as the thin strands of milk passed through the holes and into a pan. The cream that was left on top of the skimmer was added to the churn. It was my job to use the plunger until my arms wouldn't work anymore. I think Tippy thought it was his job to wind himself around my legs until a drop of cream landed where his tongue could get it. When I help Mama, I usually like to sing the churning song to make the chore go faster, but today I had lots of May Day thoughts to pass the time. When I slowed the plunging down too much, Mama took over until butter began to form and the ball thumped around in the bottom of the churn. *There will be buttermilk for Papa to drink*, I thought. *Well, at least as much as Mama will allow. The rest will go into biscuits. Or pancakes. It makes me hungry just to think about it.*

As if Papa knew how to time his entry perfectly, he walked in just then and said, "William stopped by to say he'd shear the sheep in two or three days. And the pig's gotten loose."

"Pa," Mama said, handing him a cup when she saw him turn back toward the door, "drink this first. Could be a while before you find her." It didn't take long for Papa to finish drinking the buttermilk and he was soon out the door.

"You too, Millie, drink this." When I turned up my nose, Mama said, "It's good for you. How many times do I need to say it?" Then Mama poured the rest into a bottle for later. I don't like the buttermilk just to drink, but it sure is good when it's cooked into what Mama makes for breakfast.

Papa was still out looking for the pig when Mama realized I needed to eat something soon before Luella arrived. She gave me a chicken sandwich and the last of that morning's beans.

"Can I have the other cookie from my basket after I eat?"

"It's 'May I', and yes, if you don't end up with a disgruntled stomach from eating so fast. Luella can wait if you aren't finished."

I ate as fast as I could anyway. Then I took my dishes to the cast-iron sink after I finished my cookie. Just then Luella knocked on the door. We scooped up the baskets we'd been working on for the past few weeks and put the bluets on top. Then we ran outside.

"Millie! Your boots!" Mama shouted, shaking her head. She sounded stern but she had a little bit of a smile on her face, so I wasn't worried.

"Sorry, Mama," I said, grabbing the boots and putting them on. Then I ran to catch up with Luella, who was already half the way to Nellie's house. If Nellie were to see us hang our basket, she was supposed to chase us and give us a kiss. Well, we didn't want *that*. We especially didn't want that from Harry or any of the boys, either. So, we ran through the back field to get to Nellie's house. When it looked like no one could see us, we hung her basket on the doorknob, knocked hard on the door, and then ran to some bushes and hid so we could see her get her basket. My heart was pounding in my chest something awful. Nellie's mother came to the door and saw the basket and called Nellie to come. Nellie looked all around but she didn't see us!

We weren't so lucky at Harry's house, though. We thought he was out back of his house when we ran to the front. But just as we hung the basket, he came walking around the side and saw us. He took off chasing us. We were very sure we didn't want him to kiss us, so we outran him! Even with the rest of our baskets!

By the time I got home, my feet hurt. I need new boots.

Papa was resting in the Morris chair, but his eyes weren't closed yet, so I said, "Papa, did you catch the pig? I kind of hope not because I hate feeding her. She's mean to me."

"We don't hate, child."

"Sorry, Papa. I mean I don't like feeding her because she's mean."

"Nonetheless, I found her, and she'll be fed like all our animals."

That was the end of that. I still had to feed that old sow. And I did still hate her, no matter what Papa said.

"Papa?"

"Yes, child," Papa said, without looking up while he milked one of the cows. Nearby, one of the barn cats crouched low, eyes fixed and steady, awaiting her next meal. The mouse that appeared from between two boards never had a chance.

"When will Joe be home?"

"After he graduates. Soon."

"Will he come by train into White Rock?"

"Yes."

"Can I...I mean, *may* I go with you to pick him up?"

"Yes."

"Papa?" I said more quietly, stroking Kate's soft, golden-brown neck. I was afraid his answer to my coming question wouldn't suit me. Papa was a patient man but if anyone seemed to be able to try his patience, it was me, I'm afraid. I asked questions. Sometimes a lot of them. I like to know things. If I think he's the only one who can answer a question, then I must ask and be ready for his answer.

"What is it, child?" he answered. But I could tell he was getting annoyed already. I couldn't leave now and not finish what I started.

"Well, may I help you milk? I'm tired of washing pails every day. Milking would be more fun and I'm old enough now."

"No. Your Ma needs your help, and milking isn't for girls. Go help her, or go play."

I know Papa didn't mean to sound harsh. He was busy and I think it's extra hard for him to think and speak in English when he's busy and especially when he's tired. Portuguese is easier for him but no one in the house understands very much of his language. Sometimes I feel sorry for him in that way. But girls can milk as well as boys, right? "I'm strong, too," I mumbled under my breath. Papa heard me say something, but he didn't catch what it was. He asked me to repeat it, but I was too angry, so I stormed off, heading for the swing in one of the apple trees by the side of the house. "I'm not a little girl anymore. I'm ten years old. Besides, doesn't Papa need help too, not just Mama?"

One day, not long after this, Papa announced at supper that Howdie would be home from Gorham that very night. He had graduated from the big high school in Gorham, so he would be home for the whole summer. I was so happy, I jumped for joy and started talking about all the things Howdie and I could do over the summer. I wanted him to take me fishing and go swimming down behind Forest Hall. And Luella and I decided to write a play and Howdie's real smart with words. He could help us.

But then later that evening I overheard part of a conversation Mama and Papa had. I didn't mean to hear it. I know it isn't polite to eavesdrop. But Mama said, "Manny, I'm afraid Howard won't be able to handle his civic duties plus farming." *Why not?* I thought. *He'd been going to school and coming home to help all this time.* So I kept listening for more.

"Now, Julia," Papa answered. "Our Howdie is strong. He'll be fine." This made me feel better. After all, Papa would know best about Howdie, I thought. But never mind all that right now. Howdie would be home soon!

When I heard the heavy steps of a horse, I knew he was here. "Oh! It's Howdie!" I ran out to meet him. He was in a friend's wagon so he could bring all his things home. "Oh, Howdie! I'm so glad you're home."

"Hello, little sister. Help me take some of these things inside." I gave him a big hug before grabbing some books from his hands.

Mama and Papa were very happy Howdie was home. I could tell. There were smiles on both their faces all the time we ate supper. Papa would have help all summer long now, and that made Mama happy too. I was chewing my meat, which always takes more time than other food, and the whole table felt so peaceful, like the way I feel when I sit on my favorite rock in the meadow and watch puffy white clouds float past me on their way to everywhere.

"And a letter from Josey said he'd be on the afternoon train tomorrow," Mama was saying when she passed the bread around again.

"Howdie can go fetch him," Papa added. Something made Papa look at me and I gave him my most hopeful face by raising my eyebrows and tilting my face down. I'm good at this look. Papa smiled and said, "You may go with Howdie to fetch Josey, if that's alright with your mama." I turned toward Mama and gave her the look too.

"I 'spect so," Mama answered, taking her own piece of bread and buttering it. "Millie, you will have to finish your chores first, though."

"I will, Mama! I will!"

Both brothers home for at least the summer! What joy! I'm not sure what Joe will do in the autumn now that he has graduated from such an important school so far from home. It's near the state capital all the way up in Augusta! I know he was only able to go there because somebody helped with the money. I sort of overheard this, but I don't know who gave the money to him. Surely he will find important work now. I hope it's no further than Portland, though. But never mind that. I've got the whole summer to enjoy him.

The next day, Howdie hitched the horse to the wagon while I finished feeding the chickens. They always run to the coop as soon as they hear the grain hit the ground, and that was my quickest and last chore.

"I'm ready, Millie!" Howdie called out in the direction of the coop.

"Coming!" I yelled back while I brushed corn pieces off my skirt and hands.

"We're leaving, Mama!" I yelled after I opened the kitchen door.

"I'm right here, Millie. You didn't have to shout."

"Oh. Sorry, Mama. Bye!" I saw Mama shake her head, which meant she was agitated with me, I think, but she was smiling too.

I jumped up onto the wagon seat. "Let's go!" Howdie slapped the reins on Fan's back, urging her to move.

As we headed out of the driveway, I started talking to Howdie right off. "And then I asked Papa if I could milk the cows instead of wash milk pails. Uck…I hate those old pails. They stink. Why won't Papa let me milk the cows?"

"Well," Howdie said, clucking at the horse to break into a trot, "I 'spect it has something to do with Papa not wanting you to get too familiar with farm life. He wants you to get a good education like Josey and me. Not just be a farmer's wife."

"Oh! I'd never do that! I want to be a teacher. And I want to go places and see new things. You can't do that if you have to feed the animals and milk the cows every day, you know."

Howdie laughed, "Yes, I know. That's just fine then, Millie. You *be* one. I'll bet you'll be a wonderful teacher at that. So, what do you have planned for this summer, my dear little sister?"

"Luella and me want to write a play!"

"Luella and *I*," Howdie corrected.

I rolled my eyes at him. It seems like I am forever being corrected by *some*one. And I don't have anyone younger than me to correct. Why am I the littlest? "School's over," I said. "I don't have to worry about grammar right now."

Howdie chuckled and asked, "What will your play be about?"

"I don't know. We haven't discussed that yet. We were hoping that you or Joe could help us think about it. But once it's written, we will give parts to all our friends and put on the play for everyone!"

We passed Hurricane Road with Babbs covered bridge just out of sight. "That sounds mighty fine, Millie. I can't wait to see it. I'm sure you'll have a wonderful summer."

We both heard the train whistle in the distance, signaling its departure from the station. Howdie urged Fan to pick up her speed.

"Howdie? What do you think you'll do this fall?"

"I'm not entirely sure yet, but I've applied to a business school in Portland."

"What kind of business?"

"It's a school to learn all about how to start or run a business, all sorts of businesses."

"What sort of business would you run?"

"Most likely I wouldn't start out running a business but helping the people who do."

"Oh. I'd like to run a school, I think. It seems like a pretty easy thing to do. You just find a school building and when school starts, you open the doors, and the children all come in and sit down. Then you just teach them what you know. There isn't much else to learn except how to be a teacher. And that would probably be easy for me too."

Howdie laughed.

"Why are you laughing at me, Howdie?"

"I'm laughing because I think you're cute."

"Oh. Well, that's okay then. You can laugh at me." And he did, harder this time.

Finally, we reached White Rock station and there was Joe, sitting outside on his luggage, smiling broadly, just like Howdie did yesterday. I couldn't wait for Fan to completely stop, so I jumped off and ran to Joe and gave him a big hug.

When everything was loaded onto the wagon, Joe hoisted me up onto the seat. Then the boys climbed in and sat one on either side of me. Howdie clucked at Fan, and we were on our way home.

I mostly listened to the boys talk on the way back, but that was alright because that peace filled my heart again like at supper yesterday. I was thinking that there's no finer place to be than between my two big brothers. Yes, it will be a wonderful summer.

Three

The Tempest

It was a wonderful summer indeed. I had all the usual fun—swimming, croquet, fishing (Howdie was the only one who would take me because the others say I talk too much), strawberry and blueberry picking, and playing with my friends. I love to run in bare feet and play tag or hide and seek with my friends. Sometimes I just play with Tippy or read a book when the weather is rainy. What I don't like so well are thunderstorms. Once, lightning hit the metal rod on the barn and it made such a loud sound, I thought the barn fell in. I'm sure Fan and the rest of the animals were very scared because that's their home.

But the best part of the summer was acting out the play with Luella. We decided to use a story in *My First Picture Book* called "The Little Old Woman Who Lived in a Shoe." Luella wanted to be the old woman, and I would be her oldest son, named Strong-arm. He uses an ax to cut wood, which is why his arms are strong. I asked Papa if I could use his ax in the play. He said yes, if I was very careful. I was. We needed two other people to be the old woman's husband and the giant. So, we got Annie and Clara to help. Annie wanted to be the husband and Clara said it was okay if she was the giant.

Luella wore a bonnet, and we used our dolls because the old woman had many children. I brought out the toy baby buggy Mama keeps behind her bed where the ceiling slants real low. We made a big shoe out of chairs. It didn't look much like a shoe. I wore a pair of Howdie's pants to be Strong-arm, and Annie and Clara borrowed pants from their families. Clara tried to talk in a very low voice to be a good giant. I think it hurt her voice after a while, but she was very good at it.

We worked on the play for many days. When we were ready to put it on, we made posters to tell people when to come to the play, which was on a Sunday afternoon in my yard. People had to sit on blankets to watch because we used up all the chairs. They didn't seem to mind. And everyone laughed and had a good time. We took our bows and then Mama brought out refreshments for everyone. It was grand fun. Someday I want to be in a play at Forest Hall down by Mr. Moses' Coatshop. It's brand new and has a stage just for shows!

That's what happened to me this summer. Papa and the boys did the usual things on the farm, and Mama sweated a lot in the heat when she worked in the kitchen. That's usual too, but what isn't so usual for Mama is that she joined a group of women who have meetings. It's called the Women's Christian Temperance Union. I don't know what it's about but sometimes she talks about it at the supper table. She is very excited about joining. I'm not sure Papa and the boys are, though. Sometimes it seems like they all just argue about things.

"Why are you arguing?" I asked one night.

"We aren't arguing," Joe said. "We're discussing."

But then when Luella and I were quarreling about who won a game of croquet, Mama came out to tell us to stop arguing. I said, "We're not arguing. We're discussing."

"That's not what it sounds like to me, and young ladies do not argue. I suggest that Luella go home and come back tomorrow."

I just can't understand grown-ups sometimes.

Sunday, August 31, 1890

I'm sad. This is our last Sunday together. Joe is leaving this week for ~~Conetticut~~ Connecticut to go to college and Howdie is going to start school in Portland. He gave his card to Betsy so he can call on her. She lives in Portland. Joe says he wants to be a ~~sientist~~ scientist.

This is the end of summer. I'm in 6th year now. Mama has been sick lately. Grandmam comes to help almost every day.

"Show Dr. Dunn upstairs to see your Mama," Mama's mother, Jane—we call her Grandmam—said to me. She sounded more serious than usual. She scared me. "Then come back down. I'll be there right off. And fetch your father also."

I did as Grandmam asked. Dr. Dunn was new and younger than the last doctor. I wanted to know what he would do about Mama's awful cough, so I went up to Mama's room. When I saw the cold compress on Mama's forehead, it terrified me. It reminded me too much of the fever that took Jennie. I looked at the doctor's face to see if he was scared for Mama too, but I couldn't tell. Then I bolted down the steep back stairs to get Papa. I don't always like those back stairs. Most of the time I go down them carefully. There's no handrail and if I fell, I'd end up in the wood bin. There's mice in there and probably other things I wouldn't much like. But I didn't care today. All I could think about was what if Mama was too sick to live.

I tried my best to find something to occupy my mind while the grown-ups were all in Mama's room. I wished Howdie and Joe were still home. I couldn't keep my attention on what I had been reading earlier. I didn't want to go outside in case I was needed. I wasn't hungry and I didn't think that practicing the piano would be right. What if I bothered the doctor? So, I sat and thought about things. Things like, what's Connecticut like and is college difficult? Is Betsy important to Howdie? Will she demand all of Howdie's time now? Will he forget about me?

Finally, the doctor, Papa, and Grandmam came down the front stairs.

"She'll need a lot of rest for the next several days," Dr. Dunn was saying. "Use this packet of Cooper's mustard plaster on either her chest or back. Keep it on her for no more than one hour, two or three times throughout the day. Then give her this elixir just before bedtime. If she isn't better by Sunday, see me in church. I'll come right away or the next day depending on how she is."

I followed them all to the kitchen door. We stood in line like a train. I guess that made me the caboose since I was in the back. At the door, Dr. Dunn turned around and came over to me. He bent down to cup his hand under my chin, "And you, young lady, help your grandmother all you can." I would do that, but I wanted to know if Mama would get better soon.

"Thank you, doctor," Grandmam said. Papa held the door open for him and then walked out himself.

"And you can begin by helping me with this soup," Grandmam said to me, as she grabbed Mama's apron off the hook and a few potatoes and onions from the basket. She handed me the little knife so I could scrape the potatoes.

"Are you scared, Grandmam?"

"Well, child, I guess I'd be lying if I said I had no worries. But let's just let time tell us more." I don't trust time when it comes to people being sick.

Mama coughed a lot for the next few days. Grandmam slept at our house in the front room. I don't remember that she had ever stayed so long. Usually she says she has to get back to Grandpar. That's her husband. Then one day Grandmam had Papa take her home. She told me to watch Mama closely for a while and to have Papa let her know if her condition gets worse. I didn't want to be in charge of that, but Papa said I'd do fine. I think he trusts me and that makes me feel more grown up.

Even when Mama started coming downstairs, she needed my help. Sometimes she told me what to do and she sat at the kitchen table to watch me. At first it made me nervous because Mama is so fast in the kitchen, and I am very slow. But she never seemed to mind. I helped with the spinning too by holding the spun wool so Mama could wind it into balls. Mama says she will use all the onion skins we save to dye the wool yellow. I want to knit a scarf because Mama said she can use it in her charity work.

Howdie was home this weekend to help Papa shock the corn stalks. They dug potatoes too. We all went to church. I love to watch Dr. Dunn's wife play the organ. Her feet pump while her hands pull the stops, and her fingers play the music. I don't think she ever gets tired, and the sound is so beautiful. Sometimes I close my eyes, especially if I know the words to the hymns already. Mama says that if I keep practicing piano, maybe I can learn to play the organ. Oh, I would love that! I must be tall enough to reach the pedals, though.

After church we all went to Grandmam and Grandpar's house. Uncle Almon was home. I love Uncle Almon. He's funny and so nice to me. We all went and picked apples, for pies and apple cider mostly.

When everything was harvested that fall, Papa said it had been a good growing season. More than one hundred bushels of corn went to the corn shop to be processed for canning. The black cherries, oats, turnips, and potatoes all did well. But the beans didn't. Beetles got half of them. The beets were stored away down cellar. The largest pig was killed and butchered and the piglets are growing up. I feel sorry for them. Their turn will come, poor things.

By November most of the town and everyone in our family had come down with one illness or another. I had a lot of coughing and a terrible sore throat. I saw a picture of a giraffe once and I wondered if giraffes get sore throats. I knew Dr. Dunn had been very busy because Mrs. Dunn told me so at church. She said he has dealt with vomiting, dysentery, toothaches, coughs, and sore throats. There's been one emergency surgery–to take out an appendix, I think–and two deaths just in Great Falls, God rest their souls. Papa had to drive the town hearse to pick up the dead even when he wasn't feeling well. Howdie came home to start banking the house before winter, but a terrific cold virus kept him from finishing the job until three days later. The Old Farmer's Almanac predicted a snowier-than-usual season. But Papa says his leg tells him the weather at least as well as the Almanac. He didn't say what his leg told him this year.

I usually worry about Mama's health more than anyone's. But Papa limps an awful lot. I know he tries to hide his pain but sometimes I see him wince. He doesn't complain, but I would if I were him. Sometimes I think about how hard he has worked all his life. He was tending sheep on an island in another country when he was my age. I don't know much about the things that happened to him when he was hunting for whales or when he was in the army. But when I see him limp, I just can hardly stand to think about him being shot in the leg. I sure love my papa an awful lot.

One Sunday afternoon in early November, Trafton knocked on the kitchen door. "Come on in," I heard Mama say as she wiped her hands on her apron. "Pa, Trafton's here to see you. Millie, take Mr. Plaisted into the parlor, please."

Papa put his Bible on the little table and stood with some difficulty to shake his friend's hand. *Sometimes Papa acts really old,* I thought. *I wonder if he would like me to help steady him when he stands.* But I left the room and went back to the kitchen. It wouldn't be polite for me to stay and listen to them talk, even though I wanted to. They talk about the war that they were in. Part of me wants to know what it was like.

All I could hear was their how-are-you's and then nothing at all.

"Why aren't they saying anything, Mama?" I whispered in her ear.

"They have been through a lot of difficult experiences together and sometimes all that's needed in a relationship is to sit together in silence. Words aren't always necessary. Would you please take these cups of coffee to them? Carefully! Then come back to serve them some of the apple brown betty I made. After that, you may go in the living room and read *Heidi* again."

"Here, Mr. Plaisted. Papa."

"Thank you, child," Papa said. "Now run off and play."

"I'm to bring you some cake first, then I'm going to the living room to read *Heidi*. Mama told me to." Papa only nodded.

Once I was in the living room, I tried not to watch Papa and Mr. Plaisted or listen to what they were saying, but I did see and hear some of it.

"How've you been?" Papa asked Trafton.

"Not bad. You?"

"I'd be better without this old injury talking to me," Papa answered, rubbing his leg.

"Leastwise you missed a hot summer down in them hell holes for states because of it. I was surprised you made it back just in time for Sherman to take Atlanta, though. I wasn't sure you were coming back at all. Guess you're better off'n ol' Chamberlain. I read that all his wounds keep 'im bothered."

"Even so, man's done more 'an you 'n' me put together," I heard Papa say, and that was all I heard.

After a time, Trafton left and Papa commenced reading his Bible, but not for long. He fell asleep in the Morris chair like he does every Sunday afternoon.

"Trafton is going to paint three scenes to be used in Forest Hall for plays on the stage," Papa said at supper that night. "I hear he's quite an artist."

"He is?" I asked, very interested in anything to do with plays, especially in Forest Hall. That night I dreamed I was a princess in a special play written just for me.

It turned out the winter was very snowy, which was ever so much fun. Getting to school and back home is different depending on what kind of snow we have. Sometimes when the snow is new and powdery, I use snowshoes. When I do, I have to leave extra early to get to school on time. It takes the first few big snowstorms for my legs to get used to wearing them because they're heavy and wide and they make me walk funny. When the snow on the road is packed down, I meet friends and we use our sleds. We have to be careful not to get going too fast on the really big hills. Then we use our heels to slow us down a little. But not too much because going lickety-split is so much fun. Occasionally, if Papa has to take the sleigh out anyway, he'll take me in that. When he does, he tucks the thick wool blanket under my legs, and we talk. Well, mostly I talk, I guess.

Papa likes to ask me about school. He didn't go to school very much. He can't read and write English very well, and he isn't especially good at arithmetic. When Joe and Howdie are home, they help him with the log books for the animals and the crops so he knows how well the farm is doing. Sometimes I help him when the boys are not around. Papa looks over my shoulder when I am doing arithmetic studies. I think he wants to learn but he doesn't have much time to.

Today, Papa needed to go to the mill, so he took me to school in the sleigh again. He asked me what we were learning. I told him we were studying our spelling words for the upcoming bee. And we will be parsing more complicated sentences. We were working on harder division problems and on our penmanship too.

"But Papa, you know what?"

"What, child?"

"William snickered during the Pledge of Allegiance yesterday and he had to stand with his nose in a circle on the board again."

"*You* don't snicker during something that important, I trust."

"Oh, no, Papa. I would never do that," I said. I didn't say anything more until Papa looked at me the way he does when he thinks I'm not telling him everything or the truth.

"Well, I passed a note to Luella and Miss Brackett saw me do it. She said I had to write 'I will not pass notes' a hundred times on the board during recess. But Luella didn't have to, and I think she should have because she passed one to me first. I don't think it was fair. So, I'm not speaking to Luella today."

"Did you learn anything?"

"Yes, Papa. I will not pass notes until Miss Brackett is out of the room."

Spring was right around the corner when I turned eleven on March sixth. I love real spring, but I can't say I love the month of March. It's half winter, half spring. They should call this month "Muddy" instead of "March" because it's always that. Mud is everywhere that snow isn't. Fan has a much harder time pulling in March. I feel bad for her and all the animals, except pig. That old sow loves to roll in the mud. She's happiest when she's filthy.

Everyone thought we were in for an early spring. Papa was planning his crops for the year and inspecting his plow and rakes for repairing. He sharpened all his tools and checked the harnesses. He told me to keep checking the ewes and pig for when their babies were due. Mama had me help her with vegetable starts for her garden. This is the first time I've helped with so much of the farming. I'm growing up.

By Resurrection Sunday on the twenty-ninth, most of the snow was gone. Howdie woke me at five o'clock this morning for sunrise service. It was chilly enough to need all my winter clothes. Howdie waited for me, and he held my hand as we walked out to the hilltop. He doesn't usually do that, but I think he felt the love of Christ so much he couldn't help it.

Everyone comes to stand on our hill together. Grandmam and Grandpar were there. So was Uncle Almon and Aunt Winnie and her daughter, Ella, who is my cousin, I think. But she's about Mama's age. Dr. Dunn came too. Some of my friends were there and lots of others from our church and from the neighborhood. We sang the hymns that I love and heard scripture I can recite along with the preacher.

The best part is when it's time for the closing prayer. I bowed my head, hoping that when I opened my eyes again, the sun would be right at the horizon, about to come up. When the timing is perfect like that and the sky cooperates, it takes my breath away. Everyone sighs at the same time. This year, when I opened my eyes, there were big flakes of snow falling. The clouds were moving toward the sun and hadn't quite covered the east yet. We saw just the beginning of sunrise and, with the snow at the same time, it seemed magical to me. I hoped Jennie was watching it too from heaven. She loved this service more than any of us I think.

No one expected the snow to last very long. When the flakes are this big, the snow is bound to stop altogether. So, I asked Mama if I could go ice skating on the lake down behind Grandmam's house after our big dinner there.

"Yes, if your Grandpar thinks it's safe enough," she said.

Dinner on Resurrection Sunday is wonderful. All the women bring their best foods. There is always a lot of talking and laughing. Jennie would have loved to be here and skate with me. As it was, I was the only one who wanted to skate. Grandpar walked with me down to the lake to check the ice. We could see a man ice fishing out a little ways, which meant the ice was plenty thick enough. So Grandpar checked the ice at the edge and found it to be thinning but acceptable. He stayed with me while I laced on my skates. It was snowing a bit more and the wind was picking up. Grandpar told me he would stay till I was on the ice and then he would go on up to the house because he was getting too cold. He said he would send someone down to check on me and then he waited until I was out on the ice. I waved to him before he turned to go back up the hill.

The ice was smooth and glorious, with crisscross patterns of cracks making mostly triangles. I headed toward the center of the lake, twirling and sailing across the frozen water. I know how to skate backwards too, so I raced forward and back, while the wind on my face made me feel free and alive. Except for my blades scraping the ice, I knew the lake would be very quiet and peaceful, so I stopped and just stood. I closed my eyes to listen to the quiet while the snow fell all around me. To me, this is church outside. And there's no better day for it than Resurrection Sunday.

When I opened my eyes, the trees all looked more sparkly. The evergreens mixed with the bare trees like angular exclamation points in a forest of words. I thought about how the barren trees looked like stick men and women waiting for someone to bring them their own green clothing of spring–a lighter green than the evergreen trees, though. I began to think of the trees talking to each other about their clothing, and then about their forest neighborhoods. As I skated, I was so lost in thoughts about the trees that I didn't notice the snow falling harder and the flakes becoming so small as to be almost indistinguishable, one from another. Suddenly a huge gust of wind almost knocked me over and with it a fury of snow so wild I could hardly see the shoreline.

I began skating toward Grandpar's opening in the woods where I left my shoes, but it quickly closed in and I wasn't sure where it was at all.

Small twisters swirled all around me. If I wasn't concerned about being out on the ice all alone, I think I might have thought the snow was dancing. But soon, even the twisters left and all I could see was white. I turned in all directions but I realized I didn't know which way was toward the center of the lake and which way would get me back up the hill. I could hardly open my eyes, the snow stung so. That's when I started to panic. It was getting colder every minute, and I knew my clothing wouldn't keep me warm for long. The lake was anything but quiet by then. The wind sounded like one of the trains that pull into White Rock station. I felt very small and very, very alone. I started yelling for help. It's all I knew to do. But the storm just ate my words and swallowed them up before they were even a foot from me. I yelled anyway. Again. And again. And again. All the while feeling colder and colder. I rubbed my arms and legs as fast and hard as I could because they were starting to feel numb. I covered all but my eyes with my scarf. I tucked my hands under my arms and skated in tight little circles just to keep warm.

"God! Help me! Please, help me! Where are you? Help!"

It felt like I had been out on the ice forever. I began to think about being inside Grandmam's house where it was warm and everyone was having fun being together. I wanted to be with them all so very much. I heard a loud, booming crack and knew the ice was shifting beneath me. I decided to lie on the ice, curled in a ball. For a short time, I felt the warmth of my own body all coiled together. But it didn't last, and I was afraid I would be harder to find. So I stood up again. I was afraid that if I moved, I'd move away from the shore, so I tried to stand very still, though my body began to shiver and shake.

"Oh, please don't crack open!" I yelled to the ice, as if it cared at all. "Help me! Help me!" I yelled and yelled. I started to cry and my tears froze on my cheeks. I wondered if the ice fisherman had left his post. *Maybe he will walk my way*, I thought. I listened for perhaps his boots sliding across the ice. I thought I heard him. Yes, there it was again. I yelled out to him.

"I'm here!" a man's voice called out. Did I really hear the man? Or was it the trees scraping together in the wind?

"Where?" I screamed.

"Here!" The man was getting closer. I inched toward the sound of his voice.

"Help me!" I screamed again, hoping I would hear his voice even louder.

"I'm coming! Yell again so I can find you!" the man hollered.

"Here! I'm here! I'm here!" I kept screaming.

Hands grabbed my shoulder from behind me. I turned around and fell into his embrace. I didn't know who I was hugging, but I didn't care. I cried harder.

"You're okay now."

I looked up and saw Howdie! How did I not know his voice?

"Oh, Howdie! I'm so glad to see you! And I'm so cold."

"You must be about frozen, little one. Hold onto my coat behind me. I will shield you from some of the wind. Let's go!"

"Can't I hold your hand? I'm afraid we'll get lost out here!" I yelled.

"No, I need my hands to follow this rope. Uncle Almon is holding the other end of it on the shore so we won't get lost. But we may get frostbitten if we don't hurry."

I couldn't feel my hands or feet by the time we reached the shore and Uncle Almon, who was holding my shoes. "We can't stop to let you put on your shoes," he yelled out over the storm. "You'll have to walk in your skates. Let's go!"

I walked the best I could, but I was so slow that Howdie picked me up and carried me all the way back up the hill to the house.

The door opened and Howdie quickly stepped inside and into the parlor where a crackling fire and a pile of blankets awaited all three of us.

"We were so worried," Mama said, tucking me inside blankets like a moth in a cocoon. "And then it took Howdie and Almon far too long to find you. We thought you'd all perished." I looked up into Mama's face and saw that she'd been crying. So had Grandmam.

"I'm sorry to have worried you," I said between sobs. It never occurred to me that Mama cared about me this much. I mean, really, *really* cared.

"Well, all's well now," Mama said. "As soon as you feel warm enough to let me take the blankets off you, I'm going to check for frostbite."

Then Grandmam added, "And I'll figure out how to bed everyone down for the night. No one will be leaving here today. I won't allow it."

Grandmam's word was final, though I knew Papa would worry about the animals who wouldn't see him until tomorrow.

Four

Tears

Sunday, October 1, 1893

Dearest Joe,

Papa wanted me to write you and tell you about Mama's teeth. This week the dentist came to see Mama's gums. He said they weren't hard enough to put her teeth in, so she looks funny when she smiles. She asked me not to make her laugh. I try not to.

Papa also wanted me to tell you that two of his best ewes were killed by wild dogs. Fortunately, there are other ewes to join with the rams. But he was very upset.

I mostly like school this year, except the school room. The Coatshop is too small for all of us. Howdie says he would like to see Great Falls have a new school. He wants to run for a seat on the superintending school committee next year so he can make a difference. He probably told you that.

Other than that, my grades are 80s and 90s. You would be proud of me. Since I'm in my 9th year, Mr. Brown says I must be even more diligent with my schoolwork if I want to continue on to high school next year. Papa and Mama say I must go just like you and Howdie did. And I do want to very much.

But sometimes it is hard to concentrate because there is a new boy in the 8th year. He's awfully nice. His name is Lawrence. I decided not to wear pigtails anymore. I'm too old for them. Luella is still my best friend. She likes Lawrence, too. I think all the girls do.

One of the younger scholars, a boy I won't name, gets into a lot of trouble. He put tobacco spit in one of the younger girls' ink bottle! If we had a bigger school, I wouldn't have to put up with this nonsense. So far none of the boys has given me trouble when it's my turn to teach the young ones the primer. Thank goodness for that. How are your students? I don't suppose they give you any trouble.

A few scholars have pinkeye right now. The Bailey family has diftheria and everyone is staying away from their house. Mabel Hawkins' baby died of scarlet fever. Papa took the hearse for it. It made him very sad. I hate to see Papa like that.

Are you coming home for Christmas? Say, yes. It would be awfully nice.

Love, Millie

P.S. On Sunday, the 15th I will sign my pledge to become a member of Windham Hill Church.

P.P.S. I don't know how to spell diftheria.

I've tried to be sensible about Lawrence. I really like him but so do my friends and we all covet his attention. For his part, Lawrence seems smitten by all the girls no matter what age they are. When he flirts with the younger girls, it seems so improper that my friends and I just turn our backs on him.

One day, as Luella and I walked home together, we talked about Lawrence, as we did most days, when I saw Grandpar's horse attached to a buggy I didn't recognize standing by the house. I bid Luella goodbye and ran the rest of the way home.

"Uncle Almon!" I cried and ran to give him a hug. I was overjoyed. "What are you doing here? Is that your buggy? It's nice! May I take a ride in it?"

"Slow down there, Millie! One question at a time," he said to me, smiling. Mama wasn't smiling though, I noticed. She was standing near us with her arms folded, looking concerned. I eyed both of them and knew something wasn't right.

"What is it?" I asked them.

"Grandmam is ailing," Mama said. "Your uncle has come to talk to us about Grandmam's care. Grandpar is doing all he can, but it's hard on him."

"It is," Uncle Almon agreed. "I can't be up here for long stretches at a time, so I'm asking that you and your ma stop over to your Grandmam's house to help out as much as you can."

"And you know I'm already busy enough, Millie," Mama took over. "When I'm not at Grandmam's, I will need you to help out there. And then we'll switch."

They were talking to me as if I was all grown up, which is something I've wanted my whole life. But now, I don't think I want to be grown up any more. It isn't that I don't want to help. I already do that anyway. But I can't bear thinking of Grandmam too sick to care for herself.

"As to your other questions," Uncle Almon broke in, "yes, that's my new buggy. If it's alright with your ma, I'll take you over to Grandmam's house now and you can see for yourself what needs to be done for her." Mama nodded.

"You'll want an extra layer for when I bring you back. It's getting chilly now when the sun sets."

I love Grandmam dearly. It's almost always been she who comes to care for us when Mama is sick or if Mama needs extra help. It's hard to think of her as anything but healthy, anything but the fine woman she is. I never grow tired of listening to the accent she brought with her from England. And her house! The fine porcelain dishes and dainty teacups she uses when she entertains. They are nothing at all like our thicker, heavier, too-plain ironstone dishes. Grandmam's furniture is finer as well. Sometimes when I walk into their home, it's as if I leave Great Falls far behind and enter a foreign country. Grandmam dresses in elegant clothing when she isn't at home. I like to pretend that I am a lady of means like her, sipping tea and eating the fancy petit fours she had when she was a child in Europe. Or sometimes I sit at the parlor table with a teacup in my hand. I lift my little finger up as Grandmam taught me and imagine that I am an accomplished teacher or even a professor entertaining my colleagues.

We were close to Grandmam's house when we saw the gently rolling acreage with its apple orchards always ready to yield fruit to anyone who passes by. Those orchards were Grandpar's doing. He loves to be outside and doesn't much like dressing up unless he has to. He'd rather be wearing his overalls, walking among his trees, telling them to produce well. On pretty days, I like to stroll the grounds too, and talk to the trees and flowers as if they are a clutch of very special friends. They understand me better than anyone I know. When squirrels and chipmunks scurry by I think of them as wayward children and scold them for being so mischievous.

Grandpar also loves the lake. It shimmers in all the seasons unless it's covered in ice. Then it isn't a shimmer as much as a sheen. I love that their house is right on the lake. My friends and I have the best swims there, especially in August when the lake is warmest. But its water is always crystal clear no matter what time of year it is. I still find it difficult to tell how deep the lake floor is when I swim because the bottom looks extremely close to my toes. When I was a little girl, Grandpar told me that the lake's name, Sebago, is an Abenaki Indian word that means "big still water" or "it resembles the sea." Years ago, he and I stood side by side looking at the vast waters as he swept his arm left to right, telling me about when the Indians lived on this very land. The best part of swimming here is when I come back up the bank to the house because Grandmam magically produces cookies that soothe my growling tummy. *Now I wonder if she'll ever be able to do that again.*

This day, the day Uncle Almon took me to see Grandmam, didn't feel like most other times I've visited. I was nervous because I wasn't sure how to face my grandmother. But Grandmam was just lying in bed with a very bad cold. Her eyes were closed, although I think she was awake. It looked like she was lying under too many blankets, but they didn't seem to bother her. It was strange not to see her hair put up. It lay braided on her chest. *Still, she's beautiful,* I thought. She didn't talk; she needed her rest, so I let her be and asked Grandpar if there was anything I could do to help him while he and Uncle Almon talked. He wanted me to begin supper preparations, which I could easily do. It felt good to return the favor to Grandmam.

The rest of October and into November, Mama and I took turns going to Grandmam's house because the old woman was not bouncing back as Mama, Uncle Almon, and the doctor expected her to. I began to fear the worst and tried to soak in everything Grandmam said and did because I knew what it was like to wish I had more memories of someone I dearly loved after they died.

"Mama?" I said after school one day late in November. "Will we go to Grandmam's and Grandpar's like we usually do on Thanksgiving? With all the family?"

"I don't think so, Millie. You know how poorly Grandmam is doing, and Grandpar has a cold virus now too. Both your uncles are here now to help them. When your Papa and I went to take some food this morning, Uncle Almon said that he and John were somewhat concerned that they might succumb to the virus too. He didn't allow us into the house. We didn't talk about next week. We'll have Thanksgiving here, though."

Early the day before Thanksgiving, there came a knock at our door. It was Uncle Almon, and as soon as Mama and I saw him ride in, we knew why he was there. I watched Mama tear up and sit down at the table. My tears came too, especially watching Mama. Even though it was inevitable, Grandmam's death came as a blow. I buried myself in Uncle Almon's embrace as soon as he walked in the door. Then we both sat down with Mama.

"We had the doctor come again yesterday," my uncle began, facing Mama. "He said Ma had developed pneumonia. Her fever was very high. He gave her medicine for pain and fever but said we should just keep her as comfortable as possible. The doctor suspected the end would come soon. She passed just after midnight this morning. She seemed to just fade away while we held her hands. I don't think she was in a lot of pain, thank goodness," he finished, dropping his eyes to look down at his folded hands. He too was having difficulty imagining his mother was no longer with us.

After some silence, Mama said, "I'm glad you and John were there for Ma. We need to send a telegram to Josey and Howdie and Aunt Winnie and Ella. And I think Pa once mentioned putting an obituary in the Portland Daily Press. Did he mention anything about that to you or John?"

"He did. That's one reason why I'm here. Could you help me write something up this morning? And John is taking care of telegramming everyone who needs to know."

"That's good. Let me finish getting breakfast together, then we can write the obituary. Please stay and eat with us. Millie, come help me."

While we were busy in the kitchen, Uncle Almon went out to the barn to tell Papa the sad news. He likes Papa but has told me that he finds Papa to be a mysterious man of few words. I guess he can be that way sometimes. Papa came into the kitchen soon after Uncle Almon had come back in.

After we had breakfast, Papa went back out to the barn, and I cleaned up the kitchen. It didn't take Mama long to write her mother's obituary. Then she said, "Has the undertaker been notified?"

"He has," Uncle Almon said. "He will come today to prepare her body for tomorrow's viewing. And since it's Thanksgiving, will you see to food for the mourners, Julia? It won't be a usual Thanksgiving no matter what we do with it, unfortunately. At least it will be in Ma's home where she always loved to celebrate with everyone." I had been listening to all this, and I noticed that Uncle Almon's last words had made Mama tear up. I wanted to say something to her, but I stayed very quiet for fear she would tell me to go do something else. *Why do adults still tell me that? I'm forever too young except when it comes to chores.*

As soon as Mama and her brother had finished discussing all the details they could think of, Uncle Almon left Mama to the considerable amount of work she'd have the rest of that day. Mama turned to me directly and said, "Well, Millie, it's up to you and me to feed a lot of people tomorrow. The mourners will bring food too. So first, let's sit down and decide what we need to make." By bedtime, both Mama and I were plenty tired and fell into bed, thoroughly spent.

The next day, Thanksgiving Day, was not easy for anyone. A day usually spent in gratitude, eating, telling stories, and laughing, felt choked by sadness and dampened by tears. Giving thanks did not even seem appropriate. Grandmam looked lovely but she had none of the spark that made her the grandmother I knew. Worse still, the day reminded me of Jennie's wake, which had been a painful, heart-wrenching day. *Why is it called a wake, anyway? The person who died is certainly not awake!* I mumbled to myself as I helped Mama refill plates of food and wash dishes. Grandpar looked like a ghost. He mostly sat and received people from his chair. Mama kept busy and I with her. By nightfall she and I were exhausted. I fell into a fitful sleep that night thinking about Grandmam's burial coming next.

On Friday, we assembled at Harding Cemetery where Grandmam was laid to rest. The only people who spoke besides the preacher were Howdie and Uncle Almon. Howdie read John 6:40 from the little golden Bible that Grandmam had given him when he was thirteen, like I am now. Uncle Almon read the poem that will be on Grandmam's gravestone, and it says exactly what I feel: *One precious to our hearts has gone. The voice we loved is stilled. The place made vacant in our home can nevermore be filled.* All I could do was tell Grandmam that I loved her and goodbye. I said it in my mind but felt it in my heart.

Somehow, we stumbled on through the calendar and before long it was Christmas. Grandpar came to our house and Uncle Almon, Howdie, and even Joe were there. It felt so good to have everyone home. Together. Mama made her Christmas pudding and all the foods that helped make the holiday feel special even though Grandmam was missing.

"There's one more gift!" Howdie said, holding up a small, rectangular, wrapped package. We had all assumed everything had been opened already.

"Who's it for?" I asked impatiently.

"Hmmmm…why, I believe it's for…I can't quite read it," he said, squinting rather conspicuously as he held the gift up too close to his eyes and smiled widely.

"Who's it for, Howdie?" I asked again, laughing at his antics. Everyone was now smiling broadly.

"I think, I think, I think…it's…for…" he drew out his words, "for… *Millie!*"

I squealed with delight as Howdie handed me the gift. I opened it with little care for the wrapping, even though I was taught to be more careful. But I couldn't wait. In it was a small book of gospel hymns that had been Grandmam's. She couldn't give me the little yellow Bible because she'd given it to Howdie already. But I had her gospel hymns that I could take to church. It meant so much to me to have something special of Grandmam's. But that wasn't all. Inside the little book was the tiniest, most lovely red rose that had been crafted by needlepoint. I passed it around so others could examine it.

"Grandmam made that," Mama said quietly.

Thinking that the rose had been in the hymn book to be pressed and possibly forgotten, I asked Mama if she wanted it.

"No, Millie, it's yours," Mama replied with compassion woven into her words.

I knew then that Mama knew about the rose and intended it to be mine. I got up and gave Mama a hug. "Thank you, Mama," I whispered in her ear.

"Actually, there is one more gift," Uncle Almon said. "It's in the barn. Howdie and Joe, will you boys help me bring it inside, please?"

I couldn't wait to see what grand thing had been hidden in the barn and whose surprise it was going to be. Mama, Papa, Grandpar, and I sat in silence. I looked into their faces to see if they had any knowledge of this mysterious gift, but I couldn't read their expressions at all. Soon there was a commotion in the kitchen and the scraping of chairs.

"Don't come out here until we tell you to!" Joe yelled.

More commotion. Mama's face now read confusion mixed with a bit of delight. Papa's read patience. Always patience. Grandpar's face read pure glee. *He must know something*, I thought.

"Alright everyone! Come on in the kitchen!"

I ran. Mama and Papa walked. Grandpar remained in the living room. When I reached the kitchen and saw the surprise, I opened my mouth to say something, but Howdie quickly caught my attention and put a finger to his lips. Then Mama walked in. She saw her family all crowded around something against the wall. The men all held their arms out toward the surprise, holding Mama's eyes with their own. Mama turned around to see Grandmam's Hoosier cabinet that she had long coveted. Mama reached out to caress the fine piece of furniture that would make her kitchen work so much easier. Tears ran down her cheeks, but she turned to all of us and smiled. Then I went back to the living room.

"Oh, Grandpar," I said, kneeling down in front of him. He simply looked at me and smiled.

Five

Howdie

That February of 1894, Howdie was elected to the Superintending School Committee for a three-year term. We were all so proud of him. He learned a lot of things right away. He said that where most male teachers are paid approximately seventy-seven dollars a month, women receive eight dollars and fifty cents a week, which is less than half what a man makes per year. Personally, I don't think that's fair if the women have the same schooling to be a teacher that a man has. I told Howdie this and he agreed. He also said that twelve years ago, when the canal going through Great Falls closed and our town began to dwindle in size, the number of school scholars dwindled with it. Howdie said he is grateful to be able to advocate for his hometown.

He must have done a good job advocating because Great Falls was given three thousand dollars to build a real schoolhouse! The first school was held in Mr. Hall's woodshed in 1828 with eighteen scholars. The school outgrew the woodshed and later, larger places until now, the Coatshop is too small even with the number of scholars dropping. Mr. Hall's grandsons, Edwin and Frederick, donated five hundred dollars for the bell and belfry in the new school's cupola. The work won't begin until next summer, but the excitement is already growing. I, for one, cannot wait. I will be fifteen and in my second year of high school when the new schoolhouse opens!

Then in March, I turned fourteen. Mama said that she wanted me to start making the bread all by myself. The first time I made it I was so worried that it wouldn't be good like Mama's. But Papa thought it was just fine. I haven't had to make it every week, but when I do, it's a big help to Mama, I know. She also said that since I would be spending more time in the kitchen, I should wear a day dress and change into something nicer for evening like she does. That's why she gave me a good dress on my birthday. I think I'm growing up. Finally.

Papa's ewes dropped eighteen lambs by mid-March. He was so happy with his good fortune. There were several sets of twins this year, one from the Merino and the rest from the Suffolks. But then wild dogs killed half of the Suffolk lambs and Papa was so outraged he dropped what he was doing and went directly to the town office to be reimbursed for them.

"I said to the clerk, 'When are you gonna do something about those dogs? It'll cost the town a fortune if you don't.' The clerk says, 'Yes, sir, Mr. Thomas, we know we have an issue on our hands. I'm sorry for your loss,' and handed me my payment. I didn't think he sounded very sorry at all. Probably doesn't understand what livestock means to a farmer."

Later that month, Howdie surprised us all by buying the house directly across the road. He said he planned to raise chickens, which he started doing after he built a very nice coop. It was so magnificent having him so close. I wondered at first if he planned to ask Betsy to marry him and live in Great Falls. But if he did, I never heard anything about it. I would stop by to visit Howdie when I knew he was home. Sometimes I even cooked something for him. We talked about a lot of different things, but mostly about school.

I finished my ninth year pretty well, at least as far as my end-of-year marks were concerned. But in matters of the heart, I went in and out of liking and not liking Lawrence. I found him to be coquettish with the girls, so I didn't feel I could trust him when I was the receiver of his attention. Still, I liked him when he paid attention to me and hated–well, disliked–him when he completely ignored me. I was uncertain as to whether I should invite his friendship or simply let it all go to God's will.

Meanwhile my life moved on into summer with Joe coming home again and both boys working for Papa and the town. Independence Day was different than usual only in that I learned that Lawrence's birthday is that day. I made him a card and delivered it. He thanked me with a short stroll and a nice conversation. Liking him is confusing. When we are alone, it's as if no other girl exists on this whole planet. Then, next thing I know, he's enjoying the company of someone else. Sometimes I let my anger get the better of me. But I don't much like the person I become when I'm that upset.

August saw Mama and Papa going to Papa's annual Seventeenth Maine regiment reunion in Portland. I didn't go with them this year because it's usually boring for me, even though I sometimes listen to the men talk about the war and learn a thing or two. But August is when our neighbors and friends meet at Grandpar's house to pick blueberries and eat ice cream, which is much more fun than a war reunion. Grandpar decided to host this gathering one more time even though Grandmam wasn't there. It was a wonderful day despite Grandmam's absence.

School began in the fall. I started my tenth year and longed to be in the new school. But it hadn't even begun being built. The Coatshop was slightly less crowded, as many of the boys about my age left school to work on their family's farms or businesses. Lawrence, however, remained. And even though the old issues from the year before were still there, I was happy to see him every school day. He would occasionally carry my books and walk me home. But then, he also did that for Luella, which didn't make things easy for our friendship for a while. Lawrence, it seems, has no intention of settling for only one girl.

Then in November, to my shock, Howard sold his newly purchased home to Papa. Why? I wasn't certain. He told Papa that he'd decided he was too busy to keep chickens in Great Falls, work on our farm, and keep his job in Portland. This way, he explained, Papa could rent the house out and garner some much-needed money. And he would return to the city. But something about this explanation seemed perplexing to me. It disturbed me with similar feelings I would get from Lawrence when he'd tell me he liked me and then was seen with another girl. Something didn't feel quite right. I wanted to talk to Papa about it, but in the end, I thought it best to remain quiet. If he also questioned Howdie's motives for selling the farm, perhaps he was disturbed as well, and I didn't want to agitate him further. But with Howdie gone more often, and Papa getting older, I worried that he would be stretched beyond his limit.

Before I knew it, we were celebrating the beginning of 1895. My fifteenth birthday came and went in March and the rest of my tenth year ended as well. I had begun to see Lawrence at Forest Hall events—dances, plays, and concerts. I even invited Lawrence to come to celebrate Independence Day with us, and also his birthday, which I kept secret from the family. I decided that if he wanted them to know, he could tell them himself.

Joe explained to Lawrence that we had firecrackers that Papa liked to place in a pie tin. Then he'd cover it with another pie tin and light the fuse. We all stood back to watch the top pie tin blow clear off!

"Where is your ma?" Lawrence asked when he noticed she was nowhere near our fun.

"She says it's a sin to use a pie tin for firecrackers. I think she just plain doesn't like the sudden explosion and its loud bang," I explained.

"I guess there's some sense in that," he said.

Just before he had to leave, we took a walk down to the river and I gave him the card I'd made. We were standing under the oak tree looking out over the cove, watching sunfish pop to the surface of the water between lily pads, making the water ripple. It was peaceful just standing there quietly. The surface of the water caught the rays of sunlight when it rippled, so that each tiny wave lifted up a diamond-like sparkle and passed it on. Lawrence moved closer to me. I could feel my heart begin to thump. It was exhilarating to have him stand so near me. I might have moved away from him, I suppose, in keeping with my distrust of his motives, but I didn't. After a little while, he took another step closer so that our arms touched. My skin felt little tingles all over that reminded me of the water sparkles I still watched but now wasn't really seeing. I felt so alive. Next thing I knew he'd bent down and kissed me! It happened so fast that I wasn't really ready for it. Then again, is anyone ever ready for such a thing? It felt like a butterfly had landed on my lips and then flown off. I shall always remember it, no matter what happens between Lawrence and me.

There was an awkward moment of silence after he kissed me when I wondered what to do next. Stand there? Move? Talk? Not talk? Then Lawrence leaned over again and just as his lips met mine, we heard a twig crack. Instantly, I felt my face turn crimson as I pulled away and stepped back. *Please don't let it be Papa or one of the boys. Please, please.* I wasn't sure what might happen if it was one of them. We both quickly scanned the woods that fanned out behind us as a lovely doe emerged. She stopped, cautious of us. We stood still, watching her until she turned and walked away from us and back into the shelter of the woods.

The silence remained, as I at least allowed my heart to take a rest from its wild beating. I wasn't sure if this had affected Lawrence as it had me, but I knew I was done with the kissing for now and had no intention of doing anything but walk back up the hill and say goodbye to him. Lawrence followed me.

"Millie," he said quietly, "are you alright?"

"Yes."

"Are you angry with me?"

"No."

"Do you wish to talk about whatever is bothering you?"

"No."

We walked the rest of the way in silence and when we reached the house, Lawrence simply bade me farewell and left. I had a lot of thinking to do about what had just happened. Why did I feel ashamed of myself? Had I done something so wrong in receiving Lawrence's kiss? Was there a proper age to kiss? Goodness knows my friends and I talk about it a lot, but that doesn't mean doing it. What would Papa think of me? Would he be disappointed? I couldn't imagine living with myself if Papa was disappointed in me.

By the end of that July, the new schoolhouse was beginning to take shape, and I loved walking by it on my way to pick up mail or a few items Mama needed at the general store down the hill. Howdie seemed to think of the new school as his, for all the pride he took in it. Oh, he knew he wasn't solely responsible for the building, but he also knew that his input had influenced the committee.

"Please pass the peas," Joe said, interrupting Howdie's discourse on the school's progress.

"As I said," Howdie began again, coughing slightly from a lingering cold, and pushing his food around on his plate as he talked, "I believe the building will be two stories. It seemed a shame to waste the opportunity to build something large enough to be used in a variety of ways, more than just school rooms. Of course, it will cost the town more."

"Hmm," Papa interjected. "Just how much more? Isn't the town about strapped, what with new roads going in and a bridge to repair? Are there enough scholars to fill such a lofty building?"

"There will be," Howdie said. "At least that's the hope."

"Besides, Papa," Joe joined in, "down in Massachusetts, many of the schools are beautifully crafted. Makes a soul happy just to be in such a building." He was clearly in favor of the second floor.

"The hope is that the older classes can be separated from the younger ones so that more subjects can be added to the high school curriculum. And the younger ones will be less distracted working at their own levels," Howdie said.

"Will I start school in the new building this fall?" I chimed in.

"We'll have to see, Millie. That was the plan, but with the extra floor, it may take longer," Howdie said with compassion for my crushed look.

"I hope I will at least be able to graduate from Levi Hall," I said, feeling sorry for myself.

By August, even I could tell the building was clearly not going to be finished in time for the new school year. And, according to Papa, the cost was going to be a full twenty-five percent more than the original estimate. Many were not happy with the school committee and thought Levi Hall was something of an extravagance for a place no bigger than Great Falls. I felt sorry for Howdie and wondered if these remarks were difficult for him to hear.

But Mama, it seemed to me, didn't concern herself with any of that. She didn't say a word about the growing discord between the town folk. Something else was making her uneasy.

"Millie," she said one evening as we washed dishes, "you keep close to Howdie. Do you think he's losing weight and coughing more often?"

"I don't know about losing weight, but I do hear him cough a lot. Isn't that just his cold lingering on?"

"Maybe. But it seems he isn't helping your Pa as much around here, either. Not that I hold him in judgment of that. I know he would never slack. That's exactly what has me worried. He wouldn't slack, so why is he?"

"Oh, Mama, now you've got me worried. Do you think that's why Howdie sold the house across the road? Do you think he wasn't feeling well enough to live there?"

"Maybe," she said, then stopped talking to think about it. "Quite possibly, now that you mention it. In any case, I shouldn't have worried you. Forgive me. I'll think no more of it."

"But Mama, I'm happy to share your burden of worry. Really I am." And I was. Mama had had more than her share of worry about her children. I so badly wished she wasn't upset now. But I couldn't help that one bit.

"If it's helpful, I'll keep my eyes out for any changes I see and let you know. Okay, Mama?"

"Yes, child, thank you."

Then one day in late August, Howard didn't come downstairs for breakfast. He'd been staying at the farm more than usual, which thrilled me to have him so close. But Mama grew more and more concerned.

"Do you want me to go see if he's coming downstairs?" I asked Mama.

"No, Millie, I will take him some tea and bread myself."

When Mama was out of earshot, Millie asked, "Papa, do you think something is wrong with Howdie like Mama does?"

"Well, child, I guess I have always trusted that your Ma knows things about people that I don't see."

"I guess y….."

Suddenly there was a crash from upstairs. Papa and I ran to see what it was. I made it before he did. Howdie's door was open. My eyes traced the path of bread and tea scattered and splattered all over the floor, the door, and Howdie's bed. Then I saw Howdie. He was sitting partly upright, holding his sheet in his hands like a bowl to catch the mucousy blood he'd just coughed up. Mama knelt beside his bed with her hands under Howdie's, her eyes wide with fear. Howdie's matched hers.

"Oh, son, what is happening?" she said.

"I don't know, Mama," he rasped. "I don't feel at all well. Please fetch the doctor."

"I'll go," Papa said and was already moving to the stairs.

"Millie!" Mama said sharply. I hadn't moved. I felt frozen with horror. "Millie!" she said again. I finally took my eyes off Howdie and looked at her. She had bundled the soiled bed cloth in her arms and handed it to me. "Take this out to the piazza," she said with a pinched voice I've rarely heard. "Then bring me a cold, wet cloth."

The wadded-up sheet felt strangely like a layer of protection against whatever was coming as I rushed to fulfill Mama's order. When I returned, she had covered Howdie's body with a fresh blanket and was just spreading it over his arms and legs, which were oddly mottled. But, focusing on his face, I saw now that his cheeks looked hollow. I wondered if Mama had been right about his weight loss. *How could I not have noticed his condition?* Mama asked me to fetch a warm compress and another blanket, which I did. Then I stood by the doorway waiting, in case Mama asked me to do something else. I stared at my brother, trying to make sense of what was happening and how I felt about it. Howdie didn't look up.

I hadn't heard Papa return and was startled when he appeared beside me. I looked up at him expectantly. He gently told me to go downstairs to wait for Dr. Dunn, but my feet stuck to the floor as though they'd been nailed down. I didn't want to be separated from my Howdie even for a short time.

"Go now, child," Papa said again, more firmly, then moved further into the bedroom so he could close the door behind him and close me out. *The line between being a child and grown up is maddening. One moment I am kissing Lawrence like an adult and the next I'm being shooed away from one of the most important people in my life.*

I went to sit in the parlor where I could see Dr. Dunn the moment he arrived. I could hear Howdie cough above me and I began to weep for my brother, and for me, for the two of us, and the whole family. I could hardly bear the ticking of the clock's pendulum as I waited. Papa came downstairs once to freshen the compresses. When I asked him if Howdie was any better, he simply shook his head and went back upstairs. Mama came down briefly to get tea and bread, for herself and Papa, I supposed. I argued with myself that I should have taken the food up to them, but Papa had told me to wait downstairs. In any case, I wasn't hungry in the least.

It was almost dark by the time Dr. Dunn finally arrived. Again, the wait was treacherous. When Dr. Dunn and Papa finally walked down the front stairs, I searched their faces for any unspoken words. The doctor tipped his hat as he went by and then saw himself out while Papa joined me. Quiet for the first few minutes, he finally addressed me with more words than I think I have ever heard from him at one time. "Dr. Dunn suspects Howdie has had the consumption for perhaps years when the symptoms were not showing. Now the illness is very bad. He gave Howdie willowbark for his fever and laudanum for the pain. Howdie will need mostly sleep, in the house or outside depending on the weather. The more fresh air he can get, the better. Thankfully it's summer. But Dr. Dunn cautioned us that Howdie may need stronger pain medicines soon and..." Papa choked on his next thought. "And he said that Howdie may not live much longer. Your mother is too tired to come downstairs. Please do what needs to be done tonight." He turned and left me in stunned silence to walk back up the stairs carrying his heavy burden.

Until school began for the year, I did much of Mama's work so that she could tend only to Howdie. Mrs. Hall filled in for me when I started school. Sadly, but not unexpectedly, the new building was not ready for the scholars. Nevertheless, it was dedicated on September ninth in a celebration that Howdie couldn't attend. I felt so bad for him. Every day I raced home from school to see how he was doing.

One day, the next week, I found that Mama was not at home.

"Where is Mama?" I asked Mrs. Hall.

"She went to the women's circle meeting at church to deliver the speech she promised to give–about the ways the church can become more involved with the Salvation Army, you know. I told her I thought she had every right to stay home. She has been looking so tired, you know. But she wouldn't hear of it. You know how your dear mother can be. Wonderful woman, you know, but stubbornly insistent on doing what's right. Why, not long ago, she…"

"Well," I interrupted after waiting as patiently as I could for Mrs. Hall to stop talking, "is Howdie upstairs, then?"

"Yes, dear. He told me to tell you to come up after school."

It didn't take me but a second to throw my books on the table and take the stairs two at a time. I thought I heard Mrs. Hall harrumph, but I didn't care.

I found Howdie sitting up and looking better than he had for weeks.

"Howdie!" I said when I laid eyes on him.

"Little sister, come sit beside me on the bed."

"Are you sure that's okay?"

"I'm sure," he said with a warm smile. "So, this is your second to last year in Great Falls. How is this year going?"

I sat gingerly beside him so as not to jostle the bed. "It seems about the same as other years in most respects. I sure do wish we were in the new schoolhouse. I think all our subjects would be more exciting if we were."

"How far has the schoolhouse gotten? Is the second floor completed?"

"I guess so. It looks like they are finished with the roof, but you can still see straight through the walls. But, Howdie, what I care about right now is you. You look lots better than you did. I'm so glad."

He didn't speak to that but suddenly looked serious. "Tell me about your young man, Lawrence. Is he good to you?"

I think I blushed. It felt very strange to talk about Lawrence so personally. And I wasn't sure what Howdie really wanted to know. "I don't think of him as *my* young man, Howdie. He is just my friend."

"Do you like him in a special way?"

I couldn't lie to him. "Yes, I suppose I do."

"Then I will pray for the two of you to find a pathway to genuine grown-up feelings for one another. But Millie, don't forsake your studies for such a relationship. I can assure you that it isn't worth it. Love relationships can be fickle at best, but your education will serve you well, always."

Is Howdie alluding to his relationship with Betsy? I wondered. I didn't ask, only received his wisdom as I always have.

"Well, little sister, I wonder if you could bring me more water. I need to rest now."

"Of course, Howdie. I'll be right back."

In the very short time it took me to bring Howdie more water, he had fallen asleep. I carefully put the glass on the bed table and went into my own room to have a word with my diary.

Wednesday, September 18, 1895

Dear diary, you are always a good listener when I pour my heart out to you. Howdie seems better today. Is that wishful thinking? How I long to see him back to normal, enjoying his life and all his ambitions. He's such a good man and brother, I can hardly stand to see him so sick. Yet in the midst of his illness he's thinking of me. He wanted to know if Lawrence is good to me. I didn't know how to answer him. Lawrence treats me as well as other girls. He's kind to us. I just don't trust that he has singled me out. And, truthfully, I'm not sure I'm ready for that anyway, after that kiss in the cove. He's not asked for any more kissing and I'm glad. If he wonders why I reacted the way I did, he hasn't asked.

The next day, Howdie was suddenly so much worse, it was utterly frightening. Dr. Dunn came and said Howdie needed stronger pain medicine. He said Howdie would mostly sleep after taking it. Papa sent

Joe a telegram asking him to come home. Joe arrived on Saturday. He was alarmed at Howdie's appearance. Probably more so than the rest of us since he hadn't seen Howdie's deterioration since he left at the end of August. I went to church Sunday with just Papa. I'm not sure he or I really wanted to leave Howdie, but God felt closer there. As I sat in the pew listening to the sermon, I thought, *God, is it so wrong to wish Howdie would die to end his misery? I can hardly stand seeing him like this. Is that selfish?*

Dr. Dunn asked about Howdie after the service and didn't like what he heard. He came to the farm that afternoon and injected Howdie with morphine for the pain. When he came downstairs, he told all of us to prepare for Howdie's burial, that he would be surprised if Howdie lasted through the night. Mama sat down so suddenly I thought she'd fainted. Papa sat down beside her, and she clung to him and wept. Joe and I saw Dr. Dunn to his buggy.

"Millie," Joe said after the doctor had left, "I think we need to leave Mama and Papa alone. Let's use the back stairs and go sit with Howdie."

No one slept the night through. We each took turns sitting with Howdie to spell Mama when necessary. Papa drank whiskey, which he usually only did to dull his leg pain. Tonight it was obvious there was a different sort of pain for which Papa needed relief.

The next day, September 23, Howdie was freed from his suffering. He was not yet twenty-five years old. Mama was inconsolable while I kept busy with kitchen duties and whatever else the family needed to simply exist. There was no energy but for that which was necessary. Papa would have said his farm duties were necessary because a farmer's life can't be put on hold. But it can be loaned out to caring neighbors willing to add more farm chores to their own for a time, no less than Papa has done for others. Although he hated to impose on his friends, Papa allowed them to take over his work so that he could attend to family matters. Joe fetched the undertaker and, with Mama's feeble help, selected from several poems the one they thought suited their younger brother and son best:

I do believe the same sweet face, but glorified
is waiting for me, in that happy place
Where we shall meet if only I
Am counted worthy in the by and by.

At the cemetery, Papa handed me Howdie's little golden Bible. He asked me to read the twenty-third Psalm. On the way back to the house, Papa quietly said, "Keep it. It's yours now."

Six

Mama

I recently heard a passage from Isaiah, chapter 57, verse 1, that seemed so fitting: "The godly often die before their time." Fitting of Howdie, and Jennie too. I'm unfortunately becoming used to readjusting after we suffer a family loss. But this one has been harder than any other. Nothing has seemed right since Howdie died. Joe had to go back to Massachusetts to work. I guess that one thing was normal, although I could tell Joe regretted having to leave so soon. Mama was stricken in heart and health much of the time. She wept often. At first, I thought her heart simply grieved for Howdie. But then I reasoned that all the deaths—her two baby boys, her daughter, her mother, and now her younger son—were stacked as one, a precarious tower of loss that she kept upright in her heart, but only barely. She didn't seem to care anymore who saw her heartache. I figured she was so full of grief that it simply leaked out of her, unbidden.

Papa continued his work on the farm, but his demeanor told me his heart wasn't in it. It was as if the whole house, inhabitants and boards alike, sagged under the weight of that which couldn't be helped. The power of death. And death, or perhaps just the effects of it, was everywhere, not just in Howdie's room. Although right now his room was unbearably sad to be in. Everywhere Howdie had walked or sat and everything he had touched or used felt like he was still with us, yet his absence said otherwise. I suppose I felt this when Jennie died too, but I don't remember it being this poignant. I felt so helpless to lift the spirit of grief permeating the farm. All that was left was to be as unassumingly helpful and agreeable as possible. *I need to be as small and quiet as the tiny mouse who lives behind the walls until no one is watching,* I thought. *But what I most want to do is console Mama. If she felt better, so would Papa, I'm sure. I know I would.*

I was miserable, and my friends could all see it. They were as helpful as they could be in this situation. I was given sweet notes of condolences and well-wishes and offerings to help. But it was one person in particular who came to my aid that really made a difference. Lawrence. I could not have predicted that his would be the shoulder I could lean on most. We quickly became almost inseparable, enough so that no other girls even tried to step between us.

As it turned out, I needed him more than I could have imagined. The rest of the holidays that year were difficult. Joe came for Christmas. He told me when he left that he didn't envy my position, being surrounded by that much grief. Though he was complimentary of Lawrence's attention to me and happy that I had a wonderful relationship to bring me joy.

Turning the calendar to the new year didn't bring its usual celebration; only the bleak reality that the future would still not have Howdie in it. One of Mama's friends gently pestered her to attend a Women's Christian Temperance Union meeting. Papa encouraged her to go, too. He thought that if she felt she could be helpful to others, it might lift her spirits. Perhaps it did, a little.

The day I turned sixteen in March, unbeknownst to me, Lawrence arranged for all the girls to surprise me at school. When lunchtime came, instead of grabbing lunch pails, they all surrounded me and showered me with sweets and cards that rained down upon my head. It was all so much fun. When I looked up, I saw Lawrence standing back, just watching. But until our eyes met and he cracked a wide Cheshire Cat grin, I hadn't known he had anything to do with the surprise. He walked me home, carrying my books. When we reached the kitchen door, I invited him to come in. I thought perhaps he might stay for dinner if

Mama had made enough, but she was not in the kitchen, which was strange.

"Come with me to the barn. I'll ask Papa where Mama is." But Papa was not there, either. I began to be concerned. Something didn't feel right.

"Do you want me to stay until you find them?" Lawrence offered.

"Please," I said, gratefully.

I hadn't looked upstairs yet because Mama and Papa were rarely there when I got home from school.

"Stay here. I'll go look upstairs." But just as I'd set my foot on the first step, Papa appeared at the top.

"Oh, there you are! I've been looking for…what's wrong Papa?" I could see he'd been crying. I felt panic rise into my throat. "Is it Mama? Please tell me Mama is alright."

"I will explain when we are alone." He said pointedly.

Lawrence had heard the exchange and waved to me as he headed for the door.

"Lawrence is gone now, Papa. What is happening?" I had become very frightened as I watched Papa descend the stairs and walk to the parlor to sit in his chair. He seemed to take forever to get there.

"Yes, child, Mama is sick. Same as she's been off and on now. She'd been coughing a good bit, so I fetched Dr. Dunn. He gave her something to help her sleep."

"But if it's the same thing she's been bothered by, why were you crying? Did Dr. Dunn say something else? About her future?"

"No, child, not about *her* future. But while we were waiting for the doctor, your mother and I had a difficult talk about the future of this farm."

"You're not going to sell it are you?" I asked in utter horror.

"No."

"Thank goodness. But then, what?"

"Without either of the boys around, I can't manage all the animals. Tuesday, a man you probably don't know, from Windham, will come take the sheep away."

"Oh, Papa! Not your sheep!"

"Can't be helped, Millie," Papa acquiesced quietly. I could tell he was in an emotionally difficult place. And he was finished talking.

I dreaded Tuesday. Not so much for myself. I would be in school when the sheep were herded off and I had relatively little to do with them. But poor Papa was losing perhaps the last visual reminder of his Azorean homeland. It was like watching him be torn apart, little by little. First Joe left to live in Massachusetts, then Howdie died, and now the sheep would be gone. I wondered if he had assumed the farm would be passed down to the boys upon his death. I made a mental note to visit the sheep before Tuesday.

When I returned home from school that day, the house felt as if another death had occurred, with an additional shroud of grief layered on top of the others. I simply dared not do anything to make things worse. The trouble was that sometimes I wasn't sure what might make them worse. Mama was not much better, although she resumed some of her usual duties. Nevertheless, I was not free to be with my friends as long as she needed so much help.

Winter hung on with many gray days to add to the emotional darkness in the house. The snow, which is always so welcome and beautiful in late autumn, is, by March, wearisome. The occasional snow fall, inevitable thawing, and the resultant mud feels like nature's relentless torment before spring. It was on one of these interminable gray, muddy days, walking to school, that I realized Levi Hall was finished. There were no workers there. Everyone was abuzz during class time and the teacher had difficulty keeping us on track. When I walked by it after school, folks were gathered outside, admiring its simple but pristine white appearance, with its cupola and brand-new bell. At long last Levi Hall school would open its doors! Howdie had come so close to seeing it. My heart broke all over again.

In early April, complete with the United States flag proudly flapping in the wind on its new flagpole (the one we students had raised money to purchase), my friends and I, along with the younger students, parents and townspeople all ceremoniously and very eagerly climbed the steps into the new school. We were given a tour that included seeing the younger children's area and the high school upstairs, followed by refreshments in the basement. Perhaps most delightful was watching one lucky student picked at random to pull the thick bell rope at precisely the appointed time to indicate the beginning of the school day. When we high school students finally assembled at our desks, it felt quite strange to be in such a cavernously large room compared to Mr. Moses' store. I suddenly felt a heightened sense of scholarly importance, which made it easier to be excited about my studies. I even wondered if this were how college might feel. Even better, the new school was half the distance from home.

When spring finally blustered her way past the worst of winter, Papa put the cows outside. Without the sheep grazing their way down the hill, Papa's small herd of cows looked mighty sparse. Mama was rejuvenated by the warmer temperatures and even hummed while she hung the wash outside. I was rejuvenated too. I could hear the peepers again, a sure and final sign of the seasonal shift. One day Papa asked me to go find mayflowers to give to Mama. I was able to find a few that were surrounded by stubborn granules of icy snow. Their pinkish-white petals speckled the forest floor with dabs of pastel color. I hoped I had enough for whatever reason Papa had sent me on this errand. When I handed them to Mama, she smelled them with a faraway look in her eyes. Later, I heard her ask Papa if it had really been 30 years. Apparently, it wasn't a real question because Papa only smiled and nodded. Mama pointed to the small vase where the mayflowers now rested and said, "Thank you, Manny."

Luella and I still enjoyed making May baskets and secretly delivering them, a rite of spring we just couldn't refuse. The crocuses and daffodils poked their noses up out of their earthy beds to lead the way for other spring flowers. The end of school saw several of my friends graduate, a celebration I wouldn't miss. This time next year, I would officially leave Levi Hall behind too.

The end of the school year was when it felt like summer was almost upon us, especially when Joe arrived. "How's Mama doing?" he asked me quietly when we hugged. All I needed to do was look at him and he knew I wanted to discuss this with him, sometime when Mama wasn't so close by as now. But it wasn't only Mama I wanted to tell him about.

Joe needed to run an errand for Papa one day and asked if I'd like to come along. "Mama isn't as sickly as she was in March, but she isn't really herself, either," I said. "She hasn't been since Howdie died, you know? It's been hard to convey in letters what it's been like here. Just about the time I think Mama is improving, she gets worse again. It's only me to keep us fed many days. She can't handle making bread. And with the sheep gone, she isn't spinning wool. She used up most of what she had, but even so, she can't sustain knitting for long before she tires. She isn't going out much now and friends don't often come by, due to her coughing. They're afraid to wear her out, I think.

"I'm scared, Joe. Scared she'll die. Then there's Papa. He seems to move so sluggishly that I don't think it can only be blamed on his injury. It's like he feels beaten by life. Like Mama, ever since Howdie died, he's been different. Then he sold the sheep. Oh, Joe! Papa said that that was the saddest day. I can't believe it was any sadder than the day Howdie or the others died. I think that selling the sheep was admitting that he's not young and fit enough to care for them and that Mama isn't well enough to need the wool. It's as though Papa has admitted defeat. I'm scared both Mama and Papa will die, and I'll be all alone."

I started to cry. I didn't mean to, but I couldn't stop the tears. I knew Joe would understand, but I didn't want to place all the burden on him. He was happy in the life he was living, and Papa was very proud of Joe's accomplishments, as though Joe's successes were Papa's own.

"I'm so sorry, Millie. I know things have been burdensome for you, and at your young age too. I'm also very grateful for all that you do here. Is there any way I can help out this summer, at least? I mean besides helping Papa with farm chores."

"Just having you here is help enough. If I can't handle things, I'll turn to you, and that's far more than when you are gone."

Neither of us spoke for several minutes. I felt closer to my older brother than ever before. Then in the silence, I sensed a question on Joe's mind. He said, "Do you think I should move back up here?"

I could tell this had been hard for Joe to ask, yet it needed to be addressed because I had wondered the same thing. Longed for it, truth be known. But I felt guilty even thinking it. Joe deserved an honest answer, so I considered the question thoughtfully.

"Joe, if there's any way at all that we can work things out here without you having to move back, that's what I want. I know you're happy in Massachusetts. I don't want to take that away from you. And I'm relatively certain Mama and Papa would not want you to do that. It's satisfying to them knowing you are free from farm work and doing what you love. I also know that you care about what's happening to the farm. Let's let the summer decide. Watch Papa and by summer's end, perhaps you'll know what he needs. Maybe hire someone to help Papa regularly. I'll watch Mama and do what I must in the house. Can we leave things this way?"

"Yes, Millie. And I must say, I think you've grown up mighty fast."

Lawrence's birthday and Independence Day came quickly. Mama seemed enough better to insist on going to Gorham's parade with the family. We all knew she wasn't feeling particularly well when she requested a slower-than-usual pace to and from the center of town. She enjoyed the sunshine and tilted her head back enough for the sun to reach her face underneath her bonnet.

Joe and I found chairs for Mama and Papa to sit on in the shade. Trafton Plaisted and John Evans pulled up chairs as well, so Joe and I left the four of them and went strolling through the fairgrounds. It was a delightful day. We saw many friends and enjoyed splendid foods. I especially love the orange sponge cake Mrs. Burton makes and went searching to see if she had any for sale this year. It was good for our souls to put the farm and kitchen duties aside for a time.

As the afternoon sun began its westward journey and Fan clopped rhythmically, happy to be going home, Mama said, "Manuel, will Trafton and John come by later?"

"I believe so. At least that's what they last told me."

"Will you need refreshments?"

"Something easy," he answered, realizing Mama was not feeling up to entertaining. "We'll sit on the lawn, and you may rest. Millie can see to us."

I didn't want to admit to overhearing their conversation, but I would tell Mama later that I'd purchased a lemon sponge cake–there were no more orange ones left–to share with Lawrence. I'd tell her that she could rest upstairs while I served Joe, Papa, and his friends.

After dinner, Papa and Joe put four chairs out by the maple tree. John arrived first. "My daughter, Millie, and my son, Joe," Papa said re-introducing us after we'd seen them in Gorham. "Millie, did you know that John here, uh, Mr. Evans, is a soldier I served with? He let me stay with his family after the war before I bought this house."

"Yes, I think I do remember that," I said to Mr. Evans. "How kind of you. Would you like a glass of lemonade? Or just water?"

"Lemonade would be fine, thank you."

"I'll bring some out for all of you."

As I turned back to the house, I heard John say, "She's a pretty little thing, isn't she? Polite too." I flushed and was glad they couldn't see my face.

Trafton wasn't far behind, so I brought four lemonades to the men and let them know that I'd be out with coffee and dessert a bit later. Lawrence arrived then and we sat on the piazza enjoying the breeze. He held my hand and squeezed it now and then, but otherwise we were mostly quiet, no longer needing to say much to feel our connection.

Later, I'd taken the men's glasses inside and had Lawrence help me serve coffee, when John said, "Remember how quick the colonel made us get into position our first day in Gettysburg? Didn't even *get* coffee that day! Thank you, Miss," he said, taking his cup from me.

Trafton chuckled, "Just as well we didn't have coffee or much food during that battle. There weren't enough trenches dug yet to...uh...be able to use," he finished delicately.

"I guess that's right enough," John said.

"There weren't time to even think those two days. God knows Gettysburg was awful, wasn't it?" Trafton said, dryly. "When the colonel said that bloody thing was over, I think I looked down to see if my body was still on top o' my feet. Say, Manuel, you still got yer Springfield 1860?"

"Sure do. I used that trusty musket to shoot a wildcat this winter. Something had been killing chickens in the neighborhood. When I saw that cat's eyes looking out at me from a space in the woodpile, I thought to myself, 'It's you, isn't it?' The eyes were all I could see but I knew if I aimed for 'em, I'd get the brain. War training came in mighty handy just then."

"And Papa was very brave to kill that ol' cat. I was very proud of him."

Papa waved off my compliment and said, "Could we get some of that dessert you said you had? To go with this coffee?"

"Of course," I said and motioned to Lawrence to help me.

When we'd served the lemon cake, John said, "Thank you, Millie. Say, this yellow cake reminds me of a story about bananas."

Lawrence and I took our leave and sat back down on the settee with our own cake and coffee. John had apparently finished his story when we heard Papa say, "Never have been able to eat a banana since my sailin' days. Our Cap told us bananas were poisonous on the islands in the South Pacific. I 'spect the natives told Cap that to keep us from eatin' 'em all."

"Well, yer missin' out then," John said.

"It looks to me like your daughter is helping out nicely while Julia is ill. You're lucky to have an able daughter."

Papa nodded.

The next day, Mama took a sudden turn for the worse. It was as if she had waited until Independence Day was over to give in to whatever her illness was. She began to fever and refuse food. The fear of Howdie's illness taking Mama too had been with me for weeks, but I had refused to acknowledge it. It was time to fetch Dr. Dunn.

"Yes, I'm terribly sorry to say it, but your mother has the consumption, and far gone at that. I've talked with your father already and he wants to stay up there with her. I've given her something to help her sleep and more mustard plaster for her cough. It isn't likely to help much though. Keep a close eye on her. I'll stop by again soon."

The next afternoon, after she'd slept most of the day before and then half of this one, Mama summoned me to her room. I fretted all the way up the stairs about what she might say.

"Sit here," Mama said, patting the side of her bed, while she caught her breath. *So like Howdie,* I thought, filling with dread. I sat down carefully.

Mama said, "I want to talk to you woman to woman, Millie." She stopped to catch her breath. I couldn't help but hold my own while I waited. "You must be able to see that I am not going to get better." Again, Mama stopped. My breath caught in my throat and my eyes widened which Mama saw. She softened her own eyes and rested her hand on my knee.

"I don't want to wait any longer to do this," she paused, "for fear I will be as sick as Howdie was in the end." She paused again. I couldn't take my eyes off her. "Before I'm not able to carry on a conversation anymore."

I willed my eyes not to fill with tears, but I could tell they were rimmed and shiny as I waited for Mama to speak again. I took in as much of my mother as possible to commit it to memory. Her hair was thinner now but still not overtaken with gray. Though the rest of her body had also thinned just as Howdie's had, Mama was still a very pretty woman with bluish-green eyes that once sparkled but now were subdued. Her bottom lip was fuller than the top one and I have always wondered why that didn't make her look as if she was permanently pouting. But instead, my mother had the same grace and dignity her own mother had had, impeccably dressed and standing erect in public, always in command of whatever she undertook. Even if Mama were to walk down the road in her day dress and apron, she would gain the admiration of anyone she passed.

"You're sixteen now and practically grown," Mama began again after pausing. I could see how talking was wearing her out. I desperately wanted to tell her to stop talking, that whatever she had to say couldn't be important enough to drain her body so. But instinctively I knew Mama needed to use whatever energy she had to say something that she felt couldn't wait. "You can do housework...nearly as well as I can.

When I'm gone," this time she paused when she saw me struggling with this truth, "and yes, the doctor thinks I'll be gone by the end of summer, and then this house…will be yours to run." I felt like I was hardly breathing at all now. "It's a lot to place on your young shoulders…I know…but I know you can do it, Millie. You will learn how to think ahead…to keep on top of things. Let little things go…until you can manage them. You will know…what a 'little thing' is…as time goes on. Make priorities of food and washing…and let cleaning go…if you must," Mama's raspy cough interrupted her mid-sentence. "…because it's said, you know…that you have to eat a peck of dirt…before you die," she said with a smile, "and your guests will understand…the position I've put you in."

"But Mama," I objected, "you didn't put me in this position. You aren't to blame. Isn't it God's fault you're sick?"

"Nonetheless, child," Mama said, skirting my question, "'tis my death…that will cause you…to grow up faster. And Millie…I want you to know…that I've watched you grow…strong and able. You're smart and kind…" I was about to protest when Mama added, "…when you want to be…" I dropped my eyes. I know I've been less than kind on occasion, but I'd always assumed Mama didn't know this about me.

"Mrs. Dunn claims…you're becoming every bit…as good on the… church organ as she is. Don't let that skill…get too rusty." She stopped for a time to cough and rest. How I wanted to leave the room, but I knew Mama was not finished. "And one more thing…learn to lean…on your father. You will need him. You have Joe…in the summers…but the rest of the year…you'll have Papa. He's a good man…and fair. He'll be as honest with you…as he can be. He cherishes you…as his daughter…" Mama's cough was harder now and took longer to cease. Talking this much was irritating her lungs. I desperately wanted to tell her to stop but I knew she wouldn't. So, I offered her a sip of water instead. "I know that…it seems sometimes…that he favors the boys…well, Joe, now." I winced. "That's because…he let me teach you…the household things… while he taught the boys. But he's mighty proud of you…and expects you…to do well in school…and in everything you do. So don't…let him down. That way he will learn to lean…on you as well. You will need each other."

Mama stopped to cough again, then took my hand and said, "And remember Millie…I love you very much."

This time my tears spilled over and flowed down my cheeks. "I love you too, Mama." I said, bending down to give her a kiss on her cheek. Sitting up again, I looked into Mama's eyes and saw genuine love there. Then I slowly got up and walked toward the door.

"Oh. And Millie…one last thing," I turned. "Go to my top…dresser drawer please. There's a long, narrow box…that has your grandmother's…gold beads in it. Take them. They're…yours now."

Four days later, Mama passed away in Papa's loving arms. On her gravestone in the Great Falls cemetery, Papa had chosen a fitting poem:

Oh the hope, the hope is sweet
That we soon in heaven may meet
There we all shall happy be
Rest from pain and sorrow free.

Friday, July 10, 1896

Dear diary, I simply cannot be asked to attend one more family funeral after we lay Mama to rest. Our family of eight is now three. Please, God, let no one else die before I do. Please.

Seven

Reasons to Celebrate

While the bread was rising a second time in their pans, I pulled out the washboard to do a light load so that Papa and I had enough clean stockings and underthings to wear. I needed to make butter too, but we can eat bread without butter, better than butter by itself. *That chore will just have to wait. Goodness me, if it's this difficult to keep up now, what will I do when school begins?*

I pulled the stockings onto their stretchers and took the whole basket out to hang on the line. I was grateful for little things, like enough breeze to dry the laundry even if it was a swelteringly hot, humid day. I had to wipe my face of sweat in between hanging each piece of clothing. I was also grateful to put my hair on top of my head. I just couldn't imagine all my hair hanging to my shoulders and sticking to my neck. Yet pesky stray wisps or little clumps of hair tickled the back of my neck, nonetheless. I kept swiping at them.

"Ouch!" said a male voice.

I swung around and nearly knocked knees with Lawrence, the object of my last swipe and the bearer of the yelp. "Oh! Forgive me, Lawrence! I didn't hear you walk up. I didn't mean to hurt you. I'm so embarrassed." I was sputtering and I knew it, which only made me more embarrassed.

But Lawrence was laughing. "I saw you brushing your hair away and I thought I'd do it for you with my handkerchief. But I don't think I'll try *that* again!"

I must have been blushing fiercely because Lawrence said, "Aw, it's okay. Really. You didn't hurt me. I can see you're busy, so I won't stay long. But do you have a few minutes to spare?"

"Of course. But only a few, I'm afraid. Let's sit out here on the piazza where the breeze is nice," I said, wiping the perspiration off my brow with the bottom corner of my apron. Suddenly I felt very homely in my old frock.

"How are you, Millie?" Lawrence asked me with compassion and not a hint of thinking me homely, thank goodness.

"I'm doing as well as I can be, I 'spect. Thank you for asking."

"Is there no one else who can help you with your housework?"

"Sometimes Mrs. Hall comes, you know. Luella has come over, and if she can't help me with what I'm doing, she talks to me and keeps my mind on nicer things."

"Well, the reason I ask is that school starts soon and I guess I was wondering if you were going to be able to come back with all you have to do."

"Oh, I doubt Papa would let me skip my last year. I think he'd have a conniption if I even suggested not going. I'll just have to fit everything in, that's all."

"Well, I have some news. Guess who'll be the new janitor of Levi Hall this year?" Lawrence asked with a twinkle in his eye which might have given me the answer, but I didn't catch on. So, when I only raised my eyebrows, he continued, "Me! The town's going to pay me to be the janitor!"

"Oh, my! Congratulations. But that means you'll be quite busy too, then."

"Yes, I guess we both will be. But being busy never hurt either of us, I don't think. Do you?"

"No. You're right." I'd never thought about being busy. I guess I just took busyness for granted. Wasn't everyone busy? "Well, speaking of being busy," I said, regretting the need to say it, "I don't mean to change the subject, but I must get back to the bread before it rises too much. Would you like to come in?"

"No, thank you. I really must go anyway. I just wanted to check on you and share my news." He got up to go. "Have a wonderful day, Millie."

"Thank you, Lawrence. You do the same." I watched him walk around the house and out of sight. Then I sighed. Things felt so different without Mama in the kitchen. In some ways, I didn't feel like a high school student anymore. I wondered if I would ever again feel like just a student. I walked back into the kitchen.

Lawrence and I were indeed busy throughout that autumn. I tried my best to keep Mama's household routines. I guess in some ways Mama's load and mine weren't so different, though. Where she dealt with the wool, I had my studies. Where she went to her women's meetings, I spent time with my friends.

This was my last year, and I intended to enjoy it. As if Providence herself had heard my prayer, our teacher announced that there was to be a play put on in Forest Hall near Christmas. The play was *The Snow Queen* by Hans Christian Andersen, and the older girls were welcome to try out for two of the smaller parts. Mr. Brown assigned the book in preparation, whether or not we were in the play. I desperately wanted to be given a role. I read that book some years ago and loved it. I wanted to play the part of the Snow Queen most of all, but it sounded like the bigger roles would not be available to the high school girls. After all, the older women would have more time for a lead role than I would. In any case, I would talk to Papa about it.

We sat down to a dinner of sliced ham, potatoes, and carrots. Papa was heading into the harvesting season and would be hiring extra help soon. For now, he simply looked too tired to even cut his meat after a long day's work.

"I have something I want to speak with you about, Papa," I began. "There's to be a play in Forest Hall just before Christmas–*The Snow Queen*. Remember I read that and told you about it? Well, Mr. Brown said today that there are two parts that we girls may read for. I would love to be in that play. Do you think I might have time to do that?"

Papa didn't say anything for a while. Waiting for him to think about something tried my patience something fitful.

Finally, he said, "You do have a much heavier responsibility now, with Mama gone. And I'm grateful you are so helpful around here. I'd have to hire help to do all you do." I turned beet red at such a rare compliment. I know he loves me, but he doesn't talk about it. "But you should be able to be a child, at the same time. You're not yet grown, and I understand that. Ask Mrs. Hall if she can help out on the days you can't, if you are given a part."

"Oh, Papa! Thank you! Thank you, Papa!" I saw the ends of his mouth curl up ever so slightly underneath his whiskers as he ate his meal. My heart nearly burst with gratitude.

And it nearly shook my whole body with nerves when it was my turn to read for a part. There were several women there, including Addie Moses, Luella, and me. We agreed to be happy for one another if any of us should be so lucky as to get a part. After reading, we were told to check the outside door of the hall on Tuesday for the role assignments.

It was a very long three days, but on Tuesday Luella and I walked down to Forest Hall together. It was raining and we hoped the dismal weather was not an omen of our failure to get parts. When the hall came into sight, we could see several people crowded around the front door. Addie was nearly there. We quickened our pace.

Just as we neared the crowd, Addie wiggled out from the center of it and stood with her hands together in front of her chest. She had a huge smile on her face.

"What! What do you know?" I cried out.

"Yeah, tell us!" Luella shouted.

"See for yourselves!" Addie shouted back.

Luella made it to the door first and whooped and jumped up and down. I knew then that she had gotten a part. I was genuinely happy for her. But I felt a twinge of jealousy, too. Then she and Addie danced in circles. I couldn't be sure if Addie was excited for herself or Luella or both of them. I realized that if they both got parts and I didn't, I would need to be gracious and I wasn't sure I could do that genuinely. *They must know if I got a part,* I realized, *but they don't beckon me. Oh, dear.*

I finally had the courage to take the steps up to the announcement sheet. I carefully read down through the list of names. Moses, Nason, Peterson, Smith…*Thomas!* I got a part! I was so excited, I dashed over to Addie and Luella and we all danced in the rain.

"I'm the Finnish Woman," Luella said.

"Oh! I forgot to see what part I got!" I said.

"You're the Lappish Woman," I think, Luella said.

"What part did you get, Addie?" I asked.

"I got The Princess!" Addie answered.

"Who is the Snow Queen then?" I asked.

"I think it's Mrs. Bailey. She'd be a very good Snow Queen, in my opinion," Addie said.

I could hardly believe my good fortune to be in a play in Forest Hall with Addie and Luella. I couldn't wait to begin practices.

Papa was happy for me. I was only a little disappointed not to play the Snow Queen, but on the other hand, my part would be easier to learn, and I wouldn't need to be gone from home as often with a lesser role. While I studied my lines with Luella, Trafton Plaisted began painting three beautiful winter scenes and Mrs. Appleby volunteered to help with our costumes. October and November flew by quickly with everything I needed to do for the play, in addition to schoolwork and my usual duties at home. But I was joyful and very grateful to feel happy again after a long, long time of grieving.

December came and the play was only a week away. Practices were going well, though everyone wished for more time. The final costume fittings had been happening the past month and I couldn't wait to get into mine. But I knew Mrs. Appleby was worried they wouldn't all be finished in time. The scenery boards that Mr. Plaisted painted were simply wonderful and when I was on stage I felt as if I was truly in a fantastic winter wonderland. But he too wanted more time to put the finishing touches on the last board. Most of us had fully memorized our parts, though there were those who still felt very shaky without a script in hand. One way or another, performance day was looming.

One day that week I came home from school and found a letter on the kitchen table for Papa in lovely script. He didn't often get letters addressed to him. Most of the time his mail came to me so I could read it to him. I put my books down, grabbed the letter, and went to the barn.

"Hi Papa. Would you like me to read this letter to you now or wait till after dinner?"

"Did you see where it's from?"

"No. I didn't look at it that well." I glanced at the return address and gasped. "Papa! It's from the Azores!"

"Yes, it is. From my older sister, I think. Let's read it later."

"Okay. I'm going to run down to Forest Hall right now. But I'll be back for dinner."

Later, when Papa was settled into the Morris chair with his pipe, I read him the letter written in beautiful penmanship but somewhat broken English.

"'Ponta Delgada, Island of Flores, September 8th, 1896. My dear and loving niece and brother. I have no expressions to explain to you the joy that my heart felt with the reception of your kind and well come letter of April last, in which I see that you had not forget us yet. I hope that these few lines will go and find you and your family enjoying a good health. I will say again our sadness of your son Howard's death. Please be of good cheer. Do not hold sadness for too long.

"'As for us out here we are getting along the best we can, myself, am getting old and gray, my husband the same, and the rest are like young people. The death of our brother…' Wait, Papa, which brother? Did you know this?"

"No, I didn't. I don't know which brother. Read on, child."

"Oh, Papa, I'm so sorry." My head spun and my heart reeled with this news, but I continued. "'The death of our brother gives me a great trouble for I was expecting him home from day to day as he told us in his last letter that his whaler would arrive soon, but the will of God is always the first.' José? Oh no! I'm so sorry, Papa."

"Can't be helped."

"It sounds like she thinks she told you this news before."

"Letters sometimes get lost from overseas. Keep going, please."

"'You tell us, dear brother, in your kind letter that you have a kind of notion to come out here some day. Oh my. I wish that I can see that happy day, to give my heart a full joy. It is not hard as it use to be to come here, for the steamships run between here and States every month. I wish I could afford to go and see you all. Yes my dear, you can come with your dear wife and stay as long as you can, and I beleave you both would like it.' You haven't told her about Mama yet?"

"No, child. I didn't have the heart to just yet. Is there more?"

"Yes. 'The crops are looking good at present, fruit I think will be very little this year. And now dear brother for my good news, my daughter Marie plans to see you in the spring! Yes, it is true. Look for a letter from Marie, she will say more. Now I must come to an end with my small letter by sending my best love.

"'You must beleave that this is from your ever loving sister, Maria José.' Oh! How exciting! You have never met your niece, have you? No, of course you haven't. I wonder how old she is? Maybe she will be here to see me graduate!"

"Perhaps. Patience, child."

Sunday, December 12, 1896

Dear diary, the play last evening was not only enjoyable but very good, in my humble opinion. Papa said he liked it. Lawrence did too, but he said I was the best. I think he felt like he needed to say that, but it was nice to hear. I wish Joe had been able to come. That would have made the evening perfect.

There's something about immersing myself in a role like that. I become another person and for a little while I can escape my current life, my grief and my workload. I feel as light as a breeze when I'm on stage. I pray I might be able to act again one day.

Papa got a letter from his sister, Maria, earlier this week. Aunt Maria said that their brother, José, died on board his ship. While that is terribly sad, what disturbs me is that Papa seemed to take it in his stride. He hasn't told his sister about Mama's death yet. I think he is still taking her death very hard.

But my cousin, Marie, is coming this spring for a visit! I can't wait to finally meet someone from Papa's family. I wonder how her English is? It will be grand to see her!

Eight

Marie De Silveira

Late May 1897 brought the first days of summer-like warmth and with it, my cousin, Marie. Thankfully, she docked in Portland instead of New Bedford, where Papa had docked nearly forty years ago. Papa would have found a way to pick her up no matter where she came in, but traveling to Portland only took an hour and a half, which Papa did easily. Fan might have thought differently because she was getting old and much slower. Papa had yet to trust young Fitz in front of his wagon when he was pulling ladies. At only three years of age, Fitz could be stubborn and erratic.

I liked Marie the moment I laid eyes on her as the wagon pulled into the drive.

"Hello, Marie!" I said, waving.

"Hello, Miss Millie!"

Hugging her tightly, I said, "You don't need to call me 'Miss.' Just Millie, please. Come on inside and make yourself at home. Papa will carry your things upstairs." I looked at Papa, who nodded.

Marie and I linked arms as naturally as if we'd seen one another every day. I led her into the kitchen.

"Such a fine, large home!" she exclaimed.

"Walk around a bit while I get us some lemonade and cake."

"Hopefully I won't be lost!" she said. I wondered just how small her home really was.

We all sat under the front tree enjoying our afternoon refreshment. "How was your trip across the ocean, Marie?"

"Long!" We all laughed at the way she punched that word. "But I did learn to sway with the ship."

"Were you seasick?" Papa asked.

"Just a small bit," Marie admitted. "I like the wagon ride much better."

"Your English is very good, Marie," I complimented, grateful she spoke English well enough that Papa did not have to translate.

"Thank you. Portuguese is easier, so please excuse my incorrect use. Uncle Manny told me your dear mother passed. I was very sorry to hear of that. It is just two of you here in Maine? Cousin Joe lives not too far?"

"Yes, just Papa and me here at the farm. Joe lives a long way from here but not so far as California!"

"California is placed by the Pacific Ocean?" Marie asked. I nodded. "How far away is it?"

"It's more than three thousand miles!" I exclaimed.

"I only know kilometers better than miles. Your Papa told me we rode fifteen miles from Portland. In kilometers, that number is bigger, I think?"

"Yes," Papa said. "But I'm not sure what the exact number in kilometers is."

"It is never three thousand, I am sure! Our island Flores is only twenty-four kilometers! So very much smaller than your country! I will not see Joe, then?"

"You might," I said. "He will be here to see me graduate on June 13. You will not leave before that, right?"

"No, Millie, I will be here still. I will love to see Joe. I was sorry my uncle's letter of nearly two years ago told that Howard died."

We sat in silence before Marie broke the awkward moment and said, "Uncle Manny, you promised to say about when you sailed from Flores. Did you see a lot of whales? I did, but far from our ship."

"Yes. But what would you like to know?" Papa began.

"Grandfather was angry to learn you stowed away. Was Uncle José angry too?"

"Yes, for a time. He thought he would have to watch over me. He was looking for adventure and having me there was not what he had in mind. The skipper wasn't happy with me either. Since he had no choice but to let me stay at least until we reached land, he made me a cabin boy. I determined to be very good at my job so that I might stay on as long as I could with José."

"Why did you leave Flores?" Marie asked.

I was very excited to listen to Papa's answers. I didn't know as much about his early life as I wished. Papa always seemed reticent to discuss that subject, as if talking about the life he left behind was too painful. Perhaps he was ashamed of the way he left his family. I doubt I will ever really know. But in the presence of Marie, he seemed more willing to divulge his past, as if she had towed Flores behind her all the way across the Atlantic and he was standing on his native soil again.

"Our home was very crowded, with so many of us. I have but one photograph, when there were only ten children."

"You *do*? May we see it, Papa?"

"Yes. Later. There were actually twelve of us children but one had married and one was born after that photograph was taken. I'm not sure why it was taken or by whom. I remember it was not easy to get us all to look good at the same time. Now I wonder how my Pa paid for it. We hardly had enough food or clothing that fit well. But José heard about gold in America and said he would send money home when he got there. I guess I thought I could do that, too. But I also thought I could get rich in America," Papa said with a chuckle.

"Why do you laugh, Uncle Manny?"

"You can see we are not rich. It is not as easy to keep money as I had thought. I was very hard on my pa. I know that now. It might have been better for me to stay and help him there on Flores, but I was very young and restless."

"But you have a beautiful, big home here!" Marie exclaimed. I smiled. She really had no idea how big homes could be in America.

"We do alright, don't we Millie?" It was not a question begging for a spoken answer. I simply looked into his eyes and nodded, although my thoughts were not completely kind. To me, a bigger house in the city seemed preferable to this farm.

"And too, Flores was very small," Papa continued. "I heard wondrous things about America and other lands. I thought I needed to see the world outside of the Azores."

"What lands did you see?" Marie asked.

"Islands and countries all over the world from the Arctic to the tip of Africa and beyond. I was surprised that people come in all shades from ghostly white to the darkest black. We sometimes took on new people when we stopped to replenish supplies, and I learned that people are people no matter what color they are. Some you like, some you don't. Some like you, and some don't."

"What surprised you the most about the other lands you saw, Papa?"

"Well, I guess snow, that first time I saw it. Now I see too much of it!"

"How much snow comes here?" Marie wanted to know.

"Enough so's once in five years should be good enough," Papa quipped. *He's thoroughly enjoying himself,* I thought, with a smile in my heart.

"Sometimes we get two or more feet in one storm!" I answered enthusiastically.

"How many meters?" Marie asked.

"Over half a meter, I think, if I remember my equations correctly," I answered forgetting she wasn't used to our measurement system.

"Oh, my! How do you feed your animals?"

"We can go straight into our barn from the house through the ell," I pointed to the connected extension. "The barn is where we keep our pung." Seeing the question on Marie's face I explained, "Ours is like a box on runners. There are sleighs that are much prettier than ours. I wish you could be here in winter, Marie. Everything is white and quiet except for the sleigh bells that Papa puts on the horse at Christmas. Do you know what skis are?"

"I have seen pictures in books, but you tell me."

"I'll *show* you later!" I said, catching Papa's eyes. "Oh! We have so much to show her!"

Changing the subject, I asked, "Papa, what was it like to see whales up close and on the ship?" I already knew that Marie would have seen many whales taken on shore in Flores and cut up for meat and oil. I asked this question solely for myself.

Papa stared out to a faraway place and said, "I never liked that part. There's a beauty to whales when they glide through water or breech. I hated to see them killed. But when they were on board, those creatures were monstrously big and frightening. I never could understand how the ship could hold the weight of something that big, let alone more than one of them. I looked into the eye of a whale once and that was the last time I could stand to do that."

"Did you see whales every day?" I asked.

"No, no, not at all. Most days were boring, when all I saw from the deck was water and less-than-nice things in the ship's belly. Some days there were storms, the likes of which I have never seen since. No whale in its right mind would stay above water longer than to take a breath, while the ship was tossed around like a toy. Many days I wondered if I'd traded the beauty of Flores for hell itself." When both Marie and I paled, Papa quickly said, "Oh...pardon my bluntness. Sometimes it was quite nice when the men got to singing and dancing or playing chess or checkers with each other. Some of them carved ivory or shells into mighty good-looking pieces. It's called scrimshaw, that artwork is."

"Did *you* get seasick, Papa?"

"More'n once, child."

"No wonder you don't like to go to the seaside," I said quietly, thinking how few times I've been myself.

"What did you eat on the whaler?" Marie wanted to know.

"Well, nothing you girls would like, I can tell you that. But we had to eat whatever wouldn't go bad between supply stops. Salt pork and beef, sometimes potatoes until they rotted, beans, and anything the doctor, that's what we called the cook, could make with flour that wasn't infested with bugs." Marie and I turned up our noses. "But on Sundays, we often got bread pudding, called duff. Now that was worth waitin' a week for."

"That reminds me, Papa," changing the subject which I hoped he and Marie wouldn't mind, "when Mr. Evans was here on Independence Day last year, you introduced me to him and said his family took you in when the war was over. How *did* you get up here after the war? That would have been a very long way from Virginia. Where did you muster out? Was it Appomattox?"

"No. After the war was over, we marched north from Appomattox almost to the capitol and mustered out in a little place called Bailey's Crossroads. As I told Marie on the way here, in Washington D.C., we were put on trains or steamers up the coast. I preferred not to go by ship and took the train. Once we got to Maine, we went our separate ways. I went to Portland and found a farmer selling fruits and vegetables. While I purchased some of his food, the farmer asked me questions, maybe because I was a soldier or my accent was foreign, and of course my skin was very dark from the sun that time of the year. When he heard I needed a home, he told me about a job near his farm in Standish, not far from here. That was the Evans farm, and I stayed with them until I could buy this house. I've always been grateful a stranger took a chance on me."

"So, Mr. Evans's family was not the one you lived with right after you left the ship?"

"No, that was the Varneys. José and I left the whaler when I told him I was done with the sea. He wasn't. He wanted to return to whaling, but he was willing to help me find a place to live. We made our way to Maine, asking if anyone was willing to take on a hired hand and found a farmer north of here. José stayed only a short time and then went right back to New Bedford, I presume. He wouldn't have sailed on the whaler we'd been on, though. Anyway, I stayed with the Varneys three years. When the governor of Maine called for soldiers, the Varneys didn't believe in war and, I guess by mutual agreement, I went in their stead. It was back to their house I went to recover from the bullet that went through my thigh here," he said, rubbing his wound, "at the Battle of the Wilderness." Marie winced.

"Why," Marie started hesitantly, "did you change your surname? Were you embarrassed of Valadão?"

"No, not embarrassed. I wanted to start over and be an American with an American-sounding name. I took my pa's middle name, Thomas, as my surname."

By this time, I had to take my leave to make dinner. Marie asked to help but I told her to stay and talk with Papa. As I left, they began conversing in Portuguese.

Later, when Papa was lighting up his pipe, he said, "Marie, Millie mentioned that she will graduate soon. She has done well in school, and I want her to take classes next year at Gorham High School, where the material is harder than our small school here. She would like to be a teacher. Four more years there would qualify her for that."

I turned my usual crimson, partly from embarrassment and partly from annoyance. "Papa," I said, "I've already told you I won't be going on." I suspected he brought this up so that Marie would add her own powers of persuasion to his. "You have no one to help during the school year," I reasoned. "You need me here. It's a lot of money to keep going to school too. Besides, I would have to take entrance exams, and I don't know how well I've been prepared compared to the Gorham city scholars. I could be mighty embarrassed if I fail. You could be too."

"I say you've done very well," Papa said evenly, ignoring my other two very good points entirely.

"But Papa, those exams cover arithmetic, history, English grammar, reading, writing, spelling, and geography! And they'd want me to take more Latin on top of all that!"

"You *take* those exams and see if you qualify. Then we'll talk again."

This time I knew Papa was finished with the subject. And indeed, he turned to Marie and began speaking in his native tongue. I excused myself in a demure huff.

On Decoration Day, we took Marie to the parade in Gorham. She liked it very much, but it was a swelteringly hot, miserable, sticky day. She couldn't believe that a place that could dump two feet of snow could also be a place as hot as this. She told me that the islands have nearly the same weather all year round, that it rarely gets higher than eighty degrees or lower than fifty. She said it's either raining or not, and almost always windy. That's the extent of the weather, she said, and added that it could be a bit boring. But I wish I could be bored on Papa's island for at least a little while.

The Sunday before graduation, I did a very silly thing. I decided to walk to church in my new shoes so I could practice wearing heels at the ceremony. They were not easy to walk in at all, and I wobbled all the way there and back. Practicing was a good idea, but they crammed my toes something terrible so that I lost my two big toenails! Now I shall have to bandage them to be able to wear my shoes. Mercy me, I'm such a silly goose. But at least Marie will be able to see me graduate and so will Joe. Joe gave me money to buy a new dress, and Marie helped me pick one out in Portland. Other than my hobbled gait, I should look nice next Sunday.

June 13 was warm but thankfully not nearly as hot as Decoration Day. Scholars, teachers, and guests were comfortable in Levi Hall when they opened all the windows. Since Papa had sat through first Joe's and then Howdie's graduations, the program looked familiar to him. But I pointed to where it said that I would be reciting a poem. He said he looked forward to that. I didn't tell him that I would also be reciting part of my essay that each scholar had been required to write:

> *Thus far our lives have moved along in the same direction. Now whither are we bound? We are as ships just launched on a great ocean, casting one backward look behind at the familiar scenes, yet peering ahead at the broad oceans of life, whose wave will be sometimes rendered furious by sudden storms. But however much we may be tossed, I pray we shall all at last rest in that spacious harbor of success.*

When I finished, I looked at Papa and saw that he had teared up. Joe smiled broadly and Marie looked quite content. I was so happy that Uncle Almon had brought Grandpar. And of course, Lawrence came. All of them were very proud of me. I was proud of myself too, and of Luella. She was valedictorian and I salutatorian. It was a wonderful day.

However, there was now no question in Papa's mind that I should continue my education. Marie concurred, and so did everyone else at dinner that night. But I only listened with my ears, not my heart. I could not, in good conscience, seek further schooling.

The following day, we sent Marie off in a flurry of hugs and wishes for a safe journey. Joe and Marie traveled together to Portland where Joe saw her safely on board her ship. Then he continued to East Douglas, Massachusetts, where he would wrap up another year of teaching.

When Papa and I were alone at dinner, I decided to ask him a question I've held onto for many years, for fear he might say he's been unhappy most of his life. "Have you ever regretted leaving your island, Papa?"

"Yes, I suppose so. Seeing Marie stirred up memories I haven't thought about in many a year. But through it all, I've learned that life is meant to be lived today, not yesterday." He stood then, gave me a kiss on my cheek, and headed for the Morris chair saying, "I was mighty proud of you today, child."

Nine

Beginnings

East Douglas, MA
Friday, June 18, 1897

Dearest Millie,

There is something I might have told you the weekend of your graduation. But other things seemed of more importance just then. I have someone I would like you and Papa to meet over the Independence Day weekend when we come to Maine. I met Sarah Beatrice Smith at Connecticut Weslyn College. She is from Waterville, Maine and is a public-school teacher in Douglas, right near me, as providence would have it. I began calling on her recently and she would like to meet my family. We will be up on Friday, July 2. You may join us at the Cumberland County Fair the next day and then, of course, the parade in Gorham on the 4th. Millie, please be sure to shape up around Bea (as she prefers to be called.) She is a real lady.

Yours,
Joe
P.S. Take those tests! You will do fine.

Shape up? Shape *up*! A *real* lady? Who does he think I am? I have graduated from high school! I think I'm old enough to know how to act. I showed the letter to Luella, who can keep a confidence. She was angry for me. "Angry as a bee in a bonnet," she said. And then he decided I should take those tests because *he* thinks I would do fine. No one is listening to *me* and what I want. I'm so angry, I am considering not taking the exams *just because* he wants me to!

At least I had cooled off by the time Bea and Joe arrived. I had the holiday to get to know her, and I think I know now what Joe means by a "real lady." She acts and dresses like someone well suited to city life. I wonder how she'll like staying on a farm all summer? And will I oversee the kitchen, or will she want to? She is older than I am, after all, but it's *my* kitchen.

Bea stays in Howdie's room, which feels very strange to me. I have maintained something of a strained but cordial relationship with her for Joe's sake. I can tell he loves her mightily, the way he caters to her. But I think Bea is the type of "real lady" who needs too much attention. She is soft, not used to the hard work a farm woman must endure. And she must have her tea at the start of the day. In her room! I am the one to take it to her. Begrudgingly, if I am totally honest. She gets sick headaches quite often too. For that, I don't envy her.

She is a smart woman with quick opinions and is quite talkative, which often is a nice change from being around the men who are much quieter. I don't dislike Bea, but it isn't the same as having just Papa and Joe around. I don't feel as if I can be myself completely. Take Lawrence, for instance. It isn't that Papa and I talk so awfully much about Lawrence, but I feel free to when I need to. On the other hand, I find that I never talk about him around Joe and Bea. They have seen him come around and Joe talks with him sometimes, but I've never discussed our relationship, and they have never asked. They think of me as a child.

When Bea is in the kitchen, content to do the cooking, I take the time to be with Lawrence. We always enjoy going down to the cove and sitting beneath the oak tree to talk. We talk easily about a lot of things. This summer the topic almost always comes around to the new school year, knowing that we will not see each other much if I go to Gorham. Lawrence said he would miss me, but he really doesn't seem as broken-hearted as I have felt whenever I think about it. Maybe that's just the way boys are about things, not as sentimental. We talk about the tests I finally agreed to take, how well I think I did on them, and when the results will be available. I was really very nervous when I took the exams. Some parts seemed easy and other parts seemed to completely baffle me.

One day I went to the general store to buy what we needed for cooking.

"Miss Mildred Thomas," Mr. Anderson said cheerily.

"Hi Mr. Anderson."

"I have something for you," he said in a lilting voice, which seemed a bit strange, almost mysterious.

"What is it?" I said, smiling.

He whipped a large envelope from beneath his counter and said with a flourish, "Seein' that return address tells me that whatever's in this envelope is mighty important."

"Gorham City Schools! This must be my test results!"

"Prob-ly so. Go ahead 'n' open it!"

I hesitated. "No, Mr. Anderson," I said, "I think I'd rather open it alone, if you know what I mean. I hope you understand."

"Sure do, Millie. Didn't mean t' pry. There's no more mail for your family. Was there something else I can get for ya while you're here?"

"Oh, yes, I almost forgot. We need sugar and baking powder."

"A pound of sugar, do?"

"Yes, that will be fine. And a can of Rumfords, please."

"That it, then?"

"Yes. How much do we owe you?"

"Tell ya what, if you do well on them tests of yours, these are free of charge. If you don't, your Papa can bring the twenty-five cents to me any time. I'll add it to your tab with a question mark. But Millie, I 'spect I won't be seein' that quarter. Congratulations on your recent graduation."

"Thank you, Mr. Anderson! You're so kind."

As I walked up the hill toward home, my feet had a mind of their own, and they didn't want to go very fast. I was scared to look in the envelope, but excited too. At home, I dropped the baking supplies on the kitchen table and headed to my room, very glad no one saw me come in. I sat on my bed holding the envelope gingerly, as if it contained some of Papa's Independence Day explosives. Finally, I slid my thumb underneath one corner of the flap and gently eased my index finger into the opening and across to the other side, trying not to rip the paper. I pulled out the official-looking document and read the short note that ended:

...and so, Miss Thomas, because your test scores were sufficiently high, we have placed you in our second-year Latin/English track. Congratulations on your fine achievement.

I passed! And with good scores! My hands shook so much that the paper rippled with a soft fluttering sound. This one argument I had stood on–that I might not pass the exams–could no longer be used as to continuing my education. But I was still concerned about the cost. True, I only needed to be in school for the next three years rather than four, which was something of a relief and definitely a blessing. I decided to talk with Joe the next time we were alone.

"Well done, Millie, not that I had any concern," Joe said giving me a hug. "And they even advanced you a year. You should be very proud of yourself."

"I am, Joe. I'm very pleased. But what about the cost?"

Joe told me then that he had had the financial help of a generous friend who believed in him when he continued his own education. Therefore, he had already decided to help Papa pay for my school fees and lodging. But he admonished me not to tell Papa that I knew anything about this. He believed Papa's pride would be too damaged if he knew Joe had told me. Nor did he want me to mention this gesture to Bea. It was not yet Bea's business, he reasoned. I could hardly believe what I was hearing and thanked Joe with a heartfelt hug.

I spent the rest of the summer trying to enjoy my vacation without borrowing the anxieties of the coming school year. Luella and I visited as often as we could, and of course Lawrence and I spent as much time together as possible. Sometimes they both came over and we played croquet, or we went to Luella's house to play badminton. We pitched horseshoes at Lawrence's house or went swimming in the lake at Grandpar's. I came to selfishly appreciate Bea's abilities in the kitchen that allowed me to enjoy some freedom from household tasks. But Bea and Joe would be going back to their respective homes, and I had no choice but to think about my future. What will it be like to board in Gorham, away from Papa, and begin classes again at a more difficult school? Who would I be living with? I've never lived with anyone but my own family. How should I dress?

I needed more clothes, I decided. And Bea was the perfect person to talk to. I was suddenly so grateful for another woman in the house. Bea walked me through the sorts of things I'd want to take to school when boarding and, specifically, the respectable, becoming, yet modest dresses I should purchase. I didn't have much money to spend but she said we could find things that weren't terribly expensive in Portland. My day in the city with Bea was exciting. She seemed to know exactly what to buy and where to purchase it. We had lunch down by the dock and watched the waves splash against the harbor walls and the seagulls clamor for scraps. We laughed and laughed at their antics.

We even went to Cape Elizabeth to see the majestic lighthouse there, and then to Camp King, where Papa's Seventeenth Maine regiment was organized for The Rebellion. I paused in silence knowing that I was standing where Papa had once stood before going to war for a country he'd only lived in for three years and whose language he barely knew. Then before we knew it, we had to hurry to the train station to take us back home.

When it was time for Joe and Bea to leave that summer, I could hug them both with genuine gratitude. And I believe Bea reciprocated in kind.

But always in the back of my mind was Papa being at the farm alone. Not only would Joe be gone again this year, but so would I. Papa would be alone, working the farm, keeping the house, fixing his own meals, and having no one to share his day with at all.

"I need to talk to you about something," Papa said, clucking at Fan to make her move beyond her distrust of a large puddle. Papa was taking me to Gorham to begin school. I had given my tearful goodbyes to Luella and Lawrence and was as ready as I would ever be. I looked back at the farm one last time with an enormous lump in my throat, tears held back with will power, and a thumping heart to be leaving it and forging ahead into my future. I could think of several things he might want to discuss with me but had no clue as to specifically what.

"Yes, Papa?"

"As you know, I have hired neighbor women to help at home sometimes. But people will talk, if you know what I mean, since there will be no one else at home now. So, I have decided to marry your mother's cousin, Ella."

"What? No! You *can't* do that! Do you even love her? Oh, Papa, I *knew* things would be difficult for you with me gone. But *Ella*? She's okay, but I hardly know her. Turn Fan around at once!" I said, furiously.

"It isn't your decision, child. You aren't the one marrying Ella," he said in his quiet way. "We are to marry tomorrow."

"Tomorrow?"

"Yes. I have arranged for the Reverend Aikins to marry us at Windham Hill church. Trafton and Mrs. Hall will stand up with us. We will have no celebration. There's no need for you to miss school for it."

I was stunned into silence. *Papa has given me no choice in this matter that affects me too,* I thought with righteous indignation. *He hasn't even talked to me about any of it. I don't know whether to be angry that I'm not invited to my own father's wedding or grateful not to have to attend it. I just can't imagine Papa sharing a bed with anyone else but Mama. He's replacing Mama! For that matter, what will* my *place be in our home now?* I had so many feelings happening in me at the same time that I could say nothing at all. I felt blistering anger, left out, discarded, and invisible. Before she died, Mama had said that Papa and I would need one another. It didn't seem that Papa needed me at all. And there was another feeling I couldn't quite place immediately. Fan clopped on while I stewed and thought.

Suddenly I realized what that other feeling was. Jealousy! I felt jealous of Ella! She would have Papa's heart now instead of me. I turned in my seat facing away from Papa.

"Now, Mildred Francesca, don't you go pouting. It isn't becoming for a lady. I know what you're thinking. You feel like I have forgotten you. What would you have had me do instead?" he asked rhetorically. "I can keep my good standing in our community by having a wife. And she is able in the kitchen. She is a weaver, too. Did you know that?" Still, I didn't speak. "Child," he said less forcefully, "Ella will never be to me what your mother was. And she can never replace you."

With that, my vision blurred as Papa's words began to fill the holes of pain in my heart.

"Come, child, talk to me."

With what was left of my anger I said, "Oh, why do you insist upon calling me 'child'? I'm hardly a child anymore." Although later, upon reflection of this conversation, I had to concede that in that particular moment I was, indeed, acting childish.

I turned in my seat and looked at Papa. His dark, quiet eyes that had seen so much in his fifty-six years pleaded with me to come back to him. I suddenly realized I was denying him a reasonable solution to a difficult situation. I saw his love for me in those eyes. "Oh, Papa, I'm sorry," I said quietly. "It's just a lot to take in so quickly."

"I know it is, Millie. It was decided upon in haste and I thought it best to tell you when you and I had these private moments together. We will work things out at home in due time. For now, keep up with your own life, especially your studies. School will allow you to leave farm life one day, just as Josey has."

Papa pulled the wagon up to the back side of the boarding house. I was assigned a room with a second-year scholar from Windham who needed a new roommate. We climbed the stairs to the second floor, carrying a few bundles of my things, and stood outside a room with its door open.

"Hi, I'm Lizzie Whipple! I assume you're Millie?" I nodded to the curly-haired blonde standing in what was to be my new dwelling. "Welcome to our room, Millie. You may put your things on that bed there. When you're settled, I'll show you around, since I was here last year and know this place like the back of my hand."

"This is my Papa, Manuel Thomas," I said. Papa tipped his head in response.

"Hello, Manuel. I'm pleased to meet you," Lizzie said, sticking her hand out for Papa to shake. She seemed to have no trouble with strangers!

"Papa, I think there is one more load in the wagon. Let's go down and get it. It isn't much. I can carry it up and you can head on home."

At the wagon, Fan was stomping her impatience. Papa reached for my last two bags and put them on the ground so that he could give me a quick hug goodbye. We'd not done that before, and it felt awkward to me. I wondered if it did to him, too. Then he took my shoulders in his hands, pushed himself away from me, and said, looking straight into my eyes, "You're right, Millie. You are certainly not a child anymore. You are a grown-up scholar now. I believe you will do well here. But if ever you need me, I'll be there for you."

Tears spilled out of my eyes too quickly for my willpower to stop them. I gave my father another quick hug. "I love you, Papa," I whispered.

Then he turned brusquely and climbed into the wagon. I gave Fan a pat on her neck and stepped away. Papa nodded and gently tapped Fan's back with the reins, although she knew what to do without his beckoning. I stood watching his back, wondering what this year would be like. For each of us.

The start of school was challenging, getting used to everything. But each day was better than the last. I liked Lizzie, but I sensed she and I would not become as close as Luella and me. For one thing, Lizzie was messy, while I was tidy. I decided to ignore this for the sake of getting along. She was also much more spontaneous and outgoing, while I am more reserved and like firm schedules. My political and moral views are more conservative than Lizzie's, and while these differences were stumbling blocks at times, they also served to balance us out, offering adaptability to most situations.

Lizzie was boyfriend-free, while I was, of course, anything but. She liked to hear about Lawrence in the beginning but then tired of it quickly. I think she was jealous. But as I began to trust Lizzie with my personal life, I poured out my heart to her about Papa's new marriage.

"I just couldn't believe he would do that without discussing it with me. I mean, I'll have to live with her too, when I'm home. That could be very awkward, you know."

"Don't you think you're borrowing trouble?" Lizzie said sensibly. "You might find it's quite nice to have a mother figure around again. Besides, maybe your father just wanted to spare you from the burden of talking about it. I mean, he probably could predict how you'd feel, right?"

"Maybe," I said, "but couldn't she have just come over each day and left in the evening?"

"Did it ever occur to you, Millie, that maybe he'd like to have a bedmate again? I mean, that's only normal." My cheeks reddened maddeningly. Lizzie laughed, "You're so prudish, Millie. It's almost the twentieth century!"

One especially pretty October day, I needed to go to the library to find a book for my history paper. As I walked toward the entrance to my boarding house, Amanda, who was minding the front desk, called me over and handed me a piece of mail. It was from Luella. I hadn't heard from her in quite a while. Only a small part of me wished it had been from Lawrence, but I had heard from him last week and thought he did well to write me at all. I tucked the letter in my bag for later and smiled.

As I walked briskly to the library, kicking the first of the fallen autumn foliage, I hummed. My skirt swished gaily and rustled the leaves as I thought about how independent I felt here. I was in charge of my own life now and did not have to check with anyone when making most decisions. I'd never known what freedom from farm life and chores could be. I thought I might miss home but, so far, I did not.

When I opened the big wooden door to the library, I inhaled deeply. The smell of so many volumes of books was the smell of knowledge. It was positively exhilarating to me. This library was cavernous compared to the small branch that had recently opened in Great Falls. I found what

I needed, and though I would have loved to linger, I needed to get to my next class. That evening, after finishing what studying I felt was necessary, I finally pulled out my letter from Luella.

Wednesday, October 6, 1897

Dear Millie,

I am sorry to be so delayed in writing back to you, so I hope this finds you well and happy. I received your letter telling me about your father's wedding. I can tell you I am as shocked as you are. But I know your father as a kind-hearted man. I pray you all will come to find household peace quickly.

I am well. For now, I am helping my mother around the house. Matthew calls on me some. I am not yet certain about a future with him. Time will tell.

As I told you, the library is now set up in a closet in Forest Hall. Well, I guess it's bigger than a closet, but it doesn't feel like it. I went there to see it for myself. Addie is acting librarian, but it seems her young niece, Marion, who's only nine, loves books as well. She goes there whenever her sister opens the library door.

Now I have something very difficult to tell you. There was a dance at Forest Hall, and I saw Lawrence with a girl I didn't know. I'm so sorry. If I learn anything else, I will tell you. Promise.

My love always,
Luella

I was shocked and heartbroken by Luella's news, just as I had been with Papa's. I poured my heart out into my diary rather than entrust it to Lizzie. She is quick to talk me out of my emotional pain, which is helpful in many circumstances, but I didn't want to be quickly released from this wound. I wanted to think things over carefully for any indication that Lawrence may have had a heart for another. *He has pledged his undying love for me since Howdie died and he has acted the part too. What if that's all it has been, just an act?*

I wish I could simply wait for a moment after school to talk with Lawrence face to face. I don't want to accuse him of anything by letter. I will just have to be patient until we see each other again.

Ten

Summer Stress

Lizzie and I had much to catch up on when we returned to school after the holiday break. She shared the fun she had with friends and family. I think she had a very pleasant holiday doing enjoyable things. She didn't have housework beckoning her because her family is wealthy enough to have a maid and a cook. She showed me all her new frocks, complete with fashionable shoes and fancy hats to match. Gloves to the elbow and a gorgeous sterling silver necklace made me ask her if she planned to go out on the town any time soon. She giggled and said, "Well, one never knows!"

I, on the other hand, could show her the divinity fudge and butter cookies I brought to share with all the girls, thanks to Ella's fondness for sweets. I had no fancy dresses or accessories to show off. I felt embarrassed but hid it well, I think. Lizzie fairly pounced on the sweets, saying that her mother rarely made anything herself, preferring to purchase the delicacies, clothing, and kitchen wares from charities and churches raising money.

"So, how was it being with Ella?" Lizzie asked.

"Not so bad," I admitted. "She was so happy in the kitchen, I wasn't needed nearly as much as I thought I'd be. We talked fairly easily together. She's a cousin, so we aren't complete strangers, after all. But the situation is so odd, different with Ella as my stepmother. I think we did well. Papa seems less tense, so I'm happy about that. She brought her cat. Turns out that he and Tippy were the ones that didn't get along. Tippy hissed at her cat and her cat spat back. I think they're both used to being the only object of attention within a household. Tippy stuck close to me any time he could, poor thing. But Christmas was nice. It was quiet, much more so than yours, it sounds like. I played the organ at church one of the Sundays."

"I'd love to hear you play the organ," Lizzie said. "Maybe one day we can see if the church will let us in so you can play their organ."

I colored slightly. "Oh, I don't know about that."

But Lizzie moved on and asked about Lawrence. She still didn't know about Luella's painful information from this past autumn. There'd been no need to tell her the details of my relationship with Lawrence, just basic information. In the seconds before I answered her, I quickly thought about what to say. Lawrence never mentioned seeing someone else in his letters before Christmas. When we were finally alone together after I got home, it felt like we talked about everything *but* the dance at Forest Hall. I began to believe that perhaps he had only danced with an acquaintance and nothing more. Or perhaps she was a cousin from out of town. I was willing to give him the benefit of the doubt and drop the whole thing.

But I also saw Luella over Christmas, and she confided that at the next dance she went to after her letter to me, she saw Lawrence together with that same girl. I didn't ask for details or any more information. I didn't want to hear it. My heart was breaking and if there was more information, I wanted it to come from Lawrence himself.

By the last time we saw one another before I went back to school, I'd changed my mind and had decided to broach the subject with Lawrence rather than carry it with me to Gorham. I had a difficult time knowing how and when to bring it up and fidgeted a great deal until Lawrence noticed and asked what was bothering me.

"I...well...I heard it through the grapevine...that you were seen with a girl at Forest Hall dances. I want to know if that's true."

Responding immediately, he said, "Oh, that? Yes, it's true. She's an old friend of mine since before I came to North Gorham. She was visiting relatives, and I asked her if she would like to go to the dance. I thought it would be better for her than sitting around with old folks. That's all. I was just being friendly. Nothing to worry about, Millie. Think no more of it." He kissed me and all my concerns melted away. Or so I thought.

Finally, I answered Lizzie's question, "We saw each other a few times and it was so wonderful to be with him in person." But this was the only thing I offered her, and it seemed to be all she needed before changing the subject.

To answer Lizzie, though, the mental exercise of reviewing what had happened with Lawrence over the past few months disquieted me. I had to admit to myself that the assurance I had felt right after Lawrence explained himself hadn't put things back together as completely as I had first thought. Like Humpty Dumpty falling off the wall and cracking, I wondered if there had been cracks in my heart after what Luella had told me. Nursing my pain for weeks may have widened the cracks too. If all the king's horses and all the king's men couldn't put Humpty together again, I wondered if my relationship with Lawrence was completely salvageable. Could I take small fissures into a long-term relationship with him? Or would that automatically spell its demise? *Can I completely trust him when we are apart?* I wondered. *But isn't that what Godly life means? Trusting?*

Whooping cough swept through the villages that winter, sending spasms to all of us the moment we heard a cough or sneeze. Papa's hearse was far too busy, as scarcely a household hadn't had or known someone who had died. It was a dismal season topped with several intense snowstorms. I didn't get home as often as I'd have liked to, but it was safer to stay put.

One very snowy Saturday, one of the girls in the boarding house began reading the Portland Daily Press with a couple of her friends. They made so many oohs and ahhs and oh-mys that even Lizzie and I could hear them way down the hall. When we went to investigate, several others were there, laughing and talking. So we stayed for the fun.

The paper had been distributed among the girls, each reading from different pages. We arrived when one was reading about medicine for piles which she found uproariously funny. We couldn't help but laugh along with her.

Another found an advertisement for graphophones: "They Sing. They Talk. They Whistle. $10 - $50!" We all agreed that it would be splendid if one of us could provide the boarding house with graphophone entertainment.

"Listen to this," one of the girls said excitedly, "'Portland Theatre presents "A Railroad Ticket."' We should go!"

"Well, as long as we're wishing, here it says we can get to San Francisco from Boston in only five days!" said another girl.

"Here it says the Grand Trunk can get us to *Alaska*! Oh, how I'd love to see Alaska!" Murmurs of agreement floated into the air.

But Lizzie noticed that one of the girls had covered her mouth and looked dismayed at the article she'd found. She read, "A twelve-year-old girl put kerosene on a wood fire in the kitchen to make it burn more quickly when it suddenly flared up into a great sheet of flame, completely enveloping her about the face and upper part of her body. She isn't expected to live." The atmosphere in the room changed dramatically.

I found an article of my own that left me with a sobering taste in my mouth. I silently read the story of a one-room schoolteacher named Fanny. She and her young charges were halfway through their school day when a very sudden blizzard overtook the area.

"What are you reading?" the girls wanted to know, seeing my expression.

I explained the part I had just read, then finished reading the article aloud. "'Miss Fanny decided she had time to deliver all the children safely to their homes in her wagon. She first had them bundle up in every stitch of clothing they had. Then she grabbed the blanket she kept in the room and left to ready the horse. She then shuttled all the children to the wagon, telling them to climb in and huddle tightly together all the way home.

"'At first Miss Fanny was able to make headway. But soon the road became invisible with blinding and drifted snow. The horse could go no further. So, she did the only thing she could think of to save the children's lives. She had them all exit the wagon and unhitched the horse. Then she had the children help her push the wagon over onto its side and again upside down. They dug their way underneath the wagon, out of the wind. At first this seemed to be the perfect solution. But as time went by, Miss Fanny could see that the children were getting sleepy from hypothermia and she said, "Whatever you do, children, keep each other awake!" Then she laid her own body over them to wait out the blizzard.

"'When the storm was over, a farmer, whose house was not fifty feet from the stalled wagon, saw the situation and immediately righted the wagon. He was at first amazed to find so many bodies crowded together. Then he was terrified that they had all died. Miraculously, he found that every child had survived, though most had frostbite. Tragically, however, he found that Miss Fanny had died, saving her young scholar's lives with her own.'"

Silence overtook the room. Most of us planned to be teachers ourselves. We couldn't imagine such a tragedy. But the question on each of our hearts was, would we sacrifice ourselves for our scholars?

One day in early spring, a letter came from Joe saying that he and Bea were to be wed June 22 at the farm. It was wonderful news, if Joe was indeed happy. And so far, I had no reason to think he wasn't. I rejoiced in a wedding at home. And more happy news came in a letter from Lawrence. It revealed that he planned to join me at Gorham High School next year, assuming he passed his exams. Summer couldn't come fast enough.

As is true of time, enough passed and it was finally June. I was pleased with my grades, and I was ready to come home for the summer although I had had a wonderful year in school. Then a short letter came from Joe.

Thursday, June 2, 1898
Dear Papa and Millie,

I regret to inform you that our wedding location has been changed to Chicopee, Massachusetts. Bea feels it would be closer to more of the family and to her friends. She and I, of course, would love to have you there.

We will come up to the farm in July and be there the rest of the summer.

Love,
Joe and Bea

Thursday, June 9, 1898
Dear Joe and Bea,

Papa and I have discussed your revision in plans. You know we would love to be at your wedding, but Papa will not leave the farm that long. I have decided to stay at home with him and Ella. You will need to abide my every question about all the details when we are together!

We look forward to seeing Mr. and Mrs. Joe Thomas in July.

All my love,
Millie

In the meantime, Lawrence came to call quite often, and we spent happy hours in conversations much deeper than our letters could provide. I loved the attention Lawrence gave me when he called. It served to replace any thoughts I had about not being able to trust him.

One such day, we sat side by side out in the meadow, overlooking the river, smelling the sweet earthy freshness of moss and pine. The azure sky was interrupted with cirrus clouds that reminded me of the white ostrich plumes I'd seen in pictures of ladies' fancy hats. The breeze nodded the heads of each wildflower–Queen Anne's lace, Black-eyed Susans, blue cornflowers, and the delicate daisies. I giggled thinking how neighboring blossoms looked to be whispering secrets when their heads touched. Then they'd separate to pass the message on to the next flower when a gentle puff of air forced them together.

"Millie, your beautiful, long, silky, dark hair befits you," Lawrence said, running his fingers down through the locks I had unleashed from the bun I usually wore. My face flushed. "And your eyes, so dark and piercing, as though you could look straight through me. Tell me, my dear Millie, what you are thinking?"

I was mesmerized as if in a romantic fantasy that we girls loved reading about, completely smitten, and maybe a tiny bit dangerously so, if I was completely honest with myself. It was so easy to forget to be sensible when my heart was the only organ speaking. Yet, part of me couldn't stop this wonderful, waking dream. After several seconds to think rationally, I said, "First, I was just imagining the wildflowers having a grand conversation all over the meadow. Silly, I suppose."

"Not silly coming from such a creative mind," Lawrence kindly said. "What's second?"

"Well, I'm thinking about your birthday, tomorrow. Would you like your card today?"

"Hmmm. I think I'd rather come over tomorrow, when you do firecrackers. You will be doing that, won't you?"

"Of course! And it would be wonderful to have you come over."

"Then that's settled. Is there something else you were thinking about? Your expression doesn't seem peaceful yet."

The color on my face deepened, as it gave me away once again. "Yes. I'm thinking about how lovely it is to be in your company."

"Oh, it is, it is," he replied, as if in a fantasy of his own. "Let's take a walk down to the river."

I nodded and stood, my hand still in his. I knew that taking "a walk down to the river" meant that I would receive his exquisite embraces and tender, sweet kisses. It was all I could do to keep from pulling Lawrence into a full run down the hill. *Patience, Millie,* I told myself and forced contentment with the small talk we made all the way down the meadow.

"Guess who will teach and be the next principal here in Great Falls this autumn?" Lawrence said.

"Oh, do tell!"

"Donald MacMillan," Lawrence said, as if I should know who he was talking about.

"Is he someone special?"

"Well, he just graduated from Bowdoin College. I think that's special enough. It's expensive and elite. And to think he would come *here* to our little school for his first teaching assignment!"

"That does sound impressive," I said. Though without knowing the man, I could only be mildly impressed. Lawrence, however, was obviously thrilled. "It's a shame you won't be around to see him, though." I felt sorry for him.

"But I will! I'm staying on as janitor of the school so I will come home almost every weekend. I'm sure to run into him."

Suddenly I felt deflated. All the spring in my step was gone. "But then *I* won't see you on the weekends."

"I'll be right there in Gorham the whole week through. We can see each other every week day. And if you need to come home some weekend, I can bring you back with me," Lawrence said, sensibly, but not hearing the pain behind my words.

I could tell that Lawrence didn't see the issue the same way I did. I knew that at least I would be engaged in rigorous study on most weekday nights, not seeking the distraction of Lawrence's presence. I felt a sincere obligation to Joe's commitment of financial support and wouldn't do poorly in my classes. I said no more about it to Lawrence. I didn't want to completely break the spell of such a wonderful afternoon.

Once Lawrence and I had crested the hill on our way back, I saw that Joe and Bea had arrived for the summer. I was elated to see them and couldn't wait to hear every detail of their wedding, which would most certainly come from Bea. Lawrence and I hugged goodbye, repeating our plans for the next day. Then I turned to my brother and his new wife to greet them warmly and offer my congratulations in person.

Papa, Ella, Lawrence, and I enjoyed the holiday festivities the next day at home while Joe took Bea to the Cumberland County Fair.

"Would you like to go to the fair, too?" Lawrence asked me when he realized part of the family had decided to go there.

"No, not necessarily," I said. "I could be happy either place as long as I'm with you."

It wasn't until later in the day when Joe and Bea returned that I thought about Lawrence's question. *Had he preferred the fair? What a dunce I've been,* reddening when no one was around to see it. *I didn't even think to ask him. I'll just bet he would have gone to the fair if it hadn't been for me. I will apologize the first chance I get.*

It wasn't long before the summer routine took the place of holiday festivities. There were now three women in the house who independently knew how she liked to carry out household tasks. Being the youngest and least experienced, I wasn't sure what my place was or if either Bea or Ella even needed or wanted my help. Not one of us explicitly mentioned the awkwardness of the situation, but I felt it. Ella knew she was the current head of the household as Papa's wife but also knew she was replacing Mama and felt shy about instituting her routines around me. Bea was the newer wife and family member but not in a position to claim a dominant status. I am the youngest woman in the mix but have been accustomed to the particular routines of this home longer than either of the others.

In the end, Ella and Bea divided the kitchen duties, leaving me to help them clean the house. That was fine since it meant more leisurely time for me, so I didn't argue. Luella and I were able to see one another often that summer. She was no longer pursuing Matthew and didn't want to stay at home another year, so she decided to pursue enrollment in Farmington's normal school, some eighty miles north of Great Falls. She applied for a scholarship and received one. I was delighted for her.

"Why did you decide to enroll in a school all the way in Farmington instead of Western Normal School right in Gorham?" I asked as we walked to the library one day.

"Wait till you hear this, Millie. I learned that The Farmington State Normal School is a model school that allows students to practice teaching under the supervision of experienced faculty. I thought that would give me a better start to teaching if I could begin while still in school."

"That's wonderful!" I said, sincerely happy for her. "I guess we won't see each other any less, really. Our letters will have further to go, but we will still be able to see each other in the summers, right?"

"I don't see why not."

"If I get any chance at all, I'd love to come visit you up there," I said, excited at the prospect of traveling to a part of the state I hadn't seen.

"Oh! Wouldn't that be heavenly!" Luella beamed, lacing her arm through my elbow.

"As for me," I said, "I would like to teach when I'm finished with school. I just don't know where yet. The other thing I think I'd love is being a librarian for a bigger library than this one. One more like Gorham's library would suit me just fine."

We determined to spend as much time as possible together before she had to leave, which would be shortly before my next term began.

I also enjoyed visiting Uncle Almon, who came to live with Grandpar, at least for the summer. Grandpar was not doing well enough to continue with the same duties he was used to doing. Uncle Almon's job, he told me, was to talk sense into his father as to putting limits on his physical activity. It would not be easy, he said. His father could be stubborn. Personally, I didn't experience Grandpar as stubborn at all.

As the summer came to a close, a new tension brewed in our household. Bea was sending out the message both subtly and overtly that she did not like Lawrence and did not think he was right for me. I felt more conflicted than I'd ever felt before but kept my displeasure with Bea's opinions to myself. Neither did I mention the situation to Lawrence.

Eleven

Graduation

As my second year at Gorham High School and Lawrence's first progressed, I did see him throughout the week just as he had told me, and I had to resist the temptation to see him too often. Lizzie enjoyed his company as well. They were both very outgoing and loved a crowd. But where Lizzie often substituted her studying for a good time with friends, Lawrence was driven to succeed. We were in two different tracks, he in college prep and I in Latin/English. He had tested out of his first year the same as I had and would graduate the year after me. He intended to study science in college, whereas I was happy to begin teaching the autumn after graduation. Several of his courses required his careful attention and so, while I did see him here and there, we were not able to spend much time together.

Lawrence told me that Donald MacMillan seemed to be a very good teacher for Levi Hall school and that Mr. MacMillan was very interested in teaching his older scholars about the Arctic. He even talked of wanting to go on polar expeditions one day. To go to such a place seemed utterly staggering to both Lawrence and me.

With the winter of 1898 came a new state law making education compulsory. All children seven to fifteen years old were required to be in school. The penalty for not being there without good reason meant parents could be fined twenty-five dollars or spend up to thirty days in jail if the fine was not paid. Further, the law stated that if a boy continued to be truant, he could be sent to the state reform school. If a girl was delinquent, she could be sent to the state industrial school. My education classes discussed the pros and cons of such a law, a discussion which ended with an energetic debate. While some felt the law was too abrupt and severe, most of the scholars agreed that children needed to be in school, and this might be the only way to get them there on a regular basis. I had my own opinions, but mostly I loved the very act of debating, hearing justifiable arguments from both sides.

In February, Uncle Almon delivered the crushing news that Grandpar had died on the twenty-first. It was very sad to think that neither grandparent dwelt in that beautiful home by the lake. The decision about what to do with the house lay with Uncle Almon. I felt very sorry for him. Contemplating the selling of his childhood home could not have been easy. Even though I don't plan to stay on our farm, I certainly would not want to sell it. Yet he had made his life in Massachusetts, where his work and friends were. He said that he would take his time deciding what to do because he felt no rush. That was fine with me since it meant that he would be back to Great Falls from time to time.

That spring, with only one year left in the Latin/English track, with most of us intending to teach after we graduated in 1900, the superintendent of Gorham schools, Mr. Woodman, spoke to our entire class about issues we would need to be aware of. He said that some schools were sloppily run regarding discipline, room tidiness, and overall appearance of school rooms. This was not an issue I worried about, except maybe discipline. I had not been an overly unruly child, nor did I have younger siblings who might have been. Hence, I did not witness much discipline outside of my Great Falls classroom. I supposed that if I had a very difficult child to discipline, I would just have to learn by experience.

Mr. Woodman said that subjects were not well taught in some schools. Again, I was not overly concerned until he specified that science and physiology teachers were not covering the effects of alcohol, stimulants, and narcotics on the body, as mandated by state law. Having no knowledge of any of these things, I hoped we would cover that material next year. Then my ears perked up when I heard Mr. Woodman say that Levi Hall school had done a very credible job in this. *Thanks to Mr. MacMillan,* I thought. And then he added that high praise was also due to Levi Hall for the stellar teaching of bookkeeping and the art of penmanship.

Mr. Woodman finished his presentation, warning us to make sure parents supervise their children after school and teach them chastity, moderation, temperance, and respect for the aged. He said that there should be no profanity or smoking allowed. I was somewhat mystified by this admonishment as I considered these things to be standard elements of parental responsibility. *What parents* didn't *do these things?* I wondered. *Maybe I really do lead the sheltered life Lizzie accuses me of.*

One day just before the end of the term, with summer holiday looming, Lawrence and I had a chance to take a walk around Gorham. "So, how do you think your first year went?" I asked Lawrence.

"Not bad but not as well as I'd hoped. I thought it would be easier, I guess. I did alright but I was exhausted being janitor at Levi Hall on top of my studies. I might let go of the job next year, though I hate to because I need the money. Maybe I can find ways to do small jobs in Gorham, nearer the school."

"That sounds reasonable," I said, silently rejoicing in a year together that would include weekends.

"But," Lawrence added, as if he had heard my silent thoughts, "I expect to be busy studying most weekends. I mean, just because I'll be on Gorham campus Saturday and Sunday doesn't mean I can fritter away my time, you know?"

Crestfallen, I asked for clarification of "fritter away."

"Well, you know, spending long times with you when I should be studying."

Lawrence saw my disheartened face and said, "It doesn't mean we will never be able to get together, Millie. I just need to graduate with high marks. You understand, right?"

"Yes," I said with little enthusiasm. "Do you think you'll head straight to college the autumn after you graduate?"

"I've been thinking about that. I may have to teach a few years first to earn the money I'd need for college."

It all made perfect sense in my mind but didn't make my heart very happy. I tried to hide my feelings better than usual.

That next autumn, Lawrence let go of his janitor position, as he'd said he might. He told me he was sorry he wouldn't be around Mr. MacMillan, who was teaching at Great Falls again. I think Lawrence enjoyed the adventuresome spirit of the man, among other things. I decided to make the most of this last year Lawrence and I would be together in school. If we couldn't spend much time together at dances or taking walks and the like, perhaps we could study together. Our classes wouldn't be the same, but I thought we could quiz each other when tests were due. I talked with Lizzie about this idea, and she thought it was a good and sensible one.

So my last year had begun. Some of my classes focused heavily not only on learning more in-depth information about a given subject but also on how to break the information down into smaller ideas to teach children in an organized step-by-step fashion. From time to time, the superintendent would either visit our classrooms or write instructions in his reports that we were to read and discuss in class. One such report said:

I noticed in certain schools that the scholars were idle and listless. You must realize that one of the great advantages which children derive from attending school comes from learning to work to dig things out for themselves. Do not allow children to run to you on every foolish pretext. Do not allow children to snap their fingers to attract your attention. It was noticed in many schools the children had what is known as a sing-song tone, and closed their sentences with a rising inflection. Do not place upon the walls of your schoolroom advertisements of tobacco or other pictures representing objects with which children should not become familiar. Be sure of your facts and that which you state is true.

Clearly with the new state law making education mandatory, school instruction was being taken even more seriously. I couldn't help thinking of Howdie's love of education and how much he would have contributed had he lived to fulfill his term on the school board. In fact, Howdie's birthday was coming soon, on October 10. To commemorate that date, which I'm sure will live in my heart forever, I asked Lawrence if we might do something special together. It was a Tuesday, so we couldn't be out late. But even a short, brisk walk around a nearby pond would be lovely with the autumn colors coming to peak.

"I have an exam the next day," Lawrence said. "I'm sorry, Millie. I will be studying that night. But you go, maybe with one of your friends. You're right, it would be a lovely way to remember your brother."

As the school year continued, it was more and more difficult to spend quality time with Lawrence. Something always seemed to come between us and our plans at the last minute. I became concerned that Lawrence was losing interest in our relationship. Yet on the few occasions that I mentioned my concern, he always comforted me with words of assurance that everything was fine and normal. These words would quell my fears. For a while.

"So, I'll meet you at two o'clock tomorrow afternoon, then," I had said to Lawrence one Friday when we crossed paths.

"Perfect," he said, demurely squeezing my hand before hastening to his class.

I too needed to hurry, although the snowy pathways made hurrying unproductive. Lawrence and I had decided to meet before dinner and then eat together. We didn't have firm plans but would decide in the moment, which would give an element of surprise to the day. Lawrence was more likely to create the day as we went. I generally preferred to know what we were doing, if for no other reason than to know how to prepare myself.

"I love that about Lawrence, don't you?" Lizzie said the next day, crooning a bit when I couldn't decide what to wear. "I mean, it's so romantic!"

"Well, I guess it is, at that," I said, not willing to explain my bent on things. Lizzie and I did best when we didn't try too hard to make our relationship work perfectly. We were friends after a year and a half together, but not *best* friends.

"Have a nice afternoon. I'm going to put in some time at the library, much as I'd rather not," Lizzie frowned. "So go have a good time for me."

"Thank you," I said, leaving the room to meet Lawrence in the entrance hall. When I saw that he wasn't there, I took a seat.

Fifteen minutes later, Lizzie walked by on her way to the library. "He hasn't come yet?" she asked pointing out the obvious. "Well, he'll be here soon, I'm sure. Bye."

But Lawrence didn't come soon. After an hour, I felt silly waiting downstairs any longer and told Amanda to come get me when Lawrence arrived. But not long after I'd taken my coat and boots off and settled down to study, I realized I could not concentrate because my anger was building. *Where is he now?* I thought, realizing that my faith in him was undeniably faulty. I decided to go to the library, thinking that maybe a change in scenery would make it easier to study.

It was cold and gray outside, no different than my mood. I brooded all the way to the library, thinking of all the places Lawrence might be instead of with me. It was odd to open the big library doors, inhaling the volumes-of-books smell I usually loved, feeling gloomy instead of energized. I decided to tell Lizzie that Lawrence never did show up. Maybe she could help me figure out what had happened to him. But Lizzie was nowhere to be found. I began to wonder if perhaps the two were together and my anger flared like a dragon's breath, becoming my companion all the way back to the boarding house. There was no way I would be able to concentrate on my schoolwork until I learned what was going on.

After stomping off my boots on the porch, which I must say I did with satisfying vigor, I entered the house. Before I could walk to the front desk, Amanda approached me with a very worried look on her face. "Millie, I have an urgent message for you!"

I opened the envelope immediately, while Amanda stood waiting to learn what was mine to know. I looked up at her and she jolted back and retreated to the desk. I was in no mood to be a spectacle. Instead of taking the note out of its container, I went up to my room. There, I read, *"Millie, I am at Dr. Hunt's office with Lawrence. I will explain more later. Lizzie."*

Oh, dear, I thought with remorse for having distrusted Lawrence. I grabbed my coat and boots again and raced by Amanda's desk without stopping. *Serves her right for not respecting my privacy,* I thought. *Now she'll just have to wait a bit longer.* As I ran to Dr. Hunt's office, I slipped and caught myself. *Slow down, Millie. When you're in a hurry, don't hurry!* I admonished myself thinking how silly it would be to slip on ice and land in Dr. Hunt's office as another patient. *Well, that would be* one *way to be sure of seeing Lawrence,* I thought ironically. Finally I reached the doctor's office and walked into the waiting room.

"Oh, Lawrence!" I cried, seeing him sitting there. I quickly sat down beside him and laid my hand over his. "I'm so sorry. Whatever has happened?" When Lawrence didn't answer, I looked at Lizzie and said "I'm glad you brought him here." Then turning back to Lawrence I said, "And to think this happened while I was waiting in the house for you." I blubbered a while longer until the nurse called for him. Lizzie and I were not allowed to follow him so we kept one another's minds off that which we had yet to learn.

"What happened?" I implored Lizzie.

"I was on my way to the library and saw him approaching in the distance. Then suddenly I saw him fall. He must have slipped on the ice and landed on his back. I kept walking toward him, watching to see him get up, but he didn't. So, I ran to him the best I could. He had his eyes closed. Oh, Millie, at first I thought he…well, anyway, I asked him if he was alright. He only said that his head hurt dreadfully. I looked around and no one was close by. So, I asked him if he could get up and walk so that I could get him to Dr. Hunt. He managed to sit up and then stand, thank goodness. I'm not sure what I would have done if he hadn't been able to."

I wrung my hands and tried to calm myself, but it didn't work very well. "Oh, Lizzie, what if he's truly injured? Do you think I should try to contact his parents?"

"I don't know," Lizzie said raising her shoulders, sincerely blank.

"Isn't this taking too long?" I said to myself. As I sat in a daze, Mama came to my mind for some reason. I missed her so. I wondered how she had been able to weather the storms of her life with such decorum. Even her own illness and imminent death had been no different. She accepted her fate without complaint. Would I ever become the woman my mother had been?

Finally, the door opened, and Dr. Hunt indicated that Lizzie and I could come into his office. He shut the door behind us and said, "Lawrence here has most likely concussed his head, but that is all. There are no other injuries that I can see." Neither of us could miss the white bandages across Lawrence's brow. "He will need plenty of rest in a quiet, darkened room. He should not be overly stimulated. Someone should be right with him for the first twenty-four hours to watch for blurred vision, nausea, and sickness. Barring these, at the end of that time, he may have one morphine tablet every four hours for pain." He handed the tablets to Lizzie. "He may resume his normal schedule in one week if no other complications arise. If they do, see me immediately." Dr. Hunt opened the door and called out to the nurse, "Next patient, please."

In the waiting room, I helped Lawrence with his coat and scarf. From there, we slowly walked him to his boarding house, each of us taking one of his elbows. The house mother took over from there while we waited for her to come back after settling Lawrence into his bed. We told her what the doctor had said, and she was more than happy to oversee his initial care. She suggested we not visit him before Wednesday, which seemed an interminably long time to me. And through all of this, Lawrence had not spoken a word.

Interminable or not, Wednesday came, and I went to see Lawrence at first chance. He was in the parlor, reading, and looked his normal self. I was much relieved when he smiled broadly at the sight of me, and as we talked, he laughed at all the fuss and at having fallen in the first place. He was frustrated that he couldn't go back to class until Monday, but his house mother would not hear of disobeying the doctor's orders. In fact, she wouldn't let me stay as long as I would have liked, so we parted ways.

When Lawrence was well again, we resumed trying to see one another. But as before, he remained very busy, especially having missed a week of classes. And since I was in the last few months of my last year, I became quite busy myself. Besides my studies, our class arranged an exquisite, moonlit sleigh ride through the woods, and once spring was firmly established, we enjoyed a day at the home of one of our classmates on Prout's Neck, picnicking and playing games.

While these things were more fun than I had ever had with a group of my peers, it was the senior spring exhibition, proposed by the class and approved by the principal, that was highly anticipated. Our class decided to enact the dramatic piece *The Importance of Being Ernest*. And I was awarded the leading female role! I studied my lines voraciously and when the performance day came, I was grateful to see Papa, Ella, and Lawrence in the front row. Pleased as I was, I had expected them, but not Uncle Almon, and certainly not Joe and Bea, who had traveled the distance to watch me perform!

Our class did not have time to waste after the play was over, for there were items to accomplish before we graduated. First, there were year-end exams to prepare for. At the same time, the Latin/English scholars were tasked with creating the class motto. We decided on *Non Quid Fuimus, Sed Erimus*, which translated to "Not what we have been, but what we will be." It was resoundingly approved by the faculty and the rest of our class.

The college prep scholars designed our class rings to be a wide gold band with the raised numbers "1900" on the outside and the initials of our class motto, "NQFSE," inscribed on the inside. When these scholars presented their design, one of the boys loudly declared that we should be called the "class of the double nothings." Though some thought his remark was tasteless, it nonetheless became our unofficial class motto.

I looked at the design with the somber reality that, unlike Lizzie and others who could afford the lovely piece of jewelry, I wouldn't be able to wear one. I couldn't ask Papa or Joe for this extravagance that I might not even wear very long. It was plenty enough to have been gifted with these past three years of education.

At the year-end assembly, Superintendent Woodman congratulated his class of 1900 for our achievements. He challenged us to make good use of our fine education. I listened intently to all of his words, mesmerized by the fact that it was now my turn to graduate from the same school both my brothers had attended before endeavoring to further their mark upon the world.

Suddenly, I heard my name and immediately blushed. "Mildred Francesca Thomas, will you please come up front with me." I did so on wobbly knees. "This is your class valedictorian," he continued. "Let us confer upon her the honor of our applause." I knew I'd done a respectable job with my studies but did not realize I'd done quite this well. I could hardly believe it.

Still stunned, I looked at Mr. Woodman as he said, "It will be up to you, Miss Thomas, to write the valedictory that you will read on graduation day. Please have it ready by the time of graduation practice. Congratulations, Miss Thomas. You may take your seat."

I turned and took no more than two steps when Mr. Woodman said, "Uh, Miss Thomas." I whirled back around. "One more thing before you take your seat." I returned to his podium and stood uncomfortably in the quiet while a woman who had not been there a few seconds ago, stepped before me and handed me a small box. I looked up at Mr. Woodman who said, "You may open it, Miss Thomas." When I did, I stared at its contents, stunned. "The school board has decided that our valedictorian should have a class ring." The spontaneous applause was thunderous this time, even for the relatively few people in attendance. Tears pooled in Lizzie's eyes as well as my own. Lizzie knew how I had coveted a class ring. My crimson cheeks were wet as I took my seat, staring at the shiny new ring on my finger. I would write a heartfelt letter of gratitude to the school board, but I knew that no matter what I managed to say, it would never be adequate.

Graduation day was beautiful, but I hardly noticed. I was once again as nervous and excited as I had been three years earlier, perhaps more so. As we graduates processed down the aisle of the Congregational Church of Gorham in our black robes, I saw Joe and Bea toward the back of the sanctuary with Papa, Ella, and Uncle Almon closer to the front. I did not find Lawrence and had to push my disappointment away. The energy in the room was otherwise vibrant and the decorations dazzling. Flowers, accenting the class colors of blue and white, surrounded a white silk banner on which was printed the class motto. When it was my turn to read my speech, I stood and scanned the room once more. There Lawrence was, sitting with his friends on my far left, along with an audience much larger than that of Levi Hall three years ago. Composure was slow to reach my voice but strengthened as I read:

"Family, friends, and people of Gorham, honored School Board, and beloved teachers, we realize that without your aid, your efforts on our behalf, your kindness and unselfish labor for the good of each one of us, we would not know the success we enjoy today. Not only these successes but the apparent defeats as well, have been the means of fitting us for the larger school of life which we are about to enter.

"It is with mingled sorrow and pleasure that we meet here on this occasion—sorrow that our connection with the school and with each other as classmates is to be broken; pleasure and gratification that the prescribed course of study has been completed.

"In turning to the future, let us think of the strides in civilization since the opening of the century just passed, all the advantages with which we are blessed, and which, I fear, we regard so lightly! Surely we cannot be too thankful for the opportunities presented in these last days of the nineteenth century!

"To my classmates of 1900, Johann Wolfgang Von Goethe said that 'kindness,' and I would add friendship, 'is the golden chain by which society is bound together'. In the years in which we have been united as classmates, this chain has been weaving itself about us. Let us earnestly hope that not even a link will ever be broken when we are separated. May we proudly remember our motto, it is not what we have been, but what we will be. May we strive to be a source of satisfaction to our Alma Mater and more than all else, may we be of great worth in the sight of the Father above."

Mildred F. Thomas
Valedictory speech, June 15, 1900

Saturday, June 16, 1900

Dear diary, what a beautiful, beautiful day it was yesterday. Though the graduation exercises were exhilarating, I shall miss my classmates terribly. Never again will we all be together like that. The dinner was most delectable and the party following it was great fun. Chandler's Orchestra of Portland provided the music to which I danced with Lawrence—in my new dress and fine class ring.

This morning Joe hurried into the house with the Portland Daily Press fluttering about him. He said, "Millie, look at this!" To my astonishment, our graduation exercise was detailed in the paper and that's the first time I have ever seen my name in print!

But then, I saw, in an adjacent column, a very interesting article. A woman wrote that she suffered from the grippe until she changed her diet to warm milk toast and boiled eggs over Grape-Nuts cereal. I shall have to talk with Ella and Bea about this.

Twelve

Christmas

Sunday, September 16, 1900

Dearest Millie,

I hope you are all settled into your new boarding house now and that teaching will go well for you. You must tell me all the details. I think it best that I teach next year rather than proceed directly to college, but I don't know where yet, of course. I assume you know that Frederick Dole took over as teacher and principal at Levi Hall, filling Donald MacMillan's place. I hope he is as good.

Your roommate, Lizzie, is doing well as assistant teacher, from what I hear. Isn't it odd that she is from Windham and teaching in Great Falls while you are from Great Falls and teaching in Windham?

I received your letter telling me that your Uncle Almon has sold his parents' estate. He is truly a fair and honest man to have sold for the same amount he would sell to a family member or close friend. He certainly might have gotten more than $1,000. Decent men are not a given these days.

Helen has announced her betrothal to John as we assumed she would. They have picked December 27 to wed. Are you able to accompany me to their wedding? John has asked me to stand up with him. He told me that he should not forget what year they married, since a turn-of-the-century year is an unforgettable one. I like John. I think he will make a fine brother-in-law.

With my love,
Lawrence
Sunday, December 9, 1900

My dear Lawrence,

I think I shall be more than ready to come home over the holidays. The scholars have been restless since that first big snow last week. The youngest ones are sure that Santa Claus is due each night after school! Otherwise, I think all of my pupils are learning reasonably well so far. The young ones are all darling and it is difficult for me to be too harsh, though perhaps I should be more stern with them. The teenage boys can get sassy at times and play pranks.

I read in the Windham annuals that "a teacher must thoroughly enjoy her work and must count nothing of greater importance than to bring about a healthy development of the child's mind. She should read many educational books and magazines and be willing, yes, more than willing, to forego some of her pleasures outside of the schoolroom, in order that she may assume the duties of the following day with a broader view and a deeper interest." I do hope and pray I am not overly zealous in pursuit of my "own pleasures." Maybe you and I can talk about this when we see one another next.

I have grown to love my host family, and I think they are still happy enough with me. Their children brag that they receive special care from "teacher" since I live with them. Of course that is not true. So long as the superintendent doesn't believe it, I shall let it pass.

I am excited for the holidays and being with you at Helen's wedding. I am flattered that she thinks me accomplished enough to play the organ. At least that way you and I will both be occupied during the ceremony.

I must tell you that I was home last weekend and am troubled by my visit. Ella seemed herself. But Papa did not. I have yet to determine what may be the matter. Perhaps you will notice it when you visit.

Before we know it, I will be taking your arm when we sashay into the reception party! I can hardly wait.

Love,
Your Millie

Except for an occasional rendezvous, such as Lawrence's sister's wedding, he and I have both been so busy that the times between visits have not been totally unbearable. Even my twenty-first birthday, which fell on a Wednesday, was just another day, although Lawrence had sent me a card which arrived the day before.

On Thursday, March 21, 1901, Maine adopted its first state flag. It was a simple design on a buff-colored background. A dark blue star in the left corner symbolized the north star, a mariner's guiding light. Papa said he especially liked the star because it reminded him of the many nights he sailed under the vast heavens. Its one evergreen tree, in the center, depicted Maine's plethora of white pines. The town of Gorham purchased one for each of its schools and on Saturday, May 4, Levi Hall ceremoniously hoisted hers up the flagpole to fly proudly underneath the American flag. Many turned out to witness the event. I was happy to come home and stand arm in arm with Lawrence.

A month later, after finishing my first teaching year and returning home for the summer, I went to Gorham to watch Lawrence graduate in the same church I had. Sitting with friends, I waited for his entrance, which never came. The program said that he was to read his essay on the character of John Milton. When it came time for him to deliver it, Mr. Woodman announced that Lawrence had the measles and the program continued to the next event. This saddened me greatly on Lawrence's behalf. I knew what a wonderful day my graduation had been and wanted that for him as well. I left after the ceremony, preferring not to stay for the celebration, though it had been nice to sit with Lizzie and swap teaching stories. On the way home I wondered why I had not gotten the measles myself when the affliction had spread so widely through my school that I had had to close it for a few days.

It seemed like a long summer, going back and forth between hot and humid, at least on the days when it wasn't both. And I still felt tension in the air. "I'm just not sure what this tension is that I feel here at home," I said to Luella, as we lazily sat on Levi Hall's playground swings one day. "As far as household tensions between Ella, Bea, and me, they are not as noticeable this year. I assume that's partly because we've already established a system that works. By now, I would think that both Ella and Bea should be used to living here in the country. I can't think of what else it might be, though."

"Could it be that there is some new tension between Ella and Bea? If so, maybe you feel their tension rather than your own," Luella suggested after a few moments' thought.

"I suppose so."

"Well," Luella said, "Bea has been teaching for a while now, in charge of a classroom. And Ella has been with your father several years, all year round. She must know the household very well by now. Maybe they each come to the summer thinking they might be in charge. I mean, you are very gracious to allow both of them to do things in a kitchen that's more yours than either of theirs, in my opinion."

"You're sweet to say so, Luella. But I'm quite happy for the break."

"Well, what about Lawrence? You have said that Bea doesn't like him much. Does Ella share that opinion?"

"If she does, she hasn't said anything to me. She and Papa probably talk about me and Lawrence, though."

"Maybe you could have a talk with your father, then?"

"Oh, I don't know," I sighed, "I'm not sure I'd want to hear his opinion if it isn't good. I'll just keep my nose to the ground for now, see if I can figure this out. Tell me all about school in Farmington. I could tell you were some busy when you didn't write as often as I thought you might."

We talked and talked. It seemed time was meaningless when we were together. And we were together often that summer, when I wasn't with Lawrence. I tried to be attentive to anything Papa, Ella, Bea, or Joe said or did that might give me a clue as to what they didn't like about Lawrence. By the end of the summer, I was no closer to understanding why I felt what I did. But I *was* closer to Lawrence.

Then one day in August, before all of us would need to part company to begin the school year, Luella said, "I hate to mention this, Millie, but lately I've had a strange feeling around Lawrence."

"Not you too?" I said with a sinking feeling in my stomach. "Am I to be all alone in my feelings for him?"

"I'm sorry. I don't mean to drop this on you just as we are all leaving. But it's only been very recently that I have noticed something different about him." Luella stopped talking for a moment before saying, "You know what? It's probably nothing. So, forget I said anything, dearest. Truly."

"You've always been honest with me, Luella, and I know you wouldn't say anything just to hurt me. So, I'll try to let it drop."

Autumn arrived, the air began to chill noticeably, and the leaves' annual change of colors had mysteriously begun again. Normally, I would bask in the hues of fall, but I had other things on my mind. Most days, Papa and Ella were at the forefront, second only to my teaching job. I worried about Papa. I worried that I wasn't home often enough to assess how he and Ella were really doing. And I worried that my relationship with Lawrence might come between Papa and me somehow, though I didn't know how. And I wondered if I should care at all.

Besides, I could not get Luella's comment out of my head completely. The niggling thought that Lawrence, the new principal and teacher at Levi Hall, and Lizzie, his associate, teaching the younger grades, just wouldn't stay out of the way. One day I had the sudden thought that maybe the strange feeling Luella had was because of Lawrence's thoughts about having Lizzie as a teaching partner. Lawrence and Lizzie were friends, of course, and Luella wasn't used to Lizzie's effect on Lawrence. I was quite used to their banter by now. *Yes,* I thought, *I'll just bet that's it.* With that, I put the nigglers out of my mind once and for all.

Letters flew back and forth to and from Lawrence, Luella, Lizzie, and Marion, with whom I'd become closer this past summer. I came to enjoy Lawrence's letters almost as much as being with him. I savored each one over and over again day after day. Joe, Bea, and Uncle Almon wrote occasionally from Massachusetts, but I rarely received a letter from home, which didn't help my concerns about Papa one bit.

With Christmas coming, I was as excited as the children and couldn't wait to go home. Lawrence was invited to join us for the latter part of Christmas day. Joe and Bea would be there. Uncle Almon had been invited as well. Having seven of us around the Christmas table was practically like old times. I anticipated the joy of decorating the house and tree together on Christmas Eve.

Papa arrived at my boarding house the morning of Christmas Eve. I hugged my house children fondly and wished them the happiest of holidays, slipping them each a piece of candy before getting into the pung. I wrapped myself in the old Hudson Bay blanket an Indian woman had traded us for milk years ago. Papa clucked at Fitz, who by now was quite good at pulling. As we took off at a good clip, with Fitz's bells jingling, I waved behind us at the children and called out a hearty, "Merry Christmas!" I was in a wonderful mood.

Papa and I talked about my school year so far, my successes and failures, in my opinion. He offered his bit of wisdom now and then but was quiet otherwise. Closer to the farm he said, "Millie, I have news you won't like."

My stomach lurched as it did with words like these. *Who died now?* I thought, stiffening. "What is it, Papa?"

"As I understand it from hearsay, there was a bad storm over the lower New England states recently. None of the family from down there can make it up for Christmas. I got letters from Joe and Almon yesterday, both saying they didn't want to risk the trip due to the heavy amount of snow. I'm sorry, child."

"At least no one died," I said with relief. "But it won't be as merry a day without them. Just the four of us, then," I sighed.

"Ay-uh," Papa said quietly. I wondered what his thoughts were.

At home I gave Ella a quick hug and took my things to my room. Then I went back to the kitchen to help her, grabbing the extra apron off the hook. She filled me in on what she had planned for the holiday meals. She had learned to make some of the Christmas foods that Mama prepared to make Papa happy. For that, I was grateful to her. After dinner, Papa took his place in the Morris chair and lit his pipe. The scent of his tobacco was one I would never forget, especially on Christmas Eve. Ella and I decorated the beautiful fir tree Papa had cut, probably yesterday, while the fragrance of Papa's pipe mixed with that of spiced cider in a dance that drifted around the room. The fire crackled and a light snow fell outside our windows. No wonder I thought of it as the most wondrous time of year.

Papa and Ella had gone to bed, and I was not far behind them. I stood on the winding staircase, looking around the room at the pine boughs and ribbons Ella and I had attached above the windows. The last fragrances of the evening had settled onto furniture or the floor or escaped through minuscule cracks in the foundation. Christmas Eve was ready to be replaced by Christmas itself. I stood there a moment longer, thinking about how I was feeling just then—an odd mixture of sadness and eagerness played with my heart, though I knew that my mood would not change the outcome of the next day. Whether the sadness of missing family members would overcome my joy of Lawrence's presence or the other way around, I did not know. But with all the yearning of my heart I prayed that Lawrence wouldn't be detained as well.

I ascended the stairs to my bedroom and then, with twenty-one years of practice behind me, I accomplished my winter routine of warming the bed, changing into bedclothes, brushing and braiding my hair, all in what felt like record time. I hastened beneath my blankets as quickly as possible and hoped sleep would come just as quickly.

The next morning, Papa, Ella, and I went to church to hear the Christmas story of the divine Christ child come into this weary world, to bring hope, joy, and love to all people everywhere. It did me much good to see the familiar faces of our congregation and raise our voices in unison to the carols we knew so well. All that was missing was Lawrence and I hoped he would join me at church in the future. The bells on Fitz's harness jingled merrily on our way home. Soon it would be Christmas afternoon. Lawrence would come over to take dinner with us and then we'd sing around the tree. I thought about my Christmas gift to him—a sleek, new fountain pen with several nibs. I assumed he could use one as much as I, in and out of school. I was very excited to have him open it.

Mid-afternoon, we heard a knock on the kitchen door and I ran to let Lawrence in. But it wasn't he! It was Joe, then Bea, and lastly Uncle Almon! I didn't know whether to gasp, hug, or invite them in. I think it all happened simultaneously. And then the questions. "How did you get here?" "We thought you couldn't come!" "Where is your buggy?" By this time, Papa was in the kitchen as our late-comers stomped the snow off their boots. Everyone was laughing and talking over one another as I took their coats and scarves.

"My, but it looks wonderful in here and smells twice as nice!" Bea said.

"Here, have some hot cider," Ella said with her usual hospitality.

Once everyone was seated with something to warm their hands and bellies, Uncle Almon began the story. It seems he needed to be with family as much as we wanted to have him here. He said he missed Christmas with the whole family in the Standish house even though it had been a while since we'd gathered there. But the nor'easter that came through Connecticut and Massachusetts sealed their fate. It had been a lot of snow so fast that nothing was moving for several days. He decided the next best thing was to go to Joe and Bea's house so that at least they could be together—*if* he could get there. With a great deal of help from friends and strangers who encouraged his horse through deep drifts, he finally made it to their house, surprising them as they had surprised us this afternoon.

Bea took over and said that after they'd all calmed down and heard Uncle Almon's story, she wondered aloud if there was any way at all to make it to Maine.

"I said absolutely not," Uncle Almon chimed in. "It would just take too long. We'd never make it for Christmas Day."

Taking over the story again, Bea said, "But I thought that was all the more reason we should try. I said, 'Think how fun it would be to surprise the family up there!' I guess the spirit of Christmas took over because even Joe became energized!" Bea laughed along with the rest of us. We all knew how very laid-back Joe was. Not lazy by any means, but easy-going.

"I really didn't see how we could make it," Joe said. "But everyone seemed determined to try, so we all got our things together and I headed to the barn. Just as I had started to hitch up the horse, I heard someone call for help out on the road and saw a woman, alone in a sleigh, not able to get her horse to pull through a large drift. I went out to get her started again and once she was clear she said, 'Thank you very kindly. I'm desperate to get to Maine to be with my elderly mother. I heard Maine didn't get the brunt of this storm and that the trains are able to get through going north. So, you have done me a great service this Christmas Day, sir!'

"She was about to leave when I said, 'Wait, what time is your train?' She said she had given herself plenty of time to make it to the station but wondered why I asked. I said, 'We hope to make it to Maine ourselves to surprise our family.' She said, 'My sleigh is big enough if there aren't too many of you. We can go to the station together!' She was so jolly, she made it hard to refuse the offer. 'There are three of us,' I told her. 'Well, that's perfect then,' she said. 'Get them and let's be off!' I ran back in the house and, without thinking things through any more than that, we donned coats and boots and flew out to her sleigh."

"You make it sound as if St. Nicholas himself was driving it," I laughed. "Then what happened?"

Uncle Almon said, "There isn't much more to tell. We made it to the station, bought tickets, and headed to White Rock. And here we are!"

"Wait a minute," Papa said, "how did you get here from White Rock?"

"Oh! That's right!" Bea exclaimed, "Another Christmas miracle happened. There was someone on the train getting off in White Rock too, and being picked up by his family. He was going to South Windham but if we didn't mind sitting in the back of the wagon, he was sure his family would be more than happy to swing by the farm and let us out. It was as if coming up here was meant to be. It all fit together like a hand in a glove."

"Well, we're so happy you're here!" I said joyfully. "Let's figure out where everyone will sleep, though!" A happier problem could not be had. The women followed me upstairs. We hadn't been up there long before another knock at the kitchen door caused me to peer out the window in my room to see that this time it really was Lawrence. I ran down the back stairs to reach the door before anyone else could and let him in. I opened it and flung myself into his surprised arms.

"My, my, aren't you the happy girl today!" he said.

"Oh, just wait 'til I tell you the nicest story. But come in, come in!"

"Hold on a minute. Let me bring in this large box sitting here on the piazza. I think it's from Santa for…uh…for…uh…let me see…a Miss Millie, it says." I giggled with glee.

It was hard to wait through dinner and into the evening when we'd share gifts. But the time finally came. And went. We sang carols and even played a silly parlor game called the minister's cat in which we had to describe a cat using adjectives that started with each letter of the alphabet. It was mighty difficult to come up with a word that started with "x" but we did it with uproarious laughter, especially when my cat and Ella's decided to wrestle in the center of our circle.

Before long, the day was over, and everyone headed for bed except me. Lawrence and I had not exchanged gifts with the others, so I whispered that I had something to give him before he had to leave. He said, "And have you forgotten about the big box?" I hadn't but didn't think it proper to say anything about it.

We each produced our gifts. I encouraged Lawrence to open mine first. He did so with delight and even kissed me, saying how much he'd needed a new pen.

"Now you," he said, sliding the box toward me. I could tell then that whatever was in it was heavy. I couldn't imagine what it might be. I carefully unwrapped it, trying not to tear so much as a corner of the paper. Even seeing the pictures on the box did not give me a clue.

"It's a graphophone!" he exclaimed. "It plays music. Here, let me show you."

He took a large wooden case out of the box and set it on a table nearby. Then he unscrewed two small, silver knobs on top of the case and lifted the top off the bottom. The machine looked like nothing I'd ever seen before. It had gears, metal rods, a silver cylinder, and an ornate key on one side. I watched, mesmerized. Then he took out two smaller boxes from the original larger box. In one was a strange, round, flat metal object that he connected to one of the rods such that a tiny, sharp object in the middle—a stylus, he called it—came to rest on the cylinder. Finally, he took out a large, silver object that looked like a horn and attached it to the opposite end of the rod on which he'd attached the stylus.

As if that were not enough, he produced another wrapped gift and asked me to open it. When I did, I saw another cylinder, black this time, with concentric grooves cut into it. He took it and fitted it onto the silver cylinder. Then he told me to turn the fancy key until it wouldn't wind any more.

I did, and as soon as I let go, the whole machine came to life, moving and revolving to send the most lovely arrangement of "Silent Night" out into the room. Lawrence stood up, and, taking my hands in his, drew me to my feet. Right there, in my living room, he danced with me. I was in heaven! I closed my eyes and thought that this entire day couldn't have been any more perfect.

Days later, Lawrence would tell me that what I didn't see while my eyes were closed were Ella and Bea, who had heard the music and snuck down the stairs to watch us for a few minutes.

Thirteen

A New Arrangement

It was difficult to fall asleep that night, to say the least. My mind could not stop dancing to the graphophone music in the living room. And then those images transformed into wedding music with me in a beautiful white dress. Not that Lawrence proposed to me, but a girl can dream. And dream I have!

As he had hinted Christmas night, Lawrence gave me two more graphophone cylinders for my twenty-second birthday in March. He even called on me at my boarding house in Windham to personally deliver them. There wasn't much privacy with the children around, but at least we were not where Papa and Ella could constantly watch us. That was a fair trade in both our minds. Lawrence said, and I agreed, that he felt like he was in a fish bowl at the farm. I know Papa and Ella mean well, but I feel nervous when Lawrence is with me there, as if I am being watched like a teenager. So, instead, we choose to meet other places.

And really, I think it best that we do. Public places tempt my physical boundaries less. Boundaries I am unwilling to cross. Lawrence understands me, but I'm not certain he is happy about it. At least we have been able to talk things over to my satisfaction, so far. I don't think of myself as the exceedingly modest person Lizzie assumes me to be. I think of myself as reasonable about matters that ought to be part of a marriage covenant only. If that makes me strait-laced, so be it.

I finished my second school year and packed my belongings from both the school and my boarding house. Lawrence was kind enough to fetch me. Though I was looking forward to dispensing with the responsibilities of teaching and freeing up my schedule when Bea and Joe arrived, I was not prepared for the tension I felt last summer to elevate. One day, when I took Bea's tea upstairs to her, she asked me to have a seat beside the bed.

"Thank you, dear," Bea said, taking the tea and blowing away its extreme heat. While I waited, my anxiety heightened. "Millie," she started, then paused. Still I waited. "Well, I have observed," she paused again and this time I tensed, waiting to hear her judgments of Lawrence. "Let me begin again. Do you think your father is ill?"

I exhaled rather loudly, not aware that I had been holding my breath. Thank goodness Bea was apparently not going to ask about my beau. But in the next moment, I realized that this subject was not going to be an easy one either. "I don't think so. I mean, no more than the ailments he's had for years now." I was not yet ready to divulge that I had had concerns of my own about Papa. "Why do you ask?"

"It's just that I've noticed your father seems quieter than usual, if that can be. That, in itself, isn't terribly alarming. But Joe said something last night that compounds my concern. You won't tell Joe I told you this, I trust?" I shook my head. "Joe said that when he and Manuel were working yesterday, he thought your father seemed extra tired and asked him if he was quite alright. All your father said was that he hasn't been sleeping well."

"Did Joe tell you how Papa said this?" I asked. "Was he smiling? Or did he appear upset?"

"Joe said he looked up to read Manuel's face to see exactly that. He said that Manuel looked 'sour.' Whatever that means."

"Oh, dear, dear Papa," I said, looking down at my hands, trying to think how he might have been different lately. The truth was that, by choice, I hadn't been home as often and didn't really know what was happening in this household. For that, I felt a twinge of guilt. "Thank you for telling me this. I will keep my eye on things and my mouth shut."

And I did. By mid-July, I was convinced that Papa was definitely not himself. He spent more time than usual in the barn or the fields, or down at the mill. He stayed up longer than Ella did, whereas before, they would go to bed at the same time. And Bea was right, Papa was quieter. He didn't participate in conversations around the table at mealtimes like he used to. Sometimes the conversation included things like current affairs or politics that ordinarily he'd want to engage in. The difference was subtle enough that I might have missed it had Bea not mentioned it. It was thoughtless of me to be so inattentive to everything but Lawrence most days. I decided I would need to address this. Somehow.

I thought long and hard about things and talked with Luella, Marion, and Lawrence. And then I thought some more. I sat on my contemplation rock to feel the light breezes coming up from the river. The breezes seemed so free and unencumbered by the things that cause me so much turmoil. I watched birds catch the updrafts and soar so blithely, almost playfully, although I knew they needed to be on the constant lookout for food. St. Matthew in the Bible says to "look at the birds of the air; they do not sow or reap or store away in barns, and yet your heavenly Father feeds them." This favorite verse reminded me to set down my burdens and trust in God to provide. *Provide food, yes,* I thought. *But what about answers?* From somewhere deep within me, I heard, *Yes, even answers.*

"Alright then, God," I said out loud. "What would you have me do?" I waited. I closed my eyes and let my mind drift with the birds and sway with the flowers.

Then I heard it again, that still, small voice. *What is of utmost importance to you, Millie? What decision would bring you the most peace?*

Suddenly I knew the answer. It was a plan I hoped would help the situation rather than make it worse.

"Joe, Bea," I said when we all went for a Sunday afternoon walk while Papa took a nap, "I have watched Papa this summer. I've seen changes in him that are not for the better. At least not in my opinion."

"What changes are you referring to exactly?" Joe wanted to know.

I told him what I'd been observing. He listened intently, saying nothing until I was finished.

"Do you see them too, Joe?"

After a thoughtful moment he said, "Yes, I guess I'd have to say I do. I think I just didn't want to believe they meant something more significant than general aging. But he told me that he isn't sleeping well. What do you think has contributed to this?"

I feigned thinking about what Bea had asked me not to mention. Then I said, "Well, I don't know. And I'm not sure Papa would come right out and say more than what he told you. Even he may not know why he can't sleep. But it could be caused by aches and pains, or a sudden flare-up of his war wound. It might be something non-physical, like anxiety, although he isn't one to appear anxious, is he?" I thought out loud. "Well, no matter what is going on, I have made a decision, and he won't like it. I am going to turn in my notice to stop teaching."

"Oh, my!" Bea exclaimed. "Isn't that a bit drastic, Millie? You've loved teaching, haven't you?"

"I have, yes, but I can't continue to love it knowing that something is not right with Papa."

"Do you not trust Ella to handle things?" Joe asked me, stepping long to stretch over a puddle. It had stormed that morning.

"I've had an uneasy feeling about their relationship for over a year but couldn't put my finger on why. I realized earlier this afternoon that I may never know unless I'm here. Papa means far too much to me to satisfy my own needs over his. I can't help but think that Ella is unable to address the problem, if there is one. Otherwise, I assume she would have said something to one of us by now. She's been good to Papa in her basic care of him–cooking and keeping house. And I think that she is a good woman. But I don't see much more between them than companionship. If there is romantic love there, I haven't felt it. And if that isn't there, would Ella even know enough about Papa to know when he is in some sort of subtle pain?"

"You make a good case, Millie. If you were a man, I might suggest you take up law!" Joe said, throwing levity on the serious topic like water on fire.

"Joe, do you agree with my coming back home to live?"

"Truthfully, I'm not sure. I can see pros and cons in your decision. But I know you, Millie. And I can tell that your mind is made up. So, I will give you my blessing. Bea?"

"I would be lying if I didn't say that I have misgivings. I, myself, would still be teaching if I wasn't married. I will support you, Millie, but I won't assume it is necessarily for the best."

"It's settled then. I will contact the Windham superintendent and then we'll find a suitable time to talk with Papa. I will need you both there to show him that I am serious about this decision."

When the day came to talk with Papa, it was Bea's choice to take Ella shopping in Portland so Joe and I could speak with Papa alone. Bea said she didn't think she could add anything to the conversation that Joe and I alone couldn't handle. Given her stance on my decision, I assumed she simply didn't want to be part of that conversation.

"Papa," Joe began, "Millie and I have something important to address with you. I hope you will hear us out. I have noticed, and Millie has too, that you don't seem to be yourself lately. You told me you aren't sleeping well. Do you believe the cause to be something a doctor should discuss with you?"

"No," Papa said without hesitation.

"I'm happy to hear that," Joe said, and then paused, suddenly looking lost as if he didn't know where the conversation should go next.

Out of the silence, I blurted, "Papa, are you unhappy in this marriage arrangement?" I had told Joe that since the decision to stop teaching had been mine, I should address Papa first. Joe argued that Papa would be more inclined to listen to reason if he spoke first. *Well, Joe, you* have *spoken first, so now it's my turn.* I kept my eyes locked on our father. I was determined that he see me as an adult with adult concerns.

Papa broke eye contact and looked down at his weathered and wrinkled hands as if the answer would materialize on his palms as he rubbed them together. Then he pulled at his white whiskers and finally said, "I guess so."

"Papa," I said with sincere compassion, "I cannot stand to see you like this. I know you are only in this marriage as a convenience. But just before Mama died, she told me that you and I need to take care of each other. It's time you let me stay at home. I thank you for all you have done for me to become a teacher. I'm not sorry about any of that. But now it's time I help you."

Papa's mature eyes misted while Joe and I stayed quiet. Then he began speaking, not looking directly at either Joe or me. "I have had four children whose lives ended too soon. That couldn't be helped. But I've only ever wanted each of you to have a good education. Mine was cut short and I have regretted that at times. Now it is just the two of you. Joe, you and Bea are building a life in Massachusetts. I'm proud of you. Millie, I'm proud of you too." I held my breath for the rebuttal I was sure would come. "You have as much right to a good life as Joe does. I fear you won't have it if you stay home with me. Even if you come home to stay, what would happen if that young Lawrence were to ask for your hand? I shan't stand in the way of your happiness, child. If you marry, you'll be just as absent as if you stayed a teacher. I see no good solution to what you propose. I shall stay married to Ella."

"Papa," I said quietly, "you need to know that I have already told Windham's superintendent that I will not be back this year." Watching the creases on Papa's face deepen with disappointment, I wasn't as sure about my plan anymore.

"That's right, Papa," Joe said, softly. "Millie knows what she is doing by this decision. She doesn't feel her heart would be as sincerely with her students for worrying about you. She will be fine; I truly believe that." Joe smiled at me, building back my resolve.

Papa sat quietly fidgeting with the brim of his merino wool pillbox hat that he now had in his hands. His niece, Marie, had brought it with her from the Azores. He wore it even on summer days, though it was meant for cooler weather. Papa sat silently for so long it reminded me of a day one summer when I was nine and the circus had come to Portland. I'd heard there would be clowns and wild animals, trick riding and acrobats. Joe and Howdie had announced that they were going to it, and I begged Papa to let me go with them. Then, as now, Papa was silent for a very long time. And then, as now, I could not predict what Papa would finally say.

Barely above a whisper, Papa said, "I can't argue with you both. I will talk with Ella this evening." He rose from his chair, taking a moment to steady himself on his bad leg and limped to the barn.

The only thing Joe said to me before joining him with the chores was, "If Papa had wanted to be firm, he would have been." I appreciated Joe's attempt to assure me that Papa wanted this outcome more than either of us had guessed.

Ella quietly took her leave by summer's end after a trip to the courthouse to legalize their divorce. I gave my cousin a heartfelt hug for filling in these past years and Ella received it in kind. Joe and Bea left, and I mentally moved in, tucking away my love for teaching. *Maybe I will teach again in the future*, I thought with sorrow, knowing that I wouldn't be setting up my classroom this autumn. I tucked the sorrow away, too, while Lawrence and Lizzie prepared their classrooms for their second year at Levi Hall.

Papa remained quiet for several months after that as I resumed the household duties. I tried not to take his mood personally. For now, I was pleasantly surprised when weekly bread-making seemed like an old friend, something that had been a chore after Mama died. Now I welcomed it, as did the church when the communion plate was passed. In fact, it seemed my bread was a welcome part of community events as well; everyone had missed it while I'd been gone. When one of the women complimented me on it, I laughed and said, "I think you missed my bread far more than you missed me!"

Fourteen

Fall from Grace

After Papa and I established a routine, we moved through the months in easy step with one another. He was able to manage the few animals we kept and the fewer crops. He continued to work at the sawmill down by the river as he had in past years to make ends meet. He mostly made barrel staves and often brought sawdust home for the animals' stalls. All in all, his countenance and mood were restored to the father I'd known. This convinced me that I'd been right to return to the farm.

We managed to skirt the more serious illnesses others contracted and weather the less serious ones that befell us with a slower pace and chicken soup. We attended church and other gatherings in Great Falls when we were able. The new dam down the hill brought the hope of electricity one day soon. Meanwhile, families enjoyed swimming in Great Falls Pond that was created as a result. Forest Hall and the Smith Brother's General Store seemed no worse for having been moved when the dam caused that part of town to flood. Papa was sure to be on hand to help, or at least witness the moving of those two significant buildings, and was properly awed.

Not all was happy news, however. Gambo Powder Mill, some five miles south of us, continued to have occasional explosions, killing workers. Even we could feel those blasts when they went off. Then a friend and neighbor was murdered right here in Great Falls, which shook the psyches of all of us as surely as the powder mill shook the land. We were all grateful when the murderer was captured and convicted.

I accompanied Papa to his war reunions. Mr. Plaisted and Mr. Evans continued to visit Papa. I kept in touch with Joe and Bea via letters. Luella, by this time, had graduated from normal school and taken a teaching position in Gray. I wrote to her often, as well.

In August of last summer, I thought Bea looked thicker around her waist. I suspected she might be in a family way, but I would never have asked her about something so personal. When they said goodbye before leaving for Massachusetts, Bea leaned in to give me a hug and whispered, "Joe and I are to have a baby in January!" I gasped and beamed with joy that Papa would finally be a grandfather. I longed to see him love a little one. Being born last had some disadvantages.

Outside our village we knew that many places in the country, primarily cities larger than ours, already had electricity, and even telephones. A luxury, to be sure. One day I read to Papa from the newspaper, "'The average American earns twenty-two cents an hour or between two and four hundred dollars a year. Sugar costs an average of four cents a pound and eggs are fourteen cents a dozen.' I'm grateful we have all the eggs we need from our own coop! 'With forty-five states in the Union since Utah was admitted in '96, there are some eight thousand automobiles in this vast country with about one hundred fifty miles of paved roads.' Oh, Papa, can you see an automobile surviving for long around here, driving on rutted roads in the spring and drifted ones in the winter?"

"No, but Great Falls is talking about investing in a snow roller. It would be six feet in diameter and ten feet wide to pack down the snow. I've heard it would take six to eight horses to pull it, though, poor things. I hope the town does get one. It would greatly benefit our new rural free delivery," Papa said.

We had begun to have our mail delivered right to our door. On good-weather days, Papa loved sitting on the front stoop to wait for the mail deliverer's horse and wagon. He liked to talk to the man about the goings-on in town, as if the mail carrier's job included delivering rumors along with letters. The man told me yesterday that he delivers the Sears, Roebuck and Company catalog to some households. Then he delivers the things they order! Times are certainly changing.

Walter, the mail carrier, delivered a most anticipated letter recently.

Monday, February 1, 1904

Dearest Millie and Papa,

You are now an auntie and grandfather to a beautiful baby girl we have named Doris Julia Thomas. She was born yesterday, on the last day of January. Everything went as planned, though I could tell it wasn't easy for Bea when the baby surpassed the doctor's anticipated day of birth, but my wife did wonderfully well. We couldn't be happier. When we see you this summer, Doris, or perhaps "Dotty," as Bea is already crooning to her little daughter, will be quite ready to meet you both. I must go.

Much love,
Joe, a very happy and tired father!

I knew I'd have to wait to cradle Dotty in my arms and that summer seemed like a very long time to wait. Fortunately, some of that time would be spent with Lawrence, which always served to lift my spirits. But recently he seemed bothered by something and couldn't or wouldn't tell me what was wrong. I tried not to pry but it was concerning to me. Perhaps he was simply uncertain about his future at Levi Hall with the downturn in the number of scholars. He did, after all, have to suspend teaching the high school pupils when the school board voted to dispense with that level and send the last few scholars to Gorham Village. He was still head teacher of all scholars, but Lizzie was now only his assistant. I've spoken to her about this unfortunate change and she says she isn't happy about it. She feels as if she has been demoted. I can't say I'd feel anything different.

I pray that is the basis of what worries Lawrence because I am certain he could find another job elsewhere if he wanted to continue teaching high school pupils. But if he did that, we wouldn't see one another very often if it is too far away.

On March 5, Marion, whom I have grown to love almost as much as Luella, came to wish me a happy birthday. She had come with a small chocolate cake and a card which was signed by her and Luella. While Papa enjoyed his pipe in the parlor, we visited in the living room talking and laughing about this and that and nothing in particular. It was just so delightful to enjoy the company of such a wonderful friend. Marion asked if we might listen to my new cylinders on the graphophone, which we did with glee while we indulged in the delicious cake.

When it was nearly time for Marion to leave, she became very quiet. "What? What is it, Marion?"

"Well," she began haltingly, "I hate to do this, but I have heard something I think you should know. I really do hate to bring this up the day before your birthday, you know," I nodded at her in understanding, but now my anxiety was piqued. I tried not to show it. "But," she continued, "I don't want you to hear this from the horse's mouth, either. If Lawrence comes to call tomorrow, you ought to be prepared." Marion about gave me heart failure. I wished she would just say what she needed to. Finally, she said, "It is rumored that Lawrence has been calling on Lizzie." And then she quickly added, "I haven't seen them myself, mind you, so it's all hearsay."

"Are you sure that's what you heard? Are your sources reliable? I can't believe he would do that to me."

"Rumors are rumors, Millie. I don't know who might have started them. The person who told me, though, cares about you, and that's all I know. So, until you hear from Lawrence himself or Lizzie, you won't know for sure. I just hope they aren't true," said Marion sincerely. Marion is younger than either Luella or me, with no experience seeing men that I know of. She does, however, have experience with life, her mother having died not long ago, leaving her in charge of a younger sibling. She is a compassionate person and obviously cares about my well-being.

"I hope they aren't true too," I said to myself quietly. Lawrence is a flirt, yes, but I always thought that was because he is so much more outgoing than I am. Surely he hasn't been unfaithful, though. I love Lawrence and he loves me. We love what we have together. It just has to be a rumor and only that.

Nevertheless, I could not be certain and could not keep tears from spilling down my cheeks. It was impossible to hide my feelings from someone as close to me as Marion had become. She quickly said, "I will leave you to your own thoughts now, Millie. Just remember that no matter what happens with Lawrence, I am always nearby and have a ready ear."

We stood to hug one another. "I'm so sorry, Millie. I would never have said anything if I thought the only benefit was to spread idle gossip. You know that." I nodded. "You are worth the world to me, and Luella too, and you deserve to be treated as the wonderful person you are. Always. I hope you remember that."

"I know you don't mean to hurt me, and it seems the timing of this couldn't be helped, as awful as it is. It would not have been a bit better to have heard this some other time, so I don't fault you," I said, pulling away and looking into her eyes, which were now red-rimmed as well. "Should the worst be true," I said, "*'tis better to have loved and lost than never to have loved at all.'* Although, right now, I'm not so sure Tennyson was right about that." I let out a rueful chuckle and I could tell that Marion appreciated the lightening of the mood, if only a little.

We said goodbye and I wiped away my tears the best I could before saying goodnight to Papa. I was pretty sure he saw that I had been crying. But he didn't say anything, and I climbed the stairs to my room as though one-hundred-pound weights hung from my shoulders. I dressed for bed, abandoned my diary, which I seldom do, and cried myself to sleep.

The next day I played the organ for the Sunday service, though my heart wasn't in it at all. I had no trouble pumping air into the instrument as I angrily thought about what Marion had told me. I thought about Lawrence betraying my trust, if that's what he did. Not to mention Lizzie doing the same. All I really wanted was to go home, but I wanted to keep up appearances so as not to draw attention to myself. Besides, how could I know that there might be those in the congregation who knew more than I did about the rumor? I wanted to appear unconcerned. By the time the service ended, I realized I was acting as if the rumors were true. But was that fair? Why did I distrust Lawrence and Lizzie at all, without first learning the truth? I decided I would do my best to adhere to the ideals of our country, that Lawrence and Lizzie are innocent until proven guilty.

After the service, a few people wished me a happy birthday, as did Papa on our way home. I was quiet, thinking about how to believe Lawrence is innocent, when Papa said, "Child, is there something you need to get off your chest?"

Oh, dear. What should I say? Should I say anything at all before talking to Lawrence? "Well, Papa, I assume you are asking because you heard something last night to cause you concern. What did you hear?"

"Only that the mood changed among you girls very suddenly and I heard you sniffling."

"Well, it's just that Marion told me about a rumor that Lawrence is seeing Lizzie."

"And you fear it's true." A statement rather than a question.

"Yes, I guess I do, Papa. But I don't know why. If I trusted Lawrence completely, a rumor shouldn't rattle me, right?" I fidgeted on the wagon seat and rewrapped the blanket, suddenly feeling thoroughly chilled. Papa clucked at Fitz to quicken his pace before pulling us up the hill.

"Sometimes we put all our eggs in one basket," Papa said.

"Well, shouldn't we? I mean, it sounds like you're implying I shouldn't think of Lawrence as the only man I might marry one day. Is that what you're saying?" I was feeling defensive.

"Not exactly. If you are leaning toward one person too much, remember that leaning too far can topple a tower. If you think of your relationships as a partnership, the way you would think of Marion, for example, then if she disappoints you or leaves you, you still have yourself to stand your ground."

"So, you're saying that some of my eggs should be in my own basket?"

"Yes."

"I'm not sure how to do that, Papa," I said, confused.

"For now, remember that just because you are in a close relationship with Lawrence doesn't mean he is your whole world. Don't give him the right to take you away from yourself. Remember who you are."

I waved at a neighbor and mustered a smile. But I had a lot of thinking to do about Papa's words, which I knew came from the wisdom of living life. I wondered exactly what had taught him that particular piece of wisdom.

Uncle Almon came to call that afternoon, which was certainly the surprise he had meant it to be. No one knew he had business to attend to in Great Falls. Knowing my birthday was today he'd arranged to make his trip of necessity one of joy as well. His presence was as good an elixir for me as any medicine could be. We talked and laughed and ate some of Marion's cake. Soon the gravity of my thoughts evaporated.

When the sun was nearly down, another knock at the kitchen door made me look up to see Lawrence. I had expected him when instead it was Uncle Almon. But now, it was late enough that I assumed he wouldn't come at all. My heart seized. When I let him in, Uncle Almon said he should leave. He tipped his hat to Lawrence and gave me a squeeze before heading out to his horse.

"Hello, Millie," Lawrence said, handing me a card. "Can we take a walk, perhaps? I know it's cold but there is something I want to talk with you about privately." He'd not wished me a happy birthday, which was not lost on me. I laid the unopened card on the table, grabbed my coat, boots, scarf, and mittens, and told Papa where I was going and that I wouldn't be long.

The chilly night caught in my throat, which wasn't working well for other reasons, anyway. I remained silent, waiting for Lawrence to reveal whatever it was he needed to say. I waited for some time.

Eventually, he said, "Millie, I owe you an apology."

"Apology? For what?" He hadn't yet done anything that I knew of for certain that needed an apology. And I didn't want to make it sound like I suspected him of something.

"For what I am about to tell you." I felt sick to my stomach as I waited in anguish. "First of all, since Levi Hall has so few scholars, I am seeking other employment for next year."

"That needs no apology," I said. But to myself I thought, *First of all?*

"I suppose not. But there is something else. You have been a wonderful friend all these years and I truly appreciate that." *Just his friend?* "But, well, uh, the truth is that Lizzie and I also have a friendship, and she will also be looking for other employment."

I stopped and stood statue-still for several moments, staring at him in disbelief. At that moment it didn't seem to help that I had had forewarning. I was shocked. Probably because I hadn't wanted to believe the rumors. Lawrence didn't say anything more. He looked me in the eye only briefly before staring at his feet, which were shoving sand and mud this way and that with no purpose. Suddenly, I spun around toward the farm and with short, deliberate, and determined steps, I walked quickly away from him. *So, it* is *true,* I realized. *Who are the rumor spreaders who knew this before I did?* I felt betrayed not only by Lawrence and Lizzie, but by all those who knew and hadn't the fortitude to tell me. I'd had to hear this first via rumors. I also felt like a dolt not to have seen at least something coming. I was surprised that I had no tears.

Then it suddenly dawned on me that Lawrence had said Lizzie would be seeking employment too. He *didn't* say they would be together, but he'd implied as much. I stopped very suddenly and Lawrence almost ran into me. He'd been trying to keep up.

Looking at him from a distance of inches, I spat out, "How long have you two been 'friends'? How long have you led me to believe in a lie?"

"Millie, it just happened, you know? Lizzie and I see each other every day at school, and we just gradually realized we cared for one another. I didn't want to hurt you."

"And how long have you realized this?" I asked again, punching each word for effect.

When Lawrence didn't answer right away, I turned again toward home. "I don't know," he called out to my back.

I spun to face him, "If you don't know, it's likely been longer than you care to admit. And if you thought that telling me now wouldn't hurt me, think again. Go home, Lawrence. I think you're done here. I think *we* are done here."

I reached the house, went inside, and slammed the door. Then, dropping to the floor in a puddle of melting snow and mud, the tears finally came. Papa rose quickly from his chair and walked to the kitchen. He coaxed me to get up and take off my outer things and have a seat. Then he put more wood in the stove, set the kettle on a burner for some hot tea, and took a seat beside me.

"If you wish to unload your burden, I'll gladly listen. If not, we can sit in the quiet and sip tea together."

Until that moment, I hadn't realized that Papa could extend his broad shoulders to me like this. I assumed he did so for Mama, but I guess I'd never really needed him in this way before. Either Mama, or one of the boys, or Jennie had been the ones I'd turned to. Rarely Papa, and never with something as significant and consequential as this. He spoke so compassionately, I hardly knew him. I suddenly felt shy. I had steeled myself to say nothing to him, not wanting to cause him pain. Besides, I felt foolish and ashamed. Shouldn't I have seen this breach of relationship coming? Hadn't I had inklings of doubt now and then? But Papa's calm voice and compassionate eyes invited my voice to surface. Like it or not, I spilled the contents of my bleeding heart to him, interrupted with my sobs, my tea forgotten and growing cold.

"At least the boy had manners enough to tell you the truth to your face and leave when you told him to."

That was all Papa said. When his tea was finished, he quietly took his cup and my unfinished one to the cast-iron sink to rinse them out. Then he gently kissed the top of my head and used the back stairs to his bedroom. Eventually, I rose and blew out the lamps in the kitchen and parlor. When I entered the living room to turn down the lamp there, I saw the card Lawrence had handed me. I'd forgotten about it and now I no longer cared what it said. I tore it up and threw the pieces in the air to land wherever they may.

The next morning, the pieces were no longer on the floor.

Fifteen

A New Beau?

Monday, March 7, 1904

Dear diary, I surely hope yesterday is the worst my birthday will ever be. I feel very raw and hollowed out inside. Everything I thought my life was going to be, no longer is. Lawrence and I have parted ways. Lizzie has also hurt me badly. If forgiving them is to be possible, I have much to learn about God's ways. Am I even up to the task? Thank goodness I have little Dotty to look forward to meeting. Papa said something to me yesterday about not putting all my eggs in one basket. I think he was referring to something in his own life.

"Papa, thank you for picking up the mess I made of Lawrence's card," I said, putting a plate of eggs and bacon before him. "I am embarrassed by my behavior."

"Think nothing of it, child."

"And Papa, were you thinking of a specific incident when you told me I shouldn't put all my eggs in one basket? That I should remember who I am?" I sat down to my own plate of breakfast.

"Yes, child."

"Would you tell me about it, please?"

"Well," he said, sipping his hot coffee. "When my brother, José, talked so often about the exciting life on a whaler, I wanted it too. Very badly. I decided the island was no place for me anymore. When our Pa forbade me to go with José, I thought he was wrong. I had made leaving on that whaler the only option for my life. It's taken me years to realize that my Pa was not wrong at all. I gave up schooling for something I ended up hating."

"You really hated it that much?"

"If I'd been honest with myself, I would never have gone. I didn't like being in a boat. The sea made me sick. And I hated the idea of killing anything. To make matters worse, I had no business being on that whaler as young as I was. My Pa knew that."

"Oh, Papa, I can't imagine how awful that must have been."

"Not all of the experience was bad. I did get an education in seeing the world and its people. That's more than many have, I guess."

"So, you think that if you'd understood yourself as your father did, you might have stayed on the island?"

"At least until I was older. I wouldn't have blindly followed someone else's dreams. I'd have found my own."

"Do you regret very much your life here?" I asked, knowing the answer might hurt me.

"No, child. I've had years to realize that life is what you make it."

Now I think I knew what Papa meant. He wanted me to remember that everything I might have had in a relationship with Lawrence is still possible either with someone else or just in being myself. But I also knew I wasn't nearly ready yet to let go of my dreams of marrying Lawrence.

It was very difficult for me to leave the house for several weeks after our breakup. When I had to, I prayed I wouldn't run into Lawrence, Lizzie, or anyone else my age, except Marion. She was the only friend to whom I gave my time and attention, and even then our normal friendship felt strained, which I knew was my fault. Eventually, with the help of spring flowers, the sun, and the delightful aromas of the season, I began to live my life. It was Papa who had said to me, after watching me mope about, "Millie, haven't you punished yourself long enough?" I began to realize that in protecting myself from those who had hurt me, I was also denying the good things in my life. Still, I hadn't gotten to the point of being able to see Lawrence or Lizzie and steered clear as best I could. But I wouldn't shackle myself to the house, either.

By May, I began to speak casually to Walter, the postman, and found him to be a nice enough fellow. Certainly, he provided me with the perfect break from a drama he knew nothing about. I could trust that our conversations would include nothing about Lawrence or Lizzie. In that, I felt free, as if starting all over again. Then, just before Independence Day, Joe, Bea, and five-month-old Dotty arrived. This little bundle of joy swept almost all remnants of sadness from my heart the moment Bea put Dotty in my arms.

Walter stopped by unannounced on the holiday. He had no mail to deliver and knew Papa well enough from their front-yard talks to invite himself for a short while. He and Papa, and eventually Joe, talked about crops and machines while I made strawberry shortcake. The strawberries were deliciously just ripe enough, but I wished the blueberries had come in early so that I could fashion a red, white, and blue dessert. I made enough that Walter could stay for some. We sat outside on blankets. Little Dotty practiced sitting up for as many times as anyone was willing to right her. We laughed when she rolled back down, content to stay that way if someone put a rattle in her little fisted hand. It wasn't until I was feeding Dotty her gruel, which took a while because she was not an enthusiastic eater, that I suddenly remembered Lawrence's birthday today. The memory came with grief over our good times together, and a sourness for how things turned out.

By the time Joe and his family left for their own home at the end of the summer, Walter had begun leaving his calling card. It wasn't ornate, but it was charming. At first, I wasn't sure I wanted to begin a new relationship. Talking with Walter over the mail was one thing. Having him call was quite another in my mind. Was I even ready? I decided that if I was honest with him about my intentions, I could receive him as a suitor. *At least I may as well try to have a good time again,* I reasoned.

We sat on the settee drinking lemonade one warm September day. I'd been answering the casual questions he'd asked me when I noticed that Walter had terribly long legs to my much shorter ones. And what he'd chosen to wear was drab compared to the more fashionable garments Lawrence regularly wore. I chastised myself for comparing the two men. *I mustn't do that*, I thought, shaking my head slightly at my silliness.

"No?" Walter said, looking at me quizzically. "You mean you don't know when your father bought this farm, or you'd rather not talk about it?"

My cheeks reddened when I realized I'd not heard Walter's question. From his prompt, however, I was able to answer, "Oh, uh, I think he bought it in 1866, after the war."

"Did your father serve in the rebellion, then?"

"Yes. He was in the Seventeenth Maine regiment."

"His accent is noticeable, and occasionally his English is a little off. How did he get along fighting in an American war?"

I could feel myself becoming defensive on Papa's behalf. I considered his English to be quite adequate, considering it was his second language. "He was born in the Azores and Portuguese is his first language," I said. "He did fine, as far as I know." The bite to my answer did not go unnoticed.

"I'm sorry, I didn't mean to offend you or your father. I consider it quite brave to fight in a foreign country's homeland war. I'm sure you are very proud of your father."

"Forgive me, please," I said contritely. "I *am* proud of him. It's just that his accent has made it difficult for him at times. People don't always understand what he says or even who he is. Believe it or not, they occasionally think he's dull-minded, which couldn't be further from the truth. Now, *that* really gets my dander up."

"Please, don't misunderstand me. I don't think that of him at all. Our conversations have been quite rich with all his knowledge."

I decided it best to change the subject and said, "Tell me about yourself, Walter."

"Well, I expect there isn't much to tell, really. My father, Edwin, is a preacher in Litchfield, and my mother's name is Ellen."

"Where is Litchfield?"

"About forty or fifty miles north of here."

"That's a long way! Do you see your folks much?"

"Not often. Only when father takes time away from the church, usually in the summer. Father comes down to see how the farm is doing. Sometimes I think he's checking up on me!" Walter said with a wink.

"You run the farm? It's in South Windham, is that right?"

"Ay-uh. South Windham. The farm is father's. It isn't large, by any means. Really quite humble. My younger sister, Bessie, and I live together. I don't know what I'd do without her help. Father is content with the way we've handled things. That's what I care about. Well now, thank you for this lemonade, Millie. It was perfect on this warm day," Walter said, handing me his empty glass. "I'll be going now, speaking of farming. Got things to do." He stood up. So did I.

"Oh, and what would you prefer to be called?" he added.

"Millie is fine, thank you," I said, wondering what else he might call me.

"I've noticed on some of your mail that your name is Mildred Francesca. I wondered if perhaps you preferred using your middle name as some women do."

"No, I go by Millie with friends and family. But we pronounce the second syllable of my middle name 'ses' rather than 'ches'. Papa says it with a more 's-h' sound than 's'. I think Mama found the 's' sound easier or something. I'm not really sure. But I say 'Fran-ses-ka'"

"Either way, it's a lovely name, Millie. Mine's Walter Newell Harlow. And now that we've properly met, I think we must see one another again. May I call on you?"

"That would be fine."

"Goodbye then, Mildred Francesca, with an 's' sound," he said cheerily and stepped off the piazza. I couldn't help but smile.

The next month, Walter called again. This time he suggested we go for a ride. The autumn leaves were in their colorful glory, some drifting down around us as the horse pulled at a comfortable walk. We had a very pleasant talk. I told him about my school experiences, and he shared that he graduated from high school up in Madison, a hundred miles northeast of Great Falls.

"A hundred miles!" I said, flabbergasted.

"Yes, father served a church there. I got used to moving around a lot. In the state, that is."

"Did your mother mind all those moves?"

"If she did, I never caught on. Mother is a wonderful woman and mother. She is actually father's second wife."

"Oh, that's interesting. My father has been married twice too."

"If I may be so bold, I haven't seen anyone at your farm or delivered mail to anyone other than you and your father." It was a question without asking one.

"Remember I told you that I went to Gorham High School and boarded there? Well, Mama died before I left for Gorham, and Papa married a cousin of my mother's so that she could help him with the household in my absence. When I decided to live at home, she and Papa divorced," I answered succinctly, leaving the details unsaid. "May I also be bold and ask about your father's first wife? Was she your mother?"

"No, she was not. Father's first wife was a woman named Eliza. She died after she had three daughters. My mother, Ellen, was Eliza's caretaker during the last two years of her life. The two women grew very close, and Eliza essentially asked my mother to marry my father to help him with her young girls. I think my mother and father were already quite close by that time, though, and they fit very naturally. They had me, and then Bessie."

"So, who are your half siblings then?"

"Cora is the eldest, then Myrtie, then Persis."

"Do they live close to you?"

"Cora does. Her husband is Reverend James Aikins, who is the preacher at Windham Hill Congregational Church."

"Oh, my!" I exclaimed. "We go to that church. Well, we go there some of the time, and to Great Falls Congregational some of the time too. But your brother-in-law–that's what he would be to you, right?–he married my father and his second wife. It's such a small world, isn't it? Why don't you come to Windham Hill church?"

"I do on occasion when I'm not farming. If you're wondering why we haven't seen each other there, perhaps we've just missed each other. And speaking of a small world, my father graduated from Bowdoin

College where one of his professors was Joshua Chamberlain who fought…”

“With the Seventeenth Maine!” I finished his sentence. “Yes, Papa knows him! He was Lieutenant Colonel of the Twentieth Maine, and the Seventeenth and Twentieth fought together in the battle of Gettysburg.”

“Indeed, it is a small world when you come right down to it,” Walter said, enjoying this conversation as much as I.

“You know, I haven’t seen much of the world beyond Great Falls,” I admitted. “But sometimes I don’t think I need to. The world seems to find its way to me.”

Papa said Walter and Bessie were welcome to come for our Thanksgiving meal together with Uncle Almon. Walter and my uncle got along famously. I don’t think there’s anyone who doesn’t get along with Walter. I guess farmers speak the same language because the three men talked about crop rotation and animal husbandry. Walter knows a great deal about both, it seems. They also talked about grain elevators and farm machines. Walter has used a gasoline-powered tractor, which interested Papa very much. While they were talking, Bessie and I mostly listened as we served the meal. She brought a delicious squash dish and a custard cream pie. By the portions being eaten, we decided the men ate for taste and not just to satisfy their hunger! When they retired to the parlor, Bessie and I cleaned up and got to know one another. Our conversation was easy, and I was relieved. And my, how she loves her brother! It was a wonderful day. I went to bed tired and happy.

Walter called on me a few times that autumn and we agreed to sit together at church on Christmas Day. As it turned out, I was needed at the organ, so Walter and Bessie sat with Papa. The church looked and smelled divine, with evergreen boughs tied with red velvet ribbons and holly sprigs. Christmas carols were sung with robust voices, and it felt like people wanted to sing faster than the pace I had set. Reverend Aikins had a fine sermon. Papa always thinks he goes on too long, but I thought the whole service was perfect. Bessie and Walter wanted to reciprocate and have Papa and me over for Christmas dinner. Papa isn't always comfortable at someone else's home, but he did well, I thought. We left soon after the meal, and that evening Marion and Luella stopped over. We had much to catch up on. I wanted to hear all about Luella's teaching job, and she wanted to know all the details about Walter. Both girls were so happy for me. We got out the graphophone for old time's sake. My heart beat a little faster to see the gift Lawrence had given me, but I think it did me good to use it again with friends I love.

As Walter and I continued to see one another throughout the rest of that winter, I learned to enjoy our growing friendship. On March 6, he delivered a letter addressed only to me. It was from Joe, and I assumed it was a birthday note. It turned out to be that and more.

Thursday, March 2, 1905

Dear Millie,

First of all, happy birthday! I can't believe my little sister is already twenty-five years old. I hope you and Walter will celebrate heartily. We wish we could be there.

Dotty is toddling around everywhere now and, of course, getting into things she shouldn't. She keeps her Mama busy especially since Bea is to have a baby sometime in July. Yes, that's right! We are very excited. Dotty isn't the wiser, so Bea has brought out the cradle and taught Dotty to point to it saying "baby." I suppose Dotty thinks the cradle is called a "baby", but she'll learn soon enough. And we don't know how she will take to losing her only-child status.

The hard part of all this is saying that we will not be able to come up this summer. Please tell Papa that I hope that doesn't present too much hardship for him. I wanted to be sure to give him plenty of time to find help.

I'll be in touch.

All our love,
Joe, Bea, and Dotty

One afternoon in May, Papa asked me to sit with him on the front stoop, presumably to watch for Walter and the mail. I removed my apron, then grabbed Coonie, the newest cat I picked out from a neighbor's litter of Maine coons, and took a seat beside Papa. He wore his Azores hat and a jacket, appropriate for him in spring temperatures.

"This is nice," I offered, hoping that Papa would tell me why we were sitting here.

"Do you know of Walter's intentions toward you?" Papa asked bluntly.

"His intentions? Other than having a friendship with me?"

"Yes, child."

"I've never noticed anything more than friendship and I think I would know by now. Besides, he's five years older than I am."

"Be careful, Millie. A man's heart is a tender thing. I'm concerned because, while I like Walter, I wouldn't like you being a farmer's wife. It wore out your mother, and I see how hard you work too. Your education could get you off the farm for good. Won't you reconsider teaching?"

"Oh, Papa, not this again. You know I won't leave you alone," I said patting his hand.

We sat quietly until Walter brought the mail. Then Papa left me and Walter alone and went back to the barn.

"Hello, Millie. How are you this fine day?" Walter said, patting the cat's head as if he had directed his question to Coonie.

"Very well, thank you. And you?" I couldn't help watching Walter's manner after what Papa had said.

"I'm well. There's a dance at Forest Hall Saturday evening. Would you care to accompany me to it?"

"Yes, that would be lovely." *I'll show Papa this is nothing more than friendship*, I thought.

At precisely six o'clock, Walter arrived. I finished dressing and tidied my hair with a matching bow. When I walked down the winding staircase, Walter looked at me with doe-like eyes and suddenly, with a sinking feeling, I wondered if Papa was right.

"I'll just grab my sweater," I said.

The evening was drizzly, but it didn't dampen Walter's spirits. "You look lovely tonight, Millie. But then, you always do."

"Thank you," I replied, blushing. Although he couldn't see that in the waning sunlight at our backs.

The dance was lively. Both Walter and I saw friends there whom we talked with in between dancing and eating refreshments. "You are very light on your feet, Millie," Walter remarked.

"I guess I do love to dance," I said. "You do alright yourself, Walter."

"Music is just inside me," he said pleasantly, "and wants to come out any chance it gets!"

When the dance was over, Walter went to fetch our wraps. Annie, an acquaintance of mine, caught my elbow, beckoning me to step aside in private.

"This won't take long, I promise," Annie said. "I don't mean to interrupt you, but I assume you've heard that Lawrence is living down in Scarborough where Lizzie is teaching. I don't know why he isn't teaching too, but someone said he's working as a clerk in a store there or something. Seems like a waste of a good mind, doesn't it to you?"

The bubble of happiness I had enjoyed all evening lay shattered on the floor. Annie's words stung with the hard truth of Lawrence and Lizzie's undeniable connection. I hadn't realized until just this moment what I'd wanted so badly to believe–that perhaps their relationship wouldn't last.

"No, Annie, I hadn't heard that," I said curtly, thinking, *You say otherwise, but you did mean to interrupt me, and you thoroughly enjoyed giving me your juicy news too.*

"Oh, I'm so sorry, Millie. If I'd thought you didn't know, I would never have said a word. Please forgive me. Enjoy the rest of your evening." I stood there, stunned, as she walked away.

"Are you alright? You look bothered," Walter said, walking up behind me.

I hadn't seen him coming. "Oh," I said, thinking as quickly as my addled brain would allow. "Yes, I'm…I'm fine. A friend just gave me a piece of disturbing news, that's all. We can go."

I was quiet as the horse beat a rhythm on the gravel road. If Walter noticed, he said nothing until we reached the house. "I do hope everything is alright," he said. I wondered if this was more a question than a simple statement.

"Yes," I said, hoping my tears wouldn't spill out embarrassingly.

Helping me down, he asked, "I'd like to call next Sunday if I may? I have something I'd like to discuss with you."

"Yes, that would be fine," I managed. "Thank you for a lovely evening. I did enjoy myself." I meant it and turned toward the piazza.

"Have a good week, Millie," Walter called out tipping his hat in my direction and climbed back into the wagon.

Saturday, May 20, 1905

Oh! What I wouldn't give to tell Annie what I really think of her "timely" delivery. She's never liked me because my grades were almost always better than her's and this was the perfect way to provoke me. All the anger I thought I'd dealt with once and for all is back. I'd like to throw Lawrence and Lizzie in the lake, and Annie with them. But before I go believing her "news," I shall try to ascertain the truth of it. Walter and I were having a good time at the spring dance until Annie "gifted me" (ha!) with her news.

All that next week, I was too quiet, and Papa knew it. He tried to coax me into talking, but I just wouldn't. I'd learned that Annie's information was correct.

The following Sunday, as promised, Walter drove his wagon into our sandy driveway. "Hello, Walter," I greeted him, trying to look peacefully content when I didn't feel it at all.

"Hello," he answered.

"Come in out of this drizzle," I said, "I have some cranberry pie. Pie and coffee? Or tea?"

"That would be lovely. Coffee, thank you. But please don't fuss on my account. A time to talk would be good enough for me."

I made a fuss anyway, perhaps buying time. I wasn't sure why I was not eager to be alone with Walter. Papa sat with us at the table and engaged Walter in a discussion about the year's crops and other farming issues that I only half listened to. When we had all finished our refreshment, Papa went to his Morris chair. Walter took the dishes to the sink where I said I would rinse them later and indicated we go to the living room to talk.

"Actually, I think the rain's clearing. Will you walk with me?" Walter asked.

Sudden, unbidden memories of the same request from Lawrence more than a year ago made my stomach lurch. But this wasn't Lawrence, so I agreed and gathered my wraps. We walked in comfortable silence through the meadow until we stood just over the hill. Tentative shadows stretched eastward when rays of sunlight peeked out from behind the cloud cover. Every type of weather–sun, rain, snow, fog, and wind–had accompanied me to this place on the hill since I was a child. I took issue with none of them, preferring to see the weather patterns as my friends. Welcome here, rather than being resisted. From up here, the beautiful Presumpscot river flowed down to Portland and the Atlantic Ocean. We stood as if the view could be absorbed like a sponge within our hearts and minds. Perhaps it could.

"There's my farm, in the distance, about right there," Walter said, pointing mostly eastward. "This past year and a half has meant the world to me," he said, turning to face me. "I hope that's been the case for you, as well."

Father was right! I thought suddenly. *Oh, dear. Whatever will I say to this dear fellow? I'm not ready for this!*

"You're such a good scholar from what you say," he continued, "I'm afraid I was not the scholar you were. I haven't wanted to admit this to you, but I think our relationship deserves the truth."

I stood, riveted to Walter's eyes, not sure where he was going with this. Maybe not at all where I assumed.

"As you know, my father is a preacher, and a well-respected one at that. That's all I've ever really wanted to be, the preacher of a congregation." He hesitated and then said, "I cannot be a minister because I could not pass my Greek class, which is required to graduate from seminary. So, I never went further than high school." He paused to give me a moment to respond. When I didn't, he continued, "I had to face facts and decided to be a farmer. This has been a disappointment in my life for years. But when I met you, it was like these rays of sunshine just now," he said indicating the lengthening rays. "You brightened my world again. I can't imagine a better life than having you in it with me. I have asked your father for your hand. I have only to ask you for it now. So, Millie, will you be my bride? Will you marry me?"

My heart thumped wildly as thoughts sparked chaotically through my brain. I had been so ready for Lawrence to propose. But not for this. With all my heart, I wished I could jump into Walter's arms with a sincere and resounding "yes" on my lips. I would love nothing more than to feel as he apparently did toward me. I consider him a very good friend. But I'm in no way ready to be his, or anyone's, wife.

The ever-so-slight pause in my response changed his countenance. I could see the poor man deflate as a withering hot air balloon and it made me feel simply dreadful.

"Walter, I cannot say yes. I'm so very sorry, for I can see how much that would mean to you. But I cannot."

He looked down at his hands, then back to my eyes. "I don't consider myself good enough for you, Millie, but if you'd have me, I would do everything in my power to make a good life for you."

"I know that, Walter. I do. You've been nothing if not kind and considerate to me. I just…"

"I know. It's alright. I've sprung something quite sizable on you. Perhaps as you think about it, you will feel differently. But if you don't, Millie, know this—I don't care when it is, even years from now, if you ever see fit to have me, I will make good on my promise to love you all the rest of my days."

My eyes spilled over and down my cheeks as I thought, *This is the most difficult thing I think I have ever had to do. Far harder than spitting out words of contempt at Lawrence. But it wouldn't be fair to Walter that my heart still pines for another, much as I wish it weren't so. And Papa's right, I don't* want to be tied to the farm the rest of my life. Someday, when Papa's gone, I'll leave here.

Sixteen

Mountain Highs

Mid-morning the next day, the sky began to darken fiercely. The clouds roiled over each other in shades of slate, the darkest being almost black. When the trees swayed every which way, it was obvious the storm was about to break. *Ha,* I thought, *nature's way of mimicking my mood.* I made sure all the windows were closed, then I walked through the ell to the barn. Like this storm, my anger was intensifying.

"So," I said to Papa the next morning, with a mixture of indignation and confusion, "when you asked me to sit with you on the stoop and wait for Walter to deliver the mail, he had already come to you asking for your blessing, hadn't he?"

"Yes, chi…Millie, he had."

"What did you tell him? You told me you wouldn't like it if I were a farmer's wife, so I should think you certainly wouldn't have given him your blessing. But if that were true, he wouldn't have asked me to marry him." My words came out as a round of bullets.

Maddeningly calm, Papa said, as he cleaned out the cow stalls, "I had thought about what I might say to Walter if he ever came to me, and I decided to give him my blessing because you are both adults. I suspected you'd turn him down, and I thought it was better to come from you than me."

Thunder cracked all around the farm. Papa's information didn't make me feel much better. Nevertheless, at least I knew the truth. But if he wanted details about my time with Walter yesterday, I wasn't about to give it. When a deafeningly close clap of thunder crashed, I reflexively dropped into a crouch. Likely the lightning had hit the metal rod just over our heads. *You mock me*, I said to God in my mind, though if I'd spoken the words out loud no one could have heard me over the storm.

When the noise tapered off, Papa said, "I assume you did turn him down, by the looks of things." Papa knew me all too well. "I think you need to get away for a few days, Millie. Somewhere that'll do your soul good. Think on it."

I watched Papa's back as he walked to the horse's stall. He looked more stooped and hobbled than usual and I knew, with shame, that it was probably on account of me. He was living with a moody and fickle woman. *Why, oh why can't I have a normal life like most of my friends? If I did, I'd be married by now.* I turned to go back into the house.

All of a sudden, I stopped, realizing what Papa had just said. He was giving me permission to be gone for a few days. *That has never happened before,* I thought. *He'd never deny me that opportunity, but suggesting it must mean he really does think I need to go. Maybe I do.*

I gave the matter serious consideration. I could go see Joe, Bea, and little Dotty. While that was very tempting, I was afraid Bea, especially, would coach me on how I might have done things differently with Walter or even my love life in general. I didn't feel like being coached by anyone. Besides, Bea and Joe were readying for their new baby. No, I needed to go somewhere completely new to me, a place where I could really relax and think about my life. I didn't have the money to go wherever I pleased, which limited the possibilities, but I finally thought of someone I might visit, if she'd have me. Hattie Evans, in Crawford Notch, New Hampshire. She'd introduced me to Lillian, a girl for whom she'd been a nanny. Lillian was my age, and we occasionally played together when I went to Grandmam and Grandpar's house. I pulled out stationery and my pen and wrote to Hattie immediately, hoping she would welcome a visit.

Meanwhile, Papa asked the neighbors if they knew of anyone for hire. Timmy Parsons, a favorite hired help of Papa's the past few years, was now married and starting a farm of his own. So, Papa ended up hiring the young Weaver brothers, Henry and Sam.

It was strange not seeing Joe and Papa working together. And, of course, I missed Bea and Dotty, too. And now Walter wasn't calling, either, of course. He still delivers mail, so I try not to be outside when he comes by. It just feels too awkward. Thankfully, Luella is home. She and I, and Marion, who just graduated from high school, see one another as often as possible.

One very sultry evening, when the black flies and mosquitos were particularly grievous, Papa and I sat in the parlor, windows open wide to catch even the slightest breeze. We tried not to move. Papa didn't even want to smoke his pipe but tried to read his Bible without falling asleep. I tried to continue knitting the blanket I'd started for the new baby but abandoned it when the yarn felt too hot on my lap. Instead, I picked up the Sunday newspaper to read anything I might have missed when suddenly I grew very attentive.

"Papa! Listen to this!" His eyes fluttered open a crack. "Donald MacMillan—you remember the teacher at Levi Hall a few years back?— well, he has been teaching at Worcester Academy since then, I guess. It says that Mr. MacMillan has been running a summer camp for boys on Bustins Island, off the coast of Freeport. He teaches the boys seamanship and navigation. And you know the bad storms that came through? Well, I guess some boats wrecked near the island and Mr. MacMillan saved the lives of nine people! And this got the attention of the arctic explorer, Robert E. Peary, who asked him to join this year's expedition to reach the North Pole! Imagine *that*!"

"So, will he go with the expedition?" asked Papa, now fully awake.

"Well, it says he won't break his contract with the school, so I guess not. But imagine that! Going all the way to the North Pole. Even *you* didn't get that far north on the whaler, right? My scholars from Windham would have loved hearing about this. I'm sure the youngest ones would love to ask Mr. Peary to take their letters to Santa Claus!" I chuckled.

Not long after that, a letter arrived from Hattie. I tore it open and read that she was thrilled to have me visit and suggested I come up in July. She didn't care which specific days I chose, so long as I gave her enough notice to tidy the house. That made me chuckle. I couldn't imagine her house not being tidy. After checking train schedules, I decided to go up the week after Independence Day.

I stepped onto the train with great anticipation. Traveling alone was something I had not done. Everything was new and wonderful. But it was when the train reached the v-shaped notch that climbed up through the White Mountains that the view almost took my breath away. *And to think, Hattie* lives *in these mountains!*

The climb up through Crawford Notch was slow, as the engine puffed away. There was plenty of time to breathe in not only the evergreens, but the views as well. As Papa had said, it was as if my soul really was being refreshed with every breath I took. I simply couldn't take my eyes off the hills and the occasional animal along the way. I even resented the noises inside the train that wanted to pull my eyes away from the mountains.

One towering peak caught my attention. I gasped and thought, *That must be Mount Washington.* It's always topped with snow no matter what time of year. I love to pause on the bridge in Standish just to see it on a very clear day. Even in July, there's a tiny bit of white on top like the meringue on baked Alaska! I've always wondered what it would look like up close when it sits so majestically from a great distance. I sighed with satisfaction as I caught glimpses of the great mountain through the pine trees.

The train began to work harder and slowed even more as we approached a bridge. Many men were working around it with tools and large machines. Some of them stopped to wave at us, and we waved back enthusiastically. It was all so fascinating. Just beyond the bridge was a house. Most people on the train were amazed that there would be a house hanging off the side of a cliff. *I hope that's not Hattie's house,* I thought with dismay, certain it could not be. *It's probably for some of those men we just passed.* Soon we snaked around a bend, squeezing through blasted-out rock walls, when we came upon Crawford depot. *Sure is a small building compared to the one in Portland!* I thought. *I hope someone is here to meet me.*

"Welcome to Crawford Notch, Millie!" Hattie exclaimed as I stepped down off the train. Sitting beside her was a reddish-brown dog. When I looked at it, Hattie said, "This is Rusty." I bent down to greet him.

After hugging warmly, Hattie and I set off down the tracks the way I had just come. *Maybe that* was *Hattie's house,* I thought with real concern.

"So how are you? I hope your trip was agreeable," Hattie said, breaking through my thoughts.

"Oh, yes! It was a lovely ride up here. Such views! I've always loved seeing Mount Washington from White's Bridge, but what a thrill to be right in these mountains!"

"I've said as much myself. Did you finish school?" she asked me.

"I did. I graduated from North Gorham in '97," I said, using the new name for Great Falls because Hattie had used it in her letter. "I thought I might work right away after that, but Papa insisted I go to Gorham for three years and study more Latin and English, and then go to normal school from there. I graduated from Gorham in 1900 and they called us the class of the double nothings! I always found that so funny."

"I assume you wanted to be a teacher? Where did you go to normal school?"

"I didn't end up going. I was the only one left to take care of the house by the time I graduated from Levi Hall. Mama died in '96. So, Papa took another wife to help him at home while I boarded in Gorham. But I could tell he wasn't happy with her. So, after graduation, Ella, Papa's second wife, left soon after I moved back. I knew she had only been a convenience." I chose not to tell Hattie that I had taught for two years. I was afraid that if she could tell how much I had loved teaching, she'd lean on me to return to it.

"I learned that you lost your sister and brother, but I didn't know you lost your mother too. I'm so sorry your family suffered so many deaths, Millie."

"Thank you. It wasn't easy. Only one brother is left, and he moved to Massachusetts to teach. Papa and I have fallen into a rhythm together, though. I keep house and he works the farm, as it is by now. Smaller by far without my brothers to help him. This spring I had a suitor who asked Papa for my hand, but it didn't work out. I think Papa didn't want me to marry a farmer, knowing how hard farm work is on a woman. And I don't want to leave Papa alone. He's never been entirely well after being wounded in the Rebellion. So, I decided to turn my suitor down. I guess it wasn't mean to be."

"Was it difficult to say no to the man?" Hattie asked me gently.

"Surprisingly more difficult than I would have thought. He's a nice man and I may never be asked to marry another."

"You're what, about twenty-five now? You're young. I should hope you'd have other suitors."

"Perhaps," I conceded, "but North Gorham isn't much of a town. And staying on the farm doesn't give me a lot of chances to meet people."

When the house came into view, I said, "That isn't your house, is it?"

"It is!" Hattie said, enthusiastically. "I know it looks a bit scary so close to the tracks and the drop-off. But I assure you, it's quite secure."

"What are those men doing to the bridge?"

"They are working to strengthen it. It's all being done while trains maintain their schedule too, which is amazing. Come, meet Loring, my husband."

A portly man with a kind smile walked up to us with his hand outstretched. "This is Millie Thomas. Millie, this is my husband, Loring."

"Nice to meet you, Loring. You certainly have a beautiful place to live."

"Ay-uh, we do. I'm sure Hattie will show you around. Like all the noise?" he chuckled, indicating the bridge work. "Usually the only sounds are coyotes or bobcats yowling or the trains passin' through. It'll quiet down this evening, though." He left with a wave.

"Yes, let me show you around," Hattie said.

She led me into the house on the edge of Mount Willard, which was much larger than it had looked from the outside. We walked through a lovely parlor and up a staircase to two large bedrooms. She gave me the one at the back of the house after showing me the one that faced the tracks. She said that I might not appreciate the night trains if I were to stay in that front room with the tracks a mere twelve feet from the windows. I thanked her for that!

We went back down through the parlor, the dining room, and into her kitchen, where she offered me some lemonade and a freshly-made doughnut. I'd no more than sat down when a cat was on my lap, doing figure eights while rubbing against my elbow.

"This is Boomerang," Hattie said. "We found him, well, he found us, when we lived in Lewiston before coming up here. He's a good mouser and heaven knows we need one of those."

"May I ask you a question?" I said, keeping Boomerang's internal motor rumbling with contentedness.

"Of course."

"How do you get food and supplies up here? You're awfully far from the rest of civilization."

"Mostly the trains bring orders to us from Bartlett, which you went through. I wire an order to them and they put it on the train. The uphill trains don't stop or they can't get started again. It's too steep. So when they bring supplies, they hang the bag on the pole outside as they go by or, if it wouldn't hurt what's in the bag, they just drop it on the ground."

"Do you see people much? I mean I didn't see but a very few houses on the way up."

"Yes, people in this area take the train when they come visit or walk the tracks like we did. I go visiting the same way. Loring's sister and her young son just came up for a visit from Maine. Really, the trains are the center of everything up here. The large building, a bit further than the depot that you pointed out, is a resort. Sometimes people staying there walk down here to visit. It's really quite interesting because they come from all over. If what you really want to know is whether I get lonely, I don't. Besides, the track crew lives here too."

"All those men out there?" I asked incredulously.

"No," she laughed, "most of those men come up from Portland on special assignment and stay up the tracks in their own train car. No, we house four men who work here year-round. They sleep upstairs above where we're sitting now. They eat with us, but otherwise keep to themselves mostly. By the way, what would you like to do while you're here?"

"I don't know. I've never taken a vacation before. I brought books to read, and I have letters to catch up on. I'd love to take a walk each day, if it's nice out. But you don't need to entertain me," I said.

"I take long walks myself. I have the perfect one to start with, if you're up for a climb."

That evening, I met the crew. All of them were very pleasant. And I also met my first train that rumbled by. My, oh my they're loud! The house shook till I was sure we were going to end up at the bottom of the mountain! They come so close to the house, I thought they would go straight through the living room. But no one seems to notice here, including Rusty and Boomerang. I suppose they're used to the trains by now, but I don't think I'd ever adjust to them.

I didn't sleep well that night, so I chose not to go on a strenuous walk the next day. But the day after that we hiked to the top of Mount Willard. It took us a couple of hours, but once we were there and looking down through the notch, I didn't want to leave. It was simply breathtaking. And Mount Washington was so close, I could hardly believe it!

Those few days flew by. Hattie wouldn't accept help in the kitchen at all. I dined like a queen. I learned that Hattie's husband is the grandson of John Evans, who fought with Papa. I had wondered if they were related. Sometimes I watched the work on the bridge, but mostly I wrote letters or read my book. I saw a black bear down the tracks that scurried into the woods when it saw me. Otherwise, I didn't see wild animals except a few deer, which never seem wild to me. The last day, before boarding my train, Hattie took me to the Crawford House just beyond the depot. It is an enormous hotel with wealthy people strolling the massive grounds or playing croquet and other games. Just to walk amid such extravagance made me feel out of place, even though it was fascinating to see. Hattie said she has friends who work there, so she's gotten used to the grandeur.

"Thank you, Hattie. So, so much. It's been such a wonderful break for me."

"I enjoyed every minute," she said. "Do come back anytime."

I was filled with gratitude, a bit of sadness at having to leave, and a new outlook on what I have at home. Love fills our house; I know that now. More clearly than ever. I hope I never have to leave home again to remember that.

Tuesday, July 25, 1905

Dear Millie and Papa,

Yesterday was the big day! Joseph Smith arrived early Monday morning. Once again, Bea was wonderful. She did say that if we have another, she'd rather it be a winter baby! The heat of this summer has been nearly unbearable for her. Dotty is very curious about little Joe and tries to poke her finger in his nose. I suppose that's normal, if not hard for the baby.

I am being called. Bea says she will write her own letter to you soon.

Missing you both,
Joe

Saturday, July 29, 1905

Dear diary, there seems to be at least two different mountain highs one can have—climbing a mountain to look over beautiful valleys and learning that a brand-new life has just come into this world.

Seventeen

Another Chance

Before I knew it, four years had passed since my visit with Hattie. Eventually, the pain of Lawrence's betrayal and the guilt of having turned down Walter faded. In the course of time, I was able to talk to Walter when he delivered mail as if there had never been the disheartening disruption between us. Walter's ability to forgive and go on was not lost on me. *He's a truly fine individual,* I thought one day when he clopped off down the road after handing me our mail. In the winter, I could see that his job was much easier once the town's new snow roller compacted the snow.

It doesn't seem like much has happened in Great Falls since I went to New Hampshire. I guess that's a good thing if it means nothing terribly dreadful has happened to anyone I love. Frank Morse was killed by a runaway horse. He was only thirty-three and had a wife and children. I'm sure it's been dreadful for them. Brown-tailed and gypsy moths are still ravaging some types of crops and trees. The town is debating whether or not to keep paying a bounty on any moth nests people find and destroy. There are two automobiles that putter down the road occasionally. Papa always hobbles out to the road as quickly as he can if he hears one coming. And since Levi Hall does not have the proper fire escape as mandated by law, all the pupils are being taught on the first floor. What a waste of space.

Of consequence in the best of ways is that last spring Bea and Joe welcomed little Rachel Matilda to the household. Dotty was helpful to her mother when Rachel arrived the last day of April. Young Joe calls his new sister "Tildy" like the others do. Last summer was especially cheerful with the children so alive with love and laughter.

I have long since thought of myself as an old maid, so when there was need of a librarian here in Great Falls, I happily accepted the position. I open the library on Wednesday afternoons from two o'clock to half past four. I arrive by one o'clock and do anything that needs to be taken care of before I open the door, such as updating the precise records that are submitted regularly to Gorham. I'll either mail the records or deliver them by hand occasionally when I take Papa's wagon to Gorham village. There is usually a small group of people gathered by the door, waiting for me. I love greeting my patrons and showing them books I think they'd like, making sure they see the new ones that circulate from Gorham's much bigger library. I have added what I call "Time for Tales," when I read to the children so their mothers are able to browse the books unbothered. I love being a librarian so much, I think perhaps I may even prefer it to teaching.

An inevitable outcome of being a librarian is garnering news, such as when Levi Hall's own Donald MacMillan made his first trip to the Arctic with Robert Peary. Unfortunately, both of Mr. MacMillan's heels froze and he was forced to leave the ship, which consequently never did reach the North Pole. He made subsequent trips with Peary and became one of Great Falls' claims to fame when Peary and his crew discovered the Pole this year.

One piece of news that I overheard, though the women tried to whisper, made a direct hit to my heart. Lawrence, it seems, has moved back to Portland. If this is to be believed, he is supposedly working for the Cumberland County Power and Light Company. And most surprisingly, he is not with Lizzie. It has been five years since I last spoke to either of them. Why does it feel like just yesterday?

I wasn't outside when Walter delivered Lawrence's letter at the end of the summer. I'm grateful because I can't imagine the awkwardness of having Walter hand me a letter in Lawrence's handwriting. He isn't the nosy type, and I'm sure he wouldn't ask me about it, but I'm also sure he knew. I just wouldn't want to cause Walter undo pain. *Then again, perhaps he is seeing someone himself.* That thought hadn't occurred to me before. *But, no, he as much as said he would wait in case I changed my mind. Either way, it isn't my concern now,* I finally decided.

That night I finally opened Lawrence's letter in my room.

Sunday, August 29, 1909

Greetings Millie!

I hope this letter finds you doing well. It's been a long time since we last communicated and at that, it isn't something I remember fondly. I'm quite sure you do not, either. I am sincerely sorry for the way things ended between us. I won't blame things on Lizzie. We were both swept away with the idea of seeking something new. New location, new jobs, and, yes, I'll say it, a new relationship. I truly thought Lizzie was the better fit for me. We both enjoy a hearty social life to your preferred quieter one.

But after a time, we grew tired of the very things that had drawn us together. Now, I see the beauty in two people being different and the adage that "opposites attract." I would love a chance to explain myself further if you'll let me call on you.

I sincerely hope you have forgiven me by now, although I will understand if you have not.

Missing you,
Lawrence

I read and reread his letter several times to decide how I felt about it, after the initial shock of his having written wore off. His words reawakened the anger I'd pushed away years ago. But this time my rage came back with a few friends–justification for being angry was mixed with bitterness for the wasted years we might have had together, sadness of having lost my friendship with Lizzie (yet curiosity to know her side of their story), and then, of course, a tenuous excitement for the possibility of another chance.

So many questions emerged. Do I even want to give Lawrence another chance? Can I risk being that hurt again? But doesn't everyone deserve a chance to prove that they have learned from their mistakes? He sounds humble enough, but has he truly changed for the better? Finally, after wrestling with questions I couldn't answer, I decided to sleep on them. One thing I did decide before falling asleep was that I don't want to talk things over with Papa. And I'm glad Joe's family has already left. I don't want to know what they think. I am twenty-nine years old and it's high time I made my own decisions–completely.

After nearly a week of contemplating what to do, I knew I wanted to write him back, and I knew what I wanted to say.

Thursday, September 9, 1909

Dear Lawrence,

What a total surprise to find your letter amongst my other mail. I am well, yes. Papa and I manage the farm with a bit of extra help, although the farm is some smaller than when you last saw it. I am also the librarian in town on Wednesday afternoons, which I very much enjoy.

And yes, you may come to call if you like. We have much to talk about.

Sincerely,
Millie

It had been difficult to know the best way to close the letter. Where Lawrence had signed "Missing you, Lawrence," I had not wanted to reveal yet that I had missed him too. "Sincerely" seemed neither too formal nor too intimate. And I had, indeed, written sincerely.

A week and a half after I had sent my letter, which I mailed at the general store rather than hand it to Walter, Lawrence called on me. Papa had not known he was coming and was quite surprised to see him, though he merely greeted Lawrence as he would anyone else. I could not read his expression nor the thoughts behind it.

He'd arrived in a lovely new carriage into which he helped me. We went up Standish Neck Road to the tee where we turned southward onto Chadbourne Road. Then he took a smaller road to reach the lake, and we found a quiet spot to sit and talk. He had even brought sandwiches and fruit, which surprised and delighted me.

After dispensing with the proper niceties–How are you? What is new? and so forth–we began the essence of our visit.

"Millie," Lawrence said after a pause in the conversation, "I don't exactly know how to begin. I'm sure you've had questions, though. Is there anything specific you want to know?"

"Yes. First of all, I had heard that Lizzie taught down in Scarborough. What did you do?"

"She did. She stayed with a host family, and I rented a room in a boarding house. I worked at an apothecary as a clerk."

"The whole time? You and Lizzie were living and working in the same town this whole time?"

"Yes. She loved her job. I can't say I loved mine, but the pay was adequate."

"Did you stay, then, for her sake?"

"Yes. We thought we were headed for marriage."

This wasn't easy to hear, but I decided I'd rather know the truth. "So, I guess I want to know what happened that you didn't stay together."

"Well, as I mentioned in my letter to you, we enjoyed a hearty social life, going to parties, or traveling to new places close by, that sort of thing. I helped her with school activities, like creative projects or even being her assistant teacher when she wasn't feeling well. The superintendent didn't seem to mind my doing that since I'd been a teacher before. As long as I didn't expect to be paid, he thought it was a pretty good deal. I didn't do that too often, though. I couldn't because I had to work my regular job too."

"So, then, what happened?" I asked, thinking he was trying to avoid answering my question.

"Towards the end, we didn't seem to get along as well. She was irritated with me a lot, and I felt bored with our relationship."

"Honestly, Lawrence, what you describe doesn't seem boring at all."

"The things we did weren't boring. We had a great time together. But when we were alone, not doing anything special, it seemed like we couldn't really talk about anything meaningful. That's when I began missing you. What we're doing now? Talking like this? It never happened with Lizzie."

"Actually," I said, "I experienced something similar when we roomed together. I didn't feel safe to tell her everything in my heart. Our relationship worked best when I kept my emotional distance."

"Yes, That's what it was. Something always stopped me from being able to express myself deeply."

We sat in silence for a long time, both in our own thoughts, I guessed. At least I was. How easily Lawrence and I were able to slip back into the relationship we'd had years ago. *If he hadn't fallen for Lizzie, we'd be married now,* I thought.

Lawrence must have been thinking along the same lines. "I feel like a fool, Millie. A shallow fool; what I gave up to have a good time."

He moved to kiss me, but I backed away. I wasn't ready to jump back in time so quickly. Lawrence jerked backward himself.

"I'm sorry. I just miss you so much," he said, embarrassed, I think.

"You hurt me terribly," I said, rather proud of myself that I was expressing the truth about my pain, "and you will have to earn your way back to my lips."

"You're right, of course," he sighed. "Do you mind if we just sit and talk about other things? It's so beautiful here."

"Not at all," I said, feeling satisfied with what he'd told me. Suddenly a last question formed in my mind. "But first, tell me something. Who called the relationship off?"

"Honestly, I'm not sure. She may have spoken first, but I was thinking it at the same time."

"Thank you," I said, "for answering my questions."

When Lawrence dropped me off at home, he said he wanted to keep in touch with letters since he doesn't live in Great Falls anymore and wouldn't be able to come calling as often. I agreed wholeheartedly. It seemed the perfect way to slowly gain a solid foothold into this new connection.

Papa looked up from his Bible when I walked past him. He said nothing. I began to feel guilty for keeping him in the dark and doubled back and sat down near him.

"Papa," I began, "I assume you would like to know at least something of this new association with Lawrence?"

"I guess I am curious, yes," he said. "But if you don't wish to talk about it, I won't hold you to it. I only pray you find true happiness."

"Do you not like Lawrence?"

"I don't much trust someone who could hurt my daughter as he did. But I also trust you to follow your heart. And your heart is yours alone. You must lie in the bed you make for yourself."

"Yes, Papa, I understand."

Lawrence was as good as his word. Letters came often and Walter delivered them all. How he took them or what he thought, I had no idea. He still smiled when he handed me the mail.

All that autumn, either by letter or the times Lawrence called on me, I learned more about his family than I had known before. His openness was admirable, I thought. He talked about the company in Portland where he was working and his aspirations for the future. *Papa should like the fact that if Lawrence and I marry, I won't be a farmer's wife.* But Papa was restrained where it came to Lawrence and said very little.

When the holidays came around, I sensed that Papa would rather not have Lawrence join us for either Thanksgiving or Christmas. At first I was angry, but when I thought about the resistance I might get from Joe and Bea, I didn't push it. If I was quiet about my new relationship with Lawrence, Christmas might be the wonderful holiday with Dotty, Little Joe, and Tildy that I longed for. I couldn't risk those precious days being ruined. I'd simply have to usher Lawrence back into the family a little bit at a time.

Then, once more, death came to my family. This time it was Uncle Almon in April of 1910. Georgie, Matie, Jennie, Grandmam, Howdie, Mama, Grandpar, and now my beloved uncle. So many names on so many gravestones. So many memories. So much loss. Mama's youngest sibling, John, my other uncle, was a man I hardly knew. He was alone in his immediate family after Almon's death. He knew Uncle Almon was close to me and suggested that his service be held in a church and that I see to making that happen, which I was honored to do.

A strange and wonderful thing happened after the reverend asked me to pick out hymns and play the organ. Normally, I am told what hymns to play so I look over them to refresh my mind on the key and what stops to use. To my memory, I have never really thought much about the words beyond the old familiar hymns everyone knows by heart. But I decided to go out into the meadow and sit on my contemplation rock and think about what Uncle Almon meant to me. I thought perhaps in doing that, the names of hymns would come to me there. I cried a little and laughed a little. Then, suddenly, I remembered the little *Gospel Hymns* book that Grandmam had given me when I was only thirteen years old. I hadn't looked at it in years.

I left the rock to fetch the book, which was in my bedroom, and sat on the bed with it, turning its thin pages. The print was so fine, I could hardly read it anymore. When I turned to page fifty-two, the little needlepointed rose Grandmam had made fell out. I looked at the hymn on that page and felt compelled to read its words:

> *How sweet the name of Jesus sounds*
> *In a believer's ear;*
> *It soothes his sorrows, heals his wounds,*
> *And drives away his fear.*
>
> *It makes the wounded spirit whole,*
> *And calms the troubled breast;*
> *'Tis manna to the hungry soul,*
> *And to the weary, rest.*

Dear Name, the Rock on which I build
My shield and hiding place;
My never-failing treasure, filled
With boundless stores of grace.

I would Thy boundless love proclaim
With every fleeting breath;
So shall the music of Thy name
Refresh my soul in death.

Right then, right there, I bowed my head to talk with my grandmother. "Grandmam," I said, "thank you for giving me this wondrous little hymnal so long ago. I confess I haven't used it lately, nor have I taken the time to reflect on the words to most of the hymns. But I believe it was you who led me to the hymn you would love to hear us sing in memory of your beloved son, for who else could it have been? I love you, Grandmam."

So it was that we held his memorial service at Great Falls Congregational Church in early July so that Joe and his family could be there. And I smiled as I played hymn number seventy-one on page fifty-two.

One day I burst into the barn to see if Papa was there. Not finding him, I scanned the fields, but he wasn't there, either. *He must be out,* I thought, and went into the house to start making dinner. Suddenly I began to chuckle at the irony of the situation. When I heard Papa arrive home, I decided not to wait for him to come inside. Instead, I moved the pan off the flame and quickly wiped my hands on my apron. Then I walked to the barn. While Papa took the harnesses off the horse and brushed Fitz down, I exclaimed, "Papa! Guess what?"

He looked at me with alarm at my outburst. When he saw mirth on my face, he was obviously relieved. "Sorry, Papa, I didn't mean to scare you, but Great Falls has its first telephone! It's in the general store! Just think of it, we wouldn't have to wait for a return letter in answer to questions, especially important ones. We could hear the person speaking from miles away! It's just, just, well, almost unimaginable, don't you think, Papa?"

Papa was thoughtful and then merely answered, "Yes, that is most unimaginable."

"Well, anyway, Papa," I continued, chuckling aloud, "I came home to tell you about it. I couldn't wait and I went to the barn and then the fields. I got frustrated when I couldn't find you. I wanted to tell you right away. And then I thought about the irony of wanting to tell you something right off without waiting, just like the telephone could do. Just think, we could call Joe to tell him our news immediately," I sighed contentedly.

"But at what cost?" Papa said, "Surely it can't be free."

Papa's words doused my enthusiasm like a bucket of ice water when I realized he was right. "I guess I'll keep on writing my letters," I said glumly and turned on my heels.

Once again, as when Howdie and Mama died, Lawrence was by my side as much as possible that summer, though his presence elevated the tension I felt with Bea. I could only assume she didn't like him, or trust him, or both. I understood that her approval of our relationship was not necessary, but I wanted it very badly. I felt torn. I wanted to be with Dotty, Little Joe, and Tildy so much I ached inside each time I left with Lawrence. Yet, when I was home, I often felt an iciness around Bea. So, inevitably, Lawrence and I often did things away from the house. It was easier for me that way and hopefully for Bea. But it came at the cost of leaving those I love to be with another I love. It hurt me intensely not to be with everyone I cared about at the same time.

By August, things were coming to a boiling point with Bea. Joe approached me one day to say that she thought it best they leave early for Massachusetts. I couldn't believe it had come to that. I asked him if the issue was Lawrence.

"I think it is. I'm sorry, Millie, but I'd rather not leave Papa in the lurch. Will you talk with her?"

"I'd rather not, truthfully, but I will."

"Soon," he added.

The next day, I found Bea at the Hoosier cabinet making bread. I was surprised, actually, because she usually had me make the bread.

"Would you like help with that?" I asked her.

Bea spun around so quickly, flour sprinkled through the sunlight streaming in the window. It looked like a delicate snowfall, an oxymoron to what was coming.

"OO-OO-OO," six-year-old Dotty said, walking into the kitchen. "That looks like snow!"

"Go outside and play!" Bea scolded.

Dotty looked crestfallen as she headed for the door. She looked back at me and I winked at her, hoping she wouldn't worry. I felt so sad for her, though.

"No, I don't want help with the bread," Bea said curtly. "It should have been done by now, so I thought I'd best do it myself."

I sighed. "Bea, I think we need to talk. I'll go to the children and when you are finished, come find me."

"Mama sounded angry," Dotty said, sitting on the lawn in a heap. "Did I do something wrong?"

"No, Dotty," I said. "Come walk with me. I want to show you something." I took her hand and we walked to my contemplation rock. "Here, look at this rock."

"I've seen it lots of times, Aunt Millie," she said as though she thought I was daft.

"Sit on it," I told her. She sat down and I sat on the grass nearby.

"This rock is special, Dotty. I call it my contemplation rock. I sit here lots of times for lots of different reasons. Sometimes I'm happy, sometimes I'm afraid, and sometimes I'm just very sad. But if I sit here long enough, and just talk to myself, or think about things, or sometimes even hum or sing, most of the time I feel better than when I sat down. Sometimes I get answers to questions that are on my mind. Sometimes I just feel peaceful. Maybe it would work for you, too."

"But it's your rock, not mine," she said logically.

"I like to share it with people I love very, very much. I need to go talk with your Mama right now and maybe I can learn what she's angry about. You are welcome to sit right here for as long as you like. Except you must mind whenever an adult wants you to come. Alright?"

"Yes, Aunt Millie."

I left her there and soon Bea was ready to talk. I took a big breath, praying that all would work out, and walked toward the house. Bea and I sat on the front stoop where we could see Little Joe and Dotty. Tildy was napping, but we would hear her if she woke up.

"Bea," I started, "I know you are upset. Is it something about Lawrence?"

"Yes, Millie, it is. I really don't trust him after what he did to you. I don't understand why you do. I'll admit that I have not been overly fond of Lawrence from the start. But the way he hurt you is unconscionable in my mind. I could never, ever go back to someone who was as unfaithful as he was to you. Can you explain yourself?"

Why should I have to? I thought, my own anger rising. But I knew I needed to answer her for there to be any peace in the household the rest of the summer. "I'm not sure what I can say to convince you that he is remorseful and knows he handled himself poorly."

"'Handled himself poorly?' That makes it sound like he did the right thing the wrong way. I don't think he came anywhere close to doing the right thing. Do you? I mean do you really?"

"No. I didn't say that right, I guess. He knows how badly he hurt me. He's been apologetic and attentive to me since he started calling again. I think he really has changed, grown up."

"Do you love him, Millie?" Bea said more tenderly.

I hadn't admitted this to anyone else and not even so bluntly as this to myself. "Yes, I do."

"Is there any way at all I can make you see that Lawrence may not be the best man for you?"

"No, Bea. I love him and I think he will ask me to marry him one of these days. And when he does, I will say yes."

We were both quiet, letting all of this sink in.

Finally, Bea said, "I care a lot about what happens to you. I hope you know that. I can't watch you make what I think is a big mistake. But I don't want to leave here angry, either. You've been gone a lot lately with Lawrence and the children miss you. And sometimes I feel overwhelmed with the household duties and the children. I could use more help the rest of the summer, if we stay."

"I'm sorry I haven't been more helpful." I said. But I wanted to say that I chose to be gone because of her judgmental opinions. "I will try to do better if it means you and Joe will stay. I love being with the children very much."

"And you are very good with them too. They love you."

We stood, knowing we'd said what we needed to. I didn't feel completely comfortable with our talk, but enough so that I could manage to stay home more often.

Joe thanked me privately before they left, and Bea and I hugged. The older children ran to me with open arms, and I kissed little Tildy on her sweet little cheek. As I watched them go, I thought about how messy life can get. Even with those we love the most. I needed a little time on the rock myself before making dinner.

Lawrence called on me throughout the rest of the year and into 1911. I wasn't going to make the same mistake the next summer and asked Lawrence to be patient with me. He was, and I was very appreciative. Even Bea remarked at Lawrence's maturity.

And then it happened. Lawrence waited until after Joe and his family had gone back home. He came to the farm one Sunday in September and asked me to come outside. When I did, he was standing under the tree, arms behind him, beaming a genuine smile that rivaled that of a child at Christmas.

"Lawrence?" I said, already blushing, "What do you have behind your back?"

He produced a small box and handed it to me. "Open it," he said.

I lifted the lid to see the most beautiful ring I'd ever seen in my life.

"Like it?" he said.

"No," I said, watching disappointment creep onto his face like a mask. "I *love* it!" Then I flew into his arms, and he twirled me off my feet.

Once he'd set me down, I said, "Lawrence, do you suppose there is only one right person for each of us to marry?"

"I do," he said, "and you, Millie, are right for me."

I couldn't agree more. I felt like the luckiest woman in the world.

Portland Sunday Telegram, October 16, 1911:

It was the privilege of your correspondent to attend one of the most pleasant and enjoyable gatherings that has ever been held in this place, which was in the form of a "silver shower" given to Miss Mildred F. Thomas, who is soon to become the bride of Lawrence S. Hanley. She is a young lady that has many friends, and she has been very dedicated to her church and library work. There were forty dollars showered upon her, showing the esteem in which she is held. Mrs. Addie Manchester very kindly opened her house for the occasion. The rooms were beautifully decorated with autumn leaves, goldenrod, and many lovely flowers. There were between fifty and sixty from Great Falls, Windham Hill, Windham Center, and Standish Neck. Ice cream and cake were being served when a very notable guest arrived, Prof. Donald B. MacMillan, who had just returned from his second trip to Labrador. He was stopping for a short visit with a friend on Sebago Lake and came to call on his friends in Great Falls, not expecting to see so many of them. All were delighted to see him back once more, also to see him looking so fine and healthy. A wedding date has been set for October 31, 1911.

Part Two

Walter

If I had a flower for every time I thought of you...
I could walk through my garden forever.
-Caroline George

Eighteen

Endings

He closed the Sunday paper and let it fall to his lap. She found her brother staring straight ahead in a sort of oblivion when she entered the room. "Walter?" Bessie said, with the bite of anxiety to her voice. "What's wrong?" He slowly opened the paper and handed it to his sister. "There," was all he said, pointing to a small article toward the top of the society page. Bessie took the paper from him, still looking alarmed at her brother's face. She'd never seen him look this way before. Then she read the article and knew the source of her brother's anguish. She felt her own agony for him as she simply stood looking at him in the palpable quiet of suffering.

"I'm grateful Pa is in no shape to read this or even be told," Walter finally said.

"Oh, Walter, I'm so sorry. I know how much you care for Millie. Did you have any idea about this at all?"

"I've heard this and that from idle gossip, and I've delivered many a letter between them. I guess I just didn't want to see the truth of it. Didn't want to believe it."

Bessie's brother, such a tall, tender-hearted man. She sighed and went to the kitchen to help her mother. There was nothing more she could do. She hoped Walter would get over Millie eventually.

At supper that night, Elizabeth, Bessie, and Walter sat down to a meal of soup and bread. Walter swirled his soup absentmindedly while the women tried not to watch. "Ma, I'll take Pa his supper tonight. You can sit with Walter," Bessie said, standing behind Walter screwing up her face and darting her eyes back and forth from Elizabeth to Walter and back. She hoped her mother understood her signal. Perhaps her mother could be successful drawing Walter out.

"Son, I'm very sorry to hear that Millie is engaged to another, but you need to eat. You're thin enough as it is. You work so hard here and at your other jobs and we appreciate it so. But you need to keep up your strength." Walter said nothing.

It was difficult for Elizabeth not to worry about her son. He was the primary breadwinner of the family now and had been for the past four years as her husband, Edwin's, dementia worsened, and he could no longer serve churches. Edwin gave her worry enough. But his first child, Cora, by his first wife, Eliza, began acting odd two years ago, which worried the family terribly. Cora's two sisters and her own eight children couldn't comprehend Cora's strange behavior and largely stayed away. Only Cora's daughter, Ellen, seemed able to cope and tried to help. Cora began having delusions of grandeur, telling people she was more religious than others. One day Ellen found her in the kitchen playing with fire. When Ellen tried to correct the situation, Cora became very irritable. But it was when Cora struck Ellen one day that Cora's husband, the Reverend James Aikins, realized with great sadness that his wife needed to be institutionalized. She entered the Maine Insane Hospital in March of 1910.

Elizabeth and Eliza, Edwin's two wives, had grown very close when Elizabeth became Eliza's nurse during the prolonged illness that eventually took Eliza's life. So, for Elizabeth, although she was not directly related to Cora, that part of Edwin's life felt steadfastly intertwined with hers. If Edwin grieved, Elizabeth grieved with him and for him. Elizabeth followed the lives of Eliza's children and grandchildren as if they were her own. In kind, Edwin's five children never differentiated themselves as half siblings, but considered themselves natural kin.

With Cora's involuntary confinement to the hospital so relatively recent, and Edwin's worsening dementia, Elizabeth's worries mounted when Walter seemed so devastated by the loss of Millie. She really wasn't sure how to handle this new development other than to console him. When Walter didn't speak and only played with his food, Elizabeth stood, walked around the table, and gave her son a hug from behind. Then she went into her bedroom to check on her husband. She told Bessie she would take over Edwin's care. Then she instructed Bessie to let Walter be for a time and to busy herself elsewhere.

Eventually, Walter left the table to care for the animals. He was quieter than usual for the next few days but gradually began to be himself again. He needed to gain back his strength because his father's health took a tumble. Edwin had still been able to speak in these last months, though not always clearly. At the same time, his physical health continued to worsen. Nearing the end of October, Edwin lapsed into a nearly comatose state. He wasn't taking food at all, save for a little warm milk toast they spread on his lips. The doctor confirmed that Edwin was close to death, so the family was called in and someone was by his bedside around the clock. Then shockingly, the night before he died, Edwin was suddenly lucid. Walter had been sitting beside his father and startled when Edwin opened his eyes and began speaking clearly.

"Walter, my son, you are in charge now. It is time you ask for Millie's hand in marriage and start your own family." That was all he said before slipping into unconsciousness again. Walter just stared at his father's face. He'd not had time to respond to his father even if he'd known what to say. Elizabeth and Bessie, who had been standing in the doorway, could only look on in dismay and trepidation for how Walter would react to this. Walter looked over at his mother and sister with tears coursing down his cheeks. He said nothing and then walked out of the room.

Later that night, the Reverend Edwin Harlow, pastor to so many from 1863 to 1907, took his last breath. It was Saturday, October 28, 1911. His service was a few days later in North Church of South Portland, where there was plenty of room for his many mourners to gather. Elizabeth had asked family members to read excerpts from Edwin's 1860 Bowdoin College autograph book. She wanted the gathering to hear how, even as a relatively young man, her husband had been influential. His friend Levi Leavitt wrote this, "Your straightforward and independent course, your inflexibility and strict adherence to conviction of duty have gained my respect, while the Christian character, good qualities of heart and kind disposition you possess have won my love." And from James Phillips, "Seldom has it been my good fortune to meet with one who seemed to enter so heartily and freely into my own feelings and views. I shall not devote this page allotted to me, Harlow, to vain flattery, for this does not become friends who know each other so well as we do." After a memorable hour of scripture, prayers, and reflections, Edwin's body was interred across the street from the first church he had served after returning to Maine from Kansas.

In the days and months to come, Edwin's service and burial were a blur to Walter, who had received so many friends and family dutifully alongside his mother and sisters. It hadn't been the sheer number of mourners that dulled his mind. That was something he would gladly do again for the sake of his mother. It was the host of thoughts clouding his mind as he hugged or shook hands with those he knew well or those who were simply acquaintances. He knew his father held influence with many people and he admired that about his father. But to him, Edwin was foremost a father who could be quite strict and demanding of him as if all of Edwin's dreams laid in Walter's lap alone. He was, after all, his father's only son.

Because of Edwin's many accomplishments and accolades, Walter lived in his father's shadow, never feeling quite good enough. His father had finished high school, then went to Bowdoin College, working his way through. From there he went on to Bangor Seminary and was ordained in 1863 when the country was at war. Instead of serving in his country's military to fight in the War Between the States, Edwin and his brother Lincoln, who was also ordained, felt they could serve best as missionaries in Missouri and Kansas. Missouri entered the war as a slave state, while Maine entered the war as a free state, thus balancing the power in Congress. Kansas, only becoming a state two months before the war began, also entered as a free state, yet claimed its share of slave owners.

Especially at the border between the two states, there were many bloody battles between the pro- and anti-slavery factions. Edwin and Lincoln, along with the wives they'd just married, bravely headed west to spend the next eight years in battles of their own over the inflamed issue. They all held firmly to their disagreement with slavery. After that war, Edwin returned to Maine with a very sick wife and three young girls. For the next nearly forty years, Walter's father pastored many churches up and down the coast of Maine. His service for the church had been exemplary, there was no denying that. Walter admired his father's dedication, courage, and sense of mission. Yet he felt diminished by it at the same time.

Now, however, Walter was indeed in charge, as his father had uttered before dying. In all practicality, Walter had been in charge for the past several years, but now his position was even clearer since his father's passing. It was generally understood that he would continue farming, carrying the mail, working on new town roads, shoveling coal at the Town Farm for the poor, and other odd jobs, while Bessie helped her mother with household duties and the daunting job of cleaning out Edwin's things.

Walter remained numb the rest of that year and into the new year. He was not exactly sullen but was void of his usual positive demeanor. This had been going on for too long, his mother decided. One evening in February, Elizabeth, Bessie, and Walter were in the sitting room together, each to their own diversion.

"Son?" Elizabeth said.

"Yes, Ma," Walter said absentmindedly without looking up.

"I want to talk with you and Bessie about something. Bessie, this concerns you only in that I would like your approval." At this, Walter gave his mother his attention. "Walter, I've been giving something a lot of thought lately. You are struggling, that's clear. You wanted to be a minister, like your father, but couldn't. I know that was a terrible disappointment. Now Millie has married another, which I know has been devastating for you as well. With your father's passing, I think it's time for you to move on from this house and these responsibilities. No, no," she said when Walter looked about to speak, "hear me out, please.

With the widow's pension I receive, I can hire help for the farm. I want you to take your own earnings and go on the trip you've always wanted to. Get out of Maine. See this great land of ours. Stretch your horizons while you can, Walter. You may live to regret it if you don't go now. Just give us enough time to hire help and put together what you need for an extended trip. Then Bessie and I will give you a going-away party to send you off properly. Do you approve, Bessie?"

After a long few seconds, Bessie said, "I guess so." She'd been caught off guard with this announcement. She would miss her brother dearly. Did this mean he would be gone for good? She wanted the best for him, of course, so she'd answered affirmatively, believing their mother knew what Walter truly needed. But within the privacy of her own heart, she decided to talk to her brother when they were alone.

"Walter?" Elizabeth said, looking at her son, needing to hear his first thoughts about her suggestion.

"I shall have to think about this, mother. I can't imagine being so far from you and Bessie."

"Yes. Yes, I understand. You think it over. There's no rush."

Bessie and their mother went back to what they had been doing. Walter did not, now that he had something substantial to occupy his mind. He decided to head to the barn.

A few days later, Bessie and Walter found time to talk. Bessie poured out her heart to her beloved sibling, saying that she would miss him terribly but would also fully support whatever he decided to do. She only wanted to know where he might go and how long he might stay. Then she listened intently to what he said back to her.

"You and mother have been the center of this home. You are both such wonderful and supportive women and I couldn't love you more if I tried. Mother has put me in a quandary, though. I want to be with you both to take care of you as best I can. Yet, she knows me well, and she's right when she says I've always wanted to see beyond Maine. You know this too. And she is also right that this is the time to go. You are both well and strong and if Ma can hire workers for the farm, I can let go of everything else. As to where I would go? Well, if I want to see this country, it's an easy choice—I'd go west!" They both chuckled at the obviousness of his answer. "As to how long I would stay, that is harder to answer, my dear sister. I believe what you really want to know is if this would be a sightseeing trip or a chance to begin my life over again. I can't answer that because I don't know. If I leave, I will go with wanderlust in my heart, letting the wind and Providence herself guide me. All I can ask of you is that you trust me to do what's best for me. Can you do that?"

Bessie's answer was a hug and a quiet "yes" in his ear. She didn't hide her tears. They both knew his decision had been made and held one another a moment longer.

The going away party was a happy occasion, so needed after months of heartbreak. Walter hadn't known so many cared about him. He enjoyed every moment, finally bidding his well-wishers goodbye and giving his mother and Bessie a hug for their thoughtfulness and love. He left the next day.

Nineteen

The Journey Begins

Walter stared at the ticket in his hand as if it held magical powers. Maybe it did! He was sitting in Portland's Grand Trunk Station. He could hardly believe he was really going to travel. He'd had difficulty sleeping the night before, what with the cocktail of nerves and excitement coursing through his body. One important thought came from his restlessness, however–he would go see Aunt Amanda in California. Mercy Amanda Harlow was his father's sister whom he had never met. If he could make it out there, she would undoubtedly house him for a time until he decided what to do next.

"Boarding track one, track number one. All aboard train number three bound for Montreal, Canada, and seventeen points between. Have your ticket ready for the conductor to punch. All aboard!"

Walter shivered with excitement as he climbed aboard his train. He would have thought he was too old to be so joyous, but maybe a childhood dream realized brings out childhood elation no matter how old a person is. He sat back against his seat, thinking he might catch a nap but as soon as the train lurched forward, all he wanted to do was watch the city go by, and then the countryside layered with fresh snow. *Plenty of time for napping*, he thought.

Actually, Walter thought about a lot of things as he steamed north and west toward Montreal, his first stopover. He thought about what a long trip it would be to California. When would his money run out? What sorts of jobs might he find to refresh his pockets? He thought about Ma and Bessie and how much they would like to know about his travels. Ah! He realized that if he could find beautiful postcards of the places he visited and send those home, he'd then have an account of his whole trip. He took out the diary he'd packed and the Sheaffer fountain pen he'd been given as a parting gift from Bessie and his mother. He began taking notes of things he thought they would enjoy in a postcard or a letter and added to his list as he went.

It was in Montreal that Walter had to change trains. He decided to stay in the city and look around for a few days. It was dark out when he arrived. He asked a ticket agent for the name of a boarding house or hotel. Nothing fancy, he'd told the agent, and he was willing to walk there if need be. The man said he could recommend one that wasn't too far and the price was reasonable. Walter thanked the man and set out through drifted snow. He found Freemans Hotel easily enough and decided to pay for three nights. Then he went to a recommended restaurant not far away. When he returned to the hotel, he sat in its lobby to simply be among the people coming and going. He derived great pleasure from the possibility of meeting a new friend.

After a while, he searched through the assortment of newspapers in either English or French spread on wooden tables amongst the various couches and chairs. The Montreal Tribune caught his eye. In it he found advertisements about clothing and food and household cleaning products, which were of little use to him other than being mildly interesting. He saw that the Grand Trunk Railroad boasted being the finest and fastest train in Canada and could make the trip to Toronto in only seven and a half hours. He made a mental note of that one. And there was a play at the Princess Theatre being held over that looked interesting. It was called *Bunty Pulls the String*, a comedy with Scottish actors.

Then his eye caught an article about a sermon Father Bernard Vaugn gave recently to a standing room only audience in New York City. Its subject was on the familiar topic of love. This, Walter was very interested in reading. It said, in part:

> *Father Vaugn urged a moe faithful obedience to conscience, which so often urges that we put away the hook which is not good for our spiritual welfare. It whispers to women, "Do not dress so as to bear half of one's bosom, it is not good for the men who are around you," and remonstrates with us against the careless use of cameras with which so many people take "moving pictures of their own creation" that are not uplifting. He said, "Man without love is not a man; woman without love is already dead. Love is so important that if you die without it you go to hell. With it, you go to heaven. A man may bring his bride to the altar and show her his multi-millions, giving her worldly power, but if she is a true wife and cannot command the recesses of his heart, it all goes for nothing."*

Walter quickly closed the paper and returned it to the small table. He was suddenly thinking thoughts of Millie he'd rather not have. He tried to push them away. In his befuddled state of mind, he didn't hear a man to his left give him a greeting. When the man spoke a second time, Walter looked up to see a rather short, rotund man, pleasantly dressed, though not overly so, with balding hair and cheerful eyes, smiling at him and extending a hand. Walter stood, noticing that the man took stock of Walter's superior height, and extended his own hand.

"Walter Harlow," he offered.

"Michael Leroy. Are you new in town?"

"I am, thank you. You?"

"Oh, I'm a permanent fixture around here. Today, I'm putting finishing touches on a new men's club that plans to meet here at Freemans. The Rotary Club. Have you heard of it? It was started in Chicago in '05."

"No, I haven't. What is the club about, if I may ask?"

"Happy you did. It's a group for professional men with diverse backgrounds. We can exchange ideas and form lifelong friendships. And, if I have anything to say about this club of ours, we'll put our heads, hearts, and hands together to make meaningful contributions toward our city's welfare. Sound like something you'd like to be part of Mr. Harlow?"

"It does, though I'm hardly what you'd call a professional man. I'm a simple farmer from Maine. I'm on my way to California."

"If you're a hard-working man and I can tell you must be, you'd fit right in. I'm sorry you won't be staying in Montreal, though. Remember the Rotary Club if you ever come to stay." Mr. Leroy extended his hand once more to bid Walter a good evening and strode off toward an adjacent room.

Walter decided he had best get some much-needed rest. His room wasn't large but neat and tidy in shades of tan and brown. *Tonight I could have slept on a rock*, he chuckled to himself while he took stock of what he'd hurriedly packed. He thought he might write a quick note on the back of one of the postcards he purchased at the front desk. But no sooner had he lifted his pen than he put it down again as though it weighed a thousand pounds. He was asleep as soon as he landed on his bed.

The next morning was gray. Snow was coming again, but it wasn't snowing yet. Walter set out to see the sights. He took the postcards with him to write while he ate his breakfast. The night had done wonders for him. He felt refreshed and renewed. He wrote his first two postcards:

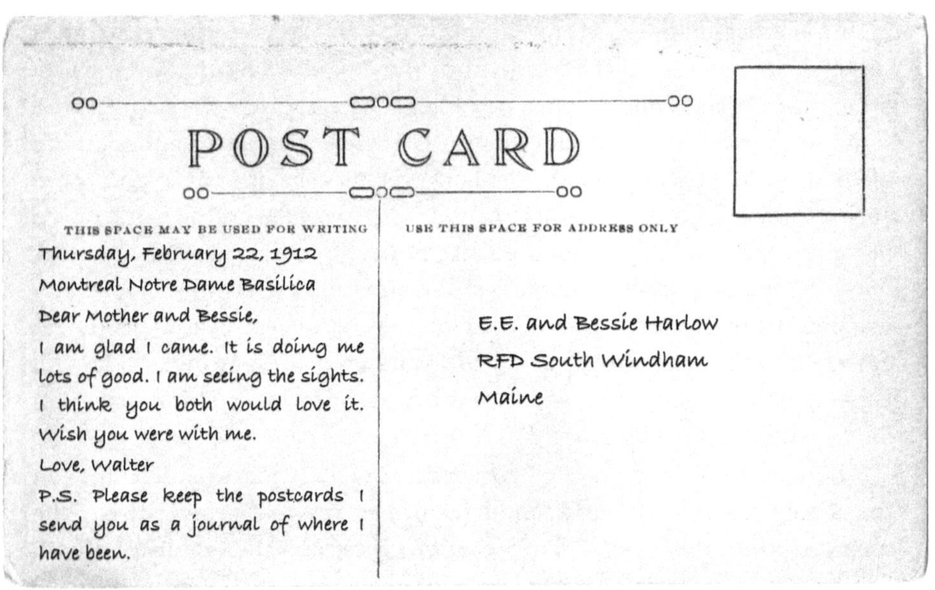

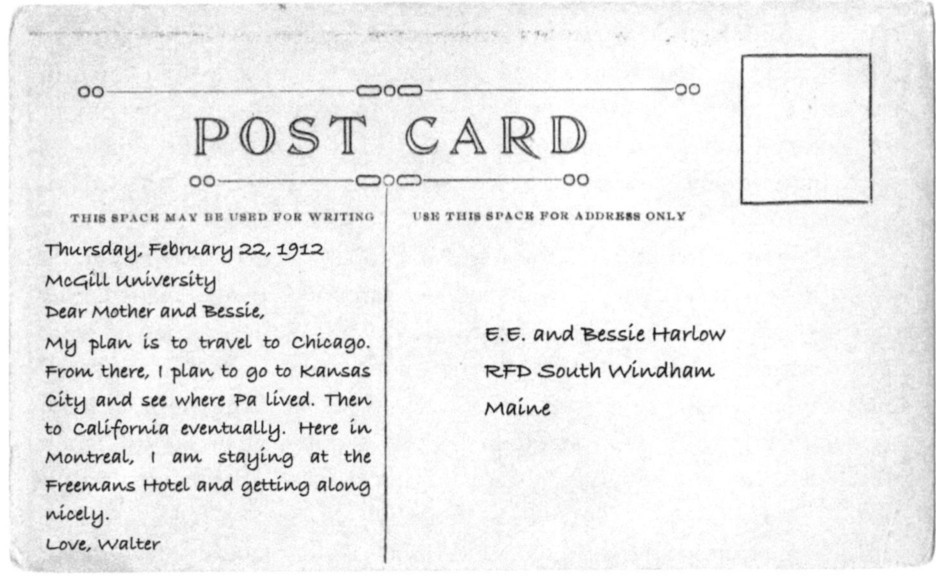

After breakfast he wandered the streets to find a place to post his cards. As he did, he saw a city the likes of which he had never seen before. In some ways it had elements of Portland, with its large metropolitan buildings. Montreal too was a city beside water, though it was the St. Lawrence River instead of the Atlantic Ocean. But in most other ways it was much, much grander. The buildings were taller, and some were much more ornate than in Portland. There were many more of them in Montreal than Walter had ever seen in one place and more varied, as well. Over the course of the next two days, though it snowed off and on, he walked through parks, by new buildings and much older ones. He stepped into the magnificent Montreal New Windsor Hotel and wondered how much it would cost to stay in such a grand place. He dared not ask and tempt himself. He wandered the grounds of McGill University and thought again, with a breath of sadness, about a path in life he would never take.

Sunday morning, Walter had a nine o'clock train to catch. He left the Freemans Hotel early enough to get breakfast and enjoy the architecture of the Grand Trunk Station. It rivaled the one in Portland, he thought, both stunning buildings. When he stepped onto his train for Toronto, he felt enriched and very satisfied with his decision to take this trip. Then he took a seat across from two gentlemen and tipped his hat in greeting.

"Hello," Walter said, offering his hand. "My name is Walter. Walter Harlow. I'm from Maine."

"Hello, I am Friedrich Strang und he is Peter, mine nephew. Vee are on ze way to Nort Dakota where I am living."

"Are you perhaps German?" Walter asked, having had a friend with a similar accent.

"Ja, I am from…ach…*vee are,*" Friedrich looked at Peter beside him, "*vee* are coming bote from Germany. I am living in Milnor since August. I send for Peter from Germany to verk for me."

"What do you do with your land? Are you a…oops…," Walter said, as the train lurched and he shifted in his seat. "A farmer? Rancher? Logger?"

Friedrich laughed out loud, "Not a logger. There exist few trees. I am farmer. I already hope to produce a healthy farm on my tree hundert acres."

"That's wonderful," Walter said with genuine interest. "I am a farmer myself, but by no means on three hundred acres."

"Tell me, vhat about your farm, Valter?"

"It is owned by my family in a small town called South Windham. We have eighteen dairy cows, a couple horses to pull our wagon, our sleigh and the plow, and a few sheep for the wool and hogs for meat. We grow mostly corn and grass for feed. Some wheat. And we have a nice garden so my mother and sister can put up vegetables for winter. It isn't a large farm, but it does nicely."

"Small but goot, ja?"

"It is. It suits us. I have to do other things to make ends meet, though. I deliver rural mail and work with road crews, cutting in new roads or fixing old ones. I'm pretty handy, so the local school hires me to fix this and that. I enjoy the variety in my schedule."

"Is Maine flat, or hilly?" Peter asked, also interested, his English better than Friedrick's.

"Maine does have its mountains up north. Many evergreen trees grow well there. One whole side of Maine is bordered by the Atlantic Ocean with a very rocky coastline. Where we live, I would say the land is hilly. Some say our best crop is rocks! And Maine can be very cold and snowy in the winter. For that reason, many of us have built our homes attached to our barns with connectors so we can get to our livestock and other things there more easily. What is North Dakota like?"

"Ah…ze land is not so hilly, no mountains," Friedrick said, knowing that Peter could not answer this question. "Vinter is same as Germany. But mine land stretches out as far as I can see with no people to see. Much peoples in Germany," Friedrich smiled. Walter wondered why Friedrich had left Germany and if he missed his homeland. But he thought it best not to pry. Friedrich's reasons might not be something he would want to discuss with a stranger.

"Do you love farming?" Walter asked, wondering if farming was all Friedrich did, or if he did other things, too.

"Ja, farming, freedom, adventure. I take Klara, my vife vis me to America to be big farmer. Ve first live in Pennsylvania. Very expensive there. America offers one hundert zixty acres free land in Nort Dakota if I build a house and stay zare. I could afford one hundert forty more acres to make tree hundert. I know some about farming in Germany. Nort Dakota is different. They have somesing called 'Better Farming' at ze Agricultural College in Fargo. I bring Peter here to learn. Ze Agricultural College has…" he spoke in German to Peter who finished his uncle's thought, "courses on ways to be successful at farming in North Dakota."

"Peter's English is better." Peter blushed when Friedrich looked over at him.

"Why do they need such courses?" Walter asked with growing interest.

Peter took over the conversation, "Uncle says that land in North Dakota isn't being used well. It is not as profitable as it might be and many farmers are selling their farms because they can't earn enough to live there. The Agricultural College believes that the farmers may not be growing the right crops and raising the right animals for that state. The courses will teach better methods of farming."

"You interested, Valter? Maybe also buy land zare?"

"Me? No. I am on my way to California to visit my aunt. I may stay there if I find suitable work. But what you say does interest me."

"Do you have a hurry to reach your aunt?"

Walter thought about that a few seconds. "No, I guess not, although I have written her that I hope to see her this spring. I want to stop in Kansas first to locate where my father lived during the War Between the States."

Friedrich looked at Peter. Peter smiled as though understanding something his uncle was thinking but hadn't yet said. "Valter, you are a goot man. And a goot farmer, ya? Help me verk my farm, ya?"

"Oh," Walter said, cradling his chin with the palm of his hand. "Well, I am inclined to say 'no'. But let me think about that."

Twenty

North Dakota

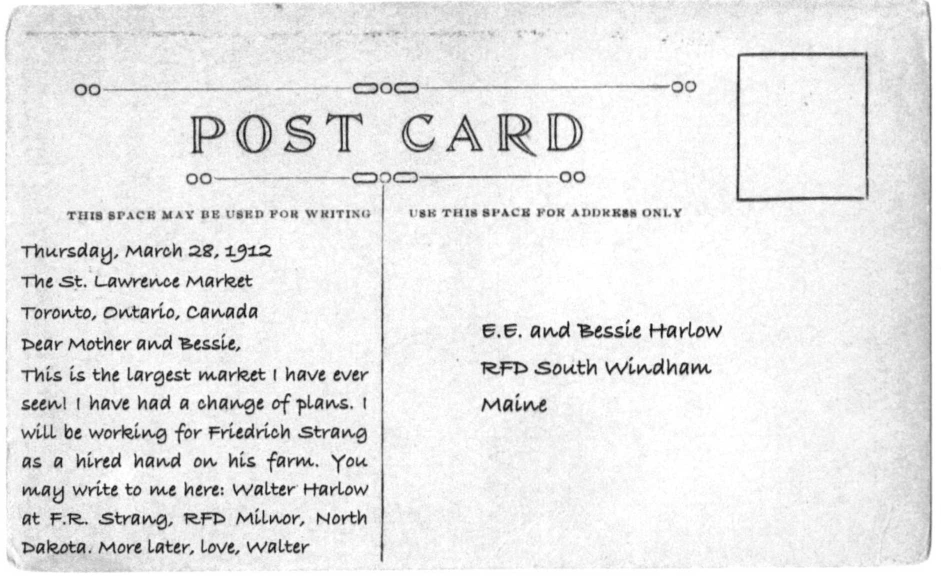

Walter needed to work out how these potential new plans could dovetail with his original plans he had no intention of abandoning. He decided he would work on Friedrich's farm until he could earn enough money to easily continue his journey west. Once Friedrich agreed with Walter's plan, both men felt satisfied and shook hands.

Sunday, April 7, 1912

Dearest mother and Bessie,

I have a little time now to write you a longer letter. I hope this one finds you both well and enjoying the start of spring in Maine. Have you heard the peepers yet? How is the farming carrying on without me?

There is much to tell you in this first letter, but I won't say everything for fear the letter will be too heavy for regular post. I assume you will want to know where I am living and with whom. We came into Milnor on a Northern Pacific train that goes through town. Friedrich's wife, Klara, fetched us with the horse and wagon and the drive to the house wasn't terribly long, maybe five miles. Friedrich and Klara are, I believe, in their late twenties and have no children. They are welcoming Friedrich's nephew, Peter, into their home. He is perhaps eighteen. You may have guessed by the names that they are all German. I can tell you some other time how Friedrich and I met.

Imagine my surprise to see a house like no other. It is called a "soddy" for the sod bricks that make up its walls and roof. One of my first jobs has been to help Peter build additional bedrooms onto the existing house. For now, things are somewhat cramped, so we have the incentive to get on with the project! The soddy is only temporary, Friedrich tells me. It was the quickest way to put a roof over Klara's head. But he is so busy I can't imagine when he will find time to build another home with wood.

The business of farming here is different than in Maine. The land in this southeastern part of North Dakota is wide open, flat to gently rolling, and far-reaching. I love watching the sun spread its rays across the vast fields in the morning. It is enough to take my breath away. They say the cold winds and snow of winter are things to experience, and perhaps only to endure. I may be here long enough for that. If I am, I will let you know if their winter rivals ours at home.

Friedrich hasn't been here long enough to have farmed his three hundred (!) acres. He hopes to begin with a reasonably-sized crop of wheat and maybe oats this year and then to expand next year. He has talked of planting *sugar beets, corn, and potatoes which, of course, I know something about. He may also raise beef cattle. Friedrich is a very intent and driven man with many dreams. I think I shall learn much here.*

This is all my weary wrist and eyes can take. Be well.

Love,
Walter

It was all Walter and Peter could do to get the additions built and help plant the wheat and oats. They fell onto their pallets by sunset. Friedrich prepared the ground for a garden nearer the house that he thought Klara could attend to easily. He decided to test it with sugar beets, sunflowers, and potatoes. If these did well enough, he'd try larger crops next year. He also hoped to send Peter to the Agricultural College in Fargo after the harvest. He was sure his nephew would come back with important knowledge.

When it was time to put the roof on the additions, Walter and Peter cut the sod into the same rectangular bricks they'd used for the walls in just the right thickness to include the prairie grass roots. To create a surface on which to lay the bricks, they interwove the sticks and branches they'd been harvesting from the few trees in the area. Once they'd secured this lattice to the tops of the walls, they laid large pieces of bark upon the sticks. Then they could begin laying the bricks side by side, grass side down with another perpendicular layer of bricks on top of the first, grass side up. As the roots intertwined and the sod settled and weathered, the roof would be reasonably water tight. Walter had yet to know how much warmth such a structure would afford them in winter.

Meanwhile, Walter's mother and Bessie waited anxiously for news from North Dakota. They had received his postcards from Montreal. They were thrilled and relieved to hear that his decision to travel, at Elizabeth's prompting, was going well and they traveled vicariously with him. Then came the postcard from Toronto with news that had surprised them. They could not imagine him in North Dakota and had no idea what things were like for him or what he was doing until his

April letter was in their hands. Waiting could be very difficult, so they were grateful their schedules were busy.

By this time, they had new information about Millie and wondered if he would want to know about her at all. It was Bessie who finally decided they should not mention anything about Millie unless he asked.

Sunday, April 21, 1912

Dearest Walter,

How happy you made us when we received your recent letter. We are well, though heartsick missing you, of course. The peepers have begun their singing! And the foliage is the beautiful light green of spring with leaves the softness of a baby's ear.

Bessie and I oversee the farming but 'tis Abel Watson and Roy Young who keep the place running. I am well pleased with the quality of their work. I must confess Roy can be lazy. He prefers talk to work. I see Abel pushing him along. At least Roy is a kind soul. They are both good to your sister and me.

Your change of plans surprised us both but we are happy if you are. I can hardly imagine what three hundred acres of land looks like without trees to block the view. And the "soddy" you speak of sounds so different as to be in another country.

Cora is no better and remains in the insane hospital, poor dear. Reverend Aikins keeps a gallant smile but I take him food now and then. Ellen is such great help to her father, from what her siblings say.

I don't know how you receive your news and I don't necessarily want to be the bearer of such. But it is disastrous enough that likely you have heard about the dreadful sinking of the luxury ship, Titanic. It was so very close to its destination and not so terribly far from here. We've heard that over half of the passengers died in the icy waters. I most certainly pray they did not suffer.

I am sure Friedrich is happy to have such an apt set of hands and good mind as yours to aid him. Tell him hello from Bessie and me, although, of course, he doesn't know us.

All our love,
Ma

One Sunday evening in May, Walter and the Strangs sat outside while the sun appeared to lower itself toward a horizon it knew not. They spoke of news such as the *Titanic* sinking, as well as the political struggles in Germany. Walter surmised from putting pieces of conversation together that Friedrich had wanted a big farm, and, because it seemed unlikely that he could find affordable land in Germany, they'd moved to Pennsylvania as many other Germans had. The fact that there was growing political unrest in his homeland sealed Friedrich's decision.

After a lull in the conversation, Klara asked Peter something in German. He translated, "Do you have a sister or brother?"

Walter had preferred not to talk about himself yet. He would answer any questions they might ask, but opening the subject of the life he'd left behind was something he preferred not to do. The ghosts of his past had been tucked away so that he might forge ahead without them. He wasn't exactly sure what he might say and how much. Finally, he said, "Yes. I can show you what my family looks like better than tell you. Just a moment."

They watched with curiosity as he walked to where he found a stick. Returning, he proceeded to draw in the clay topsoil a diagram of his family that he thought would be better understood than mere words. He drew a rough outline of the United States. Then he looked up to see if they understood what he'd drawn. They had. So he drew in and marked Maine, Kansas, and North Dakota. With his stick, he drew a line from Maine to Kansas and labeled the line with the names Edwin and Eliza Ann Harlow and Lincoln and Hattie Harlow. He said, as he traced the line, that his father Edwin and his uncle Lincoln, together with their wives, traveled this long distance to be missionaries during the war, from

1863 to 1865. He waited for Peter to translate this for Klara. Then Walter marked California and drew another long line from Kansas to the Pacific Ocean. On this line he marked Lincoln and Hattie Harlow and explained that Lincoln preferred to press on to California and, loving it, had stayed.

Going back to Kansas on his map, Walter replaced "1865" with "1871," then added Edwin and Eliza Ann's three daughters, Cora, Myrtie, and Persis. Though his audience was patiently following Walter's drawing, he tried to speed things up for fear of losing them altogether. He drew a circle, a sort of lasso, around the group of five names to indicate his father's family. Then, drawing a line from the lassoed circle back toward Maine, he told them that Eliza Ann was too ill to stay any longer in Kansas and the whole family moved back home. There, he redrew the five names in the soil. Again, he waited for Peter's translation.

Next, he scratched out Eliza Ann's name and told them she had died in 1873. He added the name Elizabeth to the circle of five in Maine. He explained that Elizabeth had been Eliza Ann's nurse, and the two women had become very close friends. Later, Elizabeth and Edwin married and had Walter and Bessie, whose names he then added to the growing circle. This took longer for Peter to translate while Walter waited.

"So," he finished, "Cora, Myrtie, and Persis are my half-sisters. Bessie is my full sister. I have four sisters and no brothers."

Satisfied that he had adequately explained the complicated situation, he sat back to let his information sink in. Klara asked Peter to translate, "Do you all love each other no matter what mother you had?"

Walter smiled broadly, nodded, and said, "Yes, we do."

Klara seemed satisfied and asked Walter no other personal questions. Her smile spoke for her, and Walter had a very good feeling that he had gained a close friend in the woman.

That night, in the dark of his new bedroom, he lay awake. Speaking of his family was just a step away from thinking of the misfortunes of his dashed dreams, foremost of which was the pain of losing Millie. That pain which he'd successfully tucked away was now staring him in the face, taunting him, stirring something so deep inside him it made him ache. He curled his body on top of his blanket, protecting his heart, lungs, and belly with the backbone he failed to detect. His body felt like jelly, a mass of tormented tissue, a belly at war with itself, little effectiveness left in his lungs, and a heart as deflated as a child's rubber ball. And then he allowed himself to shed the tears he'd kept at bay.

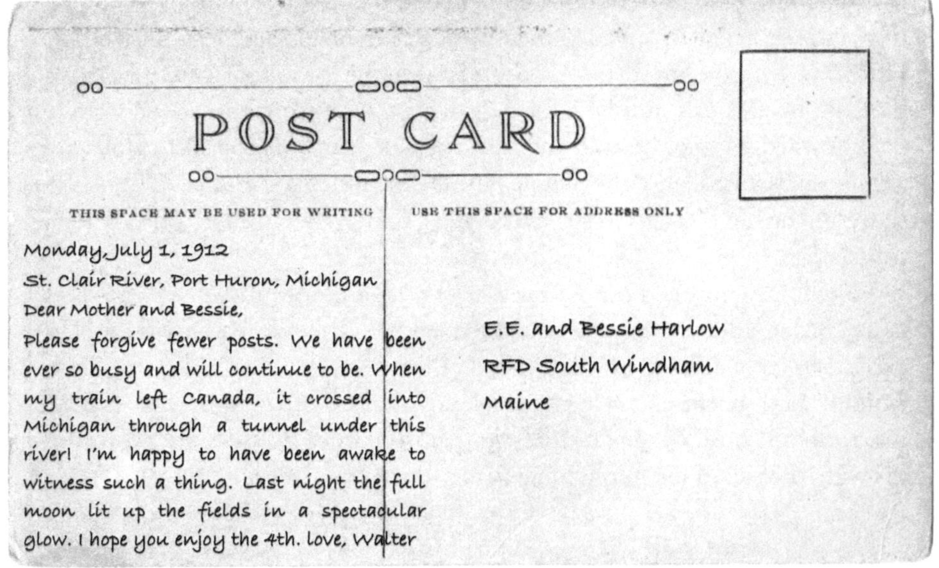

By the end of July, Friedrich and Klara were seeing returns on their sugar beets and potatoes. And the sunflowers were growing by the day. All this pleased the young couple, but it was the wheat that worried them, the crop that Friedrich had counted on. The oats, too, looked less than hardy. But it was still early so perhaps the crops would yield well in the end. Besides, Klara had news that couldn't help but buoy them all. She was with child and was ecstatic.

"Valter," said Friedrich one day, "you had milk cows, ya?"

"Yes."

"Now that my Klara is blessed in ze family way, I vant a cow. You vill help me vis cow, ya?"

"Yes, of course," Walter said enthusiastically. He enjoyed knowing he could help.

By the time harvesting was finished, Klara's belly was blooming, Friedrich and Walter were busy building a shelter for the cow, and Peter had begun attending classes in Fargo, which he could easily get to by train. Already, Peter was able to tell his uncle that the kind of wheat he had planted was bound to produce a meager crop. It wasn't hearty enough for the soil in southeastern North Dakota or the quick turn to cold weather. Durum wheat, he learned, would fare much better, or hard, red spring wheat. And barley, rather than oats for more yield. Still, their crops had done well enough to trade for a butter churn, and a few things the baby would need.

Friedrich and Walter went to look at a neighbor's middle-aged Holstein cow that didn't produce as much milk as the owner wanted it to. The farmer asked for a price that Friedrich could manage in payments. Walter looked the older cow over to make sure it was otherwise healthy. It was gratifying to Walter that he knew what to look for so that he could be especially helpful. Friedrich bought the cow. Once "Bossie" was settled in her shelter, Walter taught Friedrich how to successfully milk a cow that didn't know him. They gave the cow some feed to keep her mind occupied. Then he had Friedrich talk soothingly to Bossie while running his hand over her ribs and flank and finally her bag, always being mindful of her back legs. He showed Friedrich the milking procedure, then left to do other work. Apparently, all had gone well until Bossie kicked the bucket accidentally and the precious white liquid streamed all over the ground in every direction. What Friedrich said, as he passed by Walter, shaking his head, was an unhappy utterance in German. All Walter could do was assure Friedrich the cow would need to be milked in another twelve hours or so.

Sunday, March 2, 1913

Dear Mother and Bessie,

The long wait is over. Klara had a little boy this past Tuesday. And guess what they have named him? Walter! I am so honored. He looks like a strapping little thing and Klara is holding her own, though she is weak. After so many issues over the winter, what with Bossie having to be put down from an infection, if you remember, the snowstorms testing our dwelling, and Klara having to be in bed much of the time, everyone is very grateful for this healthy child, as you can imagine. I am happy to begin this letter with good news for a change.

You said in your last letter that a man is making waterproof boots right near you in Freeport. You said you could mail some to me. I guess I could have used them here this winter but I'm not sure how long I will stay, and I prefer not to carry them around with me when I leave. So, I'll say "no" for now.

Speaking of winter, I guess I can rightly say that winters here are not so very different than at home. There is one difference, however. Because it is so open and relatively flat here, the wind is enough to blow a person over. There isn't much to break its course. And it picks up topsoil along the way too. If I read the sky correctly, we are due for another storm soon.

Donald MacMillan, the explorer, was mentioned in the local newspaper! One of Maine's own is famous it seems. Actually, I'm not sure he was born in Maine. Do you know? But he taught in Great Falls, so he feels to me like one of our own.

I don't know when I will leave here, as I say. With the new baby and all that Friedrich is trying to handle, I hope to help him through this year's planting and harvesting seasons. Peter is fine help but another set of hands couldn't hurt.

Missing you both,
Walter

That spring, Peter mapped out a plan for the crops he had learned might fare better in their part of North Dakota. It included widening the boundaries of last year's crops. A new cow had been purchased, one that was younger than Bossie had been. Little Walter was doing well, and Klara was gaining strength every day, loving the spring weather and the chance to get outside. By mid-summer's harvest time, it was evident that Peter's suggestions were well-founded. And by mid-October, the bumper crop had afforded Friedrich not only enough money to pay off the cost of the cow and other loans but also to pay Walter a healthy sum.

Considering all this, Walter felt ready to move on, though he had developed a heart for the Strang family and their land. He'd learned a lot and taught a lot as well. It occurred to him that he could stay and make a life for himself in North Dakota, and perhaps he would return to it after seeing Aunt Amanda in California.

"Thank you, Peter," Walter said, shaking Peter's hand. "It has been a pleasure working with you." Then he turned to Klara who handed him young Walter. He gave the eight-month-old a kiss on his rosy, round cheek. "I shall miss watching you grow up," Walter said, giving the child a little poke in the boy's soft belly to make him giggle. He handed little Walter to Peter so that he could give Klara a hug. "Thank you for your hospitality, Klara," he said, and when he broke the hug and looked into her eyes, he saw that she looked confused. So, he amended his statement, saying, "Thank you for such good food. Good care." This she understood and nodded, smiling.

Crawling up into the waiting wagon, Walter waved. He noticed that Klara's eyes were full and he smiled warmly. He would miss this family. On the way to Milnor, he and Friedrich talked about farm business and Walter's next stop in Kansas. Then Friedrich said something that took Walter by surprise. "Klara vatches you since you talk to us about your family. She thinks you are maybe sad. She vonders if you left Maine because of sadness. I did not say someting before. But now I vonder ze same thing."

Walter already felt a measure of grief at leaving this lovely little family. But answering this question would be very difficult. He thought about just not answering. But Friedrich had become something of a brother to Walter and he decided he owed this man at least something of the truth.

"Klara is right. I did leave Maine in sadness." He explained how he had tried but couldn't become a minister like his father. He said that Millie's rejection had been devastating. And that his father's death had left a considerable hole in this heart. He told Friedrich that because he'd always had wanderlust and loved living in different places as a child, he'd considered leaving the farm after his father died. But he knew that his mother and Bessie could not farm their land without him.

"But ten you *did* leave, ja?"

"Yes, because my mother believed it would be best for my mental health to get away and my sister didn't argue with that. I admire my mother a great deal for having been willing to see me off and not know if I'd come back. She is a very strong woman."

"Ja, like my own mutter," Friedrich added quietly. "Now dat we haf little Valter, I see better how hard it vould be to leaf a child."

When they reached the train station, Walter reached out a hand to shake, but Friedrich pulled him into a quick embrace. "Danke, Valter. You haf been a great help to mine family. Geh mit Gott," which Walter understood.

Twenty-one

Kansas

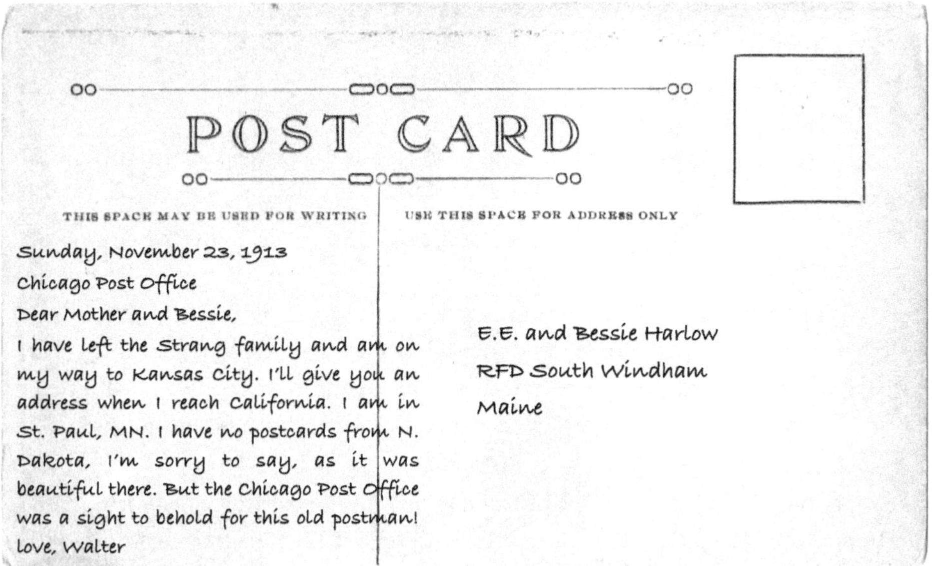

Sunday, November 23, 1913
Chicago Post Office
Dear Mother and Bessie,
I have left the Strang family and am on
my way to Kansas City. I'll give you an
address when I reach California. I am in
St. Paul, MN. I have no postcards from N.
Dakota, I'm sorry to say, as it was
beautiful there. But the Chicago Post Office
was a sight to behold for this old postman!
Love, Walter

E.E. and Bessie Harlow
RFD South Windham
Maine

Walter had nothing but time as he rode mile after mile on the rails. Friedrich had dropped him off in Milnor. He took the Northern Pacific east to Wahpeton, North Dakota, where he switched to the Chicago, Milwaukee, and St. Paul Railway southeast to St. Paul, Minnesota. From there he continued southeasterly to Sabula, Iowa, enchanted and awed by the mighty Mississippi River that chased the train a fair distance. He changed trains to head west to Cedar Rapids, then changed again to make the final journey southwest to Kansas City, Missouri.

Walter was not sure what his plan might be once he got there. He knew he wanted to see where his father and first wife had been missionaries. He'd always felt a certain mystique in the story about his sisters being born so far from Maine with the calamities of war surrounding them. By comparison, his beginnings seemed pale. But his first order of business was to find a place to eat a hot meal and bed down for the night. He would sort out the rest in the morning.

It was cold and blustery the next day, but the sun was bright. As Walter ate a hearty breakfast, he counted out the last of his money. If he wanted to get to California, he'd need to find work. The first place he thought of was a church. He asked a kindly soul where the nearest church was.

"Which denomination do you favor, sir?"

"Which ones do you have?"

"We have all sorts. Would you be looking for a protestant church or Catholic?"

"Protestant. Maybe a Congregational church or United Church of Christ?"

"Yes, sir," the man said pointing in an easterly direction. "There's a Christian church down Independence Boulevard, which is two streets that way," he said, pointing south. "If you take that east about two miles, you'll find the church on the corner of Gladstone Avenue. Can't miss it."

"Thank you, sir," Walter said, nodding.

Cold or not, it felt good to stretch his long legs after riding the train for so long. He pulled his coat a little tighter around his neck and headed out the restaurant door. He prayed God was along for the ride to open the next door.

The kindly man was right that this church couldn't be missed. It was massive compared to his little country church. It filled nearly a whole block. Made of gray stone, it stood three stories tall, with a rotunda dome in the center of what he presumed was the sanctuary. He climbed eight steps to the six, two-story ionic columns, and four more to the sizable porch. It looked like a Greek temple. Walter stood in front of four enormous doors feeling very small and pulled on one of them, which thankfully gave way. He walked into the sanctuary and stopped, completely transfixed. It seemed cavernous so he dared not make a sound for fear he might disturb someone with its swelling echoes. The enormous windows were heavenly, biblical scenes in leaded, stained glass. So enamored was he that he didn't hear someone walk up behind him.

"May I help you?" asked the clergyman.

"Oh!" Walter said, startled. "Yes. Thank you."

Before he could say more, the man offered him a pew and said, "I'm Reverend Brooks. You may call me John."

"Thank you, John. I'm not sure where to begin, frankly. My name is Walter Harlow. I am from Maine and am on my way to California."

It was Reverend Brooks's turn to look surprised. "That's quite a long way. Why did you stop in Kansas City?"

"My father came here during the civil war as a missionary for the Christian church after he graduated from Bangor Theological Seminary. I wanted to see where he served, if I could."

"BTS? I thought about going there. Was his name Edwin?"

"Yes!" It was hard not to be excited about making this connection with a stranger.

"I know about his ministry here. He was long gone by my time. But those missionaries during the war made an impact on me as a young lad. Reason I became a minister, actually. They were very brave. Things here were dangerously tumultuous. Especially for the women and children, and especially here in this border town. Most Missourians were sympathetic to the southern cause and most Kansans sympathized with the north. These people were neighbors, you understand. Sometimes even families separated by the state line. They knew each other, but the battle between them was real and harsh.

"Back in 1830, there was a Reverend Thomas Johnson who started the Shawnee Methodist Mission not far from here to teach Indian boys and girls. It was sorely needed. And Johnson was very influential. Then came the war. Johnson had been pro-slavery before the war but signed a Unionist pledge when the war began. One day, he simply opened the front door to someone knocking and he was shot and killed right then and there. They never did determine who killed him. Did your father never mention this? He would have been here then."

"No, sir, he didn't. Is the mission still open?"

"No, it closed during the war. But the buildings aren't far from here, if you'd like to see them. In fact, let me take you on a bit of a tour. Would that suit you?"

"That's very kind of you. But I don't mind walking."

"Well, it isn't every day I meet someone from Maine! I'd love to talk with you some more. But first, you seem to like our little sanctuary here," John laughed at his joke. "Let me show you around. It was built in '05, so it hasn't been here long. I feel privileged to serve this fine church."

Sunday, December 7, 1913

Dear Mother and Bessie,

Greetings this Christmastide. Friday, on the kindness of a stranger, I walked to the Independence Boulevard Christian Church to continue my search in this area. It would be difficult for me to adequately tell you about the church in great detail. Suffice it to say, it is an immense and beautiful structure on the outside. I was given a tour of the inside by the Reverend John Brooks, who knew about father's missionary work here! The sanctuary is circular, and he told me that it can hold 1,200 people! Can you imagine that? It was decked out in festive Christmas hangings and bows and lit by an overhead dome. The service this morning was wonderful.

Rev. Brooks, or John as he asked me to say, offered to show me not only the church, but also the Kansas City area. He told me some of the history here which included incidents that took place while father was here. It was obvious by his stories that father was indeed brave to come here during the war and begin his family. I told him that Cora, Myrtie, and Persis were born in Kansas City, Grasshopper Falls, and Wyandotte respectively. He took me to see Wyandotte but not Grasshopper Falls because it was too far away. He did tell me, though, that Grasshopper Falls is now called Valley Falls. If you have specific questions for me, write them down and send them to me when I am at a more permanent address.

John catered not only to my desires to see where father and Aunt Amanda were but also suggested some work I might do to earn my fare to California. He also invited me to his home for Christmas dinner if I am still in Kansas City then. God has certainly shone down upon me, and I am most grateful.

I pray your holidays are festive and warm.

I miss you both,
Walter

The Kansas City stockyards, according to Reverend Brooks, was a good place to work if a person wanted temporary employment that paid a decent wage. "But," he warned, "it isn't easy work and not for the faint of heart. But since you, Walter, are a farm boy, it might suit you."

Walter made use of the streetcar the very next day and walked into the hiring office. Jobs were indeed available. With more than twenty thousand employees, many of whom worked mindless, back-breaking, physical labor, there tended to be a lot of turnover. Walter could practically pick any of the grunt-labor jobs and begin immediately. There were mostly cattle, but also pigs, sheep, horses, and mules that numbered approximately seventy thousand total animals being processed a day. He could be a knocker, hitting the animals with a sledgehammer, rendering them unconscious, after which a man attached the animal's hind legs to a hoist and then lifted it onto an overhead conveyor belt. The sticker sliced the throat so that the animal bled out. Several knifemen removed the animal's hide after which a header beheaded it. Next, the gut-snatcher took out the intestines, and a kidney puller removed the other internal organs. Splitters sliced down the backbone, cutting the carcass in two and then the backers, grinders, trimmers, cheekers, pullers, and luggers processed the rest of the meat. But entry-level workers such as Walter moved carcasses, cut off tails or horns, and mopped up blood.

Truthfully, Walter wasn't sure he could handle the gore and the sheer gruesome nature of the job. But he needed the money, and he was ultimately familiar with the seamier side to farming. He took an entry-level job. His days were long and hard, and the sights and smells threatened to undo him at times, but the pay was adequate and he met interesting men there. Many of the people Walter worked with knew only broken English. He heard Irish, French, German, Dutch, Italian, Norwegian, Danish, and Welsh. The Australians, Canadians, and Scotsmen spoke English understandably, if their accent wasn't too thick. Workers from Russia, Bulgaria, Poland, and other eastern European nations were also represented in this microcosm of the world. Meeting new people was Walter's favorite part of the job and a whole day could go by as he listened to words he didn't understand and talked with people he could. He simply dared not think too much about what was happening to the poor, senseless animals who streamed into the stockyard on trains by the thousands every day, not knowing their fate. Walter knew the limits of his sensitive nature.

Thursday, December 25, 1913

Dear Mother and Bessie,

Merry Christmas! I am imagining the Christmas service you are undoubtedly attending. And the Christmas pudding I hope you are eating for me in my absence.

I am better than when I wrote last. My cold persists in a light cough but that is all. I am still working at the stockyard, although if it weren't for the people I've met there, I'm not certain I would still be there. It surely isn't something I would do for as many years as most of the others have. But then, they have families to feed and the necessity of steady work keeps them going.

I am getting to know this city by taking the trolley car on Sundays. You asked what shops are in this town. I walked by the cutest little milliner's shop, Bessie. I saw a pink bonnet in the window display that I can imagine you wearing for Easter, though that's a holiday we must wait some time for, isn't it? And mother, I think you would enjoy the small whatnot shops just to browse. I saw several lovely pieces on which you could display your books and curiosities. I know how you enjoy little decorations.

I will mail this tomorrow. I am going to John's Christmas service now. Be well and happy.

Love,
Walter

P.S. Happy New Year, in case I don't get a chance to write again soon.

Walter attended Reverend Brooks's church regularly and enjoyed meeting new people there as well. Sometimes, he naturally fell into ministering to people when he recognized their grief or other sadnesses. Reverend Brooks even called upon Walter to see sick people if he had too many to see himself. Walter became deeply indebted to John's understanding that caring for people helped fill the deep ache he carried within.

Finally, with the better weather of early spring came the opportunity to spend longer days hunting for the birthplaces of his sisters. Cora's was easy–within the city itself. Wyandotte, where Persis was born, was also not far. But Valley Falls was some sixty-five miles, a distance best covered by train. Walter took stock of his earnings. He decided he could afford to go on to California and would do so after a short stop in Valley Falls to locate Myrtie's birthplace. He made a point of seeing his new friends, especially Reverend Brooks, to say goodbye and to thank them for their kindnesses. Walter began to feel that as quickly as he'd made new friends, he was losing them all across the nation. He would have to stay connected by letter.

After seeing his boss at the stockyard to collect the last of his pay, Walter went to the train station to purchase a ticket on the Union Pacific to Denver, Colorado. He would change trains there and travel to Cheyenne, Wyoming, and then Ogden, Utah. In Ogden, he would need to go by Southern Pacific to Virginia City, Nevada, then to Sacramento, California, and finally San Francisco. From there he'd learn the best way to travel north to Fortuna, in Humbolt County. He decided one last postcard to his family could be mailed along the way.

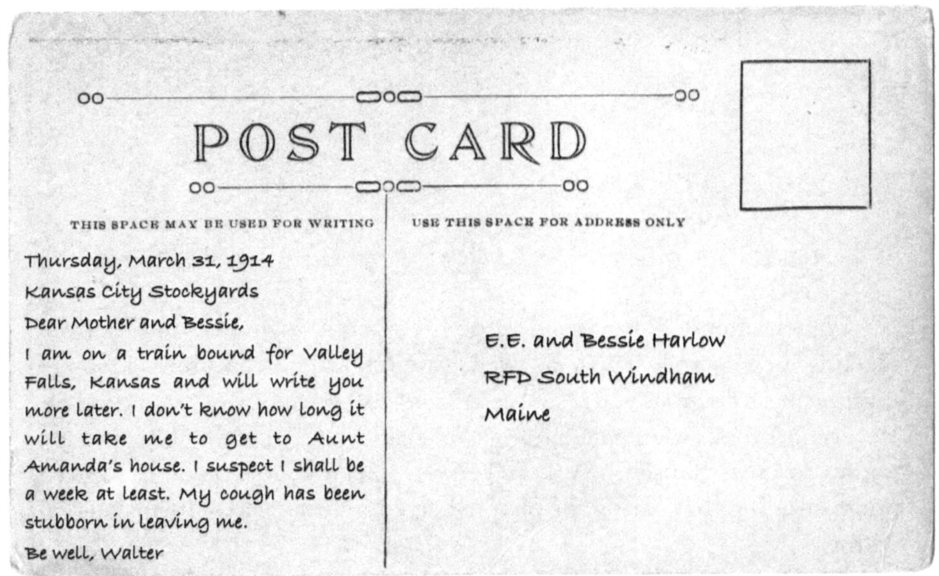

Walter's short deviation to the small town of Valley Falls was worth it. He found a small restaurant—the only one in town—and inquired about a place to stay the night. When he asked about the town's history during the Civil War, he was directed to a man who was "a walking history book" and spent a lovely afternoon being shown around, all the while hearing tales of yesteryear.

"I can't help ya much finding the house your sister woulda been born in if ya don't have an address. Chances are it's still here, though, unless a tornado took it out. Or the grasshoppers ate it!" The town historian laughed. "See, that's why the town's name changed. It was first named for the falls on Grasshopper River. The first settlers realized that those falls could power a mill. After the grasshopper plague in about 1874 that 'bout wiped out a third of the crops in this part of the US of A and Canada's as well, the town kinda figured nobody'd wanna come live here if they thought we were still covered in grasshoppers. So, the river got a new name, the Delaware, after the Indians 'round here. They renamed the town a couple of times and then finally decided on Valley Falls. Guess it sounded nice, like people'd wanna live in a town named Valley Falls."

"Any idea where my father might have had a ministry here during the war?" Walter said, followed by a coughing fit.

"Well, I can tell ya there would have been a great need for prayin' men around here. If I had to guess, because I don't know for sure, I'd say it was probably in one of the churches. See, Kansas has been known as 'Bleedin' Kansas' because of the violence between the pro-slavery and the anti-slavery peoples in the late '50s. By war time, the feuds mostly became battles. Ever hear of the Lawrence Massacre?"

"Can't say I have." Walter tried to stifle what by now was an inevitable cough.

"Happened 'bout thirty-five miles south of here in Lawrence. Y'see, Kansas was officially a Union state, but a lot of folks had slaves. So, Kansas saw a lot o' fightin' even before the war started. In '63 there was this band of Confederate commandos who just took off on their own under Colonel William Quantrill. They had some four hundred fifty of 'em who ambushed that town an' killed about 180 unarmed men 'n' boys and destroyed 'bout two hundred buildings too. Awful, just awful. What's more, Frank and Jesse James–you've heard of *them*, I presume– well, those two were mere boys when they were in that band of marauders and got a taste of outlawin'. We all know what *they* did for a living 'n' how they met their end."

"So, what could one man, like my father, do to help with all that?" Walter coughed into his handkerchief.

"Say, are you alright?"

"Yes. Pardon my cough. It's left over from a cold I've been trying to get over. Please, go on. What could one man do against so much unrest?"

"Soldiers need churchin' too, ya know. I expect he held services 'n' prayer meetings. He likely was called on to pray over the dead and wounded on battle fields and make-shift hospitals nearby. They'd take anyone who could help deliver medical supplies and even provide simple medical services. My guess is he would'a been a very busy man out here."

They were back at the restaurant where they'd started, and Walter thanked the man and walked to the boarding house. It wasn't long before he was in a room and fast asleep. The next day on the train he penned a letter home.

Thursday, April 2, 1914

Dear Mother and Bessie,

Greetings from on board the train again. I will assume with great hope that you are both doing well. I have to say that my cough persists, although I think it is some better today after a decent night's sleep.

I just visited Valley Falls and I'm glad I did. I learned that not only did the grasshoppers or locusts eat the crops and trees, but sometimes they ate food and carpets and clothing inside farmers' homes. The insects were piled a foot high in places and to get enough food they sat on sheep and ate the wool right off them. They ate the harnesses off horses, paint off wagons, and even ate pitchfork handles! As if farming wasn't hard enough! They polluted the water and sometimes caused trains to lose traction as they rolled over so many of them. I guess one settler at the time said that when they looked up at the sun, there were millions of them in the air and they looked like snowflakes. Personally, I'll take real snow over that horror.

I was given a tour by a nice fellow who told me enough about what the missionaries did during the war to make me mighty proud of father. And in truth, I feel a little ashamed that I haven't been as brave. Can't be helped now.

The woman who ran the boarding house where I spent the night had a small picture of Susan B. Anthony on the wall. She said that Anthony spent six months near Kansas City helping her sister while campaigning for suffrage. If all states are as anxious to ratify women to vote as Maine and apparently Kansas are, I should think you both will be voting soon.

I have prattled on long enough. The next city I shall see is Denver, Colorado. This is most certainly a vast and beautiful country. I am so glad to have come on this journey.

All my love,
Walter

Twenty-two

Pneumonia

Walter knew himself as a man who could make friends with a skunk if need be, but as he closed his letter, it occurred to him that he had no interest in making friends with the few people on his train car. He was grateful for a bench seat to himself. He had to backtrack to Leavenworth, Kansas, then change trains and buy a ticket to Denver, Colorado. The longer he sat, the more he realized he was feeling worse by the minute. He guessed that since he had suddenly stopped the fierce activity of the past months, his body was finally demanding the attention it should have gotten long ago. Somehow, he managed to get his ticket and board the train. All he needed to do was get to Aunt Amanda and she would take care of him, he was sure.

The cough he'd had with him for weeks was not getting better, as he'd led his mother and sister to believe. If his relentless bark was annoying to himself, he was sure his fellow passengers weren't happy about it either. On top of the cough, he felt achy and cold. The better part of wisdom told him he should get off the train and seek help, but where would he go? He knew no one in Leavenworth. Besides, his body felt like lead and all he wanted to do was lean against the cold window and shut his eyes. Even sleep eluded him as his cough woke him time after time.

From several seats down, one woman had been watching him with eyes that were knowing, though not judging; compassionate, yet detached. She sat with another woman, who looked to be her twin. This other woman was not interested in anything but her lap on which lay a thick piece of drawing paper. In her hand was a pencil.

"Anna," Alice said, giving her sister a nudge. "Look at that man down the aisle, the one who can't get his cough under control."

"Hmmm?" Anna said, not looking.

"That man there, I think he may be really sick. I wonder why he would be on a train? He certainly can't feel well. Would he be traveling to a doctor miles away all by himself?"

"Uh-huh," Anna grunted, disinterested in anything but what held her currently captive.

"I'm going to go ask him if he's okay. I'll be right back."

"Alright." Still, Anna paid no attention to her sister's concern.

Alice wasn't sure she should get involved, even to this small degree, but her background in situations like this sometimes made her as relentless as the man's cough. She slid onto the bench facing Walter who stared blankly out his window, not noticing her at all.

"Sir? Sir?" she said with growing concern. "Sir, are you alright?" Alice decided that if the man didn't answer soon, she was going to find help.

"Yes?" Walter said, coughing as though his one-word response had been poison to be rid of. Alice winced at the sound.

"Sir, what is your name?"

He answered, barely above a whisper, yet his breath fogged the window. Alice couldn't make out what he'd said and asking him again got her no further.

When he finally faced her, she saw a middle-aged, too-thin man dressed in aged clothing, his unshaven face slightly flushed and somewhat sweaty. He looked too tall to be folded into his seat. *Fever*, she thought to herself. *This man needs help.*

"Sir, may I get you a cold rag and some water?"

"Yes," Walter said without his usual humility, and not looking at Alice but at something only he could see. *He is without any affect at all,* Alice thought grimly.

She rose quickly from her seat and walked through the cars until she found the conductor. She was slightly winded by the time she found him. Her words shot forth explosively, "I am a nurse and you have a passenger in my car who needs a doctor as soon as possible. And where can I get water for him and a cold, wet rag, please?"

Then, without waiting for an answer, she told the conductor to follow her back to Walter. Her insistence stunned him into compliance. On the way, he pointed to the water receptacle with its paper cone cups and muttered something about having no rags.

Standing beside Walter's bench, the conductor said, "Sir, I'm the conductor on this train. This woman here is a nurse. She believes you might need a doctor's help." But Walter only moaned softly coughing weakly.

"Ma'am," the conductor said to Alice, nodding for her to follow him to the rear of the car, "I believe you're right. I am going to signal the engineer right now to make the next stop. I'll alert him of this situation then. But I would advise waiting until Topeka to get this man the help he needs. They will have resources the smaller towns don't have." He reached up and gave the cord above the windows three quick pulls. "Can you sit with the man until Topeka?" Alice nodded. "And if you see his ticket, let me know where his destination is. I need to go back to my job, but please come and find me if you need more help."

Alice went back to her seat to fetch her things. She put her hand on her sister's shoulder until Anna looked up. "Anna, I need to sit down there," she said, pointing, "with that sick man. Stay here. If he's contagious, I don't need you getting sick too."

Anna took her eyes off Alice to look down the aisle at the man who did indeed look quite ill. "Oh, Alice. He doesn't look well at all." Alice rolled her eyes at her sister.

"Listen to me, Anna. The conductor told me that I can get off the train in Topeka to find an escort for the man that will get him medical help. Then I'll get back on the train. So, sit tight for now, please."

"I will," Anna assured. "Please be careful."

Then Alice filled a cup with water at the cooler and wet down her clean hanky. She covered her nose and mouth with the hanky she'd been using, then went to Walter and did her best to nurse a man whose name she didn't know, who was too ill to know he needed help.

In Topeka, after all the other passengers had been detrained, the conductor stopped anyone new from getting in Walter's car until he was in the station. After explaining the circumstances to the station manager, the conductor suggested that Walter be taken immediately to the Santa Fe Hospital by cab. But there was no escort and Alice could not, in good conscience, let Walter go to the hospital alone in his condition. Since the train was not due to depart for another hour, Alice decided she could get Walter to the hospital, leave him there, and double back in enough time to reboard. The station manager pointed Alice and Walter to the first available cab. Once they were seated in the vehicle, Alice wondered if Walter would remember *any* of this, regardless of its bizarre twists.

The cabbie encouraged the horse to go faster when he heard Walter's cough. Alice was grateful not only for Walter's sake, but also for her own. She briefly wondered what her sister would do if the train was about to leave without her, but somehow Alice believed she was doing the right thing. The rest would just have to work itself out.

At the hospital, the cabbie helped Alice and then Walter down and inside the building where a receptionist processed their arrival. The first and most obvious question was one that only Walter could have answered, but he was nearly delirious with fever. His name and other important information would have to be retrieved later. Meanwhile, the receptionist motioned Alice and Walter to a seat. Alice was about to protest that she couldn't wait with him when she made an instinctive, if not hasty, decision to stay with Walter. With nothing more to do than sit and accept her fate, Alice thought about how it was that she was in this strange position.

She and her twin sister, Anna, had decided to take a trip to Leavenworth, Kansas, to visit an aunt. Not unlike Walter's trip, though she didn't know it. Their father had died some twenty years ago, leaving his wife to care for the twins. As Alice reached her teens, she saw how her mother struggled financially and decided to become a nurse to help out. Anna, always drawing or painting, was able to sell a few of her pieces. But mostly she took in sewing and mending to help. The young women stayed at home, never having married. When their mother became ill, Alice primarily looked after their mother's physical care while Anna had an uncanny knack for understanding her mother's emotional needs. The twins cared for their mother until she passed from tuberculosis just before Christmas in 1912.

Alice and Anna's aunt arrived from Leavenworth to attend her sister's funeral. She helped the twins sort through some of their mother's belongings and they encouraged their aunt to take whatever she wanted. When it came time for their aunt to go back to Kansas, she encouraged the twins to visit whenever they could, saying the change of scenery would do them good. About a year later, Alice and Anna took their aunt up on the offer and it had been wonderful to get away. After about two weeks of being pampered, they were ready to go back home to California.

It was one thing for Alice to use her nursing skills on her mother, but quite another to help a grown man whose name she had yet to learn in a town she knew nothing about. What *was* she to Walter? A companion? A guardian? If she called herself a nurse, no one would understand why she wasn't in her uniform. What must people be thinking to look upon them? That she was a wife? A sister, perhaps?

"A doctor will see you now," the receptionist said. "Have you learned of this man's identity?"

"No," Alice replied, following the woman. "I think he is too ill to know who or where he is."

It didn't take long for the doctor to diagnose Walter's pneumonia. He praised Alice for her care. "I don't know if this man would have made it this far if not for your intervention, Miss…"

"Alice Clark, sir. I am a nurse."

"Miss Clark, if you will follow me, please, I'll have my nurse stay with him."

"Since we don't know this man's name, he will be John Doe for now," the doctor said in the confidence of an unoccupied bay. "I can prescribe antiserum or X-ray therapies. Antiserum would be the more expensive because it involves more treatments over a longer period of time. But, its administration is kinder to the body than X-rays, in my opinion. Both have shown promise with cases like this but whether this man pulls through will largely be up to him and his constitution. And I am sorry to have to ask but are you prepared to pay at least part of his bill right now, Miss Clark?"

"Uh, no, doctor. I mean, well, I guess I could help a little, but I was on the train west with this man who was in my train car. I don't know him. I live in California and wouldn't have access to my financial affairs until I get home. What I have with me I need for my travels. My sister is still on the train. I need to get back to her."

"I see," the doctor said, wringing his hands in thought. "Alright. First of all, this man is contagious. You would do well to quarantine for several days. If you feel you must travel home immediately, I suggest wearing a scarf around your nose and mouth for the protection of others. I will prescribe X-ray therapy that may show results in lowering his fever even yet tonight. We will consider John Doe a charity case for now. As such, he will not be allowed to remain in the hospital after he seems able to travel and hopefully after he can tell us who he is."

"Thank you, doctor."

As her hanky was all she had to cover her mouth, Alice fled the building with only one hand to navigate doors and stairways. She began walking as quickly as possible toward the train station. That is, if she remembered correctly where it was. She thought it wasn't terribly far. It had only seemed like it when she wanted to get Walter to the hospital as quickly as possible.

At the station, she realized with dismay that her train had left. Panicking, she asked the ticket salesman when the next westbound train would leave. Before he could answer, she felt a hand on her shoulder and heard Anna say, "I thought it best I get off and wait for you."

"Oh, Anna! Thank goodness! I'd rather we both have to figure out what to do next than just me alone."

"Why are you covering your mouth?" Anna asked. "Is the air outside stale?"

"No, dear sister. Let's sit. I need to talk to you."

After Anna had heard everything, she and Alice decided together to find lodging in the city for the next few days to be sure Alice would not become ill. They found a boarding house with affordable rooms so that Anna could stay separated from her sister.

During the day, Anna wandered the town or sketched scenes in this unfamiliar city that kept her happily busy. Alice, on the other hand, first wired her employer of her unavoidable detainment. Then she wired their aunt for a bit of money she'd pay back later. Finally, she felt compelled to visit Walter in the hospital. She found a scarf in her suitcase which Anna had rescued from the train and wore it into the building.

At the receptionist's desk, Alice asked to see John Doe. The receptionist, a different man than the one she'd seen the day before, said, "We don't have a John Doe, ma'am. I'm sorry."

"But he was admitted here yesterday under that name," Alice stammered.

"Uh...wait a minute. Might his name be Walter Harlow? I was told to update the paperwork for a Walter Harlow to be admitted to the contagious ward when I came in late last night. Perhaps Mr. Harlow was John Doe? He claims to be from Maine. Though why he is in Kansas, he didn't say."

"That could be him," Alice said, somewhat relieved, although she wouldn't be entirely convinced until she saw him. "May I go to him?"

"At your own risk, ma'am, since he is not in a private room. All the patients there are considered contagious with different ailments."

Alice was not deterred. She was a nurse and had seen contagious diseases before. She headed for the ward, thinking about the man being from Maine.

"It *is* you," Alice declared under her breath when she had scanned the room for a familiar face. She was smiling, although behind her scarf. "Your name is Walter Harlow?"

Walter was still very sick and coughed with difficulty but wore a slight smile and replied, "Yes, I am." He stopped to cough again and then said bluntly, "Who are you?"

"My name is Alice Clark. I'm the one who brought you in here yesterday. Do you remember that?"

"No," was all he said.

"Do you remember being on the train from Leavenworth?"

"Yes, but barely." He coughed harder.

"Well, I will be sure to tell you all about it when you feel better. I shall visit you again tomorrow." She waved as she left the room and saw that he had waved very weakly back.

The next morning, Alice visited Walter again, still wearing her makeshift mask. Walter had improved, and was sitting up, eating watery porridge. "Ah, you're eating! Good for you, Walter."

When he looked confused, she said, "I'm Alice Clark. I saw you yesterday afternoon. I brought you here two days ago. We were both passengers on the train to Denver, or wherever you were going to be getting off. I'm glad to see you looking better today."

The porridge was soothing to Walter's throat and as long as he didn't push too hard, he was able to converse with this pleasant stranger. "I have been wondering greatly how I came to be in the hospital. It certainly wasn't on my list of places to visit."

Alice chuckled from behind her scarf. "Let me tell you everything I know, which isn't that much." It didn't take long to fill Walter in. He told Alice that he had asked his nurses to no avail; no one knew anything about his situation. The only persistent person, he said, was the social worker who was most eager to know if Walter could pay for his stay.

"Yes, the doctor asked me if I was going to take financial responsibility for the cost of your care. I can help with that, if need be," she offered.

"No. Please. I can pay. But since I'm not sure where my money and things may have landed, I will need to send a wire to my mother in Maine who will wire money back." And then, suddenly realizing his mother would be alarmed at the request without any knowledge of what his situation was, he said to Alice, "Might you be so kind as to take down a few words to accompany the wire? My poor mother will think I have gotten myself into a terrible mess," he said, and then thinking a moment longer added with a wry smile, "Maybe I have at that."

After Alice penned the note to Walter's mother, the social worker sent it by telegram to Maine asking Mrs. E.E. Harlow to please wire fifteen dollars to the telegraph office in Topeka, Kansas.

By the time all of this was arranged, Walter needed a nap. Alice left his side, thinking about what she'd learned after taking down his message–that he had a mother in Maine and was headed to California.

The next day, Walter was even more improved and was promised his leave of the hospital the following day. He asked Alice to rebook their tickets to Denver and would cover Alice's ticket to repay her kindness.

When Walter was released, he was taken by wheelchair to the hospital entrance where Alice had secured a cab. She and a nurse helped him outside and then, with the cabbie's help, got him into the cab. Walter was very weak but no longer half out of his mind. When he saw Alice in double, the look on his face made the sisters laugh heartily.

Walter insisted on paying for Anna's ticket too, and the three of them boarded the train and sat together. Then Walter was content to listen to these identical sisters fill him in on who they were. Soon he realized that, while they were identical in looks, or nearly so, they had quite different personalities. Alice was more direct and clearly took the lead. Anna was softer, more fragile-looking, and was content to follow her sister's directives. Their love for one another was clear and their trust was also apparent. Because they were all headed for California, they traveled as three. By the time they'd reached San Francisco to part ways–the Clark twins south to Fremont and himself north to Fortuna–Walter knew which sister he preferred.

Twenty-three

Aunt Amanda

Walter lay in bed that first night in Aunt Amanda's house with a parade of thoughts marching through his head. He'd arrived in the middle of the night and felt sorry to have awakened her. But his aunt had waved it off, shown him to his room, and said she'd see him in the morning. *What a journey it has been getting here,* he mused, too wide awake to fall asleep. It would take him a while to tell his aunt the whole story, but it would be a nice way to revisit all that he had experienced–those first few days in Canada, meeting Friedrich and Peter, riding on a train that went under a river, going to North Dakota for a year and a half, working in the stockyards of Kansas City, visiting Valley Falls, and then becoming so ill as to be taken to the Topeka hospital in such a stupor as to not realize where he was or why. But in doing so, to have met the Clark sisters.

There the parade stopped. The Clark sisters. Such a grace, a providential miracle to have been so sick with a nurse on his train to take over his care. He could never repay Alice, but he could at least think of something nice to send her. And Anna. She had shown Walter the artwork she'd done on the train. He was impressed. She had a way with a stylus. She could bring an object or person to life with a rendering he could only describe as having emotional depth. He wondered what she could do in color. But there was something else about Anna that captivated him–her sweet nature and the joy that bubbled up and out of her. He smiled to himself in the darkness.

He must have drifted off, perhaps with that smile upon his face, for it was light outside and nearly past breakfast when he awoke. "Good morning, Auntie," he said giving her a proper hug.

"Good morning, Walter, dear. My beds are not so accommodating for someone your height, I'm sorry to say, but I trust you slept well?"

"I did, yes, thank you."

"Sit right down, now. You're thin as a rail. Eggs and toast alright?"

"Perfect," Walter replied. "Say, Auntie, it looks to be a lovely day. Would you show me around? I didn't see much of Fortuna in the middle of the night. Oh, and I want to send mother a postcard telling her I've made it here. So, perhaps on our way around, we can post that?"

"That sounds lovely," Amanda said, placing a plate of eggs, toast, and fruit in front of him. "You write your card, and we'll leave after that."

Walking the streets of Fortuna, Aunt Amanda pointed out this and that while Walter wondered where to begin telling her about his journey from Maine. Finally, when she asked, he decided to tell her about the Clark sisters first because he intended to court one of them. "I guess you'd say I'm smitten with Anna," he concluded. "And you know, it's odd to even say that since these girls look so much alike. It's like one of them looking into a mirror and me seeing both the sister and her reflection. How can I be smitten with one and not the other?"

"My dear boy, the heart knows things the eyes can't see. It isn't about what's on the outside when it comes to matters of the heart. Let me tell you about my dear, dear John, God rest his soul. Well, better yet, I'll tell you about my own journey from Maine to California tonight over tea and dessert. John will be part of that story. Now, tell me how it was that you met these sisters."

Walter and Amanda walked and talked. Amanda was thrilled to hear so much about the lives of her brother's family that were mostly lost to her for the distance between them. She was saddened by Edwin's death, which she'd gotten word of through her sister-in-law, and mentioned that, of her six siblings, only her brother Elkanah was left. And at that, she hadn't heard from him in many years.

That night it was cool and Walter and his aunt sat by the fireplace, each with a cup of steaming hot coffee and a piece of cherry pie. It felt so good to Walter that his travels had at last reached a destination—one with a dear family member and even the promise of love in the air. He settled back to listen to Amanda tell her story and sighed with contentment.

"I was the only girl of the seven of us, and born second to last. They named me Mercy Amanda, but mostly called me Amanda. When they did use my first name it was because I was in trouble. I think they shouted 'Mercy' as much as a plea to God as to get my attention! Anyway, I was treated very differently than the others. For the boys, father had made a rule that they had to work for him, either on the farm or in the small shoe shop father had, until they were twenty-one. I was fine with that because I loved having my brothers around. But your father decided he didn't want to stay home that long. He didn't want to do any more farm chores, and he had no interest in making shoes.

"He decided to teach school to pay his way through Bowdoin College and also pay off our father instead of working for him. I've never figured out whether father was amenable to that arrangement or not, but I don't remember any fighting over it. Five years later, when Lincoln wanted to leave home before he was of age, Edwin somehow found enough money to pay our father for Lincoln's absence too. Both boys wanted to be ministers and both graduated from Bangor Seminary.

"When the war started, Maine was not involved yet. But when President Lincoln did call for Maine's young men, Edwin and Lincoln both decided to join the Missionary Society to aid the cause rather than fight. They were called to serve in Missouri and Kansas where the lines between the Union cause and the Confederate's were blurry. But they were not allowed to go out west without being married. I assume the Society wanted their missionaries to be single-minded in their work, if you know what I mean. So, your uncle Lincoln married Hattie Pritchard, a young woman he'd met in Bangor. Your father had been engaged to a young woman who died of tuberculosis, such a dreadful disease to get, God rest her soul. And I do mean dreadful. I speak from experience, but I'll get to that. Edwin was determined to go west with or without a wife. He always was a very determined person, as I'm sure you know.

"Providence stepped in and as my brothers were not to leave for the west for another two weeks after Lincoln and Hattie married, they stayed on Hattie's family's farm to wait out the time. They invited your father to stay there with them. Hattie had a sister, Eliza, who was there after having broken off an engagement with an engineer. Seems Eliza's beau planned to go west which was fine with Eliza, but since he was not a Christian, she didn't think the marriage would last. So, Eliza and Edwin married, perhaps for convenience, no one really knows and I guess it doesn't really matter, does it?

"Edwin and Eliza stayed in Kansas City, Missouri, while Lincoln and Hattie went on further west. I think they all saw their share of awful things during that war."

"Yes," Walter broke in, "I think they must have, judging from things I gleaned when I was in that area."

"Oh, that's right, you were just there, you said. Then you know where your half-sisters were born. It was not an easy life for any of them. Eliza had all she could handle with three youngsters. She was not a well woman and hadn't been for some time. But while they were out there, I came down with tuberculosis. I was still in Maine, you know, and I had a cough that lasted several weeks. I thought my insides would come right out."

"I wonder if Alice thought I had tuberculosis?" Walter said under his breath.

"What dear?"

"The cough I had that alerted Alice of my being ill. I wonder if she thought it was tuberculosis?"

"If she has been nursing for several years, she's probably seen a lot of things that would explain a cough, tuberculosis for one. I'll just bet she was happy that it wasn't that."

"Probably. I'll have to ask her. But please, go on. You had tuberculosis?"

"Yes, that terrible cough. I wasn't interested in eating, either, so I lost a considerable amount of weight. As you can see, I could stand to lose some weight now too," Amanda chuckled good-naturedly, "although *not* by virtue of tuberculosis, God forbid. Back then I was much younger and smaller, and everyone decided that I was losing too much weight. When I began to swell up in my joints, the pain was sometimes excruciating. That's when father decided I needed a lot of fresh air and sunshine. So, he put me on a horse and sent me out to Kansas City to visit your father there. I've never been able to understand how he thought I could make that long trip, but he put me on a horse and, in his words, he 'turned me out in the sunshine'. I made it with a lot of help from some very kindly folk. One very compassionate couple took me in for a couple of nights and then took me to the train station somewhere in Ohio and paid for a ticket all the way to Kansas City. I've always wished I'd written down their names and address. But I didn't. All I can say is that there are some real angels in this world." Walter nodded in definite agreement.

"Well, by the time I reached Kansas City, the disease had turned for the better and it wasn't long before I felt like my old self again. I guess I was one of the lucky ones to survive at all, let alone intact. I enjoyed being with your father and Eliza and their three little girls. It was easy to see that the workload was frightful, so I did what I could to help out. Then one day a man came to the missionary center to volunteer some time. He was a mighty fine-looking man, he was. And about my age too. That was my John. His full name was John Wesley Miller. His parents were Methodists from Indiana, where he grew up. They wanted their first born to have the name of the founder of Methodism. And I believe there was something in John that wanted to live up to his namesake. He was a wonderful Christian man."

"I wish I'd met him," Walter said longingly.

"I wish you had too, dear. He'd have liked you."

"So, did he come out west to be a missionary?"

"Yes. I think that was what was on his heart to do there in Kansas City. I don't think he meant to meet someone he wanted to marry, though. But the chemistry between us was strong and we were engaged quickly. Your father married us in October of '69. It was pretty convenient having a minister for a brother," Amanda laughed. "Do you want more coffee and pie, dear?"

"Not just yet, thank you. So, how long did you stay there in Kansas City?"

"We didn't stay there long. We went west to Council Grove on a land grant. John still had a missionary's heart, though, and he heard that the Kaw Indians out there could use help because they were being displaced from their land. The Methodist Episcopal Church South had been missionaries to the Kaw tribe and ran a school for three years just before the war broke out. But that school didn't last, so the church sought help. John felt that calling, and that's where we went. Unfortunately, Council Grove was far enough away from Kansas City that we didn't get back to see your father again before they moved back to Maine. I'll always regret that." Amanda took a long drink from her coffee before beginning again.

"So, anyway, while John and I were in Council Grove, your father had to leave Kansas City because his wife had become so ill that no doctors there knew how to help her. They told your father to take her back to Maine. I would have thought that trip alone would kill the poor woman, but they made it. She was sickly for two years, as the story goes. But you probably know how your mother and father ended up married, right?"

"Yes, I do."

"Anyway, John and I made a nice little house out in Council Grove. I kept a garden and did some sewing and mending for folks while John was helping the church. Soon enough, the children started coming. We had a son and two daughters in all. John Junior, Winnifred, and Mary."

Aunt Amanda stopped a moment and reached for her hanky. "This part of my story has never been easy. I don't tell it often. But I think you will honor it. When the youngest, Mary, was only two, there was a very strong thunderstorm that came through. Kansas certainly had its share of bad storms, I'll say. Our house was struck by lightning. Our John Junior was killed in the fire. Neither John nor I could get back to his room, which is where the lightning struck. I think he was gone quickly." She paused to wipe a tear from her face and blow her nose. "At least I have prayed so all these years. Mary, the youngest, was fine because she was sleeping nearest us. I just picked her up and ran outside. But Winnifred was panicked and froze. She wouldn't come when we called her. John was able to rescue her," Amanda said, openly weeping now. "But her little face was badly burned. She had to live with terrible scars the rest of her life, which wasn't terribly long, God rest her soul.

"After that, the three of us, John, little Mary, and me, decided to move on and as far from Kansas as we could. Which is how we ended up in Fortuna. The name alone felt like a good place to start over. John died here in our bed. I have never wanted to move again. I feel close to him here."

After his aunt was quiet awhile, Walter asked, "Does Mary live near here?" He didn't want to assume that Mary had died too.

"She's not far. Not right here in Fortuna, but in Ferndale. I know she'd love a visit from her cousin. She and her husband raise dairy cows."

"Oh! Like me. Well, like our family farm does, anyway."

"Yes, dear. That reminds me to ask you, how long do you plan to stay?"

"I guess I don't know. If I may stay with you until I develop a plan, I will find a job to help pay for my stay here. And then find a place for myself."

"Mercy no! My name does come in handy sometimes," she giggled. "You will stay for as long as you like. And you may work for me. I'm getting on in age, you know, and I could use a strong pair of arms to do things around here that just don't seem to get done. Would that suit you?"

"Of course. We can talk more about that as we go. But for now, you look some tired, auntie. How about turning in?"

"I suppose you're right, dear. Thank you for listening to me."

Amanda rose, took their cups to the kitchen, and showed Walter how she liked to close the house up for the night. Then she kissed his cheek and went on down the hall, leaving Walter to think about her story and the cousins he would never meet.

Thursday, April 30, 1914

Dear mother and Bessie,

Tomorrow is May Day. Bessie, I know it's been years since we hung baskets, but I still think of that every May 1.

I am having a wonderful time with Aunt Amanda. She is such a loving woman. I feel right at home, and I don't think she would want it any other way. I trust you got confirmation of her address from my postcard? You may write to me here at least for the time being. Soon I will go see her daughter, Mary, who lives in another town not far from here. A new cousin to meet!

I guess my biggest news is that I came down with pneumonia just after I left Valley Falls. I met a nurse on the train who got me to a hospital in Topeka. She stayed by my side until I could get back on the train. And since she was also going to California, she stayed with me to make sure I was not going to relapse. Thankfully, the further we went the more like my old self I became so that now I feel just fine. But the most interesting part is that the nurse, Alice Clark, has a twin sister named Anna. My, but they look identical!

I'll keep this short as it is late and I can hardly keep my eyes open. I pray you are both well.

Very much love,
Walter

Twenty-four

Courting Anna

Sunday, October 25, 1914

Dear Friedrich, Klara, Peter, and little Walter,

I hope this finds you all doing well. It seems like ages ago I was working on your land. How are things with the family? How did the barley yield?

Last time I wrote you I mentioned the twins, Alice and Anna. This weekend they came up for a visit. I had written them that the Northwestern Pacific Railroad had completed their tracks from Sausalito to Eureka. The golden spike ceremony to celebrate this achievement was held this past Friday in Cain Rock, about seventy miles from here. It was all very exciting, and since the girls had always wished to see the giant redwood trees, I suggested we take a trip to Eureka to see them. One could certainly build mighty fine farm buildings with the long, straight boards from just one of those enormous trees!

This morning before the twins left, we managed to get some early-morning fishing in. The Eel River has catfish and smallmouth bass in it, and we caught enough for a feast at noon.

Anna's artwork is wonderful. She encourages me to keep working on my own. Recently, I did a drawing of a farmer's horse near here. I embellished it somewhat to make it look less like a tired workhorse, and it isn't half bad, if I do say so myself. Anna called it the "cat's meow." I had to ask her if that was good or bad. I have never heard that phrase. It means she liked it very much.

I must close this now. Aunt Amanda is calling me for supper.

The best,
Walter

Though Walter worked for his aunt, he had never worked so little for so much in his life. She treated him royally. And so did Mary, his cousin. When he and Mary realized they both had experience raising Jersey cows, they felt an instant kinship sharing the successes and failures of dairy work. Walter wrote to his mother and sister how wonderful it was to feel so close to kin who lived so far away from Maine.

By now, Walter had talked and written about Anna enough that Elizabeth and Bessie suspected more than a simple friendship between them. They were thrilled for Walter if that was the case, but they also realized it most likely meant that Walter would stay in California. Elizabeth wasn't ready to ask her son what his intentions were. She wasn't sure she wanted to know. But Bessie was very eager to find out and penned a letter.

Sunday, November 22, 1914

My dear brother,
Please pardon my frankness, but your letters sound like you are enjoying California, and a certain young lady in particular. Mother and I assume you have your eye on Anna. Does Anna, herself, know this? Or are you reluctant to talk of your feelings for fear of being hurt again? I can't say I'd blame you if that is the case.
We are all doing just fine here. I too have had my eye on a young man, believe it or not. He has come calling twice. He is a farmer as well, with

mostly sheep. We met at the autumn festival in Windham. I wasn't going to go but Mother insisted I get out. I'm very grateful now that I did. His name is Ernest Moller. Do you know him?

Mother and I have been invited to celebrate Thanksgiving with Ellen this year. It's very nice of her to invite us. What will you be doing Thursday?

Please tell us about Anna. You can trust me to share with Mother only what you want me to and that which I think she would prefer to hear. Stay well.

Love,
Bessie

Sunday, December 6, 1914

Dear Bessie,

A quick note to say thank you for your kind letter. Yes, Anna is the one I fancy, although her sister, Alice, is a very fine woman as well. But Anna shares my artist's eye and heart and perhaps I long to allow the artist in me to express himself. Anna may suspect that I am taken with her, but I have not said as much yet.

I am, of course, grateful that you and mother are doing well. And I am very happy for you to be courting. I do know Ernest and have found him to be a fine chap. Perhaps a bit to himself, so I am surprised you would have met him at a festival and not at the library.

Aunt Amanda and I spent Thanksgiving at Mary's house. She has three boys who are a rambunctious lot, so the house was teeming with activity. All in all, we had a very nice day.

All my love and merry Christmas,
Walter

"I am planning to take Anna to the Exposition in San Francisco next week, unless you have specific work you need me to do," Walter told his aunt at supper one evening in May.

"I've heard some fascinating things about that. Will you be gone the entire week?"

"Probably. Alice was not able to take any more time off after her trip with Anna to Kansas. She had to ask for extra days on my behalf, too, so I feel a bit guilty about that. I've heard a person could spend days at this exposition and not see everything. I guess it will depend on Anna's stamina as to how many days we go see it. I will leave on Monday and hope to be back by no later than the following Monday evening, if that's alright."

"That's fine, dear. I was just thinking that I'd like to have you repaint the house this summer. Maybe you can start when you get back."

"I can do that."

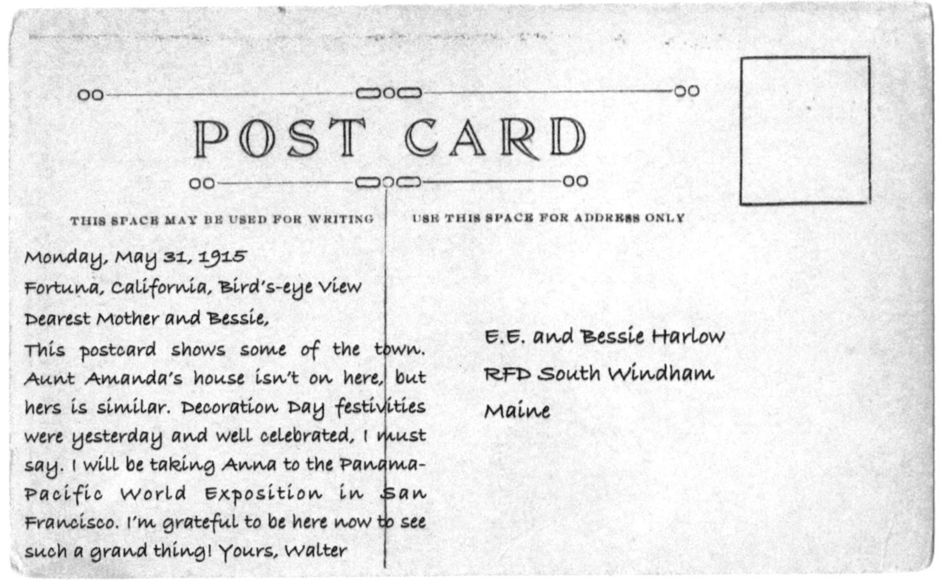

As Walter's train followed the tracks to San Francisco, singing its rhythmic click-clack, click-clack, he found himself absent-mindedly humming to the beat. He startled when he realized that he was humming one of Millie's favorite hymns. Millie should have been far from his mind, but he couldn't help thinking about her and all they'd experienced. He'd loved every minute being with her. She had spunk and character, wit and wisdom, not to mention good looks.

He recounted that last conversation he'd had with her. Why had she turned him down? He knew what she'd said, but the answer must lie in what she hadn't said. He couldn't honestly say he was a bad fellow, so that couldn't have been it. He'd been honest with her and told her he'd wanted to be a minister but couldn't pass Greek. Would she have been embarrassed by him? Perhaps she'd wanted to be a minister's wife. She loved church, church music, playing the organ, teaching children. He told her he'd decided to be a farmer instead. She obviously knew her way around a farm, so asking her to be a farmer's wife should not have been a deterrent to his proposal of marriage, he reasoned. *Unless,* he thought suddenly, stiffening. *Unless being a farmer's wife is exactly what she didn't want to be.*

She'd said she could see what it would mean to him to accept his proposal. She said he'd been nothing if not kind to her. After a moment's thought he realized that what she was saying was that she believed he was a good person but not good enough to be *her* person. He'd told her it was alright to think it over, that he would wait. But she'd never gotten back to him and in fact she'd avoided his eyes when they were near one another. Oh, how that hurt. It could not have hurt more if a doctor had surgically removed his heart with no numbing agent.

And then to read that she was marrying another. That another man would live with her, make a life with her, maybe even have children with her. He shook his head while his mind quieted. Then, with resolve in his heart, he said to himself, *Forgiving her is easy. It isn't her fault that she loves another. Love* is *what it* is. *I won't wait any longer for something she clearly doesn't want.* Then and there, Walter decided not to think about Millie again.

"How was your train trip down here?" Alice asked him when she picked him up at the station. "Anna was busy with a customer, or she would have come with me."

"It was fine," he stated, only briefly thinking about his resolve regarding Millie. "Warm. But not much could have made me unhappy today knowing that I would be with you and Anna. How are you both?"

"We are well. Still adjusting to living without mother after a year and a half. I do miss Mama's pies! I don't have the time to make a decent pie these days and Anna would rather cook than bake."

"Alice, I'm glad you came alone. I want to ask you something important. I hope now is alright to do that?"

"Yes. Go ahead."

"Well, perhaps you already know that I am fond of you both, but I have a special kind of love for Anna," Walter said. He felt like a bird in a cage whose door was open. Depending on how things went, he might hop to the door and fly, or he might stay safely inside.

"Yes, Walter. We both are fond of you as well. And I suspected as much about your feelings for Anna."

"Your father is not alive for me to ask him, so I come to you for this. I would like to ask for Anna's hand, and I'd love to have your blessing."

"Yes, Walter, you have my blessing. I could not speak for Anna herself as to how she might answer such a question. Neither of us has assumed to be married one day, though neither of us is put off by such a thing if we felt the rightness of the situation. Anna is a lovely person, as you must already feel. She is also of a more fragile nature than her twin. Her fragility, on one hand, sends her to the daybed for a time with chamomile tea or aspirin or both. On the other hand, it is her fragile essence that makes her sympathetic to most of nature, save for mice." Alice laughed at where her sister drew the line to be "compassionate to all beasts," to quote Anna's description of herself.

"That said, Walter, as long as you understand my sister and you are ready to accept her as she is, I have no misgivings, assuming you treat her as lovingly as she deserves to be treated. I can only say that I would dearly miss my twin were the two of you living as far away as Fortuna. In that case I just may have to find a nursing job up north! You'd not be rid of me so easily," Alice said, winking.

Walter's rapt attention to Alice's words were mixed with two parts excitement and one part solemnity as he considered what he'd heard. "I plan to ask for Anna's hand when we go to the exposition."

There was nothing more Walter needed to say on the subject, and Alice began talking of more mundane things the rest of the way to Fremont. He only half-listened to her. His mind was stuck on Alice's comment about he and Anna possibly living in Fortuna. Did he feel at home enough there to settle down? Would his new relationship with Amanda and Mary be strong enough to ask Anna to relocate? He didn't think so. What about living in Fremont? Could he make Anna's town be his? And then, like a small seedling poking through an arid desert, he thought, *Could I really live all this distance from Mother and Bessie? It had been exciting to travel this far from home, but adopting it permanently?* Walter had honestly never really entertained that possibility. He'd deluded himself, always keeping thoughts of never going back to Maine safely guarded but out of reach. Even the letters and postcards he'd written to his mother and sister felt more like including them in a vacation, not keeping them informed of an inevitable change of address. He realized that Bessie had given this possibility more credence than he had.

"Walter!" Anna cried out from her seat in the living room where she was engrossed in a painting. She quickly rose to give him a hug. "You're here!"

"I am, indeed, Anna," he said. And if any thoughts of Millie and returning to Maine lingered, they melted away in Anna's embrace.

"Walter must be tired and hungry, sister," Alice interrupted. "Let's have tea and cake and then send this boy off to bed."

Anna smiled at Walter and whispered, "Ever the practical one of us. I suppose she's right, but do sit down and talk to me a while. It's been too long since your last letter. How are you?"

They'd all but gotten started in conversation when Alice summoned them to get their tea and plate of cake, which they took to the parlor. It wasn't a big house, but it was more than adequate for the two of them. It was the house they grew up in, and now their mother and father's bedroom was the spare in which Walter would stay.

"This neighborhood reminds me a little of one I lived in as a child."

"How so?" Alice asked.

"There's something about the way the houses are laid out here that makes me think of Madison, Maine. 'Course you have this beautiful bay. Madison's water source was the Kennebec River and Wesserunsett Lake."

"That's quite a name, Wesser what?" Anna giggled.

"Wesserunsett. The Abenaki Indian tribe named it. Locals say the word means 'bitter water place.' That's always seemed a terrible name for something so beautiful. I wonder if it isn't the water that's bitter but maybe something awful that happened there."

"Were you born there?" Alice asked.

"No, I was born near Portland, which is downstate. We lived in Madison for a few years while my father was a minister, and I graduated from Madison High School. I lived in several towns in Maine, wherever my father was preaching."

"Did you want to be a minister like your father?" Alice asked as Anna sat dreamily watching Walter talk.

"I did," he started. Once again, he was in a position to tell the truth or skirt the issue. He decided not to tell them everything, rather a condensed version of the truth. "But I started doing other things and ended up managing father's farm for him. I love to tinker on machines. And," he said, with a twinkle in his eye, "guess what I think is the most interesting book to read?"

Anna shrugged. Alice said, "*Moby Dick*!"

"That is a good one. But I find the dictionary to be the most interesting."

"The dictionary?" Anna asked quizzically, tilting her head.

"Well, think about it. There are words whose origins cover the globe. There are words to fit any occasion, if you have the patience to hunt for them. And words to make the common man sound like a college graduate!"

"Yes, but then no one would understand him!" Anna said, closing that subject rather quickly, Walter thought. "What do you most want to see at the exposition, Walter? I am most eager to see what they have been calling the Tower of Jewels! Imagine something forty-three stories high decorated with more than one hundred thousand glass beads!"

"I can see how that would be fascinating. To answer your question, though, I guess I would like to see how they made the telephone stretch from New York City to San Francisco. At least in the small towns I have lived in, very few people have a telephone to connect them to their neighbors, let alone across the nation. I've also heard that there is an aviation field. That too, flying, I mean, seems at best impractical for much else than pure enjoyment. I hear they give people rides. I'm afraid I am too much of a land lover to dare a ride like that. I can't imagine the cost of such a thing, either."

"Well, I will just have to go some other time," Alice said, yawning. "I'll let you two kids enjoy it for me. But I think I'm the one who needs to go to bed. I do leave early tomorrow morning. Anna, would you please clean up before you go to bed?" Getting a nod from Anna, she finished, "Good night, then. Sleep well."

Walter and Anna were happy to have the downstairs to themselves. Walter helped Anna take dishes to the kitchen and wash them up. Then they retired to the living room for a bit of time alone. Before long, neither of them could stifle yawns. They climbed the stairs and Anna showed Walter where he was to sleep. Then, before retiring to her own room, she looked up into Walter's brown eyes, soft, and doe-like in the glow of the only electric lamp still on. They radiated from a man who was gloriously happy and reflected her own blue ones.

Part Three
Millie and Walter

What's meant to be will always find a way.
-Trisha Yearwood

Twenty-five

Back in Maine

"Papa! Come quickly! Papa! Something's happening south of here. Papa? Where are you?" I was becoming more and more frantic now about his absence in addition to my original concern. Having exhausted my search in our buildings and then the fields, I finally found him most of the way down the hill to the river. No wonder he hadn't heard the commotion. "Papa!" I panted, skidding to a stop before him. For a thirty-six-year-old, I was still quite spry. Nonetheless, running in a panic nearly took the wind out of me. "Papa, something's happening in that direction," I said pointing south. "People are running down the road and I saw the fire wagon heading toward White Rock. Here, take my arm, let's see if someone needs our help or our horse and wagon."

Papa is limping badly these days. His war wound has gotten the better of him, as has his rheumatism. He isn't working the fields any longer, and he and I have hired what help we need. *Thank goodness for his war pension,* I thought, taking mental stock of our situation as we trudged slowly up the hill. Papa still enjoys milking the few cows that are left, and I shan't take that away from him until I have to. I want Papa to maintain his dignity. He's a good man, just as Mama said on her deathbed. Brave and conscientious too. For not being a legal citizen, he certainly has pride in his adopted country.

"Not much further," I said, straining a bit harder to keep us moving uphill.

To learn America's language, fight in her war, serve as an elected delegate to the Gorham district of the Republican Caucus and then as a juror of the Superior Court, not to mention being at Great Fall's beck and call, it's a wonder his decline hasn't been faster.

"Why did you go down the hill, anyway, Papa?"

"Your old father was being foolish. I thought I saw the Indian woman. It's been a while since she came up to the farm to get milk for her baby. I thought maybe she needed more milk."

"Oh," was all I said. *Was he hallucinating?* I wondered, apprehensive for his future, and mine with it. Indeed it has been quite a while. At least thirty years! But there's no point telling him that.

When we finally reached the top of the hill, we both froze. In the distance, south of us but blowing easterly across the river, we saw much more smoke than I had seen before finding Papa. It was difficult to say how far away the fire was, but a few miles would surely put it right in White Rock. I shivered, nervous for friends who lived there. The longer we stood, the more I realized I was becoming chilled this early-October morning. "Papa, wait right here while I run into the house and grab my sweater. I'll get your heavier coat too."

I didn't wait for a reply but ran "quick as a bunny," as I liked to instruct my nieces and nephew when they visited. Papa had not taken his eyes off the billows of smoke rising until they were swept away by the wind and replaced by more, closer to the ground.

"Let's go sit on the front stoop. Maybe someone will be able to tell us what's happening."

As we rounded the house, I saw Effie standing near the road looking toward the smoke. "Yoohoo, Effie!" I called out while I settled Papa on the top step.

Effie turned toward us and crossed the road. "Isn't it just awful!" she said. "Bert went down there at least an hour ago. I sure wish he'd come back."

"I'm sure he's fine," I reassured my friend and soon-to-be neighbor. There was still a parade of people heading south but also a few coming back from that direction. "There's Bert!" I said, joining Effie and walking toward Effie's fiancé.

"Bert, what's happening?"

"A fire is destroyin' most of White Rock, I'm afraid. Someone said it started in Shackford's store sometime last night, so the post office and the store are both gone now. The Farmer's Union and the grist mill are all but gone too. So's the depot. I heard that the engineer of a train goin' through saw the smoke and blew his whistle long and hard. They say it nearly woke the dead. Good thing it did, though. Everyone was able to get out of their homes and I don't think anyone was seriously injured. Some animals might have been, but no people, thank the good Lord."

"Oh, Bert," I said with genuine relief for my friends' safety and anguish for their losses. "Do they need more help? Is there anything we can do?"

We were standing near enough to Papa that he heard most of Bert's report. Bert reached in his pocket for his pipe. "I'd say just wait. I imagine help might be needed keepin' the White Rock folks fed and clothed in the days to come. Right now, it's a mess there. I'd stay away if I was you." He packed his pipe and lit it, drawing in a few breaths to get it going well and contentedly puffed away, standing with his weight on one hip. One might have thought Bert didn't care at all about the fire from his calm demeanor but if they did, they would have been wrong.

Papa and I were both stunned into silence, imagining what it would be like to lose the farm and house to fire. It wouldn't be the first time either of us stressed about everything going up in flames, knowing that we could lose it all, just like that.

Wanting to change the subject now that Bert told us there was nothing we could do at the moment, I said, "Well, how are you two coming with the house and your wedding?"

"Oh, you know Effie," Bert said while putting his arm around his fiancée. "She flits around doing this 'n' that 'n' somehow things get done. The weddin's her department. The house doesn't need much, you know. Just some paintin' and paperin' to meet Effie's desires."

"I want a bright yellow kitchen," Effie said almost defensively. "I found a kitchen table and chairs painted yellow with black trim that I want ever so badly. I think they look so cheery. I've poked and prodded this guy to start painting that kitchen. If it were up to him, it would never get done."

I enjoy the teasing nature of Bert and Effie's banter. They're a nice couple and Papa and I will enjoy having them as neighbors after their wedding in December.

"Say," Bert suddenly said, "guess who I saw at the fire? Walter Harlow! Yup. He's been back a little while now, he says. He plans to pick up his RFD route soon's he can. I didn't think he'd be back here at all."

"I didn't know that," I said. *I'm surprised I haven't heard someone say something in the library,* I thought. *Maybe this is the first he's been away from his farm since he got back.*

"It'll be nice to see him if he picks up this route again," Papa jumped in to answer quickly. "Well, Bert, Effie, I need to get off this stoop and on with my day. Thank you for the news. Millie?"

"Yes, Papa, I'll be right there."

"Ay-uh, you're welcome," Bert replied. He took Effie's hand, and they walked back across the road.

"Thank you, Papa. I really didn't want to talk about Walter," I said, taking his arm and helping him up. "Sometimes I'm not sure how to get away from Effie, bless her heart. She *is* a talker, isn't she? And that fire. Just dreadful. Those poor, poor people. I'll keep my ears open for ways to help. In the meantime, Papa, don't go down that hill again without help. Please. If the Indian woman is back, maybe she will come up and see us."

Tuesday, October 17, 1916

Dear diary, what a day it's been! First a huge fire in White Rock. I've heard a rumor that it was deliberately set by people disgruntled by this election. Would that November 7 come and go quickly.

Then I found Papa wandering down the hill searching for the Indian woman. He isn't steady on his feet. What possessed him to think that woman was down there? I have no idea. That was 30, 40 years ago! What will he do next?

But then Bert said he talked with Walter in White Rock at the fire. Walter is back? I wonder if he brought a wife?

"Hell-oo? Millie? It's me," Effie said, rapping on the kitchen door.

I heard her and would have had to wash my hands off before I could open the door, so I said, "Come in. Come in out of the cold, Effie."

"It's mighty chilly for November, seems to me. How are you?" Effie asked, taking her coat off and hanging it on the hook. Then she added, " Did your father vote yet? Bert did."

"I'm fine, Effie, and yes, I took Papa to vote early this morning. I don't think he'd miss an election if he were half dead! I am baking my bread for the week, as you can see. I'll keep working on it if that's alright with you. Have a seat here and keep me company. How are your wedding plans?"

I turned my back on Effie to continue working. Bert had purchased the house directly across the road that had belonged to Howard years ago until he sold it to Papa the year before he died. Papa was getting too feeble to keep the house as rental property, so Bert's need for a home was perfect. The only difficulty was that, while relieving Papa of extra work, the house was sentimentally "Howdie's home" to all of us and always would be. At least seeing Bert with the house keys in one hand and Effie's hand in his other made the transition feel worthwhile.

"I think most everything is in order now that Reverend Aikins has said he can officiate," Effie answered. "A December wedding begs a different décor than, say, a spring wedding. I will decorate the living room with evergreens, of course. There's certainly no shortage of those! I think I'd like to include bows. Muriel says she'll help me with those. I want to carry a bouquet of one gardenia in a gathering of holly. There's that nice holly bush beside the house, if you recall."

If I recall? I could remember every little thing about that house, I thought, sadly. But Effie didn't realize just how personal that house was to us Thomases. And none of us were about to tell her that and ruin her excitement. She was relatively new to the neighborhood and had only recently spent enough time at "Howard's house" to become a frequent visitor of ours.

"I'm glad you have Muriel to help you. You can call on me, as well, if you need to," I said, putting the dough into their pans to rise.

"Oh, thank you. I just may at that. In fact, I think we may need more cookies for the reception. I'd love to have cookies in Christmas colors. Do you know of any good ones?"

"What about rainbow cookies?" I suggested.

"Oh! Yes! That would work wonderfully. Remind me what the colors are?"

"Red, green, and white."

"Oh, that's perfect! Thank you so much for making those. We'll put them out the morning of December 6. Oh, just think of it, I'll soon be Mrs. Bert Gilman," Effie purred, hugging herself.

I think I just volunteered to make cookies! I realized, with a wry smile Effie couldn't see. *But I'm happy to do it all the same.* Effie stayed long enough that I had to politely tell her I had other things to do. Once she left, I realized I didn't have long to gather all the ingredients for the cookies which I've only made once, with Bea's help. *I surely hope they will be good enough for a wedding reception.*

It took a full two weeks after the most contentious election I've ever lived through for results to finally be announced. Every day since the election, the front page of the newspaper has been splattered with election drama. Some days there has been nothing else but that. Woodrow Wilson, the incumbent, was on the ballot running against a supreme court Republican named Charles Hughes. Hughes appeared early on to have won and was asked to declare. But he remained cautious, wanting to be absolutely certain of the results.

As the days after the election progressed and California's tallies began to suggest Woodrow Wilson might win, some Republican officials began alleging possible fraud. I was aghast at so much as a notion of fraud in a presidential election. *What is this country coming to?*

Finally, today, November 22, Hughes telegrammed Wilson a gracious concession. I could feel the electric tension in the air quiet, at least for the time being.

"Hello, Manuel. How've you been since I saw you last?" Walter said when he handed Papa his mail. He noticed Papa's more pronounced limp.

"Well enough, thank you. It's nice to see you back."

"It's nice to *be* back. The man who replaced me in '11 seemed happy enough to give it back," Walter chuckled. "And I rather like having a reason to get out in the winter. But it sure is cold out, isn't it? I haven't been used to this much cold since I lived in North Dakota for a year or so. Now, North Dakotans really know how to do winter up there! And here I thought Mainers had the upper hand on cold weather!"

"North Dakota, eh? That's quite a piece away. How did you like your trip?"

"Overall, it was exciting. I saw much more of this country than I ever imagined I would. But, hey, it's mighty cold for you to be standing out here. One of these days I have something I'd like to talk to you about," Walter said, already moving toward the road. "Take care."

That last part had Manuel wondering. He wouldn't say anything to Millie, though. He couldn't be sure how she felt about Walter. *Best not poke that sleeping bear*, he smiled to himself.

But Millie had been watching from the parlor window, out of sight.

Trafton Plaisted visited Manuel in February. He wanted to see how his old friend was faring. They sat in the parlor over coffee and cake, reminiscing as usual. Two men who understood as few others could what that war had done to those who served and saw the wreckage of buildings, beasts, and bodies. They both considered themselves fortunate to have walked away from the South, mostly intact. So many hadn't.

"Remember the sweet potato coffee we were given when the real coffee ran out?" Papa said, sipping on his black coffee.

"Ay-uh. Ain't liked sweet potatoes since. Remember the way we'd get secret messages across enemy lines sometimes?" Trafton said, snickering at the unorthodox method as if he'd thought of it himself.

"You mean hiding messages inside spools of thread?" Papa said.

"That one old woman gave up most of her thread spools easy enough, but by golly she was going to keep her white thread if she had to go to war herself!" Trafton said, slapping his knee and howling in laughter which Papa echoed a little less boisterously.

It did my heart good to hear Papa laugh. He'd suffered so much loss in his lifetime and not just in watching fellow soldiers fall in battle. They sometimes spoke of the deaths of women and children who had nothing at all to do with the war. Or the enormous numbers of horses that fell in the line of duty. *Maybe that's one reason why Papa volunteers to drive the hearse,* I thought, taking their dirty dessert plates from them. *Maybe in some respects he is numb to death. Or maybe because so few of the dead in war were given proper burials, he hopes driving the hearse makes up for that.*

The laughter between the men died away and their mood changed without a word between them. It was as though the spoken word was superfluous, that only the air between them was necessary to know what the other was thinking and feeling.

"Trafton," Papa said, "I have something I'd like to get off my chest before I die."

"Yer not planning that event already, are ya?" Trafton quipped. But Manuel knew that Trafton's intent was not to stifle Papa's need to speak.

"You know that I bought my farm from a woman who hadn't owned it but two years. I got it for a decent price, too. But I always wondered why it was the woman who sold it and not her husband. And why they were here so short a time. It's a good piece of land." Trafton nodded. "Then I learned that the woman's husband had been a deserter. He apparently hid in the barn the only time officials came looking for him, so he was never caught. But they say he was never the same after that. He never really left the house and lived as a fugitive here. I guess his wife couldn't cope and up and sold the farm herself. She probably had to drag him out by the hair before I moved in."

"Well, she shoulda shot him. Draggin' him by the hair was too good fer 'im, I say."

Manuel only nodded slowly. "Most of us wanted to quit that damn war. But we didn't, did we? I'd sooner died than be a deserter."

They both remained quiet again, lost in personal thought.

"When I learned of the deserter right here in my own home, it disturbed me. I couldn't help think of all the lost limbs, eyes, bellies that so many walked home with, only to die from infections or some other horrible disease. Sometimes I've felt guilty that I survived. But mostly I've been humbled and grateful that I was only injured."

Trafton nodded. "I feel the same."

"But if I could have stopped at being thankful... Well, what that man did gnawed on me something awful."

"No wrong doin' there, Manuel."

"Yes, but I grew to hate the man. I didn't even know him, and I hated him. And all the more for thinking of him keeping safe in my own home. Then I started having dreams. A lot of them. They were always about fighting or dying. Often there was a man I didn't know in those dreams. He kept me from doing my best in some battle situation or other. It always made me so angry. In one dream, he hid my rifle; in another, he dragged me to the front. And in one dream, he was dead at my feet. I fired at the gray coat that took him out, but he suddenly stood up and took the bullet himself.

"This dream haunted me. It came to me night after night, so's I thought I would go mad. One night, after the miserable dream, I got out of bed and grabbed my shotgun and headed for the barn. It was like I was still in the dream, 'cept I only had half my wits about me. I was going to find that wretched deserter once and for all. I scoured every inch of that barn, disturbing the animals, but I didn't know that then. One of the sheep stirred slightly in the shadow and I shot the poor thing, thinking it was the deserter. Julia was behind me. I didn't know she'd heard me get up. She followed me. When she heard the shot she screamed and woke me up completely. I turned to her and wept on her shoulder. I think she wept on mine too, but I don't recall that now. She went to her grave the only person to know the truth of that night. I gave her that terrible experience. I'm mighty ashamed. She didn't deserve that. I have felt miserable over that night all these years, but I don't want to go to my own grave with it."

Papa fell quiet. And I nearly stopped breathing, covering my mouth to conceal my presence. I had heard it all. Trafton stayed quiet too. Maybe he had no idea what to say. Maybe he knew enough to let the silence speak for itself. At reunions, stories were shared, some funny, some poignant, like this one. I prayed that telling Trafton about his struggle would soothe Papa's soul because I would never speak of it.

When Papa next spoke, it was to thank Trafton for coming.

In late March 1917, when being outside began to be bearable again, Walter arranged to have that talk with Papa. I saw the two of them sitting on the piazza. I badly wanted to eavesdrop and could have if I'd stood closer to the door. But it wouldn't be right. I hoped Papa would tell me what they talked about.

"Manuel, I've been thinking. My mother is poorly. Bessie, bless her, cares for her well. And the farm is in good hands with the two men she hired. So, my work there, though helpful, I'm sure, isn't as crucial as it was before I went west. And anyone can deliver this mail. I guess what I'm trying to say is that I feel like a man without a purpose these days." Walter paused. "Well, sir, if this country enters the war going on overseas, well, I wonder if I should enlist. I can't talk to my own father about this. You may know he died in '11. But you served in war. I want to do right by my country. Now, mind you, they may not want me, since I'm not a youngster anymore. But if things get as bad as they say, maybe they'd take any able-bodied man. And I am that." He stopped there.

I noticed the silence and then heard Papa clear his throat. "Walter," he said, "war is an ugly business. It most certainly isn't something to take lightly. But I 'spect you know that. Especially someone your age. You're what, forty or so?" Walter nodded. "I was too young and naïve to have joined the military. I thought I'd seen all I needed to by then. I'd seen plenty of blood aboard the whaler I was on, most of it belonging to the whales we speared, but some of it was from men who'd gotten tangled in the ropes or some other foolish thing. When President Lincoln called for more enlisted men, war was talked about like it was an adventure, a chance to see other parts of this country. We were even assured that with as many Union soldiers as there were, we wouldn't be in probable danger. The atmosphere in Portland when I signed up was like a parade, men whoopin' and hollerin', sayin' 'Let's go, let's get them rebs.' I was a 'man without a purpose', as you say. And I had no wife or hope of one. When the recruiters said we'd have money to buy land and a house after the war, I guess I thought I may as well fight and have something to show for it. If I'd known how repulsive war was, I'd never have gone. That's the truth of it, son."

Papa paused. "Now, mind you, I'm glad I went with respect to feeling like a man, but, son, surely by now you don't need to feel like a man. Being forty is man enough, I should think."

Silence again.

"Is it possible that joining the war effort is a way to run from something in your life?"

There was a short silence and then I heard Papa's voice, "You don't have to say anything to me. That's just something for you to think about."

Twenty-six

Atonement

On April 6, the United States joined the Allied cause across the Atlantic. But Walter did not even try to enlist. What Manuel had said to him made sense, though he still didn't know what he might be running from. One evening, early that summer, Elizabeth sat in the living room as she did most evenings for an hour or so, tucked in a blanket.

"Walter?"

"Yes, mother?"

"Tell me about your travels again. I love hearing all about it. First of all, how is that family you stayed with so long?"

"You mean Friedrich and Klara? As far as I know they are still well. You asked me that last night," Walter began, irritated.

Elizabeth let out a little chuckle. "I know, dear. Silly me. I'm sorry."

Feeling ashamed to have spoken as he had, he said, "That's alright, Ma. Forgive my attitude. Little Walter should be about four years old now. Klara had another child, which was stillborn. I guess she almost died as well." Walter noticed his mother's sharp intake of breath, so he hurried on, "Of course Friedrich is grieving the loss of this second child, but he is so grateful to have Klara that he says he chooses not to complain. He's a good, God-fearing man, and they'll be fine." His mother let out a heavy sigh.

Walter continued, now in his own reflective reverie, no longer needing his mother's questions. "I grew to love the wide-open spaces of North Dakota about as much as Friedrich does. If it hadn't been for my desire to see Aunt Amanda, I might have stayed and gotten a piece of land for myself. I guess I could still go out there if I wanted to one day."

"Oh, please don't go that far away from Maine again, Walter," Bessie pleaded, staring at her brother and shaking her head almost imperceptibly.

"We'll see," was all Walter said.

At this, Bessie went to her mother, telling her that it was getting late, and she'd take her back to her room.

"Good night, Ma," Walter said with a smile. He turned back to the newspaper.

"Walter," Bessie said quietly after leaving their mother's room, "may I talk with you, please?"

"Of course," he said putting down the paper.

"Not here. Come with me to the kitchen." He followed her there.

"I don't think you're seeing what's happening to Mama, my dear brother," Bessie said, mildly chastising him. "When you came back home, and I'm very grateful you did, it was because Mother had had a stroke. Fortunately, her speech is restored. But something is happening lately that I don't think you're seeing."

"Apparently. You've said that twice now."

"It's her memory. Sometimes her thinking is clear, but more and more she isn't remembering things correctly or she doesn't remember things at all, like tonight. I hope you saw that more clearly."

"Yes," Walter said, waiting for more.

"But, at the same time, she often remembers things from a long time ago. That's what happened when you were talking about Klara's second baby. I think Mother was reliving a memory from years ago as though it just happened. Do you remember ever hearing her talk about her sister's stillborn baby?"

"No."

"Well, Ma was there, helping with the birth. There were other women too, so she wasn't alone. I don't know if she felt partly responsible for the stillborn child or not, but now I wonder because of her reaction. When she told me about it, a few years ago, she just gave me the facts. But now I think it may have been traumatic for her."

"Oh," Walter said, not without compassion.

"When you suggested you might move back to North Dakota, I tried to stop you. Mother would never let on how much she missed you. She knew that getting away was what you needed. And she'd do anything for us, even to her own detriment. But when you came back, she was so happy. It was like something in her settled. Both her "babies" were home. I don't think I could bear to see her lose you again. Or even *think* she might lose you again. She's fragile, Walter. I know you think of her as strong and resourceful. But she's rapidly losing that part of her. She doesn't even ask to see Persis or Myrtie anymore. It's not that she loves them any less. I think it's just that her world outside of you and me is shrinking."

"But I wouldn't leave until after she's gone," Walter said, reasonably.

"Maybe not, but I don't think she needs to hear you even mention it. Pretend, for her sake, that you wouldn't think of leaving this farm again."

"For her sake or for yours?" Walter unleashed his irritation and immediately regretted it. He wasn't even sure where his rawness was coming from.

Taken aback and hurt, Bessie said, "What do you mean by that exactly?"

"If Ma isn't remembering yesterday or even today, does what I say really matter?"

"So, you would hurt her again and again, because you're sure that she would forget it anyway? How Christian is that?" Bessie spat out and then walked out of the kitchen and up the stairs, presumably to her room.

Walter felt awful. He wasn't trying to hurt Bessie. He was so grateful for her attentive care of their beloved mother. But he also didn't fully understand what Bessie was really getting at. He decided to go to bed and wait for the morning to shed more light on things.

But sleep wasn't coming easily and all he managed to do was toss and turn. So, instead of trying in vain, he put his clothes back on and stepped outside. Standing in the darkness, he waited for some direction as to where to walk. Finally, he saddled the old mare and pointed her in the direction of his brother-in-law's church in Windham Hill. Churches had been childhood places of solace for Walter. He'd been able to go unnoticed into his father's churches to think and to pray. And dream. He dreamed of being a minister to a congregation like this, pews filled with men, women, and children, all dressed up to hear the Holy Scriptures. Oh, how he had wanted to preach about the love of God, to instill hope into the hearts of his parishioners.

He still loved the church, but he didn't attend regularly and wasn't sure why not. Yet he had to admit to himself that when he'd gone west, it was to churches that he'd sought direction.

As the old horse plodded slowly along as if to say, "I thought night was for sleeping," he patted the side of her neck to reassure her he'd had purpose in saddling her. As he did so, he thought about the Kansas City stockyards and his part in slaughtering so many innocent animals. He shuddered. *Why did I do that? Couldn't I have found something else to do that wouldn't have left such a caustic mark on my soul? I can never forget what I saw there.*

Suddenly, Walter realized something he'd not thought of before. *Maybe all the blood and gore in the stockyards was in some way akin to the blood and gore Manuel mentioned about war, the suffering of so many living things. What did he say exactly? Ah, yes, he said 'war is ugly business.' The work in Kansas City felt ugly, too. But why? I too have had our animals slaughtered for sustenance. What's the difference? Maybe it's the sheer immensity of a business so purely mechanical that no love is lost on the poor creatures. I have loved even the hogs we raised for meat. Does an animal somehow die knowing it has been loved? Does that make killing it any better?*

Before he knew it, he'd arrived at the church, slid off his mare, and tied her to a tree. Then he slowly climbed the front steps of the white clapboard building, with its tall, narrow steeple, and turned the doorknob.

As soon as he stepped into the foyer, the rich, familiar smell of oak boards met his nose and filled him with an instant sense of humility, which took him by surprise. Shame draped over his shoulders as he slid into a back pew. He was grateful for the night sky that allowed the moon to cast a sheen on the hymnals in the pew racks. When he looked up, the iridescent cross on the altar was staring back at him. He felt the wetness of tears on his cheeks as he sat in silence for a moment.

"I've never spoken that harshly to Bessie," he said softly, as though he might be overheard. "I would never intend to hurt her, ever. Why do I do the thing I don't want to do?"

What is this harshness you have for yourself, Walter? he heard in his heart. Surprised, not because he'd heard from God, but because he heard it now, in all his shame.

"You mean, what am I running from, like Manuel asked me?" All at once Walter knew the answer would be a sort of turning point in his life, something that would direct him repeatedly in its wisdom. Something so much bigger than himself that the answer was not in any particular place like California or even Maine.

He quieted his mind to listen for more.

It is not to be found in a particular vocation, either, the mysterious yet familiar message-giver conveyed, having heard Walter's thought.

"Not even as a minister? I'd have access to You in a special way then, wouldn't I?"

Would you? Where did your father go to find Me that you have not or could not go yourself?

"I don't know. But then why was father called to be a minister? I thought it was specifically to be closer to You and preach about You? That's why it was so important to me to be a minister like my father. That's why I'm angry that I couldn't pass Greek."

Did you want to be a minister for Me? Or for you?

These words stung with the echoes of those he'd spoken to his sister. And, he guessed, that was not by accident.

"I thought I wanted to go to seminary for both You *and* me, but I guess mostly for me. I thought it would please father. If father approved of me, I thought You would too."

Do you want to know what pleases Me?

"Of course."

Your love. That's it. That's all. Whether it's for Me, or someone else, or an animal, or most especially for yourself, sincere, heart-felt love always pleases me. Your father was a minister because he felt that calling and as he pursued that path, the way opened for him.

"I thought I felt that calling, but the way didn't open for me. Why not?"

Are you sure it didn't? What about all the people you've helped over the years? Why did you help them?

"Because it felt right to. And I wanted to."

It felt right and it was loving, was it not?

"Yes, but I didn't always mention You like I would if I was a minister."

What pleases me are your actions that have reflected sincere love and compassion, no matter where it came from or to whom you gave it. To Friedrich or Aunt Amanda, to those you tended to in the hospital, or the small boy who received your gift of a penny, to the cows on your farm or, yes, even the steers in the stockyards who received your sympathy, which was born from your great love of animals. Love comes in many shades and situations.

"So, I can live as a man of compassion without a stole?"

If you were meant to wear a stole, the way would have opened.

"So, it's okay with You that I'm not a minister like my father?"

Of course, but is it okay with you?

Tears cascaded freely down Walter's cheeks as he realized who he was really angry with and whose forgiveness he really needed. He'd thought he needed his father's forgiveness, and certainly God's. But it seemed what he needed most of all was to forgive himself, the one whom he'd been angry with all along. And he now knew with clarity that he'd been running from himself and he needn't anymore.

This realization came with an openness, a feeling of expansion, an uncluttered freedom. *Maybe that's part of the reason why the uncluttered miles of Kansas fields and grasses were so appealing to me,* he thought. Suddenly, it felt foolish to have beaten himself up for not being able to finish seminary. Suddenly, passing Greek seemed like a very narrow passageway to loving people, as if seminary was the only way one *could* love. It was *one* passageway, and it had been his father's. But it wasn't his and never would be. And, unbelievably, Walter realized that was alright.

"I sense you smiling at me," Walter said.

I am. But more than that, I am smiling with you. You have heard My Message and you have seen Me.

With a much lighter heart and heavier eyelids, Walter rode home. Just as he reached the farmhouse, he heard this: *And...I am also* not *smiling, so to speak. There are those to whom you need to reach out.*

"And I shall. Starting tomorrow." He'd make things right with Bessie, first of all. Then he would begin loving people with the heart of a minister, no matter where he was or with whom. No matter that he had no stole.

On August 18, 1917, his mother succumbed to her dementia and Walter knew that this good woman, who had loved her family so well, was at last free, roaming the halls of paradise. As grateful as he was that she no longer suffered, it didn't make him miss his mother any less. He and Bessie now had each other to lean on in their common grief.

Twenty-seven

Friendship

A week after Elizabeth's service, Bessie and Walter sat quietly in the living room, absorbed in different things, when Bessie put down her knitting and said, "You know, don't you, that Millie is living with her father."

"Yes. I deliver her mail. If you are not so subtly suggesting that I call on her again, you can stop. I won't reach out to her other than to be polite. 'Once bitten, twice shy' as they say. Speaking of which, do you ever see Ernest Moller at all?"

"If you're trying to change the subject, it won't work. No, I don't see him and I'm glad. That very brief relationship made me nervous. I don't think I was made to be someone's wife. Back to Millie, I would like to know why she is living with her father. I have never heard exactly what happened six years ago, have you?"

"Oh, so 'tis you who wants the relationship with her so you can nose about her business. I have no idea what happened between her and her fiancé, and I have no need to know."

"Oh, drivel! You're boring."

"My dear sister, it is not a matter of boredom at all. It is a matter of propriety and respect for Millie. Why don't you ask her yourself if you are so keen to know?"

"I haven't had a personal relationship with her since you left. I'm not about to start one with that question."

"Then don't. Now may I go back to my newspaper, please?"

With a snort, Bessie turned back to her knitting.

Lizzie walked into the library. I was surprised but gave her my best smile. "Hello, roomie," Lizzie said with a tilt of her head that hinted at hesitation mixed with genuine goodwill.

"Hello. What brings you here? Is there anything I can help you find?"

"No. I would like a moment to talk to you when you aren't busy."

No one else was in the library just then, but that didn't mean I wasn't busy. But I could drop what I was doing easily enough. "If you don't mind me helping anyone who comes in, we can talk right now."

"Oh, good. I was hoping to get this off my chest today while I had the courage. First of all, I hope you have no ill will about my coming to Great Falls to teach." She paused for my answer.

"None at all. Though I was surprised when I saw you outside with the children a few weeks ago. I hadn't known until then that you were teaching here." I could have asked her a question but decided to let her take the conversation where she needed to.

"Oh, that's a relief. It might have been a very long school year otherwise. I took a year off after what Lawrence did, but I decided I loved teaching too much not to continue. The job in Scarborough was taken when I decided to go back, so I looked for a job somewhere else. When I learned that Great Falls was open, I jumped at that. It has felt like coming home, I guess, after living so close to Portland. I really do love the country life in Great Falls. I just didn't realize it until I worked so close to a big city. Children are adorable everywhere, but the ones here are a bit more innocent, I guess, to the harsher realities of city life."

Lizzie paused and I held my tongue. Many questions were surfacing in my mind now.

"Um, well, that brings me to what happened between Lawrence and me. I never…"

The door opened and a woman with two small children entered.

"Hello. May I help you?" I said, impatient to hear the rest of Lizzie's sentence and trying not to sound like it.

"Yes," the woman said, "Tommy would like a book about farming. And Daisy, here, wants another book on kittens."

"Of course," I said, moving to the children's section. "Daisy, did you like the book I read last week?"

Daisy nodded vigorously, saying nothing.

"Then this one here should do just fine," I said, handing her a colorful book with wonderful pictures of a litter of kittens playing with each other. "And for you, Tommy, how about this one? There's also a few others right here. Look them over and see what you think you'd like."

I looked up at their mother, whose smile told me everything. "I'll be at my desk if you want to check the books out. But you can read them here if you like. I close in an hour." I preferred they check the books out and leave, but I couldn't force such a thing.

A few minutes later, the woman approached my desk and said, "We'll check them out. I need to get home soon. Thank you, Millie."

After I processed their books and wished them a good day, they left Lizzie and me in silence once more.

"Go ahead, Lizzie. I think you were talking about what happened between you and Lawrence."

"Yes, well, I never intended to hurt you, I hope you know that. I thought I loved him, and my feelings ran away with me. I should have at least told you then what was happening instead of you having to learn about it via gossip. Lawrence and I enjoyed our relationship for quite a while. And then it started to feel, I don't know, forced, I guess. Something changed between us. Not overnight, but things changed quickly, it seemed to me. Then he began to forget our plans occasionally, which wasn't like him at all. I made a nice dinner for him once and I waited a couple hours past the time he said he'd be there. At first, I was just angry. Then I began to think the worst, that something awful had happened to him. Finally, I just went to bed. I didn't know what else to do. But the next day, he came to the school early to wait for me. He was so sorry to have missed our time together. I believed him, of course."

Of course, I thought to myself, *this story is beginning to sound familiar.*

"So, after that, things seemed alright again. For a while. Until one day I decided to surprise him at the apothecary where he worked. I didn't see him at the clerk's desk, so I walked around to the back of the store and saw him standing there, having what looked like a very intimate conversation with a nicely dressed woman."

"Oh, my!" I said, "That must have been awkward. Did he see you?"

"Not at first but when he did, he pushed the woman aside to come to me. The woman didn't know what was happening. She just stood there with her hand on her hip waiting for Lawrence to turn back to her. And I stood there waiting for an explanation. And, well, actually, in hindsight, telling you about this, it's almost funny, isn't it? With poor Lawrence caught like a rat in a trap."

Poor Lawrence? I thought. *I think I'd rather call him reckless and say that he got what he deserved. More like poor Lizzie, I'd say.*

"So what happened after that?" I asked, praying fervently that no one else would come into the library and derail Lizzie's energetic story-telling.

"Well, I just stormed out of there. I thought he might follow me but if he did, I left too soon because I didn't see him. I was not about to be fooled by his insincere apologies again. I saw him once more and told him I was done with the relationship. Best decision of my life. Except coming to Great Falls and patching things up with you. I'm just terribly sorry and truly hope we can be friends again?"

The door opened and two youngsters came in and headed straight for the section they wanted. "I think I'd better attend to them, and I could be a while helping them," I said to Lizzie. "But thank you for your honesty. We can indeed be friends again and let's do get together soon." We hugged and a friendship temporarily frozen was thawed back to life again. I listened for Lizzie to say something that indicated she knew that I'd been jilted by Lawrence too, but she never said anything to that effect. I can only assume she knew nothing about it.

Walter and I have spoken to one another when he brings the mail, but the conversation is always short and very polite, as if we are complete strangers. It feels uncomfortable to me. *Can I set things to rights?* I wondered.

Effie and I were standing between our houses one day when Walter came with the mail. I think Effie's presence made the situation easier because Walter struck up a real conversation with us.

"Good afternoon, ladies. How are you this fine day? I see you are dressed for the weather. Did I catch you coming or going?"

"Coming back," Effie said with her usual effervescence. "Millie went with me to the store. I'm afraid I'm still trying to set up my kitchen. You'd think I'd have it finished by now, this many weeks after my wedding. But the kitchen isn't as natural a place for me as it seems to be for Millie."

"Did you walk down there in this new snow?" Walter asked, noticing the two sets of footprints leading up the hill.

"We did!" Effie answered. "It's just so lovely to be the first to walk through new white snow, isn't it?"

Not much gets that *girl down these days,* I thought, feeling a tad envious.

"I can't disagree with that, Effie," Walter said, smiling. "I suppose you two have heard that whatever this new disease is has now affected most of Europe. It's hard to believe one ailment can spread that far and wide. It must be a miserable condition, and during the war too. I can hardly think of anything more dreadful."

"Yes," I answered this time, "I've been reading about it in the paper. Papa hopes the disease won't cross the ocean. But surely it couldn't do that, right?"

"I have no idea about that. But speaking of your father, how *is* he, Millie?" Walter asked, happy to change the dismal subject he wished he hadn't brought up.

"He complains more often about the pain in his legs. They're both aching now. I can tell he feels miserable some days. I went to church without him last Sunday. Well, I guess you would know that. It was nice to see you there, by the way. But I had some convincing to do to keep him home. He can be stubborn at times."

"Would it help if I called on him? Give him company to keep his mind off his pain, perhaps?"

At first, I was going to tell him that wasn't necessary, but then I thought differently. "If you would like to do that, I'd be much obliged. He can't visit for long periods but once in a while for a short time might be good for him. Thank you."

"For you, too, Millie," Effie said, understanding my care-giving situation. Bless her for that.

"Then that's what I will do. And I'll be very happy to. You ladies need to get in where it's warm. And this mail won't deliver itself. Take care," Walter said, nodding at us and giving the horse a light slap with the reins.

If Effie thought any more of Walter's conversation than the friendliness of an acquaintance, she didn't say. But I wondered. And what would it feel like to have him visiting Papa?

Summer began. For most it was the warmer weather that ushered it in. For me, it was when Joe and his family arrived. Doris was now fourteen and a half, young Joe would celebrate his thirteenth birthday that July, and Rachel was ten. One day, soon after they arrived, the three of them came running to the piazza where I was reading. In fits of laughter, they demanded, "Say it again, Aunt Millie! Tell us about the nervous usher in church!"

I sighed as if doing this for them would be a big imposition. But secretly, I loved it. "All right. Once more. A woman walked into church one Sunday. She was fairly new and quite lovely. She tried to take a seat but found that a man was sitting in her pew box. So, she found the usher and asked him for his help. My, oh my, was the usher nervous! He was so nervous that his words came out all wrong. Do you want to know what he said?"

"Yes!" the children shouted.

"He said, 'Padam me mardon, may I sew you to your sheet? Your pie is occupewed."

The children laughed and laughed, and I laughed right along with them. None of them noticed Bea was watching out of the corner of her eye as she hung out the laundry to dry. Nor were they aware that Walter had just come to deliver the mail. He stood spellbound, watching the fun, and Millie in particular.

"She seems happier, Joe. I tell you she laughs more these days. Even Doris noticed and told me Millie was dancing a jig. Can you believe it?"

"What were you saying, Bea?" Joe yawned. He just wanted to turn over and go to sleep after a long day sorting out how to work Manuel's diminishing farm. They'd just come in from Massachusetts at the beginning of the week. Traveling to Maine with the three children wore him out, too. They were well-mannered enough but excited to get back to the country where there was no school to attend, no shoes needed, and no fences to hem them in. They jabbered incessantly.

Once they were at the farm, Rachel headed for the swing. Every day she delighted in swinging, and some days she let Dolly enjoy the ride as well. Young Joe would be a big help to his father this summer and Doris would spend a lot of her time in the kitchen. I could feel my load lessen the moment they drove into the yard.

"It's just that I sense a change in Millie, a good one."

"That's good," Joe said before giving in to sleep.

Bea sighed and pulled the covers up under her chin. As she waited for sleep to overtake her, she wondered what, if anything, was happening between Walter and Millie. *Those two have grown a lot over the years. I think marriage would be about right for them now.* Bea yawned. The next thing she heard was the old rooster crowing the arrival of the sun.

Twenty-eight

Dis-ease

Unfortunately, that summer of 1918 was not all laughter. The newspaper was passed around in hopes it would deliver good news where none seemed to be had. The war hadn't ended, and by now the influenza that had ravaged military foxholes in Europe had come over to Camp Funston in Kansas. Though the disease spread as far as Boston to the east and California to the west, Mainers were not terribly concerned. They felt isolated and away from the country's mainstream.

Even so, influenza was the start-up topic for many a conversation, mostly so that each party could convince the other that this dreaded new disease would not affect them. And so it was for Walter and me standing in the front yard when he came to deliver the mail. "I'm just sorry to hear that the disease has spread as far as the west coast," Walter said. "I hate to admit it, but I'm grateful not to be in California right now." *On the other hand,* Walter thought, *I am concerned for Alice and Anna, whom I've not heard from since I left Fortuna. Thank goodness my aunt is okay.*

Walter didn't want to leave the subject without sounding reassuring, and said, "Here in Maine, I think we'll be just fine." Then, changing the subject, he said, "By the way, speaking of the west coast, the Panama-Pacific International Exposition was quite the 'cat's meow,' to use a phrase I learned in California."

"I don't know what a 'cat's meow' is," Millie laughed, "but I've read about the exposition. What was it like?"

"It was amazing beyond words, to tell you the truth. Besides, San Francisco itself is a very beautiful city."

"I'd like to hear about it," I said, hoping to keep the conversation going a bit longer.

"I'll tell you what. I'll stop by after I deliver this mail and tell you about it. I won't have a lot of time since I need to get back to the cows. Milking time, you know. But I can give it a start."

"Yes, that would be fine. I'll see you then."

I couldn't help redoing my hair bun and freshening up before Walter came back. But I didn't change my dress because I didn't want Bea to see me making that much of a fuss. Then I put two chairs out on the front lawn rather than the side, a signal, I hoped, that I didn't want to be unduly bothered by the children.

"So, where was I?" Walter said when he returned, grateful for the tea Millie offered once he was seated. "Oh, yes, well first of all, San Francisco, you know, is on the Pacific Ocean."

"Is there a difference between oceans just to look at them?" I asked.

"Not much to the casual eye, although it did seem like the waves there were bigger. In fact, everything out west seems bigger. Wider. More spacious. But primarily I was in San Francisco to see the exposition, not the ocean."

"Yes! Tell me about what you saw there," I said, genuinely interested. In fact, I suddenly wondered if perhaps the children should hear this. I asked Walter if that was alright, and he wholeheartedly agreed. So, I went to fetch them.

When we returned, I invited the children to sit on the grass where they could hear Walter. "What's an exposition?" Joe wanted to know.

"It's like the...,"

"Where's Dolly?" Rachel said frantically, searching with her eyes. "Where is she? She was right here with me, now she's gone! Joe...did you take her? Did you?"

"I didn't take her!" Joe yelled. "Wait…what's that? Right there, Rachel. Dolly's been right next to you all the time!" He laughed, enjoying his sister's panic a bit too much, in my opinion.

"Joe, that's enough," I said. "Rachel was scared just as you would be if you thought you'd lost something of value to you. You need to apologize to your sister." Reluctantly, Joe did as he was told.

To Rachel, I said, looking at Dolly, "You know, Rachel, if 'twoulda been a bear…" Here I paused an extra second, then finished, "'twoulda *bit*-cha!" I said, pretending to bite Rachel's nose. Rachel broke into a giggle despite herself. With the mood changed for the better, I looked at Walter and said, as if nothing had happened at all, "Please, continue."

Walter smiled at me, then said, "An exposition is like the grandest fair you could ever see," Walter loved the wide-eyed looks of his audience. "There were block-sized courtyards laid out like a city. Each block displayed something from another country. There were more than twenty countries and forty-eight states represented. Most displays had buildings with at least one dome, which is how the fair got its nickname, City of Domes. Perhaps you've heard about it?"

"I read about it in a magazine!" Joe said excitedly.

"We learned about it in school," Doris offered. Rachel said nothing.

"Good!" Walter said, smiling at them. "Well, one of the buildings was called the Tower of Jewels. It was forty-three floors high, with more than one hundred thousand glass beads in many bright colors, which were strung on wires so they would blow in the wind."

"Why would it be called the Tower of Jewels if the beads were glass?" Doris asked.

"That's a great question. It's because of the way they sparkled when the sunlight fell on them. They looked like jewels, especially from a distance." Walter felt a twinge of pain thinking about how Anna had stood before this building in awe, tears welling in her eyes to look upon something so enormous that shone so magnificently. He moved on quickly. "Rachel, I think you would have liked all the different kinds of trees they planted all over the fair. So many different shades of green and shapes of leaves. Some were very tall. If they'd hung a swing in one of those, you could have swung at least twice as high as yours here in the apple tree." Rachel's eyes grew bigger. "And Joe, you might have liked to see the Ford Motor Company assembly line on display. They built eighteen Model T's every day!" We watched young Joe nearly shake with excitement. "There were so many, many things to see that it would take days to see it all."

"What did you like best, Walter?" I asked, thoroughly enjoying his presentation.

"Hm, that would have to be the aviation field where pilots did stunts in their airplanes or 'aeroplanes' as an announcer from England called them. To see them fly was one thing, but to watch them do loops and dives all over the sky was mesmerizing to me."

"What's 'mesmerizing' mean, Uncle Walter?" Rachel asked, not realizing the implications of addressing him that way. I caught Walter's eyes for a moment before he answered her, "It means to be completely charmed by what you see. I couldn't believe what I was seeing, but I had to because it was happening right before my eyes. And at night, one pilot added lights to his wings so that all you could see were ribbons of light twirling in the sky like an enormous firefly!"

"Why was it called the Panama-Pacific exposition?" I asked so that the children would know the answer.

"It was celebrating both the completion of the Panama Canal and the four hundredth anniversary of Balboa's discovery of the Pacific Ocean. But San Francisco itself wanted to show off its recovery from that horrible earthquake in 1906 too. And rightfully so. The city, as I say, is quite beautiful."

When it was time for me to help with the evening meal, the children got up slowly and walked away. They weren't ready for Walter to end his stories, and in truth, neither was I. As Walter and I walked back to the kitchen with the chairs, I whispered, "I'm sorry about Rachel calling you 'Uncle Walter.' That child is a bit of a romantic I think. No one here has used that term that I know of. So, please, accept my apology."

"Think no more of it. I quite liked the sound of it."

Tuesday, August 13, 1918

What am I to make of Walter's words after I apologized for Rachel calling him "Uncle Walter"? He said to think no more of it; that he liked the sound of it. I was embarrassed as I hadn't coached her to say anything like that. He's made no overtures to formally call on me but I'm enjoying his company, nevertheless.

Summer left us along with Joe, Bea, and the children, as usual. It was becoming increasingly difficult to say goodbye to them. The summer days of love and laughter with my nieces and nephew left a void in my heart the moment they drove away, the youngsters waving to me from the back seat. I kept my tears in check so that Papa wouldn't see my grief. My days were virtually the same without them, save for seasonal changes, except that Papa's care was progressively more difficult as his health declined.

Apart from the joy of Joe's family, it had been a largely unhappy summer in terms of world news. German U-boats snuck around the east coast, making everyone jittery, with good reason. The USS San Diego was sunk by the Germans off the coast of New York, and land mines were planted that sank thirteen U.S. ships and other vessels. We weren't far from the coast, either. It sent a chill through my body to think of the Germans coming on shore.

As for the influenza epidemic, which was being called the Spanish Flu, Philadelphia reported the highest number of deaths from the disease in the United States so far. Thankfully, Maine was unaffected. A letter from Joe shared a splash of good news, at least in his mind, when he said the Boston Red Sox were in the 1918 World Series, which would be on an accelerated schedule due to the war. "The world can't be all bad with Carl Mays, "Sad" Sam Jones, "Bullet" Joe Bush, and Babe Ruth pitching in the series!" he said excitedly. And indeed, a short letter from Joe mid-September boasted the Sox's world series win over the Chicago Cubs.

Honestly, I didn't care who won the series, only enjoying it for Joe's sake. I had too much to think about with Papa withering little by little. It wasn't so much one specific moment that I could say was the beginning of Papa's decline, but compared to a few years ago, or even last year this time, I could see the difference clearly. He was more and more frail, which meant that my work was more and more intense.

Not long after the series, I nervously read about the course of the Spanish Flu, which had entered Maine after all. The mayors of large cities, trying to preserve the dignity of their towns, clashed with Maine's health commissioner as to how to handle the spread of the epidemic. Where the commissioner favored immediate closure of all public places and asked for universal mask wearing, the mayor of Portland felt total closures would cripple his city. And he frowned on wearing masks at all. By the end of September, as the situation became more dire, Portland's mayor finally closed theaters, dance halls, and public schools. Meanwhile, up state, the mayor of Lewiston heard local physicians claim the illness was just a bad cold and that with good hygiene there was no need for concern.

September closures at times made little sense. Some churches still held services while funerals were banned. Theaters were closed, yet some remained open because there were many who lived in unheated, one-room tenements and went to the theaters to stay warm. As the illness spread, I scoured newspapers to determine what to do about my library. On October 1, my conscience told me to close it. By October 5, all church buildings in Maine were ordered to close and the mayor of Lewiston finally saw fit to lock down his own city. At first, general driving was completely banned to conserve fuel due to the war. A little later, driving into the countryside was seen as healthy, so the ban was lifted on Sundays. At least for Papa and me, driving bans in general didn't affect us.

I read that some people wondered if the pandemic had been started as a German war offensive. That felt unsettling to me. I wondered how people could truly be that egregious. Effie and I discussed whether to heed the call for able women to volunteer as nurses, no experience necessary. We would be paid regular nurse's wages and travel expenses. Both Effie and I knew that I needed to stay home to care for Papa. Effie would have to make her own decision.

By mid-October, after living with the erratic epidemic rules, there was much disagreement about how the epidemic was being handled. The reporting of cases was sloppy, making us wonder how safe we really were. Many ministers believed churches were a necessary source of spiritual health and should be the last places to close, particularly on Sundays. And besides, why was the government mandating edicts to the churches anyway? Churches that complied became hospitals. On the other hand, beer saloons flagrantly remained open because many believed alcohol and socialization were necessary to one's health. The Anti-Tuberculosis Association warned that if the health rules were not upheld, tuberculosis could spread as well. And with the casualties of war ever increasing, everyone, including me, was on edge.

So it was that one Saturday, I had a surprise visit from Lawrence. I was not worried that he might ask to begin calling again. I knew without a shadow of a doubt that I was finished with Lawrence in that sense and could not be swayed. I was, however, quite curious. I was hanging wash on the line outside when he drove into the driveway in, of all things, his automobile!

"My, oh my!" I said, still holding a clothespin in one hand and a pair of Papa's pants in the other.

"Like 'er?" Lawrence said, very proudly.

"I guess so. I'm not accustomed to having feelings for automobiles as I might for a horse."

"I just got 'er. She rides like a charm and makes my trips here and there so much faster. I'm even offered jobs just because I have a car, as people like me call them instead of 'automobile.'"

"Well, that's just fine, Lawrence. I'm very happy for you," I said, mostly sincere.

"Actually, Millie, I came to see how you and your father were doing with this epidemic everywhere. I mean, I didn't come all the way here *just* to ask you about that. But I thought I'd stop on my way to other things. Have you two been well?"

"So far we have. What about you?"

"So far, so good. And otherwise, any news?" Lawrence asked, but I didn't hear him because I had glanced at someone coming down the road and realized it was Walter. I saw his face briefly and detected a frown, not his usual smile. He put the mail in the box and hurried on. *Oh, no!* I thought. *He doesn't think I'm back together with...oh, no, no, NO!"*

I threw down the clothespin and pair of pants and raced to the road, but Walter had left so quickly I couldn't run to him. *I'll just have to catch him tomorrow.* "I'm sorry, Lawrence," I said, walking back, "but I need to go check on Papa. You'll excuse me." I didn't wait for a reply. I didn't care what Lawrence thought of my discourteous manner unless he understood that I was finished with him once and for all.

The next day, Walter's substitute delivered the mail. And the next day the same. And the next and the next. I was truly concerned that Walter had given up on me and I wore my anxiety like a wet wool coat. I thought about going to Walter and Bessie's house, but that would be too forward. *Besides, I didn't do anything wrong,* I thought. Though true, the words felt impotent. *Time will just have to prove to Walter that I am no longer interested in Lawrence.*

Seconds later, I wondered, *Why do I care what Walter thinks?*

Twenty-nine

Anguish

"Walter, it's been a week now since you have delivered the mail. What's wrong?" Bessie asked.

"I don't feel well," was all he said.

"In head or heart?"

"Maybe both," he said sourly.

"Won't you please talk to me about it? Maybe I can help," Bessie urged.

"Maybe I am coming down with the Spanish Flu," he said. And then added under his breath, "Might be a blessing."

"What was that last thing you said? About a blessing?" Bessie asked. He didn't answer so she went on. "You don't sound sick. But you're so mopey. If I know my brother, and I think I do because I've seen this before, I'd say you are heart sick more than anything else. Is it Millie?"

Silence. Finally, "Well, maybe so. When I delivered her mail last week, there was an automobile in the driveway. I was very curious who would call on the Thomases in something that fancy. I saw that Millie was hanging the wash. But she was talking to Lawrence Hanley. I fear her allegiance to him again. I haven't the heart to inquire so it seemed easier just to give the route to Benjamin. If Millie wants to be with Lawrence, so be it," he finished.

"But Walter, do you know for sure Lawrence is calling on Millie?"

"Why else would he pick her up in a fancy automobile? I surely can't compete with that," he barked. Bessie raised her eyebrows at Walter's bitterness.

She watched her brother slump further into the soft chair pulling a small blanket up under his chin. *There's no doubt Walter is sick in heart,* Bessie realized with alarm. She couldn't bear to see Millie jilt her brother again.

Another week passed and Walter had stopped even climbing the stairs to his bedroom, preferring to sleep on the couch. He had been coughing more and more every day, complaining of a sore throat, and wheezing when he breathed. Bessie called for the doctor, who had seen so many patients like this, he delivered his news with the emotionless, flat tone of having delivered a similar speech many times.

"Walter has the flu. Plenty of rest and fluids, soups are best. Anything brothy and hot that he can swallow. I can give you aspirin for his pain. I'm out of quinine, but I will give him a shot of camphor to ease his chest congestion. He's had pneumonia before and he's likely to get it now if he doesn't have it already. And it will be worse for him this time. Watch him for fever or inability to sleep and call for me if you think he is worse. I may have morphine by then. That's the best I can tell you, Bessie. This disease is not good."

To say that Bessie was worried out of her mind would be an understatement. She stayed by Walter's side day and night.

By the end of October, the epidemic was beginning to loosen its grip on Great Falls. I reopened the library and slowly life began to normalize as businesses resumed. On November 11, 1918, the Great War ended. I read in the newspaper the following excerpt from a soldier on the front:

In three hours the war will be over. It seems incredible even as I write it. I suppose I ought to be thrilled and cheering. Instead I am merely apathetic and incredulous. There is some cheering across the river—occasional bursts of it as the news is carried to the advanced lines. For the most part, though, we are in silence, with a feeling that it can't be true. For months we have slept under the guns. We cannot comprehend the stillness.

Robert Casey
Battery C, 124th Field Artillery Regiment, 33rd Division

I can hardly imagine what this man and so many others must feel. I don't pretend to know what it would be like not to be able to comprehend silence. I am grateful that this terrible war is over, but I must confess that it hasn't affected me personally. Maybe that is why I am not participating in the celebrations others are having. Or maybe it's just that my heart is heavy for imagining my life without Walter. And to think, at one time I couldn't imagine agreeing to marry him. What has changed?

"Millie," Papa said at dinner, "I know there is something bothering you. And I think you should talk about it. With me or someone else, but speak your mind. I should have learned how to do that many years ago."

"Oh, Papa," I said, putting down my fork, "how well you know me. It's just that I fear Walter may never call on me again."

"And why is that, child?" I haven't minded Papa calling me that these days. I don't know exactly when I stopped minding, but now I realize I will always be his child, no matter what age I am.

"Nearly a month ago now, Lawrence came to the house. I was hanging out the wash. He drove into the driveway in an automobile." I could see Papa's interest. "Yes, I almost woke you to see it. I might have, but while we talked, Walter came by with the mail. He saw us and, well, that's when his assistant began delivery."

"I wondered why I hadn't seen him. I feared he might have taken ill with this flu."

I suddenly realized I'd never thought of Walter possibly being ill. *How self-centered I am,* I chastised myself silently.

"Why did Lawrence call?"

"He had business somewhere around here, I guess. He said he wanted to ask about my health and yours with respect to the epidemic."

"You don't trust that's what he was after?"

"I don't know, and I don't really care. I saw Walter hurriedly stick the mail in the box and leave quickly. Oh, Papa, his face when he looked at me. I'm afraid he thinks Lawrence and I have gotten back together. I haven't heard from him since. I feel terrible that Walter may think I'm with Lawrence when that isn't the truth of things at all. I was just as surprised to see Lawrence as Walter probably was. I just don't know what to do about it." I hung my head and stared at my uneaten food without seeing it at all.

"Could it be that you love him?" Papa said tenderly.

"Who? Lawrence? No!"

"No, I mean Walter."

Too quickly I declared, "Oh, I don't know that I feel *that* strongly."

Neither of us spoke as Papa sipped his coffee.

"Well, maybe I do," I conceded. "But when did this happen? I don't remember waking up one day wanting to declare my feelings for Walter to the world like I did with Lawrence. So how can both be love? I'm confused."

"Love is more about how we treat people than about a specific feeling. Here," Papa put down his fork, got up with difficulty, left the room, and came back with Howdie's little golden Bible. He opened it to 1 Corinthians, chapter 13, and read, "'Charity,' which means 'love', you know, 'suffereth long, and is kind; charity envieth not; it is not puffed up, doth not behave itself unseemly, seeketh not her own, is not easily provoked, thinketh no evil; rejoiceth not in iniquity, but rejoiceth in the truth; beareth all things, believeth all things, hopeth all things, endureth all things. Charity never faileth.' Do you hear anything at all about feelings in what I read?"

"No, Papa," I said quietly.

I knew that Papa wasn't reading the words. He couldn't. He might have read from his Portuguese Bible but then, of course, I wouldn't have understood most of it. No, Papa had memorized these verses which, until this very moment, I hadn't known. It wasn't that I'd never heard the familiar words myself, but hearing them recited flawlessly from Papa's lips not only made the passage more deeply meaningful but made me see Papa in a whole new way. Suddenly he wasn't just Papa, the man who raised me to be the woman I am, but a man with the sensitivity of one who had experienced love in his lifetime.

"Papa, will you tell me about the love you had for Mama and Ella? Were they the same?"

He took so long to answer that I was afraid I had asked him something far too personal. But he said, "I didn't fall in love with either woman before I married them. Not the way you felt about Lawrence or the way you want to feel about Walter. Your mother and I simply felt that our union would work out well. I had property and only a small amount of money to begin a farm. She had family money and was ready to leave home. But, as it turned out, your mother and I had more in common than we thought. I grew to love her very much. And there isn't a day goes by that I don't think of her and miss her."

I saw his eyes glisten. At least I hoped so. It meant so much to believe that Mama and Papa had truly loved one another.

"As for Ella, I know I didn't handle that situation as well as I might have. And I have regretted that ever since."

"It's okay, Papa, truly it is."

"I married Ella for convenience and companionship. I tried to convince myself it might become more than that, that love would grow between us as it did with your mother. I wanted you to see that I could be happy with another wife so that you would move away from here and not think you needed to take care of me. But you knew I wasn't happy. When Ella and I discussed divorce, she said she'd rather not have ended the marriage. But I learned she was no more invested in our union than I was. We parted ways as friends."

He stopped and I began to think about what he had just admitted when suddenly he was chuckling. "What is it, Papa?"

He started laughing out loud. I have rarely seen that.

"Papa! What's so funny?" I said, now smiling, too.

"You probably think you are the one who broke us up in the end. But the truth of it is that I was getting no sleep at all because she insisted that cat of hers sleep with us in our bed! The cat is what came between us."

"Literally, as well as figuratively," I said and laughed along with him. Never have I felt as close to Papa as this.

"Well," he said, lifting his fork to finish what was left on his plate, "I want you to know–no, I want you to believe–that if a relationship is destined to be a lasting one, love will grow in accordance with the ability to treat one another lovingly. If the relationship ceases to be healthy or becomes nothing more than friendship, like Ella's and mine, so be it. You will have lost nothing if love has been your guidance."

Considering all that Papa had expressed so well, I wondered one more thing. "Papa, you seemed reluctant to let me even consider being Walter's wife years ago because you didn't want me to be 'nothing more than a farmer's wife' as you put it. Could you give us your blessing now if Walter should propose marriage and I accept?"

Pulling at his beard in thought, he said, "Yes, I could. You are much matured all these years later. I trust you to know your heart. If you believe you'd be happy with Walter, I can also believe that."

When I walked into the building, I smelled the heavenly scent of pine, which lifted my spirits considerably. The sanctuary was gaily decorated with pine boughs and red-ribbon bows, with extra ribbon hanging freely and fluttering as people walked by. In the windows were candles in glass globes on simple red wooden bases, their attached ribbons draped down over the sills. A lovely wreath hung on the pulpit. Papa had come, as I knew he would want to. Christmas service was his favorite, maybe because it was the one time he could sing along with all the hymns, having committed to memory the familiar carols. He took a seat with Joe, Bea, Dotty, Little Joe, and Rachel. I loved seeing an entire pew taken up with my beloved family. If only things were right again with Walter, the day would be perfect.

I couldn't sit with them because it was my turn at the organ. I checked the hymn numbers on the wall board to tell me what carols we were going to sing. Then I lifted the cover off the organ console. And there, to my surprise, was an envelope addressed to me. I wasn't sure whether to open it right then or not, but I had a few minutes to spare. The entire card was edged in fuzzy blue fringe. The artwork on the front was a small girl enwreathed in foliage; the back, a winter scene of evergreen trees and birds. Inside the card, an artist's rendering of two young children was surrounded by the loveliest of poems:

I've bought a prettier card than I ever saw before,
I'll hasten to the one I love and leave it at her door.
It isn't much of a present I bring you this Christmas day,
But 'twas all I had to bring you, and I could not stay away.

It was not signed, but it said, "Meet me after the service in the vestibule, please." I could not imagine who would have given it to me. I glanced behind me at the nearly full pews, but Reverend Aikins began the service, and I had a job to do. I will tell you that my mind was not fully on my playing, but, owing to my great familiarity with the organ and the carols, in addition to the robust singing of so many people, I was able to render a decent job. But I thought the service would never end.

When it did, I closed up the organ as fast as I have ever done before and hastened to the vestibule. At first, I could see no one special in the crowd of exuberant parishioners wishing each other a merry Christmas. None of them wanted to leave the church, and I was growing impatient. Finally, after the room thinned, I saw one person who stood alone, looking at me from the other side of the room. I smiled and thankfully received a smile back.

"Bessie!" I said when at last we were both on the same side of the vestibule.

"Hello, Millie. Merry Christmas!"

"Thank you for your card. It was a surprise and a very welcome one at that."

"You're welcome. But it is not from me. I have a message for you from Walter. It won't take long. Would your ride be willing to wait a few extra minutes for you?"

"I'll go ask."

The family was still in the sanctuary and said they were more than happy to wait. I told them I'd be back when I was finished. At least they would not have to wait outside. I returned to the vestibule.

"A message from Walter?" I asked eagerly. I dared to think his message contained hope for our future.

"He has been ill since October. He almost died with pneumonia."

My breath caught in my throat. "Almost died?"

"Yes, he was in a very precarious position for a while. The doctor did all he could. He gave Walter a fifty percent chance of making it through."

"Oh, Bessie, I don't know what to say. I'm so sorry for…well…all of it."

"Thank you, Millie. His message is that he wants to see you and wonders if you might come to the house soon. He is too weak to travel even so small a distance as coming here to the church, which he wanted to do, to deliver the card himself. I wouldn't let him. I don't think he realizes how sick he really was. And still is. He is not contagious now, at least, so it's safe for you to come."

"Should I come today?"

"Today or as soon as you can."

I hugged Bessie with new misery in my heart and told her I would come as soon as possible.

I decided to spend Christmas with the family, although I had to manufacture a joyous heart for the children's sake. After they were in bed, I filled Joe and Bea in on what had transpired since October. I couldn't bear to put any of it in letters to them, so they were quite heavy-hearted to hear all of it. They both said they would pray for Walter's health and for my visit with him.

That night I had a dream. I woke up not remembering much of it but what I did remember was both wondrous and mystifying. The location of the dream was stunningly colorful and very joyous and peaceful. I was in a beautiful grassy field interrupted only with flowers in a vivid array of colors. The flowers were talking amongst themselves and laughing. I noticed that the air had an aroma of perfume. Then, appearing out of thin air was a small group of people holding hands and cheerfully dancing in a circle. If there was music, I didn't hear it, but I knew the dancers did. I walked closer to them and saw, to my utter delight, Mama, Jennie, Howdie, and a child I didn't recognize. I assumed the child was either Georgie or Matie, but then why not both?

I greeted them all and asked, "But who is the child?"

"She is yours."

Thirty

Confessions

When I entered Walter and Bessie's living room, I found Walter under blankets on the couch. He was dressed, which was a good sign, I assumed, but there was a small table beside him with the principal elements one needs when ill. *He is not yet out of the woods,* I thought. Bessie had let me in but was now nowhere to be found.

"How do you feel?" I asked him.

"Better every day, but impatient to get on with my life," he said with a slight smile to his voice that otherwise sounded sick. I winced and waited.

"Primarily I wanted you to come here because I think it's time we talked. I feel better enough to do that now. In October, I think it was," I knew what was coming and inwardly cringed, "I came to deliver mail one day and saw Lawrence and his automobile in your yard. I must say outright that if you and Lawrence are seeing one another, please tell me now. I can handle anything better than these past couple months of assuming I would not be welcome to call anymore."

"I was so afraid you'd assumed that," I began. "If I'd been able, I would have told you that day or the next that Lawrence came unannounced, presumably to ask if Papa and I were alright. Personally, I think he had other motives, but no matter what he came for, I was just barely cordial to him and in no way taken in. When I saw you, I ran to the road, but you were too far away. I assumed I'd see you the next day. But, of course, I didn't."

At this point, I walked over to the couch and knelt down in front of Walter so that he would see my sincerity, "Walter, no matter what happens between you and me, I will never go back to Lawrence again. He has crippled my heart for the last time."

Walter reached out and put his palm on my flaming cheek. "That's very good to hear, Mildred Francesca with an 's' sound." I blushed even more, if that was possible. "Are you willing to let me call on you when I am fully well?" I nodded, not trusting my voice and went back to the chair.

"We will speak no more of the incident, then," he said. "But with that behind us, I feel it's time I talked to you about my trip out west. Are you willing to hear it?"

"I am, yes," I said. But I was suddenly tense because he sounded more serious than he had when telling me about the exposition.

"I went through Canada and several states and ended up in North Dakota for a time. Your father may have told you that. We talked about the difference in farms there as opposed to here."

"He did, yes."

"When I left there, I went to Kansas to find the places my father had been as a missionary. I can tell you more about that sometime. It was a stopover with all sorts of memorable situations. But it was outside of Kansas City that I came down with pneumonia. I was very sick and didn't know how badly. It was only by the good graces of a lovely young woman, a nurse named Alice, that I made it through that ordeal. She was in the same train car as I was, and she apparently realized that my cough was quite bad. She told the conductor that I needed a doctor's care as soon as possible and we stopped in Topeka where Alice got me to the hospital. I don't remember any of this. The first thing I do remember is waking up to this woman who explained to me where I was and why I was there. To me, she was an angel. She stayed by my bedside as much as possible until I was well enough to leave there. Then she took me back to the train so we could both continue our journeys."

"So, she was going to California, too?" I asked, trying not to think about what "a lovely young woman" might look like to Walter.

"Well, yes, she was, but not to the same city. The really odd thing was that when we got in a cab to go back to the train station, there was another young woman already in it who looked exactly like Alice. I honestly thought I was still sick and seeing double. It really scared me at first. It never occurred to me that Alice might have an identical twin. But she did, and that was Anna."

"So, these two women took time out from their own journeys to be with you? I mean, Alice is a nurse, you said. Didn't she have to work? And what about Anna?"

"Yes, they did," he said, answering my first question. "I'll get to Anna later. But Alice sent a telegram to her employer to say she would be delayed a few days and that it couldn't be helped. Meanwhile, we traveled to California together, which was a considerable distance from Topeka. But Alice insisted she accompany me until she felt I was well enough to part ways.

"Anna is quieter than her sister and while Alice was fussing over my health, Anna was creating beautiful drawings that intrigued me. We talked about art off and on the rest of the way.

"We parted company in San Francisco. They live near there and I needed to get a different train to go north to Fortuna where my Aunt Amanda lives. I won't tell you anything but the truth, Millie. I want you to always know that I am being honest with you." *You may never know how important these last words are to me,* I thought. He went on, "While I was enjoying my time with my aunt, Anna wasn't far from my thoughts. Aunt Amanda could see through me and encouraged me to call on Anna. She knew about you because I told her everything."

Now I was even more curious. "What did you tell her about me?"

"I said that you were a young woman I knew, that I had asked for your hand, and that you turned me down." Walter sighed.

"Surely that isn't all you told her, right? I mean that sounds very cold," I said with a growing sense of uneasiness.

"No, it isn't all. But let me finish telling you about Anna. I wanted to go to the exposition there in San Francisco and so did Alice and Anna.

But since Alice had to work, I took Anna alone. The short of it is that I asked for Anna's hand there at the exposition and she said 'yes.'" Walter paused on purpose, to see how I was doing, I think. But I did not betray anything of myself, so he went on.

"I went back to my aunt's house a very happy man and we planned to wed that next spring of '16. But then I got a letter from Bessie in March, saying that mother had had a stroke and wasn't doing well. I couldn't imagine not seeing my mother again and since she was still alive, I knew I needed to go home. I asked Anna if she would come with me. I wanted to show her Maine, anyway. I thought she might even like it well enough to stay and we would live here.

"I went to Anna's house to talk to her and Alice about the situation. They were both very quiet, I remember. I guess I should have seen what was coming, but I didn't. Anna said she needed some time to think about coming to Maine, so far from her home. So, we all slept on it until morning. I slept at their house, by the way, because they had room and it's a long day's train ride from Fortuna to their town. After breakfast, Anna wanted to walk with me. That's when she began to cry and said Alice didn't think it wise for her to travel so far, that she was too fragile. I asked Anna what *she* thought, apart from her sister.

"It took her a while to say it, but essentially, she conceded that Alice was right. She said she had been sickly all her life and that she had relied first on her mother and then Alice to look after her. She told me she loved me, but she didn't think she would make a good wife. I tried to tell her that I would care for her in Alice's absence, but in the end, I could tell that Anna would not be able to live without Alice close by. And I guess I didn't want that situation. Or maybe that's what I needed to believe in order to face another marriage refusal.

"And that was that. I came home. Mother got worse and worse and then died. It was a very rough time for me."

"I heard about your mother. I'm so sorry."

I could see the toll it took for Walter to tell me about all of that. As I looked at him, I realized that he was as tender a man as Papa had become. It also took a toll on me to know that Walter had been involved with another woman while he was gone. *Why did I think he wouldn't become involved with anyone else?*

I wanted to be angry about that but realized I had no right.

"Is there anything you want to ask me?" Walter said.

"I'm sure there will be. For right now, I'm letting it soak in that you were romantically involved with another woman enough to ask for her hand."

"If it's anything like learning you and Lawrence were to be engaged, then I understand."

"Walter, about that, I feel I should fill you in on that a little bit. Are you up for it?"

"Yes, if it isn't a lengthy story. I can feel myself needing a nap soon."

"How about if I come another day and fill you in?" *I certainly have enough to think about for the time being,* I thought.

"Yes, perhaps that would be best. Tomorrow?" he said.

"Yes, perhaps tomorrow. Meanwhile, I pray your healing gets better by leaps and bounds." I let myself out, climbed into the wagon, and headed home. On the way, I saw storm clouds in the west. *Oh, dear,* I thought. *Perhaps not tomorrow.*

It was several days before Papa was willing to get the sleigh out and let me travel the roads. We'd had two back-to-back storms, each with about two feet of new snow. As I glided along, through the new white world Nature had provided us, I thought about what I might say to Walter.

"Hello, Bessie. How are you?"

"I'm well, thank you. And you?"

"I am too, thankfully."

"Walter is on the couch. I have things to do." She left Walter and me alone.

"Well, you look more chipper than when I left," I said. "How do you feel today?"

"Much better. I think you are something of an elixir for me. The day you came, after I took a nap, I could see that we were going to get a storm. I didn't realize how much of one, though. Then I worried you'd try to come the next day. But you are more sensible than that, I believe." I just smiled. "You were going to tell me about your engagement to Lawrence, I believe?" Walter said.

"Yes," I said, taking a breath to steady myself. "Well, did you know that I was engaged to be married in 1911?"

"I did."

"The newspaper article?" He nodded. "I suppose about everyone read that article. And I imagine that was difficult for you?" I conceded, though I didn't really want to hear his answer if he chose to give one. I felt that in the interest of being vulnerable to one another I had to ask.

"Yes, it was difficult."

"For whatever pain I caused you, I am very sorry. But I cannot regret having followed my heart as I am trying to do now. I was in love with Lawrence. I loved his aspirations. He dreamed of lofty things which I assumed would have given me a glorious life in the city. At least that's the way he painted the life we would have together in Portland. It would have gotten me off the farm and at that time I was tired of working so hard to fill Mama's shoes. It was depleting me, I think. Lawrence offered a way out of all that. So, when he asked me to marry him, I was more than ready to say 'yes'. I assumed Papa would find a way to fill my shoes because he was so adamant, at that time, that I leave the farm.

"It was terribly exciting to plan a fancy wedding. Bea, Luella, Marion, and her aunt, Addie Manchester, and I put our heads together and dreamed up the flowers, the music, the decorations, and my dress. I didn't know that Addie was planning my surprise bridal shower at the same time. It was electrifying to feel like the center of everyone's attention at that shower—well, except when Donald MacMillan arrived, uninvited." I chuckled and said, "At that point, I was decidedly *not* the center of attention, you can imagine! And then to be written up in the paper like that—well, it quite went to my head, I must say. I look back on it now and I don't feel like the same person at all.

"But something else was going on during that time that I didn't know about. Lawrence was calling on another woman! I could hardly believe it. Still can't. She's from Portland and that's all I really care to know about her. They might have gotten married had the woman not called it off when she learned he was already engaged. That relationship ended maybe a month before the shower.

"Anyway, the very next day after the shower, Lawrence apparently became careless and was seen in North Windham with Lizzie. Maybe he thought he had me securely in his grasp, beyond the need to be faithful. I don't know. But one of my friends, I won't say who, told me she'd seen them together. I wanted to believe it was something as casual as the two of them running into one another. But then my friend told me they were kissing, believe it or not! That did it. Something in me broke. I took the old wagon out and went looking for him, which Papa didn't know. And I found them.

"This next part I am not proud of, but I raised my voice in anger and asked him why he would even think of doing such a thing. Lizzie, either, for that matter. Especially when our wedding was only days away. I suppose half of North Windham heard me shout but I didn't care. Then I took off my ring and threw it at him. I told him he could pick it up and give it to Lizzie for all I cared. Then I walked to the wagon and drove away as fast as the horse would go.

"The days that followed were very difficult. I'd turned you down years before and then Lawrence, and in doing so, I resigned myself to be a spinster for the rest of my life. But even that was nothing compared to having to face the people who had been so kind to me. I gave all their lovely gifts back and found ways to frame our breakup that were kinder to Lawrence and Lizzie than the truth. For a long while I felt broken and tossed aside like the ends of the boards Papa cuts at the mill–useless as good building material."

"Sounds like we both took a beating in that department," Walter said. I gave him an uncomfortable smile of acknowledgement.

"But after the despondency, I began to feel anger–no, rage–because I thought, 'I'm better than some old end piece of a board!' I resolved then and there not to allow anyone to have all of my heart ever again.

For years I have been guarded, not that most people would have noticed, but I know I'm holding part of myself safely inside."

"I've been guarded too, I think. I mean, look how quickly I assumed you and Lawrence were back together."

"We've both been hurt, I know. And if I needed more reason to let go of Lawrence, which I don't, I saw Lizzie recently. It turns out that she broke up with Lawrence because she saw him with yet another woman! I think there's something seriously wrong with Mr. Casanova."

Walter didn't honor my speculation with a remark, but said, "Assuming you agree, how do we begin to rebuild our own relationship?"

"You *do* want a relationship, then?" I asked, just to be sure I'd heard him right.

"Yes, if you do. I too have been learning and healing. Recently, I had a conversation with God that has helped me see how I have been holding myself in unforgiveness for years. I thought of myself as a failure to God for not being able to be a man of the cloth like my father. Now I see that God's work is for everyone, everywhere, every day."

"May I say something as a mother might to her child? I'm proud of you, Walter. That's a big lesson to learn. Maybe one for a lifetime, as I think that when we keep ourselves in unforgiveness, it doesn't fully open us to God's work. I think I need to have a talk with God about that too."

"I'm glad you are proud of me. Thank you. How about this: Let's treat our relationship as if it was brand new, which in a sense it is. I'll come calling when I'm able. And we'll just set expectations aside and see what feels right and where things lead. Is that alright with you?"

"It is."

"And may I call you Cesca? Has anyone else ever called you that?"

"They haven't. I like it. It can be just ours, with no other history. It will help make starting over really feel like starting over."

Thirty-one

Gaining One, Losing One

Walter began writing me letters every day. There was nothing particularly earth-shattering in them but, especially since he was not able to deliver the mail himself yet, I felt like he was close by. I, of course, reciprocated. And our new relationship was off to a good start. How I looked forward to those letters. I hoped he looked forward to mine as well.

As the new year progressed, I felt closer to Walter by the day. On February 14, the postman personally put a small envelope in the palm of my hand. The rest of the mail he handed to Papa. I carefully opened the precious little wrapper to find a card in the shape of a glove which had a child's head poking out the top of it. I believe Walter painted it himself. Inside it read:

I wish I were your soft kid glove
For then dear Valentine
As long as you'd allow it
Your hand would lie in mine!

I left it out where Papa could see it if he wished. At dinner he said, "Millie, I think you are finally happy. Am I right?"

"Yes, Papa, you are. I love Walter. I know that now and I know he loves me. He is a fine man, and I know I can trust him. This is a much more mature relationship than I ever had with Lawrence."

"That is all I have ever wanted for you, child. I can die a happy man now."

"Well, don't go dying anytime soon, Papa. Please."

Though we were making light of things, I knew Papa was getting worse and it concerned me. No matter whether Walter asked for my hand or not, I would not leave Papa.

Then one day in early March, I received a letter that would have left no doubt in my heart if indeed there had been any left at all:

Tuesday, March 11, 1919, South Windham, Maine

Dear Mildred,

Fourteen years ago I gave you a pledge, or rather perhaps I should say prophesy—for things of the heart apparently are not of our own ordering. Lately it has seemed to me that you were calling for the fulfillment of that pledge, or prophesy. Friday evening, unless I receive some word from you to detain me, I will call to see you. It may be late as the roads will be hard and I shall probably have to come with the old horse.

Walter

I took its formality as a sign that Walter was planning to formally propose to me. I tried not to hold my hopes too high, but Friday couldn't come soon enough if that was his intention.

Friday evening was cold and spitting snow. I wore layers of clothing when Walter told me he had somewhere he wanted to take me. He tucked a thick blanket over my lap and another over his own. Then he clucked to the horse. As it trotted through the snow, the clouds parted to allow the moon to give us a sliver of light. *If it was daylight*, I thought, *I'd say there was enough blue to make a Dutchman's pants*. Even at night, the parted clouds promised that the storm was ending. Indeed, the growing number of visible stars, along with the moon, graced our path.

My thoughts, though they held a growing curiosity, were mostly puffs of impotent words as we trotted along in peaceful silence. All I wanted to do was drink in this night, every peace-filled moment. Then, suddenly, a single thought replaced the impotence of all others. *"Enough blue to make a Dutchman's pants' has always meant good weather coming. But I just realized that tonight, perhaps it means that good* things *are coming! Oh, my dear sweet Jennie, thank you for your presence tonight. I promise to be happy for both of us.* Tears of happiness stung my eyes as I thought of my sister with joy rather than sorrow.

Walter steered the horse down Hurricane Road and still I didn't know where we were headed, nor did I care. My heart was at peace with this man, a peace so profound, I knew I'd never felt the likes of it before. He slowed the horse to walk down the hill into Babb's covered bridge which spanned the Presumpscot River. As we entered the bridge, the sound of the horse's hooves went from muted on the snow to a clipped echo on the bridge's wooden floor. And then Walter pulled us to a stop at the bridge's midpoint. There was silence, save for the horse's few nickers before he was resigned to standing still.

I sat quietly, wondering what was coming when Walter spoke. "Lately I've taken stock of who I've been these past forty-three years of my life. I've been a dreamer, lusting for adventure. After you turned me down and my father died, I thought that by traveling, I might find the life I dreamed of. It turns out that while I loved that journey and I'm grateful I took it, I've discovered that my heart is rooted in Maine. I've also been a romantic, which led to two failed marriage proposals and maybe even failure in school which, as I told you, I've forgiven myself for. But the most important thing I've learned is that if I can't be content with who I am, I won't be content with who I'm with.

"Do you see these two vertical boards?" He pointed to the two parallel boards in the bridge structure, distinct from the others on either side which were slanted. "There are two like them on the other side, too." We both turned to look at them. Then Walter turned to me. "These boards mark the center of the bridge and its strength. I feel a bit like them, centered and strong after searching a long time to know who I am. I accept that I am a simple man working his land. My ministry lies in the relationships I have with those whom God sees fit to cross my path. And that is plenty. So, Cesca, if you will have me as I am, a simple man who will love you all the rest of my days, will you agree to be my wife?"

"Walter," I said, putting my hands in his, "you are hardly a simple man, at least from my perspective. And if by 'simple' you mean that you are 'just' a farmer, remember that I am 'just' a farmer's daughter. But what I most cherish is knowing that I would feel safe in your hands and trust that you would put no other woman before me. For that, I gratefully say yes, of course I will be your wife."

After what felt like hours rather than seconds, his lips found mine.

I couldn't wait to write to both Luella and Marion about my engagement, so, tired as I was that night, I stayed up to capture on stationery the very thoughts and feelings I had after Walter left. Marion would easily understand, as it wasn't that long ago that she had been a blushing bride when Guy Wilson married her. Luella was still single, but she knew my heart so well, she'd understand vicariously.

"When? When do you plan to marry?" they both asked me when I saw them each.

"We aren't sure. I told Walter that I will not marry him while Papa is alive and needs my care. He understands, though he is anxious to be wed, of course. But that's one thing I love about him. He is nothing if not a patient man."

"You must be settled on the thought of being a farmer's wife, then," Marion said.

"You know, it's strange after thinking so long that I wouldn't like to be one, but, yes, I am. And I can't even imagine being happier as anything else. Walter told me that he believes everyone should be welcome around our table. His sense of community and love of mankind is admirable and being a farmer affords him the chance to put his belief in motion. Of course, it is I who will put the food on that table!" Marion laughed along with me. She knew all about being a farmer's wife. "But I see that Walter believes this is part of his ministry. I've thought about what he said, and I think it is my ministry too, to extend the arm of hospitality as far as it needs to reach. And you know what else he said? That what's his is mine. He will not be one to treat me as his maid. I believe we are to be equals in life."

"If so, and I believe you are exactly right," Marion said with conviction, "you can be sure yours will be a very, very joyous life, indeed."

Sunday, March 16, 1919 Gorham, Maine

My dear Walter,

Since I've been honored with the joyous news of your engagement, I'm desirous of telling you directly how deeply and sincerely I congratulate you. Also, of my gladness for Millie since your companionship and love will make her life happier. She is a rare treasure as you know and deserves the best in the world. Please believe that I am rejoicing in your good fortune and wishing you both happy, happy years together.

Please extend greetings and love to your sister Bessie for me.

Most sincerely,
Marion Wilson

A letter from Joe and Bea conveying their congratulations came with a few dollars to have a telephone line installed at the farm so that I could speak more privately with Walter. I'd been going over to Webster's house when I needed to. Initially ecstatic, I quickly learned that whatever I said would not necessarily stay private on the party line. Our intimate thoughts were only safe to share in person. Nevertheless, there were other times when being able to use the telephone so quickly meant possible disasters averted. And sometimes, it was simply nice not having to leave the house to call a friend. As wonderfully thoughtful as the money was, what pleased me most was that Bea wrote her own line below Joe's saying that she thought Walter and I were well-matched and could see great happiness coming.

My life after Walter's proposal included two distinct threads—one very pleasant one with Walter in the center of my thoughts, the other, a very distressing one, watching Papa slip away. I could tell, at least, that he felt deeply content upon hearing of my engagement, though he wasn't speaking much anymore.

Papa's health was of utmost importance to me, which meant that my days as his caretaker were full. Papa often insisted on walking unaided. When he'd fall, I would call a neighbor to help me get him up. He would inevitably be grumpy because he didn't think he needed help. If he wasn't trying to maintain a semblance of his normal life, milking the cow or walking the fields, he was sleeping, either in his bed or on the Morris chair. But I needed to keep my eyes on where he was at all times. Sometimes when he slept I could have sworn he wasn't breathing, which frightened me every single time. He was forgetful more and more often and many times turned down going to church when I told him it was Sunday. His appetite was not consistent either in quantity or in what he found tasteful, even if what I'd made him had been a favorite. Bert and Effie were a great help to me and Papa with household and farming needs. They were always willing to stay with him if I needed to be gone.

The doctor told me that Papa had hardening of the arteries, which he believed Papa had been dealing with for probably as much as ten years. But it was Papa's heart that was wearing out. I had Trafton come to visit occasionally but asked him not to speak heavily of war. I needn't have worried. Trafton himself was not doing especially well now and never stayed long enough for much conversation. Sadly, I realized that if Papa passed before Trafton did, Trafton would be the only one of the three friends still living, as John Evans had departed this world in 1913.

One day in the middle of May, Papa cleared his throat to talk, something I had not heard much of lately. Weakly, he said, "Millie, please sit by me." *Oh, no,* I thought. *Just like Howdie and then Mama.* "I want you to have them inscribe 'In God Have I Put My Trust' on my tombstone."

"I will, Papa," I assured him, swallowing my instant feelings of shock and heartbreak. "Is there anything else?"

"Yes, child," he said. "Be happy with Walter. He is a good man."

"Yes, Papa, I will," I said, tears flooding my eyes.

"That's good, child."

Those were his last words to me, and I was so grateful for the very last one which had become a term of endearment. On May 19, 1919, he quietly took his last breath. *What a life you have lived*, I thought, placing two coins on his eyes in keeping with a long-held custom in the Azores.

"You were but a child on a whaler for three years, seeking adventure," I said to his soul. "You forsook your family and never saw your father again." My tears flowed freely. There was no one else in the house. "You were not much more than a child fighting in a bloody war. That experience put an end to your need for adventure, I know. But, Papa, I doubt that was the adventure you'd had in mind when you stole onto the whaler. You were the father of six and a grieving father of four. You worked so hard for so little money and still volunteered your time as a civil servant. And now, it's your turn to be carried on the town hearse." This was a very difficult thought for me. "You were a good man, Papa. And a quiet one. But I know that silent waters run deep," I sniffed, caressing his long fingers, needing to dry them of my tears. "I believe you held much of your life deep in your heart. Did you ever regret leaving the Azores? Did you miss your father as terribly as I know I shall miss mine? You only voiced the most important things to me. You were so fair even when I was cantankerous and quarrelsome. Oh, how I regret myself as a young girl. But I can hear you now, saying, 'Child, there is nothing to be gained from such regret. Use it to make better choices now.' Oh, Papa, I will always love you. And I will always, always miss you. And yes, Papa, I will not fuss with God for taking you from me. But I may always wonder if you felt it was safe to die once you learned Walter would be taking care of me."

After Papa's body was gone from the house, I lifted the telephone receiver. I didn't mind who heard me tell Walter that Papa was gone. *In fact, the party line might make my job easier*, I realized. He came over as fast as he could. Together, we thought through the immediate things I needed to accomplish, which meant contacting Joe first of all. Joe wasn't surprised but, of course, very sad. He said that he and his family would be here on May 23. On Decoration Day, May 26, very appropriately, Papa was buried beside Mama and the four children they'd lost. I was grateful to Papa for telling me what he wished to have engraved on his stone. Even that relatively small duty would not be added to the overwhelm I already felt.

Later that day, Joe asked to speak to me alone.

"We will be leaving tomorrow, Millie. I am confident you are in good hands with Walter by your side now. Also, I wanted to mention two things before we go. First, as a matter of some consequence, though I'm not certain yet as to its outcome, the day Papa died was the same day that President Wilson called a special session of congress to propose a 19th amendment to the constitution that would allow women to vote. If it is ratified, you might be able to vote in November. As civic-minded as Papa was, I think he'd be pleased, don't you?"

"I'd like to think so, I guess. But *I* would be pleased!" I said with a smile.

"I know you would. The other thing is more personal. Papa's wishes upon his death were to bequeath the farm to me, as eldest." I nodded, already knowing as much.

"But since you have cared for Papa along with this farm for so long, and since I am situated well enough where I am, I want you to have it. You may do with it as you please. I won't hold you to living in it if you and Walter want to remain on his land. In that case, perhaps you'd want to sell it."

"Oh, my no! As wonderful as it is to hear this, and as kind as you are to say it, how could I possibly sell this land? It's part of my heart and soul. Isn't it part of yours, too?"

"Yes, I suppose it is. But practically speaking, it doesn't make sense to hold on to something that isn't needed. In any case, you and Walter are free to decide what to do, and Bea and I will honor whatever that is. Consider it our wedding gift to you both."

"Thank you, Joe. Oh, thank you!" I said standing to give him a heartfelt hug. "You and the family will come back up for the summer, right?"

"I assume so."

"Oh, well, certainly you *must!*" I said, "Silly me, Walter and I are planning a wedding on his birthday in August. It's early enough in the month that you'll have time to get back to Massachusetts."

"I'm glad you will marry soon. It's about time, as they say," Joe winked and walked out of the room.

"The house will seem much too quiet as soon as they have pulled out of the driveway," I pondered aloud later with Walter by my side. We were looking out over the field with the gentlest of breezes playing around us.

"My dear Cesca, perhaps you should consider asking if you can go back with them for a while."

"Oh, I don't know about that. There are things that should be done here."

"Nothing that can't wait," he said, giving me a quick kiss. "But that is for you to decide."

"I would surely miss you," I declared, realizing this stunning truth. "And I'd miss this farm," I said more quietly, grasping the fact that I'd seldom left home.

"That's what mail is for," he said, sensibly. "And before you know it, it will be our wedding day!"

"You almost make it sound like an adventure," I laughed.

"So, it could be. A mini version of mine."

The next day I searched for the skeleton key to the kitchen door which had always had the capacity to be locked but never had been. Neighbors took care of neighbors and were welcomed in with a holler. Strangers were rarely seen and, at that, weren't strangers after a handshake. But this time, since I'd be gone a few weeks, I decided to lock the door for peace of mind. Then I walked briskly to Effie's house across the street and, after a quick hug and a "Hurry back!" from Effie, I handed Coonie over to her care. Then I hurried back to Joe's waiting automobile so that we could be on our way to Massachusetts.

Walter's letters began before I even reached Joe and Bea's house and mine to him began soon after. From there the messages flew across state lines regularly, each successive letter containing more intimacy than the one before. In a letter to Walter in June I wrote about an article that stated that love develops, after marriage, into affection, which is better. I went on to say how like Papa's words these were. In the same letter I told him that it was practically settled–Doris would be coming home with me. To this, Walter responded that he supposed he must be glad that Doris would be accompanying me back but that he had thought I might come stay with him and Bessie alone using their extra bedroom. By the end of his letter, he conceded that Doris's presence would help me in my transition and that, of course, Doris would be welcome at his home, too.

"Oh, my!" I exclaimed, reading Walter's next letter and smiling sheepishly. Rachel wanted to know what I was smiling at and I probably turned crimson. Of course, I couldn't tell her what he said: *The fact is that it is so hot nights that sleep doesn't seem to do much good. If you were here, Cesca, I don't suppose I could be quite as comfortable as I am now for I am sitting in a most natural condition. But I really believe for a sight of you I would be willing to don just a few of the habiliments of civilized man.*

Two days later, I wrote: *Am glad you were able to keep fairly comfortable those hot eves or rather, more comfortable than as if I had been with you!*

The letters helped to pass the time, and soon Doris and I took a boat from Boston to Portland. When we arrived at Portland harbor, I practically leapt from the boat to the dock when I saw Walter waiting for us. After demure hugs in public, we began the trip back to Great Falls, which gave Walter and me time to discuss a few practical things that Doris's ears were allowed to hear.

I had received a letter from Marion about having a small bridal shower in her home–certainly nothing nearly as pretentious as my first one had been, which was a relief. I assumed Doris would enjoy attending it too. We decided the wedding should be held in my home with a small group of close friends and family. It would begin at eleven o'clock in the morning on August 12, Walter's forty-fourth birthday and be followed by a reception with finger sandwiches and cake. We would discuss the honeymoon privately, but decided to hold a larger reception at Walter and Bessie's farm when we returned from a week-long trip. Most importantly, we decided to begin married life on Walter's farm with Bessie to keep me company. But we'd keep my farm and decide together what its future would be.

Satisfied that most things were in order, we rode in comfortable silence off and on until we pulled into the driveway. After bidding me farewell, Walter returned to his farm while Doris and I approached mine. I fished for my key in my bag and unlocked the kitchen door, which felt so odd to me. The house smelled normal but for a bit of mustiness from being closed. I had been afraid it might smell too much like Papa. Even if it had, there was too much to do to stand and fret about the past. I wanted to start right in.

In mid-July, a small group of my friends gathered at Marion's home for a lovely tea and bridal shower. It was there that I received one of my most precious gifts, one I knew I would treasure for a lifetime. Unbeknownst to me, a crazy quilt had been started when I was to marry Lawrence. It was to be given at the shower Addie Manchester held but it wasn't finished quite yet, so it wasn't mentioned. When the wedding was called off, Addie packed the quilt in a trunk in her attic. As soon as Marion spread the word that I was engaged to Walter, out came the quilt to be finished and presented at Marion's tea. It was stunning with all its rich colors and fabrics. One piece was hand painted with daffodils, which would always be a favorite of mine. Through tears of gratitude, I thanked everyone with words far too inadequate for such love as the tea represented. And as I'd thought, Doris loved every minute of the shower.

Walter's prediction was true enough. The time flew by, and Joe and his family returned a few days before the wedding. All was joyous mayhem as the house was readied for our guests. I laid my dress over the end of my bed to smooth out the wrinkles and Bea, Doris, and Rachel did the same with theirs, happily anticipating wearing them soon.

Thirty-two

Tender Tears

The day before the wedding, Walter arrived unannounced. I wiped my hands and hurried out to see him, surprised and delighted. Then suddenly worried.

"Walter! Is everything alright? Is Bessie ill?"

"No, everything is fine," he said, wrapping me in his arms. "And now everything is perfect."

"I'm so happy you're here," I said, "But why *are* you?"

"I just wanted to see you once more before I behold you on our wedding day." Then he held me out at arm's length, his tone more serious, "And I wanted to give you one more chance to tell me if you are indeed ready and willing to be my wife tomorrow."

I looked into his eyes that held mine with unmistakable adoration and said, "Walter, can we walk in the meadow, please? There is something I have wanted to ask you for years."

Though his look betrayed a touch of panic, he took my hand as we walked toward the edge of the hill. "What is it, Cesca?"

"As I said, I've had a question on my mind for the past eight years. Up till now, I guess I didn't want to know the answer, but now I think I do. Before tomorrow. And I am indeed ready and willing to be your wife tomorrow, so put that worry out of your mind, once and for all." I paused to see his eyes register relief. I secretly guessed that anything I asked him now would pale in comparison to the fear he'd just had. So perhaps, then, this was exactly the right time to finally ask him my question.

"Why *did* you go out west, Walter? Was it because of me?"

I could see him pondering an answer. "Yes, Millie, in large part it was. I couldn't bear the thought of seeing you as another man's wife. When I read in the paper about your engagement to Lawrence, I felt hopelessly lost. But when Father died two weeks later, I didn't know which end was up anymore. If it weren't for my mother and Bessie's understanding, I don't know what I would have done. I was a broken man, Cesca. Mother finally suggested I get away for a while. I hadn't any intention of being away for so long. But as that journey evolved, I was presented with more and more opportunities. And frankly, I had to admit that the opportunities felt God-given. The further I went, the surer I was that mother had been right; I did need to get out of South Windham and see things with new eyes.

"I know now that getting away emotionally saved my life. If I'd stayed, I would not have been fit as a husband for anyone, least of all you. For a long while I felt guilty about running from my troubles. But on the way back home, I realized that if I *had* run away from my troubles, I was now running back through them. I relived those years and saw myself as a seminary failure, a disappointment to father, and as a man who failed to gain the acceptance of marriage from two women.

"Then, just before Mother died, I had that heart-to-heart talk with God where I finally forgave myself essentially for being me. I realized that if I couldn't live with myself as I was, I couldn't expect anyone else to, either. Does this make any sense to you?"

I took his hands in mine and said, "Yes, Walter, it makes perfect sense because I have had to forgive myself too. Let's be forgiven together. For the rest of our lives."

That night, I donned my nightgown and, sitting on the edge of my bed, I picked up my comb lying on the nightstand beside me. Combing through my long, graying hair I began to count the one hundred strokes as I'd done almost every day of my life. Before long, I realized I wasn't counting at all. I was imagining myself twenty-four hours from now and wondering if I would bother combing out my hair at all. I laid the comb back on the nightstand, wondering if I would have a nightstand on which to lay my comb in Walter's room. I had not, after all, ever seen his bedroom. Then I braided my hair to the nape of my neck and whipped it around in front so that I could finished plaiting. I squeezed the comb along its spine with my thumb and first finger to empty it of stray hairs and wondered if Walter had seen a woman ready herself for bed as I do. I took the stray hair and rolled it between my fingers to make a strand that I used as a hair tie with which to wrap the end of the braid. Finally, I whipped the braid behind me, and lifted my legs into the bed, pulling the sheet up over me. My nighttime routine was comforting, and I couldn't imagine not finishing my day that way. So, I decided that even if I didn't perform this routine tomorrow night, I would begin soon after.

I was about to blow out the lamp when I suddenly thought about my diary. *How could I not write about this day?*

August 11, 1919

Dear diary, this is the last day I will be Mildred Francesca Thomas. Tomorrow I will pledge an oath to have and to hold, for better or worse, richer or poorer, in sickness and health, to love and cherish until one of us dies and we are separated. Then I will be Mildred Francesca Harlow, Walter's wife.

It's a very strange thought that I will be someone's wife; that from now on I will, by definition, be living as a team. I suppose Papa and I did that too for the past twenty-three years. But that feels much different than how I am about to live.

Mama and Papa, how I wish you were here to see me get married. But if I pledged to myself not to do so until you were gone, it wasn't meant to be. The two of you prepared me well, though. I know how to be a farmer's wife, to cook, to keep house, to raise chickens, to make butter. You wouldn't let me milk the cows or I'd know how to do that, too. Can you hear me laughing now, Papa?

You taught me so much more than that. I have learned to know when it would serve me best to consider others first and when I need to stand up for myself. I'm not ever going to be the more patient one in this marriage, I fear. Walter is far better at that than I. But I know something about what forgiveness does for a relationship from the many times you offered that grace to me, over and over again. And I know and am grateful to you both that I am an educated woman, and no one can take that away from me. I'm so grateful that Walter sees me as his equal in a time when we women have so few rights of our own and are legally dependent on husbands.

Oh, but the suffragist movement is strong now and I may be able to vote for our country's next president. Imagine that! Walter and I can go to the polls together and return home having had a voice in something as enormous as this country.

I have the rest of my life before me as I have had every day I've lived. Now it seems I am to live it differently. I don't know yet how it will differ. But I know that Walter is steadfast, trustworthy, and compassionate. And together we will weather the storms of life.

Good night, diary. Next time I write, I will be a married woman.

Earlier than usual the next morning, I was awake, even before the rooster crowed. I considered trying to go back to sleep, but I knew it was futile to try. While the rest of the family still slept, having gone to bed later than usual the night before, I decided to spend these quiet moments reflecting on this special day about to dawn. I felt a mixture of nerves and excitement, but not overly so. I dressed in a simple housedress and undid my braid. With experienced fingers, I quickly twisted my hair onto my head in a figure eight, poking a few hair pins in the unruly places that always threatened to unravel.

Tying on my sensible black shoes and slipping into my sweater, I quietly walked down the back stairs and opened the door of the ell to the pre-dawn aromas of late summer in Maine. The sweetness of the meadow grass met my nose first and I breathed it in deeply. The sky was just beginning to lighten so that to my right, the cobalt blue morning glories were still asleep, too. But they would soon unfurl and grace the trellis beside the piazza.

I stepped down onto the driveway and slowly walked over the lawn to my contemplation rock in the meadow. Some evenings, the rock offered a view of gorgeous sunsets. This morning, I sat looking eastward to await the sun. A soft breeze caressed the back of my neck. It would be a long, wonderful day and there would be much to be grateful for.

The eastern sky was just beginning to turn the merest shades of orange, pink, and yellow as the earth turned to meet her life-giving companion. Once the sun was fully up, I would have many tasks to attend to. But right now, these few moments were mine to savor. What does one think about on her wedding day? What doesn't she think about? I heard a sparrow somewhere in the woods and saw what I think was a chickadee flitting from branch to branch of a small white pine just over the hill. The birds were already beginning their day. They greeted the sun long before I did. I heard the killdeer call out its name and land neatly in the meadow, perhaps caring for its last clutch of the season.

Children. I hadn't given much thought to us having children, what with our ages. People my age already had children who were having children. *No,* I thought, *let the young people have the babies. Walter and I haven't talked about a family. I hope he will be satisfied to live without one of our own.*

I hugged my knees waiting for the sun to break through the horizon over the river. How many times had I and so many others stood in this very place to watch the Easter sun rise over Great Falls? Some years we watched through snowflakes, others through rain. The ones I remember best were days when the sun poked through low-hanging clouds on the horizon that were just breaking up after a storm the night before. This thought reminded me of Jennie. She would hold my hand and together we would look at each other and sigh when the sun hit our faces.

And you, Howdie, I think you loved Easter more than any of us. I remember you following the scripture readings before I knew how to read. One time you bent down low to whisper what the word "resurrection" meant. You may have done that because you knew I'd pester you if you didn't. But I wanted to know what that word meant. It had to be mighty important to be spoken as often as it was. I like to think you are resurrected with your beloved God right now.

And Grandmam, do you know I have Howdie's little golden Bible now? I was so jealous when he got that. It was fuzzy yellow and just my size. I couldn't understand why I didn't get it instead. I smiled. So many memories of Mama, Papa, Jennie, Howdie, Grandmam, Grandpar, and Uncle Almon. I looked forward to sharing them with Walter over time.

And Walter. His steady character, unwavering devotion, quick wit, curiosity preceding a new gadget or invention, and ceaseless compassion. How is it that I am lucky enough to win his favor after all I put him through? How had I not seen the goodness in this man from the very first time we met? *Ah*, I realized, *because my heart was still blinded by my love of another. Oh, how could something that felt so right be so deceptive?*

In these past few seconds, I could see that the horizon had gotten heavy with the brilliant, whitish-yellow semi-circle that would very soon spray its contents across the meadow in a ritual as old as time. I closed my eyes to the visual symphony before me and waited to feel the first beam of warmth bathe my face. I smiled, my heart full. Then I felt it. My face was kissed so gently by the first rays of sun on my wedding day. I opened my eyes, stood, and looked out over the hill and river I loved so dearly. I could never sell it to another. Ever.

"Thank you. All of you," I said aloud to everyone and no one in particular. "I am a better woman for the love you gave me without hesitation or reserve. I will take it with me, and with Walter as my husband, I know I shall be a very contented woman."

Then I turned around toward the house and saw that Walter had already arrived. He had been watching me. Tears flowed down my face, my love spilling over. I slowly walked home to my beloved, never taking my eyes off his. When I was close enough, I saw that his face was also wet with tears.

{ 326 }

Epilogue

Love does not consist of gazing at each other,
but in looking outward together in the same direction.
-Antoine de Saint-Exupery

The cascading white ribbons were nearly four feet long and laced with sweet peas. They hung from a ball of flowers that forced me to hold my bridal bouquet right at my bosom, lest I trip. I wore a white wedding dress layered in Georgette crepe, and around my neck, the choker of gold beads my mother had bequeathed me. And in my hair, instead of my simple hair pins, I wore the exquisite ivory comb my beloved gave me this morning.

He'd met me outside the house just after the sun had crested. All my eyes saw were the tears in his, not that he had his hands behind his back. When the sun lit up the yard enough for me to see it, I noticed he was dressed for our wedding; a sleek black suit that fit his stature well with a Middlesex, standalone collar that made him look even more handsome than he already was. He embraced me tightly, a thing I wanted more than anything else, yet my mind screamed that I would rumple his suit. When he pulled away, his hand remained in front of me. It revealed the small box he'd been holding.

"Walter! What is this?"

"If you open it Cesca, you will see," he said with a profound twinkle in his eye.

In the box was a creamy-white, ivory comb for my hair. As much as I loved my dress, bouquet, and necklace, I couldn't wait to redo my bun and slip the comb into it. I knew I would need no other head covering.

I hugged him again and whispered, "You're too good to me, Walter. But keep being so. I love the comb. And I love you."

We drifted apart and I said, "It's a good thing I didn't leave the house in *my* wedding attire, Mr. Harlow, as it is bad luck to see me in my dress before the wedding! Let's go in the house. I have much to do. Have you eaten breakfast?"

"I haven't, but I'm too nervous to eat, I think."

"Well, the others will need to eat. I have enough to feed everyone. Please join us, so you don't faint from lack of sustenance."

"Already giving me orders, Cesca?" He kissed my cheek.

"Of course, when you are being too silly for your own good." I smiled and walked through the kitchen door.

The others were up now and milling about the house. Bea was making eggs and bacon. I put on my apron.

"Oh, no you don't, Millie," Bea said with a warm smile. "Today is one day you are *not* to be working. So, shoo! Doris will help me."

"Thank you, Bea, for everything. You, too, Doris." I hung my apron on the hook and went into the parlor. I really wasn't sure what to do with myself.

"The ferns and goldenrod make beautiful decorations in here," Walter said, standing between the parlor and the living room.

"Doesn't it look wonderful? Everything is ready, thanks to Bea and her girls. All we need is for eleven o'clock to come."

After breakfast, Bea wanted to help me get dressed. Doris and Rachel both insisted they be there too, which I loved. The air in my bedroom was electrifying as I was made ready to be a bride. *Finally.* I sighed, letting out a breath I'd been unaware I'd been holding. *But everything in its time,* I thought, chastising myself for my impatience once again. When we heard the piano playing Mendelssohn's "Wedding March," Bea gave me a quick hug and a smile. Doris and Rachel could barely contain themselves and hurried down the back stairs along with their mother.

I stood for a last moment at the top of the winding staircase, thinking about all the times the doctor had had to hold the grim news he'd have to tell those of us waiting below. But these stairs had seen good times too—times when expected or unexpected guests had arrived, and I took the steps two at a time. I could hear Mama scolding me to slow down and "be a lady, for goodness sake." *Mama, am I a lady now? Are you proud of me, Papa?*

Slowly, so very slowly, I made my way down the staircase. Such a ceremonious event to mark the ending of singlehood and the beginning of marriage. My guests could see my dress before they saw my face. I knew one guest was holding his breath, waiting for all of me to be standing next to him. He wasn't smiling exactly; he showed no teeth. But his whole face was poised in eternal radiance. I wondered if mine matched his.

After our reception, we left for a week-long camping trip by the lake. Every night we slept in each other's arms and every morning we awoke to a chorus of birds greeting us. A pot of hot coffee over an open fire with a cold biscuit or slice of my bread, leftover finger sandwiches and the sweet taste of Effie's cake; stepping over fallen branches or the occasional misstep into an inland bog; finding a pathway through a field of ferns; spontaneous conversations and long embraces; a bit of rain, a thunderstorm we watched together; a wary doe and her two youngsters nervously eying her forest mates, the bellow of a bull moose and the moan of his cow in the distance, the wailing of loons; the smell of rotting wood, tiny white pine saplings, animal droppings; a leisurely paddle in a canoe, a walk along the shoreline, skinny dipping under the moon. Heaven.

We returned to Walter's farm and were treated to a delightful reception of many friends. We lived with Bessie while Walter farmed his land. I occasionally went home to make sure things were in order there and to visit friends. Spring of 1920 came and with it, budding flowers and trees, newborn animals and sowing new crops. One night as I was combing my hair before crawling into bed, I said, "Walter, spring is one miracle after another, isn't it?"

"I would have to agree with that, Cesca."

"You know what else is a miracle? Our baby."

"Our baby? What baby?"

I turned around to look at him and I just smiled until revelation dawned on his face. Neither of us thought such a miracle might be ours. But our baby flourished under our watchful eyes and my belly grew and began to move.

I took a short walk that autumn by myself, contemplating the arrival of this miracle child. I was forty years old and feeling fine, though the doctor always seemed concerned. "Mama, Papa, I'll soon give you another grandchild, can you imagine that? How I wish you could hold my baby. Of course I don't know if it will be a boy or a girl but I'm sure you would have been thrilled with either."

"Remember your dream?" I heard this in my heart and gasped. *This baby is a girl!* How I wanted to share this revelation with Walter, but I wasn't sure he'd believe me or even want to know, if he did. Instead, I wrote this information on a piece of paper and put it in a sealed envelope.

"Walter, you may open this the day our baby is born, but not before." I grinned. He looked confused and then amused and put it on his nightstand.

On November 1, All Saints Day, Francesca Ellen Harlow was born. She bore my middle name as well as her paternal grandmother's. And we couldn't have been prouder parents. Walter stared at me in awe after reading the note I'd written him.

Bessie couldn't wait to spoil her niece and did, every chance she was allowed. But when Francesca was nearly one year old, Eliza Pritchard Harlow, or Bessie, as we called her, passed away at forty-one years of age. Darkness fell on Walter's family farm. The happiness of our first year together was suddenly washed in sorrow. In due time, we made the decision to sell Walter's farm and move back to mine.

For the most part, we enjoyed a blessed life. Not perfect, for whose life ever is, but blessed is how we chose to see ourselves. We had both learned to place our trust in God's provisions, even when dark shadows of pain and grief threatened to extinguish the light for good. But shadows eventually drift apart, as enough blue to make a dutchman's pants take their place. And through it all, as Papa said it would, my love for Walter deepened. Together we were ministers without certification. But what guest would ask for certification when gathered around a table of good food, abundant laughter, and genuine good will?

Walter added a large barn to our property and attached a hand-painted sign saying, *Dundee Heights.* He named our land after the 1913 dam on the Presumpscot River below the house. That dam created a wide spot in the river and a lovely cove at the bottom of our property. We filled the barn with animals, among them, dairy cows, specifically Jerseys. His small herd produced the finest milk, with twenty percent more butterfat than other breeds, which made the creamiest and richest butter and ice cream around. Some of our regular customers came all the way up from Portland. Our young Francesca had fun telling the "city folks" that their chocolate ice cream was brown because it came from the black bull.

I chose to step away from my job at the library so I could give my full attention to raising our daughter. Francesca and I were both fascinated by Walter's inventions. He rigged a rope tow for winter skiing using his tractor to pull customers up the hill after a pleasant trip down to the river. For this convenience, he charged twenty-five cents a day.

One morning Francesca awoke atop a hay mound. She'd asked the night before if she could sleep there under the stars. I allowed her only a short portion of the night there. Her father, however, assured me he would sleep beside her once she had nodded off. That next morning, she found a father-sized dent in the hay next to her own.

When she was a teenager, she was taught a difficult lesson in grace and the legal system. She had been to a youth function at church that invited teens from away. The visitors spent the night with hosting parishioners. One of the teens was found to be in legal trouble, which would be dealt with in the morning. Lay members were slow to volunteer hosting that boy. But not Walter. To Francesca's horror, her father declared that the boy was "innocent until proven guilty" and, as such, he would be welcome in their home.

As it turned out, Francesca was our only child but she grew up loving her cousins, Doris, young Joe, and Rachel, as siblings and coveted their summer-long visits just as much as I did. Eventually Fran, as she preferred to be called, grew up and went to college, at which time I returned as librarian in our small community. After she graduated from Bates College, Fran married her wartime sweetheart and had five children. She would turn out to be an uncertified missionary throughout her entire life, just as Walter and I tried to be. She helped throw us a thirty-sixth wedding anniversary on August 12, 1955, which doubled as her father's eightieth birthday.

One blustery day in March, 1956, my beloved Walter died in the bed we had shared for many wonderful years. I was grateful to have given

Walter a birthday/anniversary card just a year and a half before, professing, "My love, this day must not pass without my telling you how much you mean to me, and have meant for thirty-five years. How contented and safe I have felt with you! And I trust we may travel on together for a goodly number of years yet. Yours always, Mom." He'd called me "Mom" once Francesca was born, leaving the name "Cesca" behind, except for pillow talk, to be completely honest. Yes, my face is red now.

In 1962, I visited Francesca at her Pennsylvania home, not far from Gettysburg. The family took me to see the imposing monument situated in what was named the Wheatfield, honoring Papa's Seventeenth Maine regiment. I stood looking out over the expanse where Papa and so many others fought for two days. I chose not to think too much about what I knew of those Civil War battles, but the many conversations Papa had with his friends still come back to me at times.

In July 1969, I watched as a man walked on the moon. I told my grandchildren how amazing it was that I had been born before cars and was now watching, from a television, something I could not even comprehend.

I began living with Francesca and her family year-round after necessity forced me to sell Dundee Heights. I never imagined I could do such a thing. But the older I get, the more I realize that it isn't the farm itself I take with me but my memories which fill me with gratitude and peace. My good memories bring me limitless joy while the difficult ones remind me that I have loved deeply and completely in my lifetime.

Fifteen years after Walter died, Millie quietly slipped away in her bed at Fran's home. She was ninety-one years old.

The Joseph Thomas Valadão Family on the island of Flores, the Azores.
Young Manuel stands among his brothers and sisters.

Manuel and Julia Blake Thomas

The Portland (Maine) Daily Press reports on an August, 1894 reunion of the
Seventeenth Maine Infantry Regiment formed for the Civil War

Manuel's Civil War ribbon in
brilliant, deep purple with a rich,
red diamond beneath a golden "17"

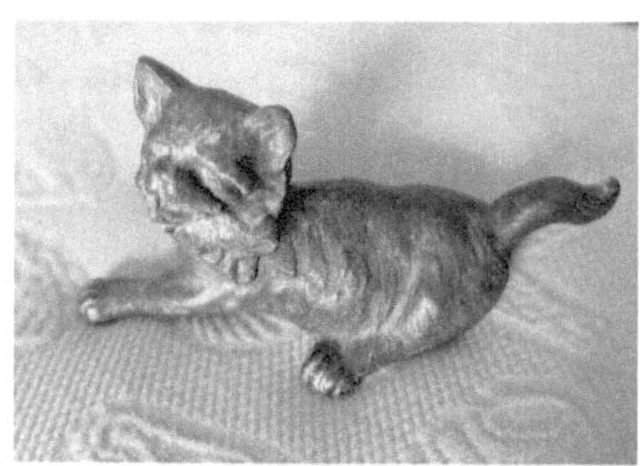

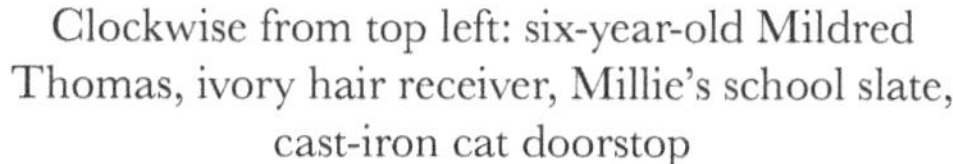

Clockwise from top left: six-year-old Mildred
Thomas, ivory hair receiver, Millie's school slate,
cast-iron cat doorstop

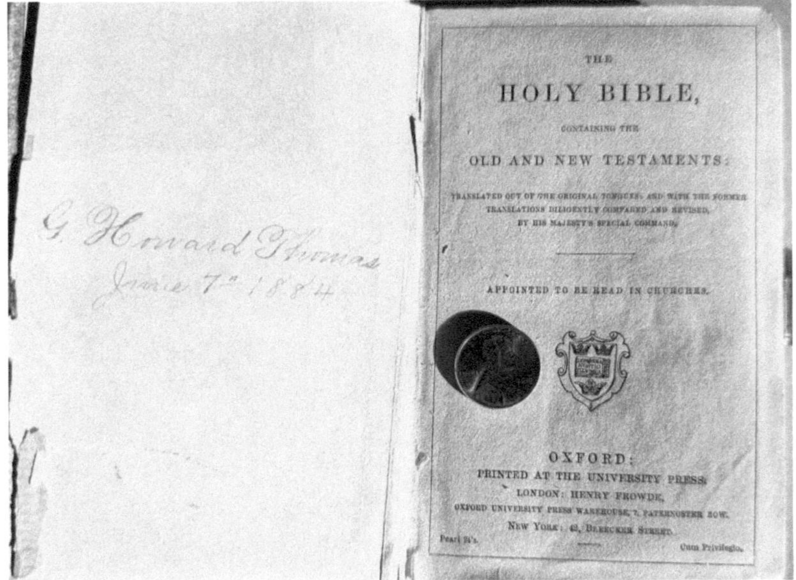

Howard Thomas's little golden Bible

Top: a graphophone c.1900 and
three graphophone cylinders
Bottom: graduate photograph of Millie

Valedictory.

It is with mingled sorrow and pleasure that we meet here on this occasion — sorrow that our connection with the school and with each other as class-mates is to be broken; and pleasure, and gratification that the prescribed course of study has been completed, and an opportunity given to enter a larger field of labor. For perhaps now, more than ever, does ambition sway the youth. So much of life and activity, of great thinking and noble acting, cannot help but be an incentive. Think of the strides in civilization since the opening of the present century! Think of all the advantages with which we are blessed, and

Gorham High School

HALF-TERM REPORT.

OF *Mildred Thomas*

Winter TERM, 1899–1900

Studies, Etc.	1st hf	2d hf	Ex.	Av.
English Literature	97	97		97
Latin *Virgil*	97	98	97	97½
History				
Algebra				
Geometry				
Chemistry				
Physics	97	95	100	97
Botany	98	98	98	98
Astronomy	97	97	90	95
Civics	95	95		95
Spelling	100	100		
Rhetoricals				
Drawing	95			98

WOODMAN, Principal.

Clockwise from top left: First page of Millie's valedictory address, Millie's class ring, Millie's high school report card, Millie (far right) in a dramatic play.

Top: the Thomas farmhouse and family
Bottom: Millie's schoolmarm photograph

Top: Walter Harlow as a nine-year-old and as a teenager. Left: Thirty-year-old Walter in California. Above: A charcoal drawing by Walter

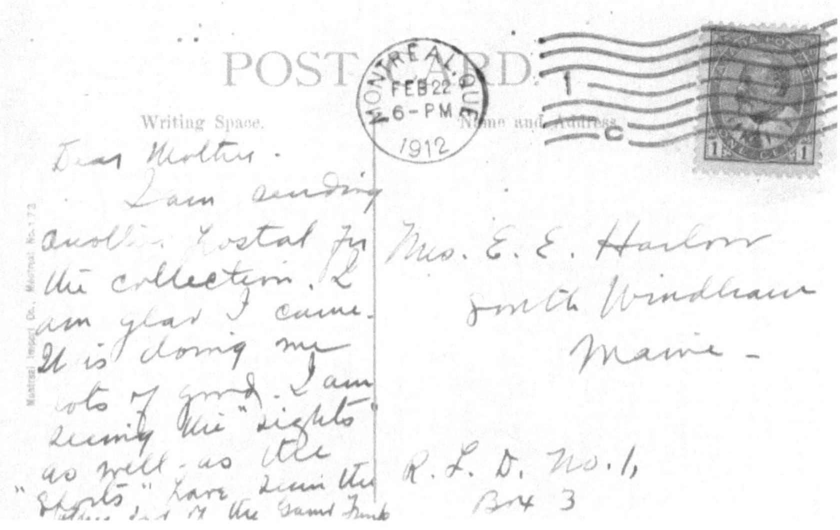

Walter's first postcard home to his mother on his trip west. (Front and back)

The Entire Village of White Rock Burns with Loss of $40,000

Manuel Thomas and his daughter Mildred Thomas (Harlow) and Coonie the cat

October 17, 1916 newspaper article

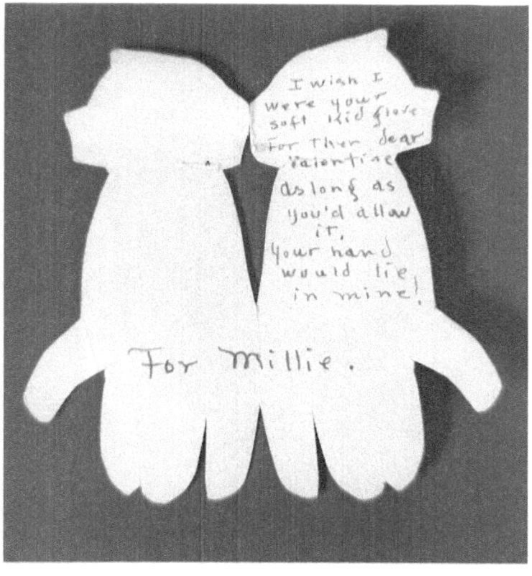

Walter's Christmas and Valentine
cards to Millie

So. Windham, Maine, Mar. 11, 1912

Dear Mildred,

Fourteen years ago I gave you a pledge, or rather perhaps I should say prophesy—for things of the heart apparently are not of our own ordering.— Lately it has seemed to me that you were calling for the fulfillment of that pledge, or prophesy.

Friday evening, unless I receive some word from you to detain me, I will call to see you. It may be late as the roads will be hard and I shall probably have to come with the old horse.

Walter.

Walter's penned letter to Millie requesting an important visit with her

Top: A letter from Millie's friend Marion Wilson
to Walter. Above: Walter's intimate
correspondence with Millie

Top: Crazy quilt. Above: Gold bead necklace.

Millie and Walter marry and
enjoy their honeymoon

Clockwise from top left: Walter milking one of his Jersey cows, a cancelled ski tow ticket, Millie and Walter enjoying their thirty-sixth wedding anniversary party

Top: The author's brother, the author, and Millie at the
Seventeenth Maine Infantry monument at Gettysburg, PA,
Millie playing her pump organ at church

Millie enjoying her elder years in Francesca's home

Afterword

I only knew Grammy for the last eighteen years of her life. She was soft-spoken, gracious, very kind, and unpretentious. She was not outspoken about religion, but she demonstrated her deep faith and wisdom by the way she lived. For too long, I assumed she was born that way. I do not remember my grandfather, Walter, only stories about him. But he too was known by many as a good person, grounded in peace. It was only when I learned a few unsettling facts about their younger years that I realized no one is born wise. Wisdom is learned the hard way and if we work at life or get lucky or both, we just might end up like Millie and Walter did.

So, I decided to weave the facts I knew, be they bitter or sweet, into a largely true yet ultimately fictitious account of Millie and Walter's early years. In many cases, my readers can check for facts or fiction but let me say that Great Falls was North Gorham's first name until 1873 when it was changed because there were too many "Great Falls" post offices in the United States.

By 1900, the year Millie was valedictorian, she was one of only eleven percent of people in the country who graduated from high school, a testament to her mother and father's belief in the value of education for all their children. However, the school year, in rural towns especially, revolved around crop seasons rather than the nine-month system most common today.

That same year, Millie's Uncle Almon sold "Grandmam" and "Grandpar's" estate in Standish, which eventually became the site of Saint Joseph's College of Maine. I think it only fitting that former family land became an educational establishment.

I was fortunate to be able to visit the area where my great-grandfather lived on the island of Flores. Generally, I believe the homes in the Azores are smaller than ours in the United States. But the green of those islands and the inactive volcanoes with their iridescent blue lakes are as spectacular as anything we have here. My only regret was not being able to see the wild blue hydrangeas and calla lilies in bloom all over Flores.

I had many handwritten letters and newspaper articles at my disposal. They were indispensable pieces to this story. One I particularly love is Walter's letter to Millie that suggested his intention to propose to her. But one document was pivotal to the story. I used the newspaper article at the end of part one, about Millie's silver bridal shower, almost verbatim.

I personally have always loved covered bridges and Babb's is one of my favorites. The structure of Babb's bridge is not as I've described it. It actually happens to be the structure of a covered bridge near my home.

I kept some names and changed others. The deaths of my family members are all accurate, even to their burial days in some cases. I contemplated how Millie might have dealt with her losses. Was an early death nearly inevitable in the late 1800s and early 1900s? Unfortunately, yes. But the death of a loved one is still an enormous loss, regardless of the age at death.

In writing this novel, I felt as though I was walking beside my characters, listening to their sincere thoughts and feelings about the many peaks and valleys they must have gone through. Because I didn't know my grandmother and grandfather in their early years, I relied on research to make them come alive. As such, it was as though the two-dimensional personalities I knew only from research became three-dimensional; as though I was there with them. Who knows, maybe time travel is a real thing.

Acknowledgements

For any book written, the list of credits is quite long, considering all the facts we accrue in the years leading up to the document, simply by living life. So it is with this book. But I will name a few who factored into this project most directly.

I must begin by thanking Millie, Walter, Joe, Howdie, Francesca, Doris, young Joe, Rachel, and Warren Gilman, posthumously, for their careful handling of historical facts and artifacts which have been passed down to my generation. Sewn together, these are the makings of family folklore and, sometimes, written stories.

Those still living who have been helpful in gathering information are Katherine Corbett and her son John, Doris Bristol, Forrest Evans, Lucy Smith, Jennifer Doran, and Stan Davis, along with certain historical societies and libraries.

Thanks go to Kirsta McElfresh, for channeling information from her great-grandmother, to Josh Howe for helping me with German-accented English, and to Lucy Smith for her deeper understanding of Millie and willingness to dialogue about these things.

Special thanks to Lucy Smith for rendering the lovely silhouettes, digitally created from actual family photographs. Marking the beginnings of each section of this book, they perfectly fit this time period when silhouetted portraits became popular.

Many thanks to my editor, Aimee Adams, who once again smoothed the many rough edges of my early draft, keeping my intent at the center of her work.

And to my husband, Stan, for his unwavering faith in my ability to understand people and then capture them in writing.

I love you all.

About the Author

Mary Anne Evans has been a trained spiritual director since 2009. She leads retreats and workshops on listening skills, telling our stories, dreams, and spirituality. She loves to read and write in her spare time. She lives with her husband, Stan, and together they try not to dote on their grandchildren too much.

Find out more at www.spiritofriverwind.com.

{ 357 }